continued . . .

ENGAGED TO MURDER

The Inside Story
of the
Main Line Murders

LORETTA
SCHWARTZ-NOBEL

JOVE BOOKS, NEW YORK

This Jove book contains the complete text of the
original hardcover edition. It has been completely
reset in a typeface designed for easy reading and
was printed from new film.

ENGAGED TO MURDER

A Jove Book / published by arrangement with
Viking Penguin Inc.

PRINTING HISTORY
Viking Penguin Inc. edition published 1987
Published simultaneously in Canada
Jove edition / November 1988

ISBN: 0-515-09839-6

Jove Books are published by The Berkley Publishing Group,
200 Madison Avenue, New York, New York 10016.
The name "JOVE" and the "J" logo
are trademarks belonging to Jove Publications, Inc.

PRINTED IN THE UNITED STATES OF AMERICA

10 9 8 7 6 5 4 3 2 1

Author's Note

I have changed the names of individuals to whom
Jay Smith refers incidentally in his letters.

ACKNOWLEDGMENTS

All of the material in this book was taken from court records, trial transcripts, official police reports, confidential FBI accounts, secret grand jury testimony, and the personal letters of key participants and victims, or was the result of countless exclusive interviews over a three-year period.

I am grateful for the hundreds of hours of time and assistance that people on every side of this case have afforded me. I want to thank private investigator Russell Kolins for arranging meetings with Jay Smith, Florence and John Reinert for the use of treasured family photographs, Vincent Valaitis, Pat Schnure, Sharon Lee, Ken Reinert, Donna Formalt, Steve Crockett, Ed Sparrow, Alice Campbell, Joshua Lock, Bill Costopoulos, Rick Guida, Jack Holtz, Lou DiSantis, Stanley Gochenour, Nick Ressetar, and especially Jay Smith and William Bradfield, who, over the years, turned down all other requests for interviews, even when offered substantial sums of money. I have never made any agreements of any nature with any of these people, nor did they ask to read any part of my work in progress or the final manuscript. They simply trusted me to try to uncover and report the truth.

This book could not have been written without the support and help of my father, the late Abraham Rosenberg; my mother, Fay Rosenberg; my husband, Dr. Joel Nobel; my mother-in-law, Dr. Golda Nobel; and my daughters, Ruth and Rebecca. I also want to express my appreciation to the friends and colleagues who assisted

Acknowledgments

me over the years—Randi Boyette, Michael Boyette, Jeff Lerner, Nora Newcombe, David Bradley, Peggy Anderson, Gloria Hochman, Ralph Keyes, Michael Pakenham, David Boldt, Mattie Gershenfeld, Yoko Johanning, Peggy Markow, Cindy Hansberry, Barbara Fazio, Donna Doyle, and Nanette Butler. My deepest gratitude to agent Ellen Levine for her boundless energy and belief in this project, and finally, but actually foremost, my thanks to Nan Graham, whose confidence, enthusiasm, and fine editorial judgment made this book a reality.

*This book is dedicated to the memory of my father,
who taught me to treasure life,
and to my mother, whose bravery in loss
showed me the meaning of courage.*

CONTENTS

CAST OF CHARACTERS

THE DEAD AND MISSING

Susan Reinert
The shy, gentle English teacher whose naked and battered body was found stuffed in the trunk of her car

Karen Reinert
Susan Reinert's eleven-year-old daughter, missing since the night of her mother's murder in June 1979 . . . presumed dead

Michael Reinert
Susan Reinert's ten-year-old son, vanished with his sister . . . also presumed dead

Stephanie Smith Hunsberger
The convicted triggerman's daughter, disappeared in 1978 . . . presumed dead

Eddie Hunsberger
Stephanie's husband, vanished with her in 1978 . . . also presumed dead

THE CONVICTED KILLERS

William S. Bradfield
Susan Reinert's intended husband. Former chairman of the Upper Merion High School English department; and sole beneficiary of Susan's $750,000 in life insurance. Serving three life sentences for murder.

Dr. Jay C. Smith
Former principal of Upper Merion High School. Former colonel in the U.S. Army Reserves, convicted triggerman. Sentenced to die in the electric chair.

THE INVESTIGATORS

Joseph Van Nort
Pennsylvania State Police sergeant. Homicide investigator.

Jack Holtz
Pennsylvania State Police trooper. Van Nort's partner.

Louis DiSantis
Pennsylvania State Police trooper. Assigned to assist Joe Van Nort and Jack Holtz.

John Riley
Court-appointed executor of Susan Reinert's estate

Richard L. Guida
Deputy attorney general and prosecutor for the murder trials of William Bradfield and Jay Smith

Matthew Mullen
FBI detective assigned to the Reinert murder case

Carlos (Chick) Sabinson
FBI detective working with Matt Mullen

THE JUDGES

Judge Isaac J. Garb
Presiding judge during William Bradfield's trial for murder

Judge William Lipsitt
Judge during Jay Smith's trial for murder

THE DEFENDERS

John Paul Curran, Esquire
Lawyer representing William Bradfield during the theft case

Charles Fitzpatrick, Esquire
Curran's law partner, also representing William Bradfield

Joshua Lock, Esquire
Court-appointed defender during William Bradfield's murder trial

William Costopoulos, Esquire
Attorney for Jay Smith's murder trial

Nicholas Ressetar
Assistant to William Costopoulos

Stanley (Skip) Gochenour
Private detective for William Costopoulos

WILLIAM BRADFIELD'S FRIENDS AND COLLEAGUES

Vincent Valaitis
Fellow English teacher and Bradfield's neighbor and confidant

Christopher Pappas
Former student who became Bradfield's friend and confidant

William Scutta
English teacher at Upper Merion High School

Richard and Carol Manser
Teachers at Upper Merion High School

Marian Taylor
Owner of the Heirloom Hotel. Rented Bradfield rooms
for the alibi weekend.

Stephen Crockett
William Bradfield's professor and friend

Margaret Crockett
Steve Crockett's wife. William Bradfield's friend.

WILLIAM BRADFIELD'S WOMEN

Susan Myers
William Bradfield's friend and lover for twenty years.
The woman he lived with.

Susan Reinert
Expected to marry Bradfield the summer of her murder

Wendy Zeigler
Former student expecting to marry William Bradfield

Joanne Aitken
Harvard graduate student, also William Bradfield's lover

Frances Bradfield
William Bradfield's first wife

Muriel Bradfield
Bradfield's second wife

Nona Bradfield
William Bradfield's mother

Maria DiCavalcanti
Bradfield's first love

DR. JAY SMITH'S FAMILY
AND FRIENDS

Stephanie Smith, Sr.
Jay Smith's wife of twenty-eight years

Stephanie Smith, Jr.
Smith's missing daughter

Edward Hunsberger
Smith's missing son-in-law

Harold Jones
Jay Smith's colleague and friend

SUSAN REINERT'S FAMILY
AND FRIENDS

Patrick Gallagher
Susan's brother

Patricia Schnure
Fellow English teacher and Susan's closest female friend

Sharon Lee
English teacher and close friend

Kenneth Reinert
Susan's former husband and father of the missing children

John and Florence Reinert
Susan's in-laws, the grandparents of the missing children

Mary Gove
Susan's next-door neighbor

Elizabeth Brook
Mary Gove's granddaughter

Donna Formalt
Susan's neighbor and friend

THE INMATES

Proctor Nowell
Star witness against William Bradfield. Claimed that Bradfield confessed to him.

Arnold Weidner
Also claimed William Bradfield confessed to him

Raymond Martray
Former cop turned convict who told police that Jay Smith admitted killing Susan Reinert. Later worked with investigators to record conversations with Smith.

Charles Montione
Inmate who claimed that Smith confessed

Joseph Weiss
Another convict who claimed that Smith confessed

THE EXPERTS

Samuel Golub
Hair and fiber expert. Testified for the defense at Smith's trial.

Jacquelyn Tachner
FBI cryptologist. Testified for the prosecution at Bradfield's trial and at Smith's trial.

CHRONOLOGY

Fall 1974
William Bradfield allegedly begins having an affair with fellow Upper Merion High School English teacher Susan Reinert while living with teacher Susan Myers.

August 19, 1978
High school principal Dr. Jay C. Smith is arrested on weapons and drug charges.

October 26, 1978
Susan Reinert's mother dies, leaving her $30,000.

Fall 1978
William Bradfield begins to tell friends that Smith, now suspended from the high school, is being framed on charges of theft from two Sears, Roebuck stores. Bradfield offers to testify on Smith's behalf. He also claims that Smith is a hit man for the Mafia and says that Smith wants Reinert dead.

March 3, 1979
Jay Smith is convicted of the attempted theft of a Sears store in Abington, a suburb of Philadelphia.

Susan Reinert buys a $250,000 term life insurance policy, with a $200,000 accidental-death rider, listing Bradfield as her "intended husband."

May 4, 1979
Susan Reinert changes her will, excluding her two children and brother as beneficiaries and naming William Bradfield as her sole heir.

May 30, 1979
Bradfield testifies as an alibi witness for Smith at his trial for theft from a second Sears store in St. David's, Pennsylvania.

May 31, 1979
Smith is convicted of the theft from the St. David's Sears store, despite testimony by Bradfield that he had been with Smith in Ocean City, New Jersey, on the day of the theft. Smith is free on bail.

June 1979
Susan Reinert obtains another term life insurance policy, this one for $150,000.

June 20, 1979
Susan Reinert obtains a third life insurance policy for an additional $100,000.

June 22, 1979
Susan and her two children are seen for the last time about 9:20 P.M. by a neighbor as they drive away from their home. Later that night, Bradfield and three teacher friends, Sue Myers, Vince Valaitis, and Chris Pappas, leave for Cape May, New Jersey. Bradfield tells the teachers he fears that Smith will kill Reinert over the weekend.

June 25, 1979
Susan Reinert's naked body is found at about 5:30 A.M. in the trunk of her car in the parking lot of the Host Inn in Harrisburg. Her children have disappeared.

Later that morning, Smith appears in Harrisburg for sentencing. He is sent to prison to begin serving a five-and-a-half-to-twelve-year term.

In the afternoon, William Bradfield and Chris Pappas fly to Santa Fe, New Mexico, to attend the summer session at St. John's College.

Summer 1979
Dozens of state police and sixteen FBI agents are as-

signed to the murder investigation and search for the children.

August 22, 1979
Vincent Valaitis, one of the three teachers in whom Bradfield confided, goes to police and tells them of Bradfield's "fear" that Jay Smith intended to kill Susan Reinert.

July 28, 1980
Bradfield files claims on Reinert's insurance policies and attempts to probate her will in Delaware County Court.

August 3, 1981
Bradfield is convicted of stealing $25,000 from Susan Reinert. Charges against Wendy Zeigler, a former student, also expecting to marry Bradfield, are dropped when she agrees to testify against him.

November 24, 1981
A statewide investigating grand jury is empaneled and a special prosecutor is named to investigate Susan Reinert's murder and the disappearance of her children.

December 22, 1982
William Bradfield is sentenced to up to two years in jail for the theft conviction and is sent to Delaware County Prison.

January 1983
While in prison, Bradfield allegedly confesses involvement in the Reinert murders to inmate Proctor Nowell.

January 28, 1983
Bradfield is released from prison after Joanne Aitken, his current girlfriend, posts the bail, which was set at $75,000.

March 29, 1983
A statewide investigating grand jury recommends that Bradfield be charged with the Reinert killings.

April 6, 1983
Bradfield is arrested at the home of friends.

October 11, 1983
Bradfield's murder trial begins.

October 28, 1983
A jury finds Bradfield guilty on three counts of conspiracy to commit first-degree murder in the Reinert slayings. Police vow to continue the search for the accomplice who, they believe, actually committed the murders.

November 10, 1983
Inmate Charles Montione informs police that Jay Smith has told him about his involvement in the Reinert murders. He agrees to testify against Smith.

February 3, 1983
Former inmate Raymond Martray claims Jay Smith has made a critical statement, implying guilt in the Reinert murders, during a taped telephone conversation.

June 25, 1985
On the sixth anniversary of the discovery of Reinert's body, Jay Smith is arrested in his prison cell and charged with the killings.

August 3, 1985
After a preliminary hearing, Jay Smith is ordered to stand trial for the murders of Susan, Karen, and Michael Reinert.

March 31, 1986
Jay Smith's murder trial begins.

May 1, 1986
The jury finds Jay Smith guilty of the murders of Susan, Michael, and Karen Reinert and sentences him to die in the electric chair.

PROLOGUE

It started with a newspaper clipping that caught my eye as I walked past the kitchen table one crisp October morning in 1983. A major trial for a triple murder was about to begin. I was an investigative reporter between books and intrigued by the idea that a classics scholar, an honored graduate of the exclusive Haverford College, and a former student and friend of the internationally acclaimed poet Ezra Pound was about to stand trial for his life. The victims were a shy, gentle English teacher and her two young children. I called the *Philadelphia Inquirer* and arranged to cover the trial and write a feature article on the case. I didn't know then how profoundly William Bradfield and the murders would affect my life.

During the second week of the trial, the small courthouse became so jammed with spectators that the judge allowed members of the press to move inside the spectator gates and sit next to the defense table. I took the seat closest to William Bradfield and quickly found myself locked in his gaze. What I had heard about the man was true. He had a quality in his face and eyes that drew people to him. What had so often been described as the steel-blue eyes of William Bradfield were in fact remarkably changeable. Sometimes there was a dark intensity in them; at other times, they seemed to turn a brighter blue. His expression changed from troubled to childlike in a matter of seconds. William Bradfield leaned over and asked his attorney who I was. The attorney handed Bradfield a packet that I had prepared. It contained samples of magazine articles I had written and a copy of my book on hunger in America, along with a letter asking if he would talk to me. He smiled at me and whispered, ''Come and see me as soon as you can.''

Eight days later, after fifty minutes of deliberation, the jury found him guilty of conspiring to commit three first-degree murders. Several months passed before a prison visit could be arranged. William Bradfield had not yet been formally sentenced and was not allowed contact with visitors, but I had finally gotten permission to see him in the company of one of his attorneys, the only people with whom he was allowed direct meetings. The guards on duty assumed I was also an attorney.

We waited for what seemed like hours in the prison's long, low basement with an armed guard's booth at one end. The visitors and prisoners sat next to each other on long rows of vinyl chairs. Hungry for connection, they kissed, caressed, and explored each other's bodies. In a room crowded with strangers, men sat with coats covering their laps and their women's hands. They shared their intimacies, moaned, and panted while babies slept on the floor and children ran and screamed unattended.

Finally, in the midst of this passion and chaos, William Bradfield appeared. "My God, it's good to see you," he said, laughing and shaking my hand so hard that it hurt. "What a treat, how wonderful this is! How did you manage it? Usually, they only allow me to talk to visitors through a wire cage, because they think I'm so dangerous. I can't believe I'm out here with you." Then he noticed me looking around, still stunned and fascinated by the sights in the visitors' room. He laughed again and said, "Welcome to *One Flew over the Cuckoo's Nest*."

As the room roared behind our backs, William Bradfield began to talk. "This place does strange things to a man. After a while, you don't know who's crazy. The fellow next to me in cell five had no toilet in his cell. He'd scream when he had to go to the bathroom. No one would come. He'd urinate in cups. He'd defecate in cups and throw them out on the tier. I complained. I wrote letters. I said the man had no plumbing facilities. Finally, a full month later, in answer to my complaint, I got a letter saying that there were *no* cells without toilet facilities. I asked my counselor if my complaint could be reentered, since there was still no toilet. 'No,' he said, 'that complaint has already been answered.'

"I asked to be allowed to go to church on Sunday. They told me I was a security risk. I said I would go in handcuffs and shackles. I was refused. It's a card game in which they don't have better cards than you, they have *all* the cards. I'm in what they call administrative custody—we call it the hole. It's really solitary confinement. I just sit in the cell all day, day after day. They're afraid I'll try to escape. When I was out on bail and I *knew* they were coming to arrest me for murder, I didn't run, but my folder says 'maximum high-security risk.' Loretta, I'm in jail for something I didn't do. To run would be an admission of guilt.''

"Would you be willing to talk to me about it?'' I asked. The question jolted him.

"I'm afraid not,'' he said. "At this point, I have some thoughts about the criminal justice system I would be willing to talk to you about. But if it has anything to do with my case, I don't think so. You have to understand, the press has done a job that is impossible to undo. I feel very much a pariah and that feeling shocks me.''

He paused and then looked directly at me. "Do you know that there are people out there who *really* believe that *I* killed a woman and her two children? That makes me tremble. What I want to do now, *all* I want to do, is to deal with my situation in such a way as to be a better person. It is undeniable that this experience has been priceless. It has given me a core, a marrow knowledge that I *never* want to lose. I have my up days and some very, very black days. I am studying the Gospel of John now. A seminarian comes to the prison. He comes into the hole to see me. I have begun to talk to the father about Judaism. On Tuesday, he picks up my questions. He does the research. He returns the following week with the answers. I have Homer and Pound and my Bible work. They give me some really good days, as good as those I can ever remember. Once I get into the general population, I can be of service. Right now, it's difficult to justify my existence because I feel I am not helping anyone.''

"Mr. Bradfield,'' I said, pressing him, "you can be of great help to me by talking to me. This is like any other life drama. The characters here represent all of us. It is as much a mystery and a challenge as any great piece of literature. What happened to Susan, to you, to Smith, and to the others? How did it happen to a man of your intelligence and your talent? You are the only one who can help me to understand that.''

There was a long pause. William Bradfield turned to his lawyer. "Can it hurt me, Josh?'' he asked.

Joshua Lock pursed his lips and then shrugged. "I don't think so,'' he said.

William Bradfield looked directly into my eyes for what

seemed like a long time, then he said softly, "If I can be of help to you, Loretta, I will."

It meant getting on his official visitors' list, and that was difficult. I had to go through a security clearance, which took another three months. It was May 1, 1984, almost seven months after the trial ended, before I next saw him. This time, I came without his attorney. William Bradfield was still being kept in isolation. When the day of my visit arrived, I became, as all visitors must, a prisoner for the day. After I had surrendered my pocketbook, briefcase, and all other personal possessions at the reception area the guard said, "Just take off your belt and that jewelry you are wearing." Finally, I passed through the metal-detector and underwent the body search. I emptied my pockets into a tray, signed in, and had my hand stamped. As I entered the prison itself, I heard the gates lock behind me. Then I heard the heavy steel door slam shut. I walked across the walled and wired courtyard to the visiting room. This time, since I was not with Bradfield's attorney, I walked to the far end, past the attorney's table. I sat outside a small wire cage and waited. A huge armed guard led William Bradfield into the cage, limping, in handcuffs and leg-irons. The guard stood right behind him with his hand on his gun. We had one hour.

"It's not as bad as it looks. Thanks so much for coming," Bradfield said. We talked for a while about life in prison and how he'd been, and then he said, "Listen, I try to remind myself that how I perceive my situation is of extreme importance to my mental health. You see, a good deal of my life was very religious. By the time I got to junior high school, I'd become interested in Catholicism. I began to learn about the monks. In many ways, this is not unlike monastics. So, I tell myself that the gods that be have said, '*William*, this is your monastic period. This is a time to hone your discipline.' This is my first principle. My second principle is thankfulness. It is very difficult to be thankful when you haven't done what you've been convicted of doing. It is truly difficult. So, I have to keep in mind that on this continent, thousands of people have fates *far* worse than mine. In Africa, twenty thousand die each month from malnutrition, with their bellies distended. If I keep that perception ahead of me, it makes it less difficult. I had fifty years of unparalleled freedom. Sometimes, I have to block thoughts of the future. To survive here, you find yourself putting things out of your mind, certain pieces of music, for example, Schubert's Eighth 'Unfinished' Symphony, or Bach, especially Bach. They are so highly evocative and moving, they stir me without aiding my control. They are provocative, but what they provoke leads to self-pity.''

''Hey man, it looks like your time is up,'' the guard behind him grunted.

William Bradfield thanked me profusely for having come to see him, and apologized for not having more time. Then, hands and feet still shackled, he struggled to stand. I watched as he was led from that cage down a long hall and out of sight to his cell. Then I walked back past the couples still clawing at each other and the babies still crying, through the guarded and wired courtyard. When the last locked door opened and I stepped outside, I felt enormously relieved, grateful that I was free to return home to my husband and children, free to walk in the woods.

The next day, I called the prison superintendent, identified myself as a journalist, and asked why, despite Josh Lock's inquiries, Mr. Bradfield was still being denied normal prison visits. ''I really don't know,'' the superintendent said, ''I'll have to check into it.'' A week later, the superintendent told me that Mr. Bradfield could now have normal full-day visits without handcuffs or leg-irons. There had been, in fact, no reason to keep him in isolation or ''administrative custody,'' as prison authorities called it, for seven months. But no one had reevaluated his status. Bradfield was exuberant. I had helped him gain some small measure of freedom and now he seemed to think of me as a friend.

In the years that followed, I visited him as often as prison regulations allowed. I would arrive in the morning and spend six or seven hours with him. At some point during the afternoon, we'd walk to the vending machines where prisoners and visitors could buy food, coffee, and cold drinks. It was part of a ritual we'd established. I'd given him dollar bills. He'd get the change from the change machines and take charge of buying the hot sausages or turkey franks. Ignoring the roaches, he would set the attorney's table, marked for official use only, with napkins and plastic forks, then hold the chair for me as if we were in some fine French restaurant. He'd often say, ''God, how I treasure these moments.'' These afternoons were the closest thing to freedom that William Bradfield could experience. They were the closest thing to imprisonment that I had ever known. Lunch was the break in a more solemn ritual of discussing his life or the case. "What should I do?" he would ask. "Where did the trial go wrong, why did the judge and jury think I was guilty?"

In all those months that ran into years, William Bradfield never asked me if *I* thought he was guilty. The truth is, I *wanted* him to be innocent. I wanted to discover, but never could, some new evidence that would allow me to prove, at least to myself, that this gentle scholar, this man who seemed so appreciative of my visits, who was so warm and who seemed so genuine, was not sitting three feet away from me lying about the most brutal crime I could imagine a man committing: the cold-blooded, greed-driven murder of a woman who loved and trusted him and of her two children.

There was also another question that troubled me. If this man, who appeared to be so honest, was looking me straight in the eye and lying to me, then who and what could I believe? I had been an investigative journalist for a dozen years. I had covered many tough stories and dealt with a lot of people in trouble. But, for the most part, they were what they seemed to be. I had learned to trust my instincts. Now I was no longer sure. I liked and admired the person that William Bradfield *appeared* to be. But I had no way of knowing what was real. The man I saw seemed to bear no resemblance to the man who had been convicted or even the man I had watched on the witness stand whose explanation of events frequently seemed confused, illogical, or simply unbelievable. The Bradfield I was visiting seemed to have the values of a saint. These values were combined with intelligence as rich as I had seen in any man or woman. No doubt, these were the qualities that had made students, colleagues, and especially women, adore him, and remain loyal to him. Even after his conviction, he had a group of followers who believed in him beyond a trace of doubt. Without exception, they were highly educated, religious, and cultured people. The former dean of St. John's College, for example, and several of St. John's faculty members; graduates of Yale, Harvard, and Bryn Mawr; men and women who invested their life savings in his defense, and trusted their young children with him, even after he was a suspect for triple murder. People who would bet their own lives on his innocence.

This, I was sure, was the William Bradfield that Susan Reinert had known and trusted. It was easy for me to understand her vulnerability and easy to identify with her. Susan and I were the same age. Each of us had two children and had been divorced. We studied and taught English. We were also from the last generation of girls raised to believe that someday our "prince" would come, the last generation to grow up believing that we *had* to be married. Sometimes I asked myself, If I had met William Bradfield eight or nine years earlier, when he met Susan, when I, too, was a single parent, could I, could any of half a dozen women I knew, have been charmed by the man, enough to become his victim? *If* he was actually guilty?

His manner, his intelligence, his sensitivity constantly surprised me. "After leaving you today," he wrote on October 31, 1984, "this most lovely last quarter day of the year, I looked at the long slanting sunlight and felt terribly sad. If you think of it, pause for a moment and drink in some of the seasonal beauty for me."

In May 1985, when my father died, I received many letters of condolence. But few were quite as reassuring or came so close to understanding the pain of that loss as William Bradfield's. He wrote, "I wish I could somehow soften the awful hurt you must feel. There is, for me, a terrible sense of unfinished and strangely urgent business remaining between me and my now-dead father. I imagine that must be true for you, too. I wish you well with that ghost. I have constant commerce with it." The letter went on to say, "I think of you *so* often day to day in here, and sometimes have long internal conversations with you. I see many things and people and situations through your eyes, and often think that you, like Henry James, would more surely catch the 'tone of things' in here than I. I miss seeing you and talking with you. I'd love to see you. Do write when you can. Yours, Will."

If William Bradfield was what he now appeared to be, a tragic injustice had occurred. If he was not what he appeared to be, how could I be charmed by a man capable of such horror? Again and again, I tried to sort it out. He loved literature, art, and poetry. He was an avid student of Greek, Latin, and the Bible. He was thoughtful and kind whenever he spoke to me. Those things were real. Was it possible that some of the very best of values could exist right alongside the very worst? Victim or killer?—the question continued to haunt me. Was William Bradfield innocent? Was he guilty, but so deluded that he had somehow genuinely hidden the truth from himself? Was he a sociopathic personality who felt no guilt, or was he the cold-blooded diabolical murderer that the judge and jury believed him to be? When I arrived at the prison, he would often tell me that I was like a second sister to him, a treasured friend. He began to call me at home, collect, and to tell me that if he ever got out of prison, he would love to come and visit me. At about that time, I began to have nightmares. The dreams took many forms, but the substance was always the same. The gentle, kind William Bradfield became the other William Bradfield, the tried and convicted killer. I was the first victim, my children were next.

Sometimes, when I visited him, I felt certain that he *had* to be innocent. Everything about the man was absolutely irreconcilable with the act of planning a triple murder; everything, that is, *except* the facts that had been used to convict him, and his strange, uncharacteristic hostility when he talked about Susan Reinert. Nothing in Bradfield's descriptions of Susan matched the impressions of dozens of other people who knew her at least as well as he did; he spoke of her as disturbed, desperate, and pathetic. He denied ever having been her lover. The evidence that convicted him was circumstantial, but, why, I wondered, would anyone in his right mind have taken it upon himself to try to control Jay Smith, the man he said was threatening to kill Susan Reinert? Why would he have bought guns and practiced what he said were Dr. Smith's techniques for murder? Why would he have spent so much time trying to "help" a woman he now claimed he hadn't even liked? It made no sense. Nor could anything change the fact that William Bradfield *was* the sole beneficiary of nearly a million dollars in term life-insurance policies, or that Susan's estate was missing $25,000 that, months before her death, she said she had given to him to invest. There were dozens of other pieces to the puzzle that were equally damaging and impossible to explain by coincidence alone. Worst of all was the fact that he had been predicting her murder for nine months, but had neither gone to the police nor warned Susan. He had also deliberately left town on the weekend he believed the murder would occur. William Bradfield freely admitted this much, yet still swore that he was innocent.

One day in the fall of 1985, William said sadly, "Judge Garb and Richard Guida told me what a terrible person I was. They said, 'You are a dangerous man, you are diabolical.' Even now, when I remember that, it shocks and hurts me." It was one of our typical visits. Delighted to have company, he would talk, I would take notes, ask a question now and then, mostly just listen. "I have my cell painted bright white now," he said cheerfully, "and I tell myself, I'm in a monk's cell. Certainly, I have to be celibate, but I had considered that anyhow. Even when I was caught up in a career, I knew I didn't give a damn. Look at the things I value," he said earnestly. "Which one of them can't I do in here? Aren't there people in here for me to love and help?" He laughed. "Mother Theresa and I have a corner on the market. Where else would I find people more desperate for love? If I want to study and learn, where, at my age and situation, could I find the chance to do it any more than in here? There are distractions, yes, but there were distractions out there, too. The fact that I cannot pick up my belongings and go to the sea, which was always a source of inspiration—that bothers me. I think a lot about the other people who've been in my situation and that gives me great comfort. St. Paul and Socrates died in my situation, so did Christ and Martin Luther King. There were hundreds of men throughout the ages who have been imprisoned or killed. Look at Galileo. You see, I view all of us, *all* of us, as silly little children. We fool ourselves in so many ways. We dress up in costumes. We mistreat each other. We pretend to be powerful, smart, wise. We get a little money and we lord it over our playmates. But the truth is all we want are the things that little children want. All of the things that are most worthwhile in life are things I can *still* do.

"If I ever get out of here, I see my life in an urban center, clothing people, feeding them. Reading my books and working on my inner life. If I said I'd like to have clams diablo, if I said I'd like to go to the Bahamas, if I said I'd like to make a lot of money, yes, then I'd be unhappy. But the truth is, I've *never* been a materialist, so I don't feel the loss of these things as great sources of pain. The public perception of me is ironic. I can't think of a more *unlikely* person to have valued money over human life. I've always tried to help people; I was trying to help Jay Smith and I was trying to help Susan Reinert. Should I have turned away from the people who needed my help? Perhaps I should have, but that was not my way. I was never in love with Susan Reinert; I was never engaged to her. I simply felt sorry for her and was trying to help her straighten out her life. I am as much a victim in this whole thing as she is. Yet, in a sense, this experience has been a great fortune. It has stripped me naked. I know myself so well now. I am so fortunate to have related to some people from absolute need. I am so fortunate, for example, to know you, Loretta. Sometimes, I sit in my cell and I think this is what it takes to be wise. It takes suffering to be wise. I wouldn't trade what I have learned through this for anything. I wouldn't trade it *even* for my freedom.''

This conversation preceded a turning point in my relationship with William Bradfield. From the start, he had known I was a journalist under contract to write a book about his case, but he seemed not to want to deal with that. On this day, I mentioned the book and the deadline I had for writing it, and the smile faded from his face. "I feel so sad," he said. "I guess this really defines the parameters of our relationship if you stop coming." He corrected himself. "When you stop coming, it's going to be a great loss to me, more than you will ever know. You'll go away and write your book. I hope it will be good. I think it will be good, but if it's not good . . ." His voice drifted off.

The lights blinked, announcing that visiting hours were over. "Think of a quest," he said, with urgency in his voice, "something you want to learn. Something we can study together."

"What do you mean?" I asked.

"Maybe if we're in the middle of learning, say, Sanskrit, you won't leave me."

A young guard came to collect our passes. "I wish you weren't writing a book," he said, as we walked toward the visitors' exit. Unexpectedly, he embraced me. "Oh, God," he whispered, "I wish you weren't writing a book." I pulled away.

I *was* writing a book, and I knew that, finally, my obligation was not to William Bradfield, or Jay Smith, or the state police, or the FBI. It was to the truth or as close as I could get to the truth, and that was something I *had* to follow, wherever it led me.

Ultimately, three separate stories emerged. First, there were the facts revealed by the investigation as it proceeded, what witnesses, police, and the FBI recalled and swore was true. Second, there was the story that William Bradfield told. And finally, there was the story according to Dr. Jay Smith.

Dr. Smith was quiet, subdued, and courteous when I met him at prison. He spoke about the hardships he'd endured and the great need he felt to establish his innocence and to spare his family the pain that this scandal had caused them. Dr. Smith denied everything William Bradfield had said. He also denied everything the police had said. Like William Bradfield, he claimed that he was a victim and an innocent man. He, too, was complex, and difficult to understand. He said he had been intentionally framed by William Bradfield, and he asked for my help.

I was committed to reporting the facts, but often, it was impossible to tell what the facts were. I settled upon the only solution that allowed everyone involved in this case the freedom of the First Amendment, the freedom to his story. I have not attempted to prove that one man was being framed, or that another was fabricating his evidence. The web of contradictory statements became so bizarre that I did not feel it was possible for me as a journalist to also be judge and jury. It was easier, I think, for the jury, which was presented with a limited amount of highly selected material designed to make a *specific* point.

And so, I have reported, as accurately as I could, three separate and totally contradictory versions of a crime so complex that it will never be fully resolved, and so tragic that it can never be fully comprehended.

PART I

The Murder

Standing next to me in this lonely crowd
Is a man who swears he's not to
blame.
All day long I hear him shout so loud,
Crying out that he was framed. . . .

—BOB DYLAN
"I Shall Be
Released"

1

It had been hot all day—damp, sweltering, oppressive heat. Suddenly, toward evening, the heat broke, the sky turned black, the wind began to swirl furiously through the darkened street. A savage summer cloudburst forced the children to stop their games. The front door was closed and tightly latched against the rain and wind. The lights flickered on inside Susan Reinert's modest, neatly kept house.

By 9:00 P.M., a new series of thunderstorms was moving in from the northwest. Huge hailstones battered the windows and rooftops. At about 9:30 P.M., on this, the last night of her life, Susan Reinert's telephone rang. After the call, the small, slender woman with luminous eyes and dark hair hurriedly gathered her life-insurance policies and rushed out into the storm with her children. It was a strange time for Susan to be leaving the safety of home. But she was in love and she was vulnerable.

Mary Gove had been standing at her window with her granddaughter, Elizabeth, watching the hailstones. The cautious, gray-haired lady wiped the foggy window and squinted. She was amazed to see Susan and the children run across the front porch and climb into their car. When Susan saw Mary Gove peering out of the window, she paused for a moment, adjusted her glasses, smiled, and waved. "That was the kind of neighbor she was," Mary Gove later recalled. "Always friendly, always thoughtful, never too busy to be kind." But this time, Susan was clearly in a hurry, and by the time Mary Gove had waved back, even the lights of the small red car had vanished into the darkness. Mary Gove shrugged in dismay, closed her curtain, locked her door, and went upstairs to bed.

Except for the killers, she was the last person known to have seen Susan or her children alive.

Two nights later, on Sunday, June 24, 1979, James Mooney, a field service technician, picked up his friend Dale Kennedy at Harrisburg International Airport and dropped him off at the Host Inn, a well-kept, ultramodern, three-story building near the Pennsylvania Turnpike. While circling the parking lot at 7:00 P.M., the men passed a small red Plymouth Horizon parked off by itself with the hatchback up. They stopped, looked at the car, and talked about shutting the hatch. Kennedy had heard that if you left your trunk open up north, you were likely to be robbed. He knew the hatch should be closed, but he was afraid that if he fiddled with the car, someone might think that he was trying to rob it. He noticed what looked like a white laundry bag sticking out of the trunk. He'd have to move that before it would shut. It would be better, he decided, to mind his own business and just leave the whole thing alone. Several months later, Kennedy would learn that the ''laundry bag'' was actually Susan Reinert's right hip. But on this night, he knew only that he didn't want any trouble. Dale Kennedy had taken the careful man's route, and within minutes he had stopped worrying about the car.

Several hours passed before Joseph Ruddy, a patrol officer with the Swatara Township Police Department, noticed the red Plymouth. He pulled up behind the vehicle and, without ever looking into the open hatch, he ran a routine check on license number 634 458. Ruddy learned that the vehicle was registered to Susan G. Reinert at 662 Woodcrest Avenue in Ardmore. He then went into the hotel to see if she was staying there. He was told that no one named Susan Reinert had registered as a guest. Immediately after that, Ruddy received an emergency call telling him that there was a fatal collision on Route 322. He left the Host Inn and sped to the scene of the accident.

At 5:25 A.M., an anonymous caller dialed 911. The man was whispering, but it sounded as if he had a Spanish accent. ''There's a sick woman in a car in the parking lot of the Host Inn.'' There was a silence for several seconds. Then the phone clicked. That was the last time the police would hear from the man. The weary dispatcher shook his head. ''Probably another drunk,'' he said before he relayed the message. The call was automatically tape-recorded, but for reasons that no one can adequately explain, it was erased. Since Ruddy was still tied up with the auto fatality, the call was dispatched to Lower Swatara Township. Ten minutes later, Niles Keene and Jeffrey Cope, two tired patrolmen about to go off duty, stood in the cold early morning fog, staring at the naked, mutilated body of Susan Reinert.

"Her knees were pressed up against her chest, her head was bent forward, and her body was jammed into a fetal position," Keene later recalled. "At first, I figured she'd probably gotten herself picked up in the bar at the Host Inn and then been raped and killed. But as soon as I moved closer, I could see that she'd been dead for quite a while, possibly as long as several days. She'd been lying in that position for at least twelve hours. I could tell by the degree of lividity, the way the blood had settled, glowing red like a sunburn across her back, then turning white again on the fleshy part of her thighs and hips. Out of habit, I bent over and touched her just once for a pulse. When I leaned toward her, I could see that dried mucus or sperm was smeared around her mouth and nose. Her face had been brutally beaten. Her eyes were black and blue. Her front teeth had ripped her lower lip. There were chain marks on her wrists and ankles, and bruises on her back that made me think she'd been chained to a tree or a platform and had been rubbing against it trying to break free. The cuts and bruises on her forearms were defensive wounds. She was a tiny lady, but at some point she'd obviously tried to fight against her killers."

After twenty years on the force, Keene was good at recognizing the signs of a struggle. But this wasn't his case. It wasn't even his township. He'd simply taken the call as a favor because Ruddy was tied up with the traffic fatality. Keene took one more look at the body. Then he walked to the patrol car and picked up the phone.

Within minutes, Joseph Ruddy was contacted. The message was short, the order direct: "Return to the Host Inn. There's a dead woman in the trunk of the car you reported earlier, third row, tenth stall." When Ruddy reached the hotel, the hatch of the Plymouth was still open and now, in the morning light, the slender, broken body was immediately visible. Badly shaken, Ruddy returned to his patrol car and called Dauphin County police. "Contact the detective on call, the district attorney's office, the Pennsylvania State Police Criminal Division, and the coroner's office," he said, stammering. "I'll stay here and secure the scene."

The crowd that gathered watched in horrified fascination as Thomas Dacheux, Troop H Identification Unit, photographed the limp, nude body and transferred it to a stretcher. Then Coroner William Bush pronounced Susan dead and ordered that the corpse be removed to Community General Osteopathic Hospital.

2

Jack Holtz was sleeping deeply. Recently divorced, he enjoyed being a bachelor and he'd been out late the night before. When the phone rang, Holtz opened his eyes and closed them again, wondering who would be calling before 7:00 A.M.

"Yeah," he said, still groggy.

"Got a homicide for you, trooper—the Host Inn."

"Be right over," Holtz answered, suddenly alert. He showered and dressed quickly, then jumped into his car, but it was already too late. Susan Reinert's body had been moved. There was no way to know what evidence had been destroyed. Holtz, who would become the chief investigator for the case, had lost forever the opportunity to see for himself how Susan Reinert had been found. He suppressed his anger and grabbed Trooper Dacheux to make sure that photographs had been taken. Then he walked over to the corpse, still lying on the stretcher, and uncovered it just long enough to see that the hands were bagged in clear plastic. There was no reason to look at the body further now. It would be safer to examine it away from the wind, in the hospital morgue. Holtz didn't want to risk losing another speck of evidence. Since there was no way to know what might be destroyed by closing the trunk, he left it open and arranged to have the car towed by Cresier Towing and Wrecking Service. Then he issued routine instructions. "Check the car for fingerprints; question all employees of the Host Inn to see if anything unusual was observed last night; secure a list of guests and the license plates of all cars in the lot."

After supervising the towing of the car, Holtz drove to Troop H Headquarters. "Hey, buddy, take it easy," he said, raising his hands and smiling when he saw his partner, Joe Van Nort, pacing and nervously waiting for details of the murder.

John Holtz, known to everyone as Jack, was a skinny young traffic cop when fifty-eight-year-old Joe Van Nort started taking him out on homicides and teaching him how to track down suspects. Some people joked that Van Nort spent more time with Holtz than he spent with his wife. It was probably true. Van Nort had married late and never had a child. Holtz, ambitious, eager, and nearly thirty years his junior, filled an empty place in the older man's life. It was one of those close friendships that occur when the needs of the mentor mesh perfectly with the needs of the man he is training. Since they'd become partners, there had never been a murder they hadn't solved.

Jack Holtz had grown up in a small steel-mining town. His father was one of 1,100 people working in seven square miles of gray steel mill. When there was work, the living was good, by blue-collar standards. But there were always risks and, too often, there were layoffs and long strikes. After years of uncertain employment and economic insecurity, Jack's father quit his steel job and became a conductor with Amtrak. When Jack finished high school, he, too, landed a job with the railroad. Jack was on the tracks. It was hard, dirty work, and it was often dangerous. When an engine knocked him under a car and almost killed him, he decided to leave. He was twenty years old when he walked into Troop H Headquarters and asked how he could join the state police. Now, twelve years later, confident, well groomed, with thick salt-and-pepper hair, broad shoulders, and large muscles carefully cultivated by frequent workouts, Jack Holtz walked proud. With a revolver hidden in his conservative three-piece suit and just the right amount of fine gold jewelry, he looked more like a corporate executive than a cop.

At 1:40 P.M., Holtz and Van Nort met the coroner and the pathologist at the morgue. Routine swabs were taken from Susan Reinert's vagina, anus, and mouth. Scrapings were made from under her fingernails. Three cubic centimeters of urine were obtained from her bladder, ten cubic centimeters of blood were taken from her heart. The body was X-rayed and photographs were snapped. Then Bair made the incision, a *Y* that started just below the neck at the clavicle. One at a time, Susan's organs were lifted out, examined, and weighed. The scalp was incised, the skull was sawed open, and Susan's brain was removed. It appeared to be normal, there was no sign of bleeding. Her stomach was empty. There was hemorrhaging in the pancreas, left kidney, and both lungs. At that time, Dr. Bair also made note of a small amount of thick, creamy material on the surface of the vagina. It was never identified. He concluded that Susan "could have been" dead for as long as twenty-four hours before her body was discovered. The cause of death was tentatively listed as "respiratory depression, secondary to an injected opium alkaloid, combined with asphyxiation caused by a tight and forceful adhesive binding." In other words, Bair believed that Susan had been sedated, then strangled to death. He was wrong. For some reason, never adequately explained, this incorrect preliminary finding was entered into the official report. Six long months would pass before a minute sample of Susan's frozen blood was finally tested: it contained ten times the lethal dose of morphine. The erroneous cause of death was just one in a series of costly, frustrating mistakes.

3

It was midafternoon when Lou DiSantis arrived at the Fidelity Bank in Philadelphia where Ken Reinert worked as personnel manager. DiSantis, a tall, sharp-featured, rough-hewn state trooper, was carrying an Upper Merion High School yearbook. "Is this your ex-wife?" he asked Reinert, pointing to a picture of Susan.

Reinert's face darkened, his knees buckled, as he stared at the photograph. "Yeah, what's wrong?" he asked, as casually as he could.

"She's been murdered, sir," DiSantis said.

Ken Reinert clenched his fists. "Oh, God," he managed to say, as the color drained from his face.

"I'm afraid you'll have to come to Harrisburg to identify the body."

Reinert spoke to his secretary, packed his briefcase, and followed DiSantis out to the patrol car. It was a long, silent drive. Neither man was prone to talking much, especially to strangers. For years, DiSantis had kept quiet until he knew exactly who he was dealing with. Ken Reinert, always shy and withdrawn, now repressed the growing wordless fear, the terror that his children too had been murdered. Only his eyes betrayed his anguish—they were tired, bewildered, and filled with occasional flashes of pain that seemed to be provoked by sudden flooding memories. DiSantis saw the other man's distress, then turned his own eyes back to the road.

At 6:50 P.M., Holtz and Van Nort met DiSantis and Reinert at Exit 29 of Interstate 83. When they got to the morgue, Holtz went in first. He was surprised to find Susan's body completely uncovered. "Who the hell's been in here?" he wondered aloud, as he pulled the sheet up to her neck. Then he led Reinert in.

"Yeah, that's her," Reinert whispered.

"Take a good look," Holtz urged gently.

Reinert looked again very quickly, winced, turned his head, and drew in his breath. "I'm sure," he said. "It's her."

On the way from the morgue to the station house, Holtz and Reinert separated from the others and stopped at Archie's Bar and Grille on Route 22 and Prince Street. Reinert ordered coffee, Holtz had steak. When they arrived at the station house, Reinert explained that Susan had asked him for a divorce several years earlier. "We always had a wonderful marriage," he said, "until this teacher, this guy Bradfield came along. I never understood what the hell she saw in him." He was talking faster now, as if the years of bottled-up feelings were about to be vented. "That bastard destroyed our marriage, completely destroyed it. She fell in love with him. She, uh, got involved, and after that I couldn't even talk to her in a sensible way. She became like a different person. Nothing I could do, nothing the kids could do, made a difference.''

"Kids?'' Holtz echoed.

"Yeah, that's what I want to ask you about,'' Ken said, finally forcing himself to raise the subject. "See, as far as I know, they left with Susan on Friday. I haven't heard from them since Friday night and I'm getting worried. I mean, I don't know where the hell they are.'' His face was pale and his hands were beginning to shake. "Karen, my daughter, she's eleven, and Michael is ten. Michael is what you would consider . . . what I consider, a typical boy. He is outgoing, interested in sports, doesn't like to do his homework that much, but does good in school. Has a lot of friends and does what boys normally do.'' Reinert continued talking rapidly to cover his apprehension. "Karen is a little more quiet than Michael. Not quite as outgoing. She is interested in gymnastics. I think she really does a lot of things that her mother wants her to do. When she comes over to the house, she pretends she is a teacher and things like that.''

"When did you last see your children?'' Holtz asked, speaking carefully, tactfully, but with a new level of intensity.

"I saw them on Friday, last Friday, you know, the evening of June twenty-second. There was, uh . . . Michael was active in Cub Scouts and they were having a father-son softball game. We met at the church where the game was.''

"How was Michael dressed at that time?'' Holtz asked.

"He was dressed to play baseball. He had a Phillies shirt on, which had pinstripes and a *P* on it, and blue jeans and sneakers.''

"Did you say that Susan had dropped Michael off? Is that right?''

"Right.''

"Did she stay for any part of the game?''

"No, Michael just got out of the car. Susan didn't say anything to me. She just drove off, like, in a hurry. Then we walked to the game. We played a couple of innings and then there was a lot of thunder, so they canceled the game. We went inside for the normal Cub Scout pack meeting they were having that night. There were thirty boys running around up front, and Lynn—that is, my second wife—and I were sitting in the back of the parish hall in the church. I happened to look over and I saw Susan standing to the right, over by the door, like about fifteen feet away from us. I said to Lynn, 'I wonder what the hell she is doing here,' because I was supposed to take Michael home. I guess she had gotten Michael's attention. Michael came running back to his mother. They then walked out of the church together.''

"How was Susan dressed at that time?"

"She had on blue jeans and it was like, I guess, what I would consider a white, knit blouse with short sleeves, with various thin, colored stripes running across it, red-, green-, yellow-type stripes. I think she had sandals on.''

"After she left with Michael," Holtz asked, "what did you do?"

"Well, all these little boys were running around, which was quite loud, so I said to Lynn, 'There is no sense us staying anymore.' So we left the church. At that time, I guess, it was between eight and eight-thirty.''

"Did you go right home?"

"Yes, we went right home. As we went out, we could see Sue turning the corner with Michael, and it appeared that Karen was also in the car with her going back home.''

"This would have been approximately what time?"

"It was probably about quarter after eight—you know, a good average. I think she came somewhere around eight, eight-fifteen. We left shortly thereafter. Then at approximately a quarter of nine—I remember because there was a bad thunderstorm—we happened to be standing out front and there was a fire across the street, or at least they called the fire company. I happened to hear the phone ring. I went in and it was Michael on the phone. He said, 'I just called to apologize for leaving the game without telling you. I had to go home to scrub my floor because I am going away.'

"I said, 'Where are you going?' There was a long pause. 'Just a minute, Dad,' he said. Then he checked with his mother. I heard him say, 'Mom, Dad wants to know where we are going.' Then I heard her say in the background, 'Why don't you tell him we are going to Parents Without Partners.' After that, we said good-bye and that was it.''

When Holtz finished questioning Reinert at the station house, DiSantis offered to take him home. Before leaving, Ken Reinert called his father in Phoenixville.

"Hello, Dad," he said. "I think you and Mom better meet me over at the house in a couple of hours.''

"Why? What's wrong, Ken?" his father asked. There was a

long silence. "Ken, hey, what the hell's wrong?"

"Dad," Ken finally stammered, "it's Sue. Sue was in an accident and they can't locate the children."

After the call, Ken Reinert climbed into the car beside Lou DiSantis and as they drove from Harrisburg to Philadelphia he slumped down in the seat, looking tired and numb. Sue was the first girl he'd ever dated. They met at a sorority party during the fall of their senior year at Grove City College. She was a thin, shy girl, not exactly pretty, but delicate and feminine, with fine, chestnut hair, a toothy smile, and large, dark translucent eyes that shone like black opals when she was happy. Ken found her immediately likable. She was, he later recalled, very sweet, yet at the same time, really smart. Someone he could protect and also look up to. Very soon, she was his best friend. He was the first boy who had ever noticed her.

She graduated with a major in English and highest honors, and they became engaged that night. The next day, Ken, who had been accepted for the ROTC program, left for military training in Texas. Soon afterward, Sue started graduate school at Penn State. It was a lonely year for both of them. They were married the following July at her house in Ridgeway, she in a long, white gown and veil, with her college roommate and sorority sisters forming the bridal party. After the wedding, they took a short honeymoon to Niagara Falls and then drove to Mathers Air Force Base in California, where Ken was now stationed.

It seemed, to this quiet young man, like the romantic fulfillment of the American dream: a girl, a boy, a marriage, then going off to serve the country. Ken thought Sue adapted well to military life. After finishing her master's degree, she became active in the officers' wives club and worked as a substitute teacher at a nearby high school. They spent weekends at Lake Tahoe, or drove to San Francisco. In 1966, they left California and were stationed in Rome, New York. Ken was in the Strategic Air Command and one week out of every three, he had to be on night duty. Sue often visited him and never complained about being left alone. Karen, their first child, was born on September 23, 1967, a beautiful, six-pound, eleven-ounce girl. The next year, they were sent to Puerto Rico. Ken had been given a choice: one year without family or three if he brought them. Sue decided to go. She taught college English at the base extension of the American University until blond-haired, blue-eyed Michael was born. The children were what she valued most in the world. She gladly gave up the stimulation of working just to play with them and watch them laugh. They were the heart of her world. It was, Ken remembered, one of their happiest periods.

In 1971, after they left the military, Sue and Ken would sit at the kitchen table in Ken's parents' house in Phoenixville working late into the night, preparing their résumés. Money was short, the children were no longer babies, and Susan had decided to return to work. She had two or three teaching offers. After carefully considering the options, she chose Upper Merion High School because it had the highest number of merit scholars in the country. She liked the job, and, at first, Ken thought their marriage seemed better than ever.

Ken was not quite sure when things began to go wrong. His guess was that it was 1974, when Susan began seeing a marriage counselor. At first, when she asked him to go, he said no. It seemed like a waste of money; besides, talking to strangers about personal problems was not his style. Then, realizing that the marriage was in serious trouble, he agreed. Now, in retrospect, Ken realized that right from the start there was only one problem, "that son of a bitch, William Bradfield," the teacher Susan seemed to be obsessed by.

"I know now that Susan was in love with him, but she didn't say so. She just suggested that we separate. At first, I didn't fight her. I figured she needed a little time to come to her senses, so I moved out and lived in an apartment for two or three months, then I returned to the house. I was paying the bills and I insisted that I had the right to stay. 'It's my house, too,' I told her. I was angry and hurt. 'I never wanted this separation, I'm moving back.' That's when I found the love letters that she'd written to Bradfield." They were written by his wife, but the words were those of a woman he did not recognize. Susan's deep love for William, and her growing need for him, had brought out a side of her personality that no one who knew her had ever encountered. He seemed to release a hidden erotic aspect, a passionate core that had been buried deep within her.

Dearest Bill,

So many places I want to touch you. So many places I want to be touched by you . . . Wish I could convey my images

of making love to you as well as you have to me. I love you.
I miss you. I think of you constantly.

Love, S

As if Susan were learning to be more explicit and erotic through
the process of writing to her lover, she added later: "Just wasn't
satisfied with that letter. . . . Know why? I love the top of your
head. That's what I see and feel when you're kissing my
breasts. . . . I would never have known it was possible to feel so
good. . . . Just thinking about you has me so excited that I
would come as soon as you touched me."

Susan also clearly believed that she was loved and needed by
Bradfield: "Don't be depressed. If we both want it, we can
arrange to have more time together this fall. We'll talk about it
when you return."

Now, as he sat in the darkness next to Lou DiSantis, driving
toward Philadelphia, Ken Reinert felt the old anger and pain rise
and surge. Then, once again, he put the memory of Susan's
letters to Bill Bradfield out of his mind. Tonight, even more
painful thoughts replaced it. The memory of Susan's lifeless
body lying on that cold steel table, and the fear, the relentless,
overwhelming nightmare of fear, that Karen and Michael were
also dead.

4

By midmorning of the following day, Susan's car had been
processed. Most of the articles found in it were routine for a
mother with two young children: a small pink raincoat with two
pennies and one fifty-cent piece in the right pocket, a woman's
guide to emergency car repairs, a Cub Scout pamphlet, a Great
Adventure ticket, and three stuffed toy animals. But there was
also a hollow rubber dildo, snap-on variety, under the front

seat, and a man's blue comb stamped *79th USARCOM,* which had been placed or accidentally dropped directly under Susan's body.

While Joe Van Nort and Jack Holtz were trying to piece together Susan Reinert's story, her brother, Patrick Gallagher, a chemist from Pittsburgh, who'd been notified of the murder by state troopers, began making arrangements to claim her body. Coroner Bush agreed to release the remains to the family and an undertaker arrived the next morning, Tuesday, June 26. As soon as Van Nort heard about the plan, he called Bush. "Hold on to the body until the lab has fingerprinted it and the police have completed a thorough investigation," he ordered. Bush, in turn, told hospital officials to keep the undertaker waiting, but by early afternoon, Susan's body had been fingerprinted, and the undertaker was back. No forensic pathologist had examined the body, and the criminal investigation would forever be without the critical information he could supply. The hospital was under a standing order from the state police, as well as a state law, *never* to release a body without the coroner's specific permission, but somehow, someone apparently misunderstood, and as soon as Susan had been fingerprinted, the undertaker left with her body. He cremated her immediately. When Holtz and Van Nort returned later that afternoon, startled hospital officials, who, to this day, claim they did nothing wrong, stammered, "What body?"

By now, furious state troopers realized that they were confronting not only the murder and unauthorized cremation of Susan Reinert, but the probable murder of both of her children as well. That night, Holtz prepared a news release with firm instructions that it was not to go to press for twenty-four hours. He was hoping someone would report Susan's death *before* the statement appeared in print. But, by the next morning, news of the murder dominated the front pages of Philadelphia's papers. MOTHER'S BODY FOUND IN CAR TRUNK. ARDMORE MOTHER SLAIN, TWO CHILDREN MISSING. Having received the incorrect autopsy report, the *Main Line Chronicle* wrote, UPPER MERION HIGH SCHOOL TEACHER . . . CHOKED TO DEATH.

James Mooney and his friend Dale Kennedy read those headlines and immediately realized that the car they had seen in the Host Inn parking lot that Sunday night held the body of the murdered woman. Kennedy cursed himself for his earlier reluctance to get involved. Anxious to correct his error, and help in any way possible, he immediately wrote to state troopers, informing them that he had observed the vehicle at 7:00 P.M. on Sunday night, at least six hours before Officer Joseph Ruddy had first spotted it, and roughly ten and a half hours before the anonymous call was received. That note, which would have provided police with a new set of critical facts and perspectives, was placed unopened on a pile of papers in Joe Van Nort's office. It was not noticed or opened until after Van Nort's death more than two years later.

Within forty-eight hours of the discovery of what looked like a routine homicide, state police were dealing with one cremated corpse, two missing children, a critically important erased tape, and an incorrect cause and time of death.

5

Jack Holtz asked Lou DiSantis to obtain a search warrant for Sue Reinert's house and serve as a local Philadelphia guide. It was DiSantis's first opportunity to be involved in a major murder case. The lanky kid with the dark hair had grown up in the streets of Philadelphia and had struggled through high school. "Don't waste your money on college, Pop. I ain't never gonna be no student," he had told his father. "Any marks I get, I gotta bust my shoes to get, 'cause nothin' comes easy to me." His father agreed, and Louie had taken a part-time job in the bakery at a local Acme supermarket earning $104 a week. He thought it was good money and he liked the job, but there was a restlessness in this street-smart young man, a quiet yearning for more.

In January 1967, DiSantis left the bakery and joined the state troopers, working on patrol—first on the Pennsylvania Turnpike, then the expressway. The way he figured it, falling into this homicide case was his first lucky break. DiSantis knew it would mean being away from his wife and two little girls, who were only two and four. His wife hated to have him traveling and missing the girls' growing up. "Ain't nothing gonna stop me now," Louie told her with determination. "This is the opportunity of a lifetime. I gotta take it."

Two men from different backgrounds, drawn together in their search for a killer, Jack Holtz and Louie DeSantis did not yet know how well they would work together. Dressed in a three-piece corduroy suit, six-feet-four, gaunt as a weathered fence post, and covering his excitement with a studied calm, DiSantis, search warrant in hand, met Holtz at 662 Woodcrest Avenue in Ardmore. It was four days since Susan had left her house but barely more than twenty-four hours since her body had been found. The white clapboard twin, with its stone chimney and concrete front porch, was indistinguishable from the other houses on the block. The small rock garden, with its azaleas and daffodils, was framed by a tall green hedge. The house looked as sedate and safe as any family dwelling could be. Inside, children's drawings and school papers decorated the walls, symbols of their mother's pride.

Holtz and DiSantis walked past the cherry dry sink, the Queen Anne wing chair, and brown tweed couch, toward the kitchen. It looked as if the family had left suddenly. There were dishes in the sink, a bowl with a little cereal and a glass of milk on the kitchen table. Holtz hurried up the stairs. In Karen's room, clothing was neatly folded, a small overnight bag was packed. The clothing Susan had been wearing when Ken had last seen her was in the bathroom hamper. Holtz also noticed a diaphragm in the medicine cabinet. That was something he figured a young single woman would have taken if she was planning to be away very long.

The men moved through the house quickly. They were looking for signs of a struggle, or the possibility that the kids might still be there, injured or dead. After finding no sign of them, they left. If the children were still alive, there might not be much time to find them.

Donna Formalt, a next-door neighbor, told Holtz and DiSantis she had seen Susan at about 6:00 P.M. on the last night of her life, a few hours before the thunderstorm. "She was out on the porch. She said she was going to a Parents Without Partners meeting in Allentown over the weekend and wondered if she had enough gas. She was worried about getting stuck on Sunday with the even-odd gas-rationing shortage. She said she *had* to be back before Monday. Michael was going to be baptized next week and Karen had to get ready for gymnastics camp. Susan and I were also planning to have a garage sale together next Saturday to get rid of some of our junk.''

The women had been friends since 1977. Donna would watch Karen and Michael each morning when Susan left for work. They would also check in with her after school. "Susan's kids are vibrant, very bright, and full of energy," Donna said. "Michael is feisty, with blond hair and blue eyes; Karen is shy and well behaved, just entering puberty and growing prettier every day." Even after a long day of work, Susan never seemed to tire of driving them from place to place. When she watched Michael hit a home run, or Karen win a trophy for gymnastics, she was radiant with pride.

When Holtz asked Donna if she knew Bill Bradfield, Donna's expression became grim. "Yeah, I knew who he was, but I don't think anyone really knew him. Susan was madly in love with him. Except for her kids, he was the center of her life. She'd have done anything for him. I, for one, always worried about that relationship and about his intentions. Once, after she first moved next door, we had gone to a mall together. She saw a store—a little arts and crafts store—and suddenly she began to cry. We sat down on a bench and she told me she was in love with this man Bradfield, but he had dumped her for another woman. She said he and the other woman, Sue Myers, owned this store together. She told me Bill Bradfield had lied to her, said he was breaking up with the other woman, but then she found out he was still living with her. For a while after that, she was trying to get over him. She dated one or two other people. Then suddenly, when her mother died and she inherited all this money, he came back. He was there at her house constantly. Susan became very quiet and secretive about their relationship. She said he had told her not to talk about it. I was hurt because our friendship had changed. Like I said, I had my doubts, but I hoped things were finally working out between them. Then on May 5, she said she was changing her will. She asked us to be witnesses. My husband, my mother, and I were in our living room.''

"Did you read the document before you signed it?" Holtz asked.

"No, I didn't," Donna said, with a troubled expression. "Actually, Sue told my husband that he could read it, but you just don't read somebody's will. We didn't read it, no. We thought it was strange that she was changing her will again, because sometime earlier in the year, right after her mother died, we had witnessed another will for her, and at that time, she told us that her brother Pat was the trustee. I figured she was changing it for Bill, but I didn't think she seemed happy with him.

"I remember this one afternoon, just a few weeks ago. It was sometime in late May or early June, she was out on the front porch. It was a warm day. I saw Bradfield hurrying out of her house. He wasn't exactly running, but he was moving quickly and you could tell he was determined to leave. As he got down the steps, Sue came out on the porch. Her eyes were all red, she was crying and trying to keep him from leaving. She called to him, but then when she saw that the neighbors were on their porches, she turned around and went back in.

"A short time after that, something really strange happened. Karen and my daughter, Louann, came back from a softball game Michael was playing in. They each had a water ice. Karen decided to go home to put her water ice in the freezer, but both the front door and back door were locked, which was very unusual. Her mother didn't answer the door when she knocked, so she climbed in a window that was off the back porch, a low window. I don't know what happened to that poor child, or what she saw, but suddenly we heard her begin to scream. She screamed and screamed, and then raced out of the house. There was panic, real terror, in her voice."

"Do you know whether Mr. Bradfield was in the house at the time?" Holtz asked.

"Yes, he was," Donna answered.

"And how do you know that?" he asked.

"Because I saw him go in."

Conversation with
William Bradfield

I was never in love with Susan Reinert, I never intended to marry her, and I was never her lover. I wanted to be her friend and to help her. She would often say that I should marry her and that I was the only one she would ever love. She was much more troubled after her mother died, but she had been writing to me and coming to see me for years and years. She wrote to me and badgered me in the summer of 1975 when I was in Santa Fe. She wrote that she would make my life complete and our sex life would be great.

In the summer of 1976, she did it again. I was in New York studying. I was there living with a young lady. I had a pinched nerve, I was in pain and taking a cram course in graduate Latin at NYU. We'd begin at seven-forty-five, classes went on all day until five or six at night. On the first day of class, the professor said, "You're going to live, sleep, and eat Latin. If you came thinking you were going to do your laundry, you won't have time," and he was right. It was the most intense classical-language course I had ever taken. In the midst of this, Susan Reinert called from a hotel. She was in New York and begging me to spend the weekend with her. I was nice, but I said I couldn't. She wouldn't accept no for an answer. Finally, I had to take the phone off the hook. She kept saying that without me her life wasn't worth living. She would look for love wherever she could find it. After that summer, she would come home bruised. She would be absent from school because she would have bruises on her face. She'd say, "You've got to come over, I'm having problems, I can't keep any food down. The children haven't eaten." I'd come over and she would be vomiting. She looked like she was ready to die. I had lost control of the situation, but I wouldn't admit it.

In 1977, I was building a store and I couldn't see her very often.

· In 1978, she came down to Annapolis where I was studying. This time when she called, I wouldn't even answer the phone, and after a while, she changed her will and put me in it and put it in my mailbox. She named me as guardian of her children, but she never told me she had life insurance.

It's my fault that I tried to play God. Overreaching and hubris, those are my great crimes, but not murder. I thought I could help her clean up her act and put her life together. I liked her more at first, but as the years went by, she was just too much for me. Her letters were like adolescent pornographic descriptions.

After her mother's death, she became really insistent that we marry. I tried to put limits on the relationship. I'd say, "I'm your friend, I'll help you, I'll baby-sit for you, but we are not dating." She'd press me. "Can we just go to a movie?" And I'd say, "No, we're not going to do that." She was very insistent, calling me, begging me to make love with her. She'd make a scene and cry and whine. She would send me notes. Things like, "I'm lying here thinking of you coming inside of me." She'd write five notes in a day and send them over to my classroom with five kids. I got all kinds of notes from her, but among them, notes of complaint. She'd say, "All I need is someone to love. I must see you, I'm going crazy." She was a needy person, terribly full of needs. I'd come over and she'd be in a housecoat, shoulders hunched. I'd say, "Let's clean a messy room," and she'd say, "Messy rooms aren't my problem. First of all, could you give me a hug?" I'd hug her, she'd cry and hold on for dear life. She'd say, "If we could live together, you would see how happy I would make you. If I had you here all the time, then things would be different. Could we at least talk about it?" I'd say, "I don't love you in that way, Sue," but she still kept on hoping. She was just too much for me to help.

6

It was Tuesday, June 26, the day after Vincent Valaitis started his summer job with a truck supplier. He was putting linings on brake shoes when Sue Myers called. As soon as she said his name and he heard the desperation in her voice, he knew exactly what had happened.

"Vince," she whispered, "her body was found stuffed in a trunk in Harrisburg. The police are on their way over here looking for Bill."

Vince sat on the edge of the chair rocking back and forth, with the telephone in his hand. The room was growing blurry.

"Vince, can you hear me? She's dead," Sue Myers repeated.

"Oh, God, no," he finally gasped.

Vince knew it was not an ordinary homicide. He had been listening to Bill Bradfield predict Susan's murder for the last nine months, but hadn't believed him. He was also absolutely certain he knew who the murderer was. Bill had even told him the weekend on which it would occur, but the prediction was so bizarre, so ludicrous, that he hadn't taken it seriously. Now, as the reality tore through his guts, he crossed himself. "Dear God," he whispered, "help us all."

Vincent Valaitis had been raised a Roman Catholic. His mother, a housewife of German descent, had been orphaned when she was eighteen months old; she believed in staying home and mothering her children. She lived by the adage that the family was the most important thing in the world. His father, a quiet man with an Old World ethic, ran Valaitis Motors, a small family business. Vince was a shy, dreamy child who enjoyed swinging on the pole that ran up through the basement of their modest house. He thought of that pole as the center of his world. It made, he reasoned, four quadrants. In the first quadrant, he'd grow up; in the second, he'd get married and have children; in the third, he'd become famous, perhaps a movie director or a lawyer; and in the last quadrant, he would grow old, die, and go to heaven. When Vince swung around that pole as a child, he dreamed of someday being the best man he could be. The worst thing he ever imagined was accidentally hitting someone with a car and being responsible for a death.

Now, as he drove through the summer heat with the news that Susan had been murdered, Vince felt a desperate need to reach Bill and tell him that he had been right, that Jay Smith, principal of the high school where he and Bill, Sue Reinert, and Sue Myers all taught English, had actually done it. Whenever Bill talked about it, Vince had said, "If you really think Dr. Smith is going to commit a murder, call the police." But each time, Bill had refused, saying, "Smith has contacts in the police department. He'll find out, then we'll all be in danger. I will have to control him myself, but I'll do it. Whatever it takes, I won't let anything happen to her." Vince had heard rumors at the high school that Bill and Susan Reinert were having an affair. "Why would anyone want to have an affair with a mousy little lady like that?" Bill had said. Then he had added, "I feel sorry for Susan Reinert. She is a frightened woman, desperate for love. She often begged me to make love to her, but I never did."

In the months preceding Susan's murder, Bill was hardly ever home at night. Vince, who lived in an apartment in the same house, often remembered the calm evenings when he would join Bill and Sue Myers upstairs for dinner. Vince recalled the smell of lemon chicken filling the room while Bill discussed Ezra Pound, ancient Greece, and the sonnets of Shakespeare. In those days, Bill had been avidly interested not just in literature, but in what other people thought and said. He had always shown concern and delicate care. Then, everything had changed. Bill would knock at Vince's door early in the morning, pale and exhausted, saying he'd spent the whole night trying to control Jay Smith.

Vince was relieved when he heard that Bill and his friend Chris Pappas, a substitute teacher at Upper Merion, were planning to spend the summer at graduate school at St. John's in Santa Fe, New Mexico. Bill would be taking courses, and working toward his second master's degree. It would be, Vince admitted, both a personal relief and a change Bill badly needed. Suddenly, it seemed peculiar to Vince that after all the months

Bill had tried to protect her, Susan Reinert was found murdered on the very same day that he left for New Mexico and on the same day that Jay Smith was committed to prison for theft.

Vince parked his car and raced up the stairs toward the apartment that Bill Bradfield and Sue Myers shared. He was so lost in thought, so intent on reaching Bill in New Mexico, that he didn't even see the state police pull up right behind him.

When Sue Myers opened the door for Vince, her phone was ringing. She motioned to him to come in, and ran for the receiver. "It's Bill," she said a moment later. "He wants to talk to you." Vince grabbed the phone and stammered out his news.

"Bill sounded very calm, very remote," Vince later recalled. "Yes," he said, his voice as cold as dry ice, "I've already had two phone calls about the tragedy. Don't talk to the police. Don't tell them anything at all." And in the same steady tone, he added, "Don't even mention Dr. Smith's name over the phone." Then for the first time, the pitch of Bill's voice changed. It cracked. "If you do," he warned, "you'll put me in the electric chair."

Vince heard the doorbell, spun around, and saw the door open. Holtz and Van Nort were standing there.

Conversation with Jay Smith

I was born on June 5, 1928, and raised in Chester, Pennsylvania. I feel I had a good family background. We had five brothers and one sister. My father was a good regular worker—worked in Sun Shipbuilding and Drydock Company, was a union leader and organizer, and, I felt, was a good father—a good parent. My mother was a good person. We lived with our grandmother and grandfather on Horton Avenue in Chester and so we had this extended family, rather than a nuclear family.

My grandfather was a caner of chairs. Now, there's a trade that's lost, but chairs were often made out of cane that would be brought in from palm trees and other kinds of trees, and he was probably one of the best caners of chairs and had his own business in Chester, Pennsylvania, and probably one of the first things I learned was how to make chairs. I was pretty good with tools. My people were, you might say, fundamentalist Protestants. We used to go to Madison Street Methodist Church and I guess I was more of a churchgoer than my brothers. My mother and grandmother used to take me to church. I enjoyed that and used to even sing a lot. Seems strange looking at me now, but I was more like a showoff, more than really a good singer. I liked the idea of singing hymns, so I would be the one who would—on Wednesday nights—always be getting up and doing a lot of the singing of hymns.

I was a newsboy, a very active, very well known newsboy in Chester and I used to be very speedy. We used to beat out a paper called the *Philadelphia Record*. I would get my thirty or forty papers. I would know all the taprooms and nightclubs and everyplace, and would go through them and sell the newspapers.

I think the thing that changed everything was the war. I was about thirteen or fourteen when the war broke out. I was frustrated because I couldn't go. My brother Wilmer went, my brother William went, my brother John went. My biggest frustration, I feel, was that I was just too young to go. But I did enlist as soon as I was seventeen. We all hated Japs and I guess we believed all the propaganda. I was eighteen—I'm trying to figure out the time now. You couldn't go in until you graduated, so I enlisted in the National Guard and I was in the National Guard for about six months, then I graduated and went right into the regular army. I was sent to Japan in the occupation, and I was in for about twenty months, but I was never engaged in combat. Never, never in my life. Never been in any combat.

What I would do is go out in the morning and round up Japanese and bring them in for labor groups, to clean up the cities. We cleaned up part of Hiroshima which was bombed. They knew where they could come to get food and where they could come to get money or aid or medical treatment. And when they came there, we would take out the healthy ones and we would pay them, of course, and then take them and help clean up cities or do whatever work or labor we wanted done. Most of them were very much afraid of us, so it wasn't too difficult to get obedience. We were armed. I had an M1 rifle—I was youthful and probably overly aggressive and stuff like that, and the Japanese were very obedient, subservient, fearful. I was only a private, so that I was at a very, very low level. At one point, I was in an infantry squad, and the electrical lines had broken down. This one fellow in my squad went over and picked up the line and got electrocuted. I remember that must have been—I think that was New Year's Day—I can see that vividly—him grabbing that line and getting electrocuted.

The military was my life. Except for being an educator and a principal, it was my whole life. When I was arrested in August of '78, I had completed my course at the National Defense University and was a colonel in the army reserves and being considered for general. I've always felt that being a general was the best kind of achievement that you could make. I would have considered that as important as my doctoral degree. I was a military student, a very top military student. I went to all the military schools—the Officers Infantry School, General Staff College, the War College—I'm a graduate of all those schools. At the time that my world fell apart, I was very close to my lifetime goal of general. I was right next door to it.

7

For a dozen years, Dr. Jay Smith, principal of Upper Merion High School, protected his private life so well that even co-workers who had known him for more than a decade could not say with certainty if he was married or how many children he had.

Smith's military superior, General John Eisenhower, son of the late president, drove with him from Valley Forge to their reserve duty near Lansdale, two Sundays a month, from 1973 to 1975. Eisenhower later recalled Smith's intelligence and his sardonic sense of humor. He praised his outstanding administrative ability as the commander's chief of staff in charge of personnel. Like other colleagues, he referred to Smith as a loner who rarely talked about anything but his work.

In August 1978, Jay Smith sent shock waves through the conservative Upper Merion community. A young couple at a local shopping center saw a man with a hood over his face and a gun in each hand swagger toward a parked van. They called police, who arrived within minutes and later identified that man as Dr. Jay Smith. The arresting officer, Lieutenant Carl Brown, Jr., approached Smith's car and saw a .22-caliber pistol lying on the seat. Smith inched back, picked up the pistol, and put his finger on the trigger. "Drop your gun, man," Brown shouted. Smith, still wearing his hooded mask, hesitated for a moment with his finger shaking on the trigger, then he dropped the pistol.

On the passenger seat was an open black bag that contained a .38-caliber, a .22-caliber, and a .25-caliber handgun, all loaded. Jay Smith told police he was looking for his daughter and son-in-law, who, he feared, were being held in the van by heroin dealers. Smith, who had no license to carry handguns, was arrested. While held at police headquarters, he placed a call. An officer standing behind Smith heard him whisper, "Get everything out of the basement, especially the file cabinet." The officer alerted two detectives, who hid in an unmarked car across from Smith's house. They saw a 1974 tan-and-white Plymouth pull up to the rear of the house. The detectives crept through the shrubbery and trees and watched a man run back and forth, carrying items out of Jay Smith's house. He made five or six trips. Then, as he closed his car trunk and prepared to leave, the officers approached him.

"I'm a friend of Dr. Smith's," the man stammered. He identified himself as Harold Jones. "He called me while I was at work at my part-time job at the Globe Security Company and asked me to run an errand for him. I didn't remove anything from the house. I couldn't even find the gun permit he asked me to look for."

"We'd like to search your car."

"You have no right to search without a warrant," Jones answered indignantly.

"Listen," the detective said, "we've been standing here watching you ever since you arrived."

"I didn't do anything wrong," Jones responded, suddenly panicky. "You can have whatever you want. Search my car without a warrant if you want to. I only did what I was told to do. Everything in the trunk belongs to Dr. Smith. None of it's mine."

When Jones's trunk was opened, the detectives found army manuals issued by the War College in Carlisle, Pennsylvania. There were also three paintings belonging to Upper Merion High School and a file box containing two white plastic bags. Each bag held about one pound of marijuana. Jones was arraigned by Justice Bernard Maher and later released on $50,000 bail.

When Smith's car was processed, the items found in it stunned the police force and instantly created speculation about bizarre criminal behavior. There were four .22-caliber cartridges, seven .25-caliber cartridges, ten high-speed Mohawk .22-caliber cartridges, a box containing another fifty high-speed Mohawk cartridges, and a military-style blue raincoat with eight cartridges in one of the pockets. Police officers also found five black empty plastic garbage bags tied with rubber bands, a pair of white gloves, one Biger .22-caliber rifle, a Colt Cobra revolver, and a black-and-red bolt cutter. Under the seat was a notebook that said, "Brinks 3:30, 7/26 (Wednesday), Wanamakers, King of Prussia."

Convinced that they had stumbled across a master of criminal activity, police searched Smith's house. They found seventeen bottles of pills, most of which were hidden in a blue woolen sock in the left-hand side of the second drawer of a file cabinet. They also discovered another large bundle of marijuana, five oil filters adapted as silencers for pistols, and, most important, a dark blue Brinks security-guard hat, a security badge, and an employee identification card with a photograph of Dr. Smith and the name Carl S. Williams.

While Jay Smith remained in Chester County Prison unable to make the $50,000 bail, Upper Merion police were rapidly piling up charges against him that dealt with a number of unsolved crimes. Among them was a December 1977 security-guard robbery of about $100,000 in cash and personal checks from a Sears, Roebuck store in nearby Abington. Police were also linking Smith to the theft of $34,000 in cash and $19,000 in checks from another Sears store in St. David's. In both cases a man wearing a Brinks security-guard outfit had come to collect the day's cash. Only after he had departed with the money and the real guard had shown up did store officials realize that they had been robbed.

Another search of Smith's ordinary, middle-class brick-and-cinder-block house, overlooking Valley Forge Industrial Park, turned up a collection of pornographic and bestiality magazines, among them *Animals As Sex Partners*, *Animal Fever*, *Carla's Puppy Love*, *The Four-Legged Lovers*, *The Beastial Erotics*, *Herbie's Dreams*, and *The Canine Tongue*.

Conversation with
Jay Smith

There was no pornography, nothing I would call pornographic. See, Loretta, you gotta remember, my daughter was involved in sexual activities very heavily as a prostitute to support her heroin habit. Her husband, Eddie, was also an addict, so they may have had a book like, let's say, *Hustler,* but there was nothing in *my* library or *my* stuff that they found or saw that I would consider unusually pornographic and, I'm going to make up a word, beastialistic. Is that a word? I don't know. Where did they come up with the idea of pornography or that I was fooling around with women on my faculty? Where did they come up with the idea that I was part of a satanic cult?

All right, yeah, I was working on an idea. I was working on a lot of ideas. At the time we're talking about, 1975 to 1978, I had felt that the homosexual issue was going to grow because it was already a big issue. Riots had occurred in New York at a homosexual nightclub. So I was working, and had about four chapters finished on how to prevent homosexuality in a child. It was to be a little pamphlet of about seventy-five pages and that was the topic of it. If they were ill-willed and wanted to, I had a book by Dr. Thomas Ralph called *Animal Physiology.* See, most of what we learn is from animals, O.K., so I had Dr. Ralph's book on animal physiology and I had, uh, I'm trying to think now. I had a book of humorous sayings, a book titled *Animals, Animals, Animals.* It was humorous sayings or cartoons. I can't remember the name of the author, but it had three words—animals, animals, animals—in it. Aside from things like this, I can't think of anything. I am denying that I ever had pornographic or beastiality books in my library. There was never a book about, let's say, black garters or whips or chains.

They said on television that they found pornographic books. All right. They define something as pornographic. Does their definition agree with yours? Here is the criminal justice system. It knows that if you can smear a person sexually and get that spread around, you're influencing the jury. See, all the prosecution and the police care about is the jury, everything else is secondary. And the sexual smears are one of the most common ways to influence the jury.

I think one of the things is, and this is a negative on my part, that being a principal of a high school, the expectations of me might be different or higher from a standpoint of, let's say, conventional morality than they would be of others. Like, if you said, for example, the pope of Rome was reading *Playboy*, that would sound bad, so, the principal of the high school has pornography. But what is it?

Even women have to pretend they are interested in it, just so their man is pleased. It's been my impression that women are much less interested in pornography than men are. Even though I hear that has changed, I don't think it has. So, they put this out, they gossip about it, see. Even Bradfield picked it up. He started saying Smith had sexual relations with some of his staff. Well, I know many principals who do have sexual relations with their staff, but I'm not one of them. That's the kind of thing that I think hurt. I didn't feel at the time when I was arrested that it would be as devastating as it was, but then I found that every place I went they kept bringing it up. It then dawned on me that this was one of the criminal justice system's techniques— widespread smear, especially sexual smear, to influence the jury that this is a bad guy. Therefore, it is then believable that he could do these other things. Do *anything*. There is something about sex that's special. If they make you out as sexually loose or sexually promiscuous, or a sexual nut, then they can almost get you on anything. And that's exactly what they did to me. I think there are a lot of people out there that think Smith is a member of a sexually promiscuous group, and he was fooling around with his teachers, that he may have fooled around with students sexually, and that he was basically a sexually promiscuous and even a kind of kooky, nutty guy. Capable of anything— any kind of crazy crime. All I'm saying is that it's not true, and there's no proof of it, but still I think that impression prevails.

8

Within a week of his arrest, Smith was formally suspended by the school board. But the action did not satisfy the crowd of several hundred frantic parents who attended a specially called meeting later that week. They wanted to know how a man who was in command of their children's educations, a man who had served as high school principal for twelve years, could have led such an incredible double life.

Bill Bradfield was the only person who rushed to Jay Smith's aid. He wrote to him at Chester County Prison, offering to send him books and help him in any way he could. Smith responded promptly.

Dear Bill:

Please cut out the Dr. Smith stuff, Jay or Jack is what my friends call me. I prefer Jack. Send me a copy of Warriner's [book of composition and grammar]. I can tutor here and make a couple of bucks for cookies, etc. Also, a copy of *Ivanhoe* if you have it, and *Moby Dick* . . . and you, *especially* you, be alert. I'll see you when I get out and give you a full story.

Smith raised his bail and, within a week of his arrest on drug and weapons charges, he was released from prison. Soon afterward, William Bradfield visited Smith at home. "Bill seemed upset," Vince later recalled. "He told me that Jay Smith was innocent and that the police were twisting evidence and unjustly harassing him. Bill said, 'I know he couldn't have robbed the Sears store at St. David's because the day the theft occurred I was with him. That was the day I bumped into him at the shore. The realization came to me last night in a dream. I dread getting involved in Smith's case, but I have no choice. After all, it's my moral responsibility to tell the truth.' "

Vincent Valaitis accepted the explanation because it seemed honest and ethical, and in keeping with Bill's high standards. Then, about three months later, somewhere around Thanksgiving of 1978, as Vince remembered it, "I was driving with Bill to the local shopping mall. Bill said he had to confide in someone. Then he turned to me and began talking almost in a whisper. 'Remember when I told you I was with Smith that night at the shore? Well, I told him about it too, but I said, 'I won't help you unless I'm sure you're telling me the truth. You have to come clean with me.' Then Smith admitted he'd been a hit man for the Mafia and had killed scores of people. He said he keeps a list of people who don't deserve to live. Vince, one of them is Susan Reinert.''

"My God," Vince gasped. "Why would Smith tell you these things?" Bill's blue eyes were troubled. "I don't know, Vince," he answered. "I just don't know."

Later that night, Vince discussed the situation with his parents. His father shook his head in disgust. "Stay away from it. The whole thing sounds too crazy to deal with," he warned. Vince agreed. He promised his father that he would not get involved, but throughout that winter and the following spring Bill told him again and again that Susan was going to be killed by Smith. Then, on what turned out to be the last weekend of her life, as he and Vince drove toward the shore, Bill slammed his fist against the car seat, and moaned, "This is it, Vince. This is the weekend that Susan will be killed." By this time, Vince had decided that either Smith was a madman making insane threats or Bill was imagining things. Vince humored his friend. "Hey," he said soothingly, "calm down. You did the best you could. No one can control a nut like Smith."

9

As soon as Susan's close friend Sharon Lee heard that Susan had been murdered, she telephoned William Bradfield. "It was Tuesday afternoon, June 26. I called St. John's University in New Mexico. They said that he was out, but they expected him back shortly, and would leave a message. Around seven o'clock that night, Bill called back. He was talking very softly as if he was afraid that he'd be overheard. He said he'd been told about the tragedy, but he wanted to know the details. I told him essentially what I knew—that her body had been found nude and beaten in the trunk of her car—and I asked him if he knew what she was doing in Harrisburg, or where she was planning to go that weekend. He said he had no idea. I said, 'Well, when were you planning to see her again?' He said, 'Not until September, when school started.' I was shocked because Susan told me they were getting married in England in July. 'But you were supposed to go to England with her this summer,' I said. I didn't mention that they were going to be married because that was still being kept a secret. Bill acted surprised. 'No,' he said, 'Susan was pursuing me and trying to persuade me to go to England, but I told her that I wasn't interested.' I was completely stunned. Not knowing how to handle it, I changed the subject and asked if he had any idea where the children might be, who might be taking care of them. 'The children?' he mumbled, like he was in a daze. 'Oh, yes, the children. How old *were* the children?' This was crazy. There was no doubt he knew those children very well. I had seen them all together several times. I remember one day in particular, Sue and Bill and I were at Sue's house talking about *The Great Gatsby*. Karen came home from school. He called her over, sat her on his lap, and started talking to her, playing up to her, telling her what a great kid she was, a really terrific little girl, and Karen was eating it up, having a wonderful time. Now, suddenly, he was acting like he wasn't planning to marry Sue, didn't remember the children, and even more alarming, he was talking about them in the past tense as if, somehow, when the rest of us thought they were still alive, he *already* knew they were dead.''

With a lot of hunches and very little specific evidence, Jack Holtz and Joe Van Nort drove to Cape May, New Jersey. They met with local detectives and distributed photographs of the children. Then they paid a visit to Marian Taylor, owner of the boardinghouse where William Bradfield and his companions had spent the weekend of Susan's death.

''Bradfield, Valaitis, Myers, and a substitute English teacher, Christopher Pappas, arrived at about 5:00 A.M. on Saturday morning. I was asleep at the time,'' Marian Taylor explained, ''but when I woke up at seven-thirty, Bill Bradfield and Chris Pappas were waiting for me in the hallway. At about eight-fifteen, Sue Myers and Vince Valaitis arrived. They said they had walked to the Lobster Pot Restaurant for coffee. Bradfield paid me for the two rooms, then asked for a receipt for four days. I thought it was strange and kidded him about it. I said I would put Friday on the receipt, but I wouldn't charge him for it, since he wasn't there. I figured it was for tax purposes. But I was still confused because on Tuesday, the nineteenth of June, Mr. Bradfield had come to the hotel and asked me to reserve the rooms for him. He said he would be arriving late Friday and wanted the keys left in the rooms. I've known the man for years. He has stayed at the Heirloom many times, but this was the first time he had ever made a reservation.''

Holtz slipped word of the backdated receipt to the press. When questioned, Bradfield refused all comment. Contacted by reporters, Charles Fitzpatrick, one of Bradfield's newly hired attorneys, would only say, ''I don't know what the police have found. I know my clients were in Cape May. I know it was that weekend. I'm positive they were there when the police indicate the death occurred, that is, on Sunday, June twenty-fourth.''

Deluged by reporters, Marian Taylor remained mute, telling them only that the four teachers had been ''very nice guests.'' When asked about the request for a receipt dated Friday, she answered, ''I have nothing to say. If they, the authorities, want to tell you, O.K.''

On Thursday, the twenty-eighth of June, Peter Kelly Jenik, a claims investigator for New York Life Insurance Company, telephoned Jack Holtz and informed him that, about two months before her death, Susan Reinert had purchased several short-term policies totaling $750,000: $250,000 from New York Life and another $250,000 from USAA, with an accidental-death rider of an additional $250,000. He said she had named William Bradfield as her "intended husband" and sole beneficiary. Holtz listened intently. When he hung up, he turned to Van Nort and said, "We've got our motive."

While state troopers were absorbing the news of $750,000 in life insurance, Vincent Valaitis and other friends of Susan's were attending a memorial service held at the Main Line Unitarian Church in Devon, Pennsylvania. Valaitis sat in the back row, next to his friend Bill Scutta, who was also an English teacher. As a huge grand piano played somber classical music, and people sat with their heads lowered in silent contemplation, Pat Gallagher stood, red-eyed. With his voice breaking as he spoke, Gallagher recalled his sister, a tiny gentle girl with long, brown pigtails, tagging along after him. "She grew up to be a quiet, sensitive person who loved her children and her work," Gallagher added.

Toward the end of the service, Pat Schnure, who had taught at Upper Merion with Susan for years, rose from her seat and addressed the group. "We've got to get to the bottom of this," she said urgently. "With the help of God, this crime will be solved." She did not need to point out that Susan's "fiancé," Bill Bradfield, had not returned from New Mexico to attend the service. Everyone who knew him had already noticed that he was absent.

Pale and trembling, Vince leaned over and whispered to Scutta, "I've got information about the murder and I don't know what to do."

"Go to the police," Scutta answered evenly.

"I can't. Please, let me explain it to you," Vince begged.

Scutta's eyes were suddenly cold. "I don't want to hear anything about it. I don't want to know. I don't want to be involved. It's better if we don't see each other until this thing gets straightened out."

After the service, Vince dropped Scutta off at his house and drove toward the rectory of Mother of Divine Providence

Church. He had to confide in someone. As he drove, a violent thunderstorm erupted. Heavy rain made it almost impossible to see the road, but the turbulence and intensity of the storm only increased his sense of urgency. He ran with all the speed of his youth as the torrents of rain drenched his best suit, and lightning flashed overhead. He pounded on the door of the rectory until a startled priest peered out.

"Something very terrible has happened, Father," Vince cried, his voice filled with panic. "I must talk to you."

The priest looked at him for a moment without responding.

"It concerns the Susan Reinert murder."

The priest's face instantly flashed recognition. "Come in, son, and dry yourself," he said. "Then we can talk."

Vince was barely inside the rectory when his story about Bill Bradfield poured out. "He was my closest friend; he tried for months to keep Dr. Smith from killing Susan Reinert," Vince said, "but the effort failed. Bill warned me that I must never go to the police. He told me Smith was a madman who had killed many people. He said Smith had Mafia ties and would have me and my parents killed. Please help me, Father, tell me what to do."

Father Daley looked directly at the tall, boyish, young man with the huge, horn-rimmed glasses. Then he put his hand on Vince's shoulder. He chose his words carefully. "You've done nothing wrong, son, and it's probably best not to go to the police, because everything you know is hearsay. Try, instead, to get Bill Bradfield to go to the police." The advice confirmed Vince's instincts and comforted him.

As soon as he got home, he called New Mexico. "I've talked to a priest, Bill," he said. "The priest told me that it's important for you to go directly to the police and tell them everything you know about Smith." There was a long silence at the other end.

"Maybe it wasn't Smith," Bill said finally. His voice sounded strange and distant. "There's someone else who might have done it, a black man named Alex that Susan dated. Listen, Vince," he added a moment later, "I think these lines are being tapped. Thanks for your call. I'll be talking to the police as soon as they submit their questions."

10

Pat Schnure hadn't realized that Susan Reinert was in love with William Bradfield until one afternoon during the fall of 1975 when she found her in the teachers' room at Upper Merion High School, weeping. By then, Susan told her, she and Bradfield had been lovers for more than a year. "As soon as I came through the double doors and saw Susan, I could tell that something was wrong," Pat later recalled. "Usually, Sue was thoughtful and sensible. She was a devoted mother and a wonderful teacher. A bright, quiet, calm person. But this time, she was running wildly. I followed behind and saw her fall to the floor. She was hysterical, absolutely hysterical. In my whole life, I had never seen anyone crying like that. She was trying to talk to me, but I couldn't understand what she was saying. I sat down next to her on the floor and held her, rocking her like a baby, until she became calm enough to speak. Finally, she told me that Bill was her lover and that she had written him a letter, begging him not to move in with Susan Myers. Part of it was very passionate and very explicit. Sue was still married and she was frantic because somehow Susan Myers had found that letter and read it."

Despite repeated rumors that William Bradfield had been living with Susan Myers since 1974, Susan Reinert had tried hard to believe Bradfield's denials. Now he was admitting that he intended to move in with Susan Myers. Sue was desperate for a committed relationship, and her letter was an unguarded statement of her love and despair.

> I can't sleep. I'm tired of crying, so maybe if I write, I can try to get some understanding of what's happening. I remember how upset you were last year when I told you everyone assumed you and Sue Myers were living together.

I also remember what you told me about your relationship with her, in contrast with your feelings for me. I was able, with your assistance, to explain away why you chose to spend so much time with her. Now that you are taking deliberate action to solidify your relationship with her, I cannot avoid the reality of it. I don't want to be part of a triangle either . . . while you are providing yourself with the opportunity to make love whenever you want to, you are depriving me of the only opportunity I wanted for that. You are ensuring that many things I had hoped for would never happen. You're making sure that Michael will never play football with you, and that Karen won't get the hugs she so badly needs and wants. I'll never hear you play your piano. That's terribly hard for me to accept. When we're alone together, we each feel at peace. You know that I want to be with you as much as you want to be with me. Why can't you remember that when you're away from me. . . .

8:00 p.m. I'm hot with desire for you. Do you think it's normal, whatever that is, to want each other as much as we do? My body smiles and opens to receive all of your love, you can touch any part of me and I am ready. I want you to touch all of me. I want to kiss and caress all of you. . . . Bill, I ache for your comfort and love and tenderness and passion and strength. I love you.

In the years that followed, Pat Schnure watched helplessly as Susan Reinert's marriage broke up and her relationship with Bill deteriorated. Over and over, Susan had tried to separate herself from Bradfield because he was unwilling to make a commitment to her. For years, Pat had serious doubts about his sincerity and trustworthiness. They began a year or so after that day in the teachers' room. Pat had offered to drop him off at home after school, since he was without a car that afternoon. While they were driving, she decided to express herself directly. "Why don't you choose one Sue or the other?" she asked, meaning Susan Reinert or Susan Myers. "Bill touched my hand and smiled sadly," Pat later recalled. "He said, 'My life is fragmented, Pat, and I don't really love either Sue.' Then, when we arrived at his house and I stopped the car, he leaned toward me. 'Pat,' he whispered, 'I'd like to know you much better. I'd like to know you inside and out.' He tried to kiss me. I called

Sue and I told her what had happened. Naturally, Bill denied it, but after that, for a long time, the relationship between them was on and off, largely off.

"Then suddenly everything had changed. After Susan's mother's death, she inherited money and land. In March of 1979, Susan said, 'Bill has finally asked me to marry him. I gave him the diamond ring that I inherited from my mother to reset as a wedding ring, and money from her estate to invest.' 'Why are you doing that, Sue?' I asked. 'Why don't you just invest your money yourself?' 'Well,' Sue answered, 'Bill asked me what I wanted to do with the money I inherited from Mother and I told him I wanted to invest it in my children's education.' 'I support the idea completely,' he said. 'In fact, I will match your investment. If each of us contributes twenty-five thousand dollars, we can buy a high-yielding certificate for fifty thousand dollars that will secure the children's education.'"

Now, eight days after Susan's body was found, Pat sat alone in her living room, and wondered what had become of Susan's $25,000 and of the diamond ring. Filled with a new level of concern, Pat ran downstairs, picked up the phone, and called the state police.

Conversation with William Bradfield

I knew that love for a woman was impossible for me after Maria. She was different. She was everything. I had just finished eighth grade and was living in Baltimore when I met her. I was fourteen. She was a huge chapter in my life. We used to sit in Baltimore and look out over a pond with geese in it. It led to the sea, and over that sea was her home. She had come from northern Italy, Venice. She was so different. She never played the coquette. I wanted a girl I could talk to and share my deepest thoughts with. When I first met her I was hitchhiking to the city, seeking adventure. It was August 1946. I got lost. A beat-up old Ford truck came along. It stopped. I got in. There was an old guy driving. Next to him was this girl. She was his interpreter. I talked with him through her. They'd been out getting vegetables. I began to talk to this fellow, but I was looking at the girl. She had eyes that were gray-green and long dark hair. I thought she was absolutely marvelous. I didn't want to leave her. With my heart in my throat, I said, "What's your name?" "Maria DiCavalcanti," she answered. Her grandfather said, "You must come down and visit us." She said, "What about Saturday?"

We began to spend time together. We talked about the sea. I told her her eyes were the color of the sea, her sea, the Adriatic. We had three years together. The most marvelous years of my life. My father would lock me in my room. I would sneak out to see her. I'd climb out the window. A lot of it was dreaming together, and reading books. I had discovered Homer and when I talked about *The Odyssey,* she would listen in just the right way. We'd walk through the streets together and talk about music—Schubert's *Unfinished Symphony* and Bach. I introduced her to Bach. When I met her parents I asked them endless questions. I also asked them if I could marry her.

I was holding her hand at St. Joseph Hospital in Baltimore when she died of polio. I walked out of the room and told her parents that their daughter was dead. It was August 1, 1949. I didn't go to the funeral and I never saw her parents again. I was so furious at God for doing that to me. After that, it was never authentic again. Never complete. Her life and death were just shatteringly important to me. I think the reason I played football was in large part due to her death. I didn't care about getting hurt, and I enjoyed the rough physical contact. I'd hit someone as hard as I could to expiate my rage. She was my solution and I had lost her. Maria's death changed the way I came at women. After that, any other little casual affair had to be just that. Nothing could ever be the love I had promised Maria.

Twenty-nine years later, when I was expecting to be arrested, I went back to retrace my steps. I walked down to the boats. I looked for the tree that Maria and I used to lie under. I couldn't find it, but I found the pond. I needed to go back one more time to try to work it through again. To address those conflicts again. To understand why it had never been the same after Maria. Why it had never been complete again. Why I began every relationship with constraints. I told every girl from then on, don't expect this, don't expect that. After Maria, it was all a matter of commerce. My experience with Maria scarred me with a wound that never healed, but why did I keep licking at it, picking at the damned thing? It didn't help me learn how to love. It just kept raising hopes in people that were bound to be hopeless.

11

Joanne Aitken, a quiet, intellectual graduate student in architecture at Harvard University, spent the first three weeks of June 1979—the last weeks of Susan Reinert's life—registered in a cheap Philadelphia hotel under the name Mrs. William Bradfield.

Joanne had met Bradfield the same year Susan Reinert had. It was the fall of 1974 and Joanne, who was working as the director of admissions at St. John's College in Annapolis, had come to Upper Merion to recruit students. At first, the relationship was casual. Several times a year Bradfield would bring small groups of high school students to see the college and at the same time he'd visit with Joanne. By the following September, she was deeply in love.

Addressing him as "Dear Wonderfully-incredibly-dear to me William," Joanne, who had always prided herself on her strength and independence, was now consumed by her love and passion for Bradfield.

> I want to say that you can't imagine how wonderful Sunday was to me (but of course you can) . . . no one can stop my constant thoughts of you—but you can stop my thoughts of everyone and everything else. I love you beyond belief.
>
> J.

As the years passed, Joanne's dependence on Bradfield grew, and so did her loneliness. She seemed to become almost desperate and to feel that she could barely survive without him. In December 1978, six months before Susan Reinert's murder, she wrote:

> This morning was the bottom of a great depression. I felt that there was no way I could get through the next hour. And hundreds of them loom before me. Until I can see you at Christmas . . . and after that, through a doubly terrible time till Easter and then summer. And what about next year? How can I return to Boston without you? I'm frightened to act without you around. I want to have you there to comfort me.
>
> Please take care. I need to see you. I don't feel as if I care what else happens as long as I can be with you.
>
> Love, J.

On June 25, the same day Susan Reinert's body was found, Joanne Aitken took William Bradfield and his friend Christopher Pappas to the airport. Bradfield and Pappas were catching a flight to New Mexico. Joanne was driving Bill's Volkswagen across the country and joining him at summer school in Santa Fe.

Twenty minutes into the first session of the science of natural mathematics, which was a discussion of Plato and the creation of the cosmos, William Bradfield challenged his professor, Steve Crockett. Crockett was impressed by Bradfield's intelligence and liked his spirit. The men quickly became friends. Not only was Bradfield the best student in the class; for years he had maintained a straight-A record in all of his seminars. Joanne Aitkin would frequently join the classes. Afterward, Crockett and his wife, Margaret, Joanne, and Bill would sit in the cafeteria and argue about obscure philosophical questions. Bill Bradfield and Margaret, a slender, blue-eyed blonde, with a beautiful sparkling smile and two small children, became close friends and often spent their free time walking together in the woods, jogging, or just talking about things they both believed were important. However, neither Margaret nor her husband, Steve Crockett, knew anything about what William Bradfield had left behind in Pennsylvania. Bradfield never mentioned that a woman he had been trying to save had just been murdered. Crockett had noticed that Bill was on the phone in the dormitory hallway for long periods of time, often speaking in hushed tones. Once Crockett saw Bill engaged in solemn conversation with the director of the university, but he was not aware that the conversation concerned a visit from two out-of-state homicide detectives.

On July 4, Joe Van Nort and Jack Holtz flew to Albuquerque, rented a car and drove to Santa Fe. They met with University Vice-President Dr. J. Avlt, and told him that they wanted to talk to Christopher Pappas alone, *before* meeting with William Bradfield. Fifteen minutes later, Avlt returned apologetically, with both Pappas and Bradfield. Bradfield, Avlt said, had insisted on being present.

Chalk-white and sweating in the dry New Mexico heat, Bradfield listened as Holtz advised him of his rights. He nodded, indicating that he understood. Then, speaking softly in an effort to sound calm, he said, "Chris Pappas, Vince Valaitis, Susan Myers, and I were in Cape May on Friday, Saturday, Sunday, and Monday, the entire weekend of the murder. I'd like to answer your questions and help you, but I have been advised by my attorneys, Charles Fitzpatrick and John Paul Curran, not to answer any questions or give any statements to the police. If you submit written questions to me, I'd be happy to forward them to my lawyer. Chris Pappas and Sue Myers are also being represented by the same firm, and will be following the same procedures.'' Bradfield and Pappas then walked out of the meeting. Holtz and Van Nort exchanged a wordless glance. The battle lines were being drawn.

Jack Holtz was livid. He had just flown halfway across the country, only to be cut off before he could start. Having no other option, he drove to the New Mexico State Police barracks, borrowed a manual typewriter, and pounded out a dozen questions.

How well did you know Susan and her two children?
When did you last see Susan and her children?
What was your relationship with Susan and her children?
What were your activities over the weekend of the 22nd, 23rd, 24th, and 25th, and with whom?
When did you leave Philadelphia for St. John's College in Santa Fe?
What type of transportation did you use?

Despite his rage, he was purposely making the questions easy, nonincriminating, the kind he figured any innocent man would answer.

What was the time and date of your arrival at St. John's College in Santa Fe?
What time did you leave Philadelphia en route to Cape May, and with whom?
What was the time and date of your arrival at Cape May, New Jersey, and departure time on the above dates from New Jersey?
Do you have any information on the whereabouts of Karen and Michael Reinert?
When did you first learn of Susan's death, and from whom?
Do you have any information of importance, relevant to Susan's death, that would aid us in the murder investigation, and in locating the two children?

Holtz reread the questions, pulled the list out of the typewriter, and dialed Bradfield's attorney. A secretary told him that Mr. Curran was out of town. "He represents Mr. Bradfield, but he does not represent Chris Pappas," she said. "Would you like to speak to his partner, Mr. Fitzpatrick?"

Holtz read the twelve questions to Fitzpatrick, who listened carefully, then said, "I have no complaints. As far as I'm concerned, Bradfield can answer them."

The night was hot. Holtz and Van Nort sat around in front of a lonely, sandswept motel, drinking Coors beer and looking up at the snow-covered mountain peaks. It was one hell of a way to spend the Fourth of July.

Normally, Holtz loved his work. He had struggled hard to get to this point in his career, getting up at 5:00 A.M., five days a week, cleaning and watering police horses, studying vehicle codes and criminal law, practicing shooting, riding, then taking fingerprint and first-aid classes. After completing that training, he was still just a young trooper on probation, riding with a senior trooper, an ex-Marine who scared the hell out of him the first time they met. Everybody used to call them Bulldog and the Pup. Finally, he became a uniformed officer and joined the patrol. It had taken another five years to move from the highway patrol to the criminal section. This murder case promised to be the highlight of his career. Even so, once in a while, on nights like this, he longed to be at home with his son. Jason was only eight when Holtz and his wife were divorced. She had been a salesgirl in a department store in Harrisburg when they began dating. After the marriage, she stayed home, took care of the boy, and kept house. She was a pretty girl, five-foot-eight, slender, with auburn hair. She'd once done modeling. Now, nine years into her marriage, she'd decided that being the wife of a cop was difficult, frustrating, and lonely.

When she left, Jack Holtz spent the weekend trying to explain to the boy that his mother wasn't coming home anymore. "We'll be on our own now," he had said, "but we get to keep the house and the dog." When Holtz was away like this, his son stayed with his mother. Usually that worked out fine, but July 4 would have been a good night to be with his boy, watching the fireworks and setting off some of their own. Instead, he was looking up at these giant, lonely mountains and worrying about getting Bradfield to talk.

In the morning, Holtz and Van Nort drove back to St. John's. This time, they asked to see both Chris Pappas and William Bradfield.

"We've spoken to Curran's office and learned that you are not represented by him," Holtz told Pappas sharply.

"Yes, that's true," Pappas admitted nervously, "but if you'll excuse me, I would like to go to a phone and call an attorney."

"I would also like to talk to my attorney," Bradfield added quietly.

About fifteen minutes later, they returned. Pappas looked considerably relieved as he said, "I am now being represented by Mr. Curran's law firm."

Holtz nodded casually and handed Bradfield the twelve questions. William Bradfield glanced at the list, and a look of consternation and anger crossed his face. Once again, when he spoke, his voice was quiet and highly controlled, but his answer, as Holtz recalled it, was firm. "I can't answer any of these questions. I'll submit them to my attorney. I'd like to help in this investigation, but I can't say when I will be able to provide my attorney with the answers. My first concern at this time is with my studies."

Conversation with William Bradfield

I wanted to be cooperative, I started out being cooperative. The first time after the murder that I called home—what I thought was home—Holtz and Van Nort were there. I asked to speak to them. They wouldn't talk to me. Later, they said it was because they had no way of knowing who was really on the phone. The next day, Sue Myers got John Paul Curran as a lawyer. He advised me not to talk to them. I said, "But I can help them." He said, "You're not there to help them, and they're out to get you. If you talk to them, you're putting yourself at risk." My position had been that I wanted to lay everything out for them, but my attorneys felt that I shouldn't. When the authorities came to visit me in Santa Fe, I said, "I have some things I want you to know." They said, "We'll ask the questions. Have you ever been in Susan Reinert's car?" I said to myself, "Hey, wait a minute. This is exactly what Curran said they would do." I looked at Chris. He shook his head. I was direct with them. I said, "Am I a suspect?" They said, "No, you are not a suspect." But the next time they saw us, they took us in separate cars so they could turn Chris and me against each other. That was their technique. One after another they tried to separate me from my friends and turn my friends against me. I reject Jack Holtz, I reject the system for which he is the cutting and coercive edge. I reject the court, and I'm here for something I didn't do. They worked on my friends for four years. They convinced them that I was just a rotten human being. It was like *Alice in Wonderland* when I sat at that trial and watched the poor little scared witnesses. You take one witness and you have him fudge a little, and you take the neighbors and you have them fudge a little, and pretty soon it adds up to a mathematical chain. The police aren't passionate seekers of the truth. I would have been willing to talk in detail about my relationships with various people, but they weren't interested in the truth. They were interested in getting people to say what they wanted them to say. At first, Pat Schnure's statements to police may have been wrong, but they were honest. Then, after she got together with others and decided I was guilty, she had me making a pass at her. That's really absurd, just absolutely absurd. One by one, they broke off all the trust of all my friends. Joanne Aitken is the only one who had the strength to resist the pressure. They worked on everyone. They even worked on my brother-in-law to chip away at my support system. He knew nothing about the case, but they worked on him anyhow. When people start hearing things about you from the FBI, very few have the backbone to resist. Most people will go along with authority no matter what the authority says. What I resent most is having this fiction hardening into a reality in people's minds. Everyone thinks I did this. I can handle staying in jail the rest of my life, but it's raising that fiction to the level of truth that really gets to me.

PART II

The
Killers

Now does he feel
His secret murders sticking on his
hands . . .
Those he commands move only in
command,
Nothing in love. Now does he feel his
title
Hang loose about him, like a giant's
robe
Upon a dwarfish thief.

—*Macbeth*, Act 5, Scene 2

12

As days moved into weeks and the case dragged on, practically every detail became public knowledge. Reached by telephone at his dormitory in Santa Fe, New Mexico, on July 7, 1979, William Bradfield was told by a reporter that he had been named beneficiary to what appeared to be well over half a million dollars in life insurance. Bradfield gasped. "Money—I know nothing about it. The first I heard anything about insurance policies is when you told me just now."

Vince Valaitis also telephoned William Bradfield with the news and later remembered the conversation. " 'Bill, she left you all this money, she left you almost a million dollars.' 'You're kidding. She did what?' 'Let me read this to you.' I read the entire article. When I was finished reading, Bill sounded incredulous. 'What? Read that again.' I read it to him again. 'I can't believe it. My God, I just can't believe it,' Bill said."

Two days later, reached again by telephone, Bradfield told another reporter it was "incredible" that he had been named beneficiary. "Is it really true?" he asked. "I have no idea how she could have taken out that much insurance. It seems incredible that she could have had that much. I still don't know if the policies really exist."

Bradfield also told the reporter that no marriage to Susan Reinert was ever planned. When asked to clarify his relationship with her, he said, "My lawyer has advised me not to discuss it. The death is a tragedy and I can tell you this—I was certainly never interested in Mrs. Reinert's money. If there are any insurance policies, the money should be used to seek the safe return of the children."

The safe return of the children, growing less likely with each passing day, had become the primary concern of everyone close to the case. Reporters covering the story were becoming as obsessed with finding the children, or their bodies, as were the police themselves, even to the point of digging on their own time for small shallow graves in the thickly wooded areas of Chester County, in landfills, and in the apple orchard across the street from the home of Dr. Jay Smith. Occasionally, late at night or on weekends, off-duty reporters would run into off-duty cops following the same leads and digging for the small bodies wherever they noticed that roots or animals had left an uneven surface in the earth.

At about that time, Jack Holtz began to have a recurring dream. In it, he would find a grave, open it, and discover the children. At first, he would be excited and proud to have found the clues that led him to the bodies. Then he'd be filled with an overwhelming sense of emptiness and sorrow because he knew for certain that, although they had been found, the once bright and joyful children were now lost, irrevocably and forever.

13

When word leaked to the press that in addition to the "routine" items found in Susan Reinert's car there had been a snap-on rubber dildo, reporters went wild.

SEX RING LINKED TO MURDER; SWINGERS GROUP PROBED

State Police have uncovered explosive new evidence in the Susan Reinert murder case, linking the Upper Merion teacher to a bizarre sex ring. The [*Philadelphia*] *Chronicle* has learned that Mrs. Reinert's knowledge of a love cult may have been a motive for the slaying. Three individuals contacted this week by the *Chronicle* said that between 20 and 30 men and women regularly participated in swinging sessions that included homosexual and sadomasochistic acts. One police source said that Mrs. Reinert may have been killed because she was about to expose the existence of the group and its members, all of whom were reported to be "professionals."

Reporters from the *Philadelphia Bulletin* suspected devil worship. "Investigators believe Mrs. Reinert may have been stripped, tortured, and sexually assaulted as she lay on a makeshift 'sacrifice altar' during a black mass devil-worshipping ceremony. . . ." Cult members were described as "intellectual professionals, not necessarily the types of individuals you would think of as fanatical sex perverts. But they did not blink at using animals for sex exhibitions and encounters. Investigators are not sure whether Susan Reinert was actually a member of the cult, or whether she attended the black mass rituals and other cult ceremonies out of curiosity, but they said they were certain that Mrs. Reinert knew about the cult and the identity of many of its members."

Satanism and devil worship, the press pointed out, is as old as Christianity itself. Traditionally, its members dress in dark hooded robes and gather at narrow altars. Usually a cult ringleader, dressed in satanic garb, performs a sexual sacrifice on an unclothed maiden. In modern times, the ceremony has often included the use of a sexual device, like the one found in Susan Reinert's car. As "Satan" performs sadomasochistic acts on his victim, who is often heavily drugged, other cult members hold lighted candles and chant ancient prayers of satanic worship.

As the murder became more bizarre each day, this new twist went national when Rupert Murdoch's *New York Post* claimed that the cult centered in Upper Merion might have carried out the murder as part of a black-mass ritual, recording it as an underground snuff film to be sold and circulated commercially.

The FBI was alerted that an astonishing triple homicide was baffling Pennsylvania state troopers. Even without the issue of a satanic cult whose membership might well cross state lines, the fact that Susan Reinert's two children were still missing was enough to raise the federal kidnapping issue. A former FBI special agent in charge of the Pittsburgh Bureau of State Police, decided that his old colleagues from the FBI should be in on this. They didn't need jurisdictional approval to lend their assistance or to investigate the possibility that an underground snuff film was circulating commercially, possibly in New York City's Times Square area. The FBI also began to look into recent revelations about Dr. Smith's secret life that were linking him to these bizarre new developments. By early August, they were working full-time on the case.

A confidential informant reported that Dr. Smith frequented a wife- or girlfriend-swapping house located on a farm outside of Quakertown, Pennsylvania. FBI agents also contacted a prostitute, who told them that when she wanted to start her own business, Smith's long-time friend, Harold Jones, had told her that he knew someone with money.

The first meeting between Smith and the prostitute took place at McDonald's in the Andorra Shopping Center, near Valley Forge, in August 1978, about three weeks before Smith was arrested on drugs and weapons charges. Jones introduced the prostitute to Smith. "I told him about my plan to open a massage parlor," she told FBI agents. "He gave me eight hundred dollars in cash, all in hundred-dollar bills. I was to be half owner. Smith and Jones would each have one-fourth shares. Smith told me I was not to concern myself about money because he had plenty."

The FBI was still tracking down leads on Smith's double life when his wife, Stephanie, died of cancer on August 10, 1979. Stephanie Smith, a frail woman in her forties, with short red hair and delicate features, had been an alibi witness for her husband. Like William Bradfield, she testified that Jay Smith had spent the day of the Sears robbery in Ocean City, New Jersey.

In the months before her death, Stephanie Smith had refused to talk publicly about her husband; however, the previous August, during a search of Smith's house immediately after his arrest, she did speak to a reporter. "Although I have been married to Jay Smith for twenty-seven years," she said, "he is so secretive that I do not feel I know him. Jay doesn't talk much, and spends much of his time closeted in the family's den, which he uses as an office. The room is always kept locked with a combination padlock. I left him and moved in with a woman friend in 1977, but in June 1978, when I became ill, I returned."

Two days after Susan Reinert's body was found, Stephanie Smith, who was fighting for her life at The Bryn Mawr Hospital, received a letter written from her husband's prison cell. Referring to their home, he wrote: "We must clean out 705 totally, Steph. We must *throw away* most of the stuff. I can't stress the importance of this. *Clean out* and *clean up*. Things that *must* go: *beds* and *rugs*. Every time I walk on that rug, something new pops out of it. It must go. I will write later about disposal." The letter was signed, "I love you. Jay."

A few days after Mrs. Smith's small, private funeral, police found a diary among her personal effects. The entries detailed her husband's life as a "swinger" and his growing contempt for his family, who, according to the diary, were referred to as "rats" and "vultures" whom he threatened to kill.

Mrs. Smith wrote about her daughters in a shaking hand: "Jay said he will kill and get rid of Steph and Cher. They will jeopardize his job anyplace he goes, especially as superintendent. Can't have a rotten family as he has, ruin his career and future." Then she added, "Will kill me because I know too much about his swinging, fucking, and mail fraud. If I behave, he'll think about it."

A rough draft of a letter that Dr. Smith had written to a female public-school principal in New Jersey was also found in Mrs. Smith's bedroom. The final draft of this letter was later obtained by police. Written inside a Hallmark graduation card, it displayed the split personality and the penchant for obscenity that had caused colleagues to nickname Smith "The Prince of Darkness." With the public façade stripped away, another, more bizarre Jay Smith emerged. The printed message read: "With love, dear, on your graduation." Smith had titled the letter "Status Report."

Love woman, we've been working, loving, fucking, and sucking, etc., etc. for over a year now, so I thought a status report would be in order on your graduation. Our relationship has been the greatest thing that has ever happened to me and, as you see, it's the only thing worthwhile in your life. No matter what we've done, I still love your blowjobs the best, and get red hot looking in the mirror, watching my cock go in and out of your precious lips, and I hate to think of Bernard kissing your lips. I don't mind his fucking, but I hate to share your lips. Even though I got your ass virginity. We'll do some fist fucking this summer.

I prefer your mouth to your cunt or your asshole. Remember, *we* share sex only with ourselves, no two-timing. I don't count our spouses, but nobody else. I'm not Bernard, so if you fuck around on me, I'll beat your ass, instead of fucking it. Don't worry about me, I'm done with cunt, you're my last woman. In addition to our special, full, suck, fuck agreement, we are a professional team . . . we should do at least six seminars, three in New Jersey and three in Pennsylvania. (Professor Evil and Discipline.) That's enough for '76 and '77, and still take care of our families and jobs, so we are sexual and professional. Now, there are some areas that we still don't agree on, *marriage*. I still don't think I would marry you, even though I love you more than any woman (my love for my wife is special, so it doesn't count). I like being with you, even when it's not suck fuck, but you still tend to fib a little and like to produce some deception . . . I want total honesty in all things. Think it over again. I don't mind sharing your pussyality with Bernard, so why can't we be open. My wife will accept it if it's open. If Bernard finds out, as eventually he will, he's going to kick your ass; he might even kick you out or leave. Don't think he's dependent on your cunt, there's plenty of that around . . . and you'd be out in the cold. From the way you described his fucking, we could help him. Don't spread your lips so wide and keep them high, it makes your cunt tighter, also . . . shit, that's his problem. For now . . . don't needle him, love him good, keep his balls empty. Well, that's a long report, but I thought I'd review some highlights. Let's take a vacation day next week or so. I love you, always will. Your love cock forever, Jay.

Conversation with
Jay Smith

Let me say this to you—I was married for twenty-eight years to one woman, my only marriage. O.K., twenty-eight years. We were married on June 10, 1951. My wife died on August 10, 1979; I was never unfaithful to my wife until the beginning of 1974, maybe 1975. So, I was unfaithful once during twenty-eight years of marriage. Yes, this was with a school principal in New Jersey, who has been interviewed by the FBI, and I've told the FBI this. My wife knew about it. She was upset about it, called the girl's school about it and told her superintendent, called the girl's husband and told him; this kind of thing. Women get to know these things, women are smarter than men when it comes to this. They seem to know, you know what I mean. I don't know what it is, your reaction to something they say has a little inflection in it that wasn't there before. You're a little bit later coming home from New Jersey than you normally were, you know. When you live with a woman for so many years, she usually knows all about you, and in romance matters, women have better instincts and knowledge and stuff; they can sense it in about half a minute. Well, it's the only woman I ever went with. See, I was giving seminars in hotels on administration and discipline. That was another big issue I was writing on—discipline in the schools. So I gave seminars, and one of the principals I worked with was this woman. She and I gave seminars together. We gave a seminar at the Sheraton in King of Prussia and at the Hilton in Hightstown [New Jersey], and I think we gave one in New Brunswick [New Jersey]. Anyhow, I think my wife may have overheard a phone call and the woman's name was on the brochure along with mine. I would send a brochure out to all the administrators, saying I was giving a seminar. It would be a six-hour seminar, and it would be $150 for each person, and I would send them an outline, and then a brochure. She would be the New Jersey and elementary-school expert. She knows elementary, and I know secondary, see.

She was pretty, maybe not as pretty as my wife was, but, yeah, I would call her pretty. She wore long skirts, she was more like Gloria Steinem. She was an intellectual, she was well read, literary. I was never attracted to the *Playboy* types; I was more attracted to the, in her case, bright, intellectual, educational types, stuff like that. I never pursued women that way, even as a military officer, where there were lots of opportunities. The FBI went to her and she said she never did kinky things with me, and we never used sexual devices, and we never did any bondage or stuff like that. They asked her all those questions. That's what they were after, see. She was married, but her husband knew. There was a book that came out in 'seventy-one, 'seventy-two, that influenced our generation, at the time, called *Open Marriage*. Her husband was a psychologist at Rutgers University, and he had a lady friend. I had been to her house a lot. He knew who I was and that we had seminars together. He knew what was happening and he accepted it, my wife didn't.

I was involved with her, I'd say, at least three years. I felt I was in love with her. I felt she was in love with me, but you never speak for what a woman feels, you know. I felt it was so; I mean, I felt it was a love affair. We had eventually planned to get married once we got divorced, stuff like this. My wife and I had separated because she was trying to force me to give up this woman and everything. This was before we knew my wife was developing cancer. My wife and I got back together in 1977. My wife was ill and the romance with the other woman was over. My wife was starting to move back into the house completely. She had all of her stuff there. I think that the other woman had felt that it was getting to be too big of a problem. When my wife found out, she even sent my daughter and her boyfriend to the woman's husband to tell him. They actually went to this husband and told him about us, and gave him a couple of letters that she sent me. I think that's what caused her to feel that we should end it, but we didn't end it until the end of 'seventy-six. She didn't want to break up at first, but when she saw all the problems that were occurring, I think that's what finished it.

14

Several evenings in a row, when Vince Valaitis returned from his summer job, he saw two men at the end of the long driveway that led to his apartment building. They were sitting in unmarked cars, watching him intently. Later he learned that they were state troopers, but at the time, he thought they were Smith's hit men. Frozen with terror, he locked his apartment door, quit his job, and withdrew from the outside world.

In a trancelike state, Vince clipped, mounted, and laminated each article about the murder as it appeared in the press, then placed the pages in large black binders. FBI ENTERS REINERT'S MURDER CASE. TEACHER MAY HAVE BEEN STRANGLED AND RAPED BY MADMAN BEFORE BEING KILLED. CULT LINKS PROBED IN UPPER MERION CASE. Often, under these headlines, Vince's picture would appear along with Bradfield's, Smith's, or Susan Reinert's. Vince had received one letter of consolation. "Dear Vince," William Bradfield's mother wrote, "My husband and I want you to know how grieved we are that you are being subjected to such anguish. We know you as a fine, good, and sensitive person and we love you as a son. Please do come by and see us at any time, we will be happy to see you. You and your family are surrounded by our love and prayers. With much love and affection, Nona Bradfield."

Mounting the articles became Vince's primary activity. Now and then, he would boil some rice or watch his favorite movie, *South Pacific*, on his video cassette machine.

By late August, when Carol and Rich Manser telephoned, Vince had lost thirty pounds. The Mansers were among the last people from the high school faculty who were still talking to him. "For goodness sake, stop by and see us, Vince," Carol said.

"I went to their house," Vince recalled, "and told Carol the things that Bill had been saying. 'My God, what's with Bill?' she responded. The next morning, she called and said, 'Come on over for breakfast.'

"While she was serving me eggs, she put an FBI card in front of me and said, 'The FBI has been here. They want to talk to you. But they have been told by the state police that you will not cooperate. I'm not going to tell you what to do, Vince, but they just want to talk to you, and there can't be any harm in that.'"

Vince was relieved to learn that the FBI had entered the case. Bill had made him promise not to talk to the state police. He said that Jack Holtz was harassing him and treating him unfairly. "Bill would probably not feel the same way about the FBI as he did about the state troopers," Vince said to Carol. "In any case, I can't hurt Bill Bradfield because I don't know anything that can put him in a bad light. I can't take any more of this. I'm gonna do it." He walked over to the phone and dialed the number on the card.

"This is Vince Valaitis," he said, his voice as tight as a violin string. "I'm at Rich and Carol Manser's house in King of Prussia. I called to say I'd be happy to talk to you, but there is one condition—I want two FBI agents and no state police to conduct the interview."

"Stay where you are," Chick Sabinson answered, "we'll be right there."

Sabinson was delighted. This was exactly the kind of opportunity the FBI had been hoping for, their chance to break the case. He also knew that it was probably the first of several occasions when the inevitable conflict between the FBI and the state troopers would surface. From the start, the troopers feared the FBI was taking over. The state police hadn't been given a choice. No one asked them if they wanted help; they were simply told that eleven FBI agents had been briefed and were joining the investigation. It was a particularly sore subject for Jack Holtz, who had been out of town when the FBI confidently announced that they would have the murder solved in two weeks. As it turned out, eighteen FBI men, five state troopers, and two Swatara Township police—twenty-four full-time people in all—worked on this case for three years before the FBI finally pulled its men out, saying that the murders were unsolvable. But then, back in August 1979, Jack Holtz was taking a stand. With unshakable conviction he warned, "There will be no interview with Vincent Valaitis unless I am present.''

After asking Carol to be his witness, Vince sat on the deck outside the Mansers' kitchen waiting for the FBI to arrive. Vince, who never smoked, picked up Carol's cigarettes and began chain-smoking. From the deck on which he was pacing, he could see a short, slender man in a gray suit approach the house. Next to him was a taller man with thick salt-and-pepper hair, broad shoulders, and a three-piece brown suit. When Carol opened the door the men flashed their badges. Vince nodded, without really looking. The short man was talking to Carol Manser.

"Do you understand, ma'am, that if you sit here, you may be called to testify?" Then he turned to Vince and said, as casually as possible, "Do you mind if a state policeman is here with us?"

Vince looked at the other officer. "You mean him? Bill Bradfield told me that the state police have been harassing him and they are really difficult, especially Holtz."

The short man looked amused. "Well, if you don't want him here," he said, smiling, "I can ask him to leave."

Vince paused for a moment, not wanting to offend the trooper. "Oh, well, it's O.K.," he said. "He can stay."

They started out with very basic questions. "How do you spell your name?" "Where do you live?" "Where do you work?" Vince looked up at the tall man, and asked, unexpectedly, "You aren't Jack Holtz, are you?"

"Uh-huh," Holtz said, looking at him directly and almost challenging him.

Vince lit another cigarette and apologized profusely.

Now, gaining confidence, Sabinson spoke more sharply. "What do you know about Jay C. Smith?" he asked. Vince's hands began to shake. Suddenly, he was completely choked up and struggling for breath. He wanted to speak, but no words would come.

"Come on, Vince," Holtz pressed, half kidding, "we've been bored ever since we got here."

Vince's mind raced with fear and indecision. His position terrified him. Then, suddenly, he was crying. "I'm afraid I'm going to be killed. I had nothing to do with this, but I know about the murders." He buried his face in his hands and sobbed brokenly. "All I ever wanted to do was teach English."

Sabinson and Holtz stood up. They walked around to where Vince sat huddled in his chair.

"Maybe we should take a break," Sabinson said.

Holtz gestured frantically. The kid was finally breaking, he was about to talk. This was no time to stop. Then he put his hand on Vince's shoulder and said reassuringly, "Vince, when this is over, you can teach English all you want to. No one will hurt you, you're under our protection. Please go on."

Vince looked up at Holtz, then with an air of fatalism, he wiped the clammy wetness from his face, and began.

"Bill Bradfield told me that Dr. Smith was a hit man for the Mafia, that he had been threatening a number of people, including Susan Reinert. He said Smith said Susan Reinert knew too much about him and his trash and that Dr. Smith was chopping up dead bodies and putting parts of them into trash cans around the high school."

Holtz looked at Sabinson and raised his eyebrows. "And what was your impression of that story?" he asked.

Staring straight ahead, Vince said, "I was stunned. I thought Dr. Smith must be making it up. Just the same, I told Bill to go to the police. He said that he could control Smith and that he could convince him not to do any harm to anyone. He also said that he thought that Dr. Smith would kill me or anyone else who was privy to this information.

"Then Bradfield told me that one day when Smith was with him near Stouffer's Restaurant in King of Prussia, he took out a gun with a silencer, and fired it into the ground, saying, 'See how I can shoot a silencer gun in broad daylight and no one can even hear me?' "

Holtz listened without reacting and then said, "Vince, did you ever ask Bill about any personal relationship he might have had with Susan Reinert?"

"Yes, I asked him," Vince answered. Then he shook his head. "Well, no, I didn't exactly ask him, but at one point, Bill said Susan Myers thought he was having an affair with Susan Reinert. He told me that it was ridiculous because he'd never be involved with her."

"Vince," Sabinson asked, leading him, "did Bradfield ever mention anything about a will that Susan Reinert had?"

"Yes," Vince said, "he did. Around April of 'seventy-nine, Bill and I went to see a film, *The Deer Hunter,* and that night

Bill told me that he was upset because Sue Reinert wanted to make him beneficiary of her will and guardian of her children. He also said he had a copy of it. He was very distressed and annoyed that she was doing this.''

15

When summer school ended, Bill Bradfield and Joanne Aitken reluctantly left St. John's in Santa Fe and wound their way across the country in Bill's Volkswagen. Joanne was to return to graduate school at Harvard, and Bill Bradfield, who could see no other viable option, would return to Philadelphia and the murder investigation. Professor Steve Crockett and his wife, Margaret, had already left for Indiana, where Steve taught at Notre Dame. On the night of the twenty-fourth of August, Bill and Joanne were houseguests in the South Bend home of their new friends. That evening, Bill confided to Steve and Margaret that he was being investigated for triple homicide. He was suspected, he explained with urgency in his voice, of killing one of his colleagues and her two children. Later Steve recalled, ''Bill told us that the murdered woman had left insurance money to him which had made him a sitting duck. Margaret and I were stunned and terribly sad. The question 'Could he be guilty?' flashed across my mind just once, then I dismissed it as impossible.'' Both Joanne and Margaret sat on the couch, crying as Bill explained. ''The reason I'm telling you about all this now is because I think the police will soon be coming here to question you.''

William Bradfield planned to arrive in Philadelphia on Labor Day. Fearing that he would be arrested upon his return, he had asked Vince to meet him outside of the city and go immediately to visit John Paul Curran, the well-bred, highly respected lawyer Sue Myers had hired to represent herself, Vince, Chris Pappas, and Bradfield. ''When I told them I was meeting Bill,'' Vince later recalled, "Holtz and Van Nort considered wiring me for sound because they thought he would tell me where the children were. 'I'll do anything you want me to,' I said, but they decided not to because they thought that Bill might embrace me, find the mechanism, and kill me."

Actually, state troopers and the FBI were not awaiting Bill's return with an arrest warrant, nor did public scorn seem immediately apparent. Bill's most urgent problem, when he got to Philadelphia, was controlling Vince.

"I wanted to talk to you. I wanted you to come home. I wanted *you* to talk to the police," Vince said as soon as he was alone with Bill.

"We'll go to the lawyer now and he'll tell us how to proceed," Bill said soothingly. "Good God, I can't believe that woman, Susan Reinert, could affect so many people like this." Bill's attempt to diffuse Vince's feeling had the opposite effect.

"God damn it!" Vince exploded, as he started the car. "Do you know what I've been through while you were away and refusing to talk?"

What Vince didn't say was that for weeks the police had been showing him material and evidence that had half convinced him that Bill had been lying and was involved in the murder. He began again to plead with Bill to talk to the police. Once again, Bill refused, saying, "The police will twist the information and hurt us all." Then he suggested for the second time that Smith might not have been the killer at all. "I think it might have been the black man named Alex, who Susan met through Parents Without Partners. I know for a fact that she dated him."

As Bill spoke, Vince slipped into confusion, despair, and finally desperation. "Then tell that to the police," he begged.

"No," Bill repeated sternly, "I can't trust the police."

Vince looked closely at the friend to whom he had been intensely loyal for so long. My God, he thought, I can't keep up this pretense that I'm still his friend while I'm betraying him.

"Bill," he said suddenly, "I've talked to the police." Bradfield's face froze in a contorted mask of disbelief and pain. There was dead silence for what seemed like several minutes.

"You've killed me," he spat. "You couldn't wait two more weeks. Who else did you talk to? Bill Scutta, your parents, Carol Manser? Well, you've killed them and you've killed yourself." They drove a little further. "You've put me in the electric chair, you've killed me."

Vince slammed his foot on the brake. "I didn't kill you," he shouted. "All I did was tell the truth."

They drove the rest of the distance in silence. By the time they arrived at the lawyer's office, Bill had hardened. He gathered his pens and pencils and picked up a small paper bag from the floor of the car. "Are you coming?" he asked, his voice as brittle as cracking glass.

"No," Vince answered, "I'm not."

"You've killed me," Bill yelled again, as he slammed the car door.

After that, the bitterness and feelings of mutual betrayal intensified between the two men. Vince drove home, believing that his whole world had been forever and irrevocably changed. He wondered how any of this had actually happened, and how *he* had ever managed to get mixed up in it.

Then, a horrible, previously unimaginable concept surfaced into consciousness. If the police were right, if what they said was true, then the person he admired most, the man who had befriended him five years earlier when he started teaching at Upper Merion, may have been deliberately using him as a tool and an alibi in a monstrous plot to murder a woman who loved and trusted him.

Vince thought again about the weekend of Susan's death, the "alibi" weekend, as the police now called it. He remembered Bill smashing his fist against the back of the car, and saying this was the weekend Susan Reinert would die. "I followed Smith around her house fourteen times, then I lost him in the hailstorm."

"Oh, God," Vince said out loud as he remembered, "why didn't I take it seriously?"

They were supposed to leave for the shore right after dinner, around seven on Friday night, and return on Monday. But Bill didn't come home until nearly eleven, an hour and a half after Mary Gove, Susan Reinert's neighbor, watched her leave her house with the children.

"Have you been with Smith?" Vince asked, instantly aware that Bill seemed unusually withdrawn. Bill wouldn't answer. He seemed to be dazed and was staring straight ahead without blinking. A few minutes later, his mood changed. He became agitated, snapping his fingers and shouting impatiently, "Come on, Sue, I'm ready. Damn it, it's late." Sue Myers had been waiting for hours. She had also cooked dinner and entertained Bill's son and girlfriend, who had stopped by to visit.

It was after 3:00 A.M. when Sue, Bill, Vince, and Chris finally arrived at the old Victorian house in Cape May, with the hairdressing establishment downstairs and the rooms for rent upstairs. It was a pleasant place, a couple of blocks from the ocean, not well cared for, but comfortable. Thinking back, Vince could recall sitting on the bed with Bill talking until the sun came up. "You know, Vince," Bill said, sadly and nostalgically, "I think you're the best friend I've ever had." A few hours later, he was running around frantically, collecting receipts. "We're going to need every one to prove that we were in New Jersey if Susan Reinert is killed this weekend." On Saturday night, Bill suggested that Vince go to church with him to pray for Susan. Vince lit a candle and there, in the quiet half-light, they prayed together that no harm would come to Susan or to anyone else. The next morning, still restless and troubled, Bill said that he wanted to go back to church. "Vince, a storm is coming," he mumbled. "My life will never be the same again."

In retrospect, Vince remembered other strange events that had occurred during those days. He recalled that on Monday, as they drove back from the shore, Bill had unexpectedly turned off the main road, into an apartment complex, and stopped the car. He walked over to a large green metal trash bin, lifted a layer of trash, and buried a brown envelope. Then, as soon as they got home, Bill ran upstairs to his apartment saying he had to call Smith's lawyer. A few minutes later, he returned, grabbed Vince, and hugged him. "I did it, I did it," he laughed joyfully. Then, suddenly, Bill was crying, sitting in a chair with his broad shoulders heaving, and his big strong hands holding his head. When he finally looked up, the tears were glistening wet on his beard. The sobs started again, only this time, they were absolutely dry. A long time passed before the words came. "Thank God it's over," Bill gasped, laughing and crying at the same time. "Smith's in jail. I saved that fucking woman's life."

16

Every lead was promising, every new clue significant, every shift in the case hopeful, but still no arrests were made, and no one could supply any answers that would explain the fate of the children. It had been a long, frustrating summer, and by the time school started again, some people were describing the disappearance of the two children and the murder of Susan Reinert as the "perfect" crime. Only Joe Van Nort appeared to be optimistic. "This is an inch-by-inch investigation," he said calmly, "but one I am confident will be solved. It's just a matter of time."

Signs at the entrance to the ever-growing suburb in Montgomery County read, UPPER MERION TOWNSHIP IS A GOOD PLACE TO LIVE, WORK, AND WORSHIP. But most of its thirty thousand residents, many of whom had moved there specifically for the fine public schools, were now wondering about that.

Geographically, Upper Merion forms the end of the newer part of the traditional Main Line. The area is upper-middle-class, bordering on affluent. The high school has a larger library, more laboratories, bigger and better athletic fields, more advanced audiovisual aids, more functionally designed classrooms, and a better cafeteria than many of the private high schools or colleges in the area. It is, without a doubt, one of the state's finest and best-equipped upper-middle-class, contemporary suburban high schools.

Yet, in the year following Jay Smith's arrest and conviction, and the months following Susan Reinert's murder, allegations of everything from teen orgies and satanic cults to sex between teachers and students ripped through the high school and its surrounding suburban neighborhoods. Reports that Dr. Smith had amassed a huge pornography collection, dabbled in swingers' sex clubs, where he was known as Colonel J., and sometimes wore a Satan's costume during his escapades, added to the panic. On top of everything else, parents learned that Smith's twenty-year-old daughter and son-in-law had also vanished. The couple had not been seen for nearly a year and a half, and police believed that they, too, had been murdered.

By the start of the school year in the fall of 1979, the former principal of Upper Merion High School had been convicted first on drug and weapons charges, then for posing as a Brinks security guard and robbing two Sears, Roebuck stores; there were four missing bodies, two of them children; and one murdered English teacher. Hysterical parents, looking for parallels between the Smith and Reinert cases, soon found them. They had all heard that in May 1979, the month before Susan Reinert's murder, William Bradfield had provided Jay Smith's alibi at the principal's second trial for theft. Many had also read published reports stating that Susan Reinert had been very upset about Bradfield's testimony because she believed he was perjuring himself. Susan told her friends that she had been with Bradfield that day in Ocean City. But Bradfield testified under oath that on the day of the theft he was with Smith, looking for the summer home of another English teacher. Bradfield's testimony had not convinced the jury; after listening to the other witnesses they convicted Smith.

Jay Smith, who had been free on bail until summer, was scheduled to start serving his prison sentence on Monday, June 25, 1979, the same day and in the same city that Susan Reinert's body had been found. This followed the weekend Vincent Valaitis, William Bradfield, and Sue Myers spent at the shore after being told by Bradfield that Susan Reinert would soon be murdered. Now, all three teachers were scheduled to return to high school classrooms.

The week before classes resumed, nearly three hundred frightened and angry parents gathered at a school-board meeting, demanding that Bradfield, Valaitis, and Myers be removed. Superintendent Charles A. Scott told the crowd that the teachers could not legally be fired. He said, however, that he was considering taking them out of the classroom, away from direct contact with the students. "At this time, we have no information that would permit us to discharge, suspend, or take any disciplinary action against any employee in connection with reports that have appeared recently," Dr. Scott said, carefully avoiding even mentioning the teachers' names. "But we must recognize that, while protecting the rights of our employees, our primary obligation is to provide an atmosphere within which students may learn. It may, therefore, be necessary to transfer or reassign the teachers. I have been given full authority by the Board of School Directors to take such action when it is deemed warranted by me."

Scott paused for a minute and looked out at the crowd, then he asked them to stick by the school district at a time when it was under fire. "Clean up the school, take action against the teachers," someone called out. Scott was tired and tense. "Look, we're as concerned as you are," he said. "It's our community too, and we're trying to build a community we can all be proud of. We're trying to move to the limits of our authority. We need your help, your support."

Suddenly, he had an idea. "We need you to send in letters to tell us how you feel. We're not shy about taking action. We just took action to get rid of a principal we felt was wrong, and we knew that we would need round-the-clock police protection as a result of that action."

Earlier in the same meeting, the board accepted the resignation of Jay Smith, who had been suspended since his arrest. Now one of the parents spoke out sharply. "Why didn't the board take stronger action against Smith, instead of just allowing him to resign after a dozen years, without even a statement?"

Growing visibly impatient, Scott answered, "The alternative to accepting Smith's resignation would be to 'reject it,' which would mean that the board would have to initiate its own investigation, a costly and time-consuming process which would require many trips to the prison to conduct hearings."

Another parent, still dissatisfied, called out, "The board's just moving from one cesspool to another. These teachers' names have surfaced in connection with a *murder* investigation. We won't allow our children to attend classes taught by any of these teachers." Several angry mothers and fathers in the back of the room shouted their approval and began to chant, "Cesspool, cesspool, clean up the school, cesspool."

"Vince, if I could pay you to leave, I would," Dr. Scott told Vincent Valaitis the next afternoon, "but since I can't,

I'm going to remove you from the classroom."

At first, Vince said nothing. He just stared at the wall, with his fists clenched. Then he rose and began to pace back and forth. Suddenly, urgently, he said, "Why? For God's sake, tell me why."

For a moment, Scott seemed moved. "Vince," he said, his voice softening, "if you were hearing rumors about Smith killing Susan Reinert, why didn't you come to me and tell me?"

"Because, Dr. Scott, they were just rumors," Vince answered. Then his eyes filled with tears. "Look," he said, "I'm a teacher, I want to teach. I don't want to leave the classroom." He was begging now. "Please don't send me away. I haven't done anything wrong. Can't you give me another chance?"

Scott hesitated for a moment, then shook his head. "Report to me in this office on the opening day of school."

That was all he would say on the subject until a public announcement was made the following day: "The decision to reassign the teachers has been made. It is in accordance with the many requests we have had from parents not to have their children placed in classrooms with certain teachers."

On the opening day of school, Scott emerged from his office looking relieved, and told waiting reporters that the teachers had accepted their new assignments. Susan Myers would be evaluating a new curriculum devised for English classes. William Bradfield and Vincent Valaitis would be rewriting and editing bulletins and reports. All three would be transferred to Bridgeport and would no longer have any contact with students.

Despite the transfers, the anxiety of parents and students continued to escalate. Along the strip of fast-food restaurants on nearby DeKalb Pike, waitresses openly wondered if the bodies of the children would ever be found. Even after the teachers were gone, rumors and speculation continued in pleasant suburban kitchens and afternoon exercise classes. Some people were convinced that Susan Reinert had been sacrificed in a black-mass ritual conducted by a satanic cult. Others felt certain that she had fallen victim to a sadomasochistic sex ring operating out of the high school itself. "Back to school" had taken on a new meaning. Students now spoke about the "devil" in Upper Merion, and a guessing game was being played in the high school corridors: who could identify the teachers who were "the closet killers and cult leaders"?

William Bradfield had always been a towering figure at Upper Merion High School. In fact, a teachers' union campaign the previous year had been so successful that he had been elected president of the Upper Merion Educational Association. On the day that Scott made his announcement about the transfers of Bradfield, Myers, and Valaitis, William Bradfield made his first and last public statement about the case. It was read for him by another teacher at a meeting of the teachers' association.

As you are all aware, over this summer, our school, and some of us in particular, have been mentioned in the press in regard to the tragic death of Mrs. Susan Reinert. Because of this, my effectiveness in the position of the president-elect is in serious question to the point of my considering resignation, even though I have not been charged with any wrong-doing and have, indeed, been told that I am not even a suspect. I want to assure you that I had nothing to do with Mrs. Reinert's death, and that I have no idea as to the whereabouts of her children. I also want to assure you that I am doing everything I can in order to bring this matter to a speedy and just resolution.

17

John and Florence Reinert rarely left their house in the Philadelphia suburb of Phoenixville. They stayed close to their telephone, close to the hope, growing slimmer each day, that the phone would ring and the voice of some savior at the other end of the wire would tell them that their grandchildren were still alive. Each day was a void, each night a new night of sorrow.

Even after the divorce, Susan had remained close to her in-laws, and on Friday, June 22, the night she and her children disappeared, she had asked them if they could take care of Karen and Michael over that weekend. As it happened, it was the weekend of the Reinerts' wedding anniversary, so instead of saying, "Yes, of course, bring them right over," Mrs. Reinert had made a decision that would haunt her for the rest of her life . . . the decision to wait until Monday.

After dropping Michael off at his grandparents' on Monday, Susan was going to drive Karen to gymnastics camp and then come back to visit with her former mother- and father-in-law. Together, they were going to make plans for Michael's baptism that week at the Washington Memorial Chapel in Valley Forge Park.

"Susan was a wonderful mother," Florence Reinert said, her soft blue eyes brimming with tears. "She was always taking the children places, always doing things for them. She was also a wonderful wife to our son, Ken. She was as loving, thoughtful, and kind as any daughter-in-law could be. We just could never understand what happened. Right up to the end, Ken and Sue always defended each other. When Ken remarried, I remember being on the phone with Sue and saying something about it. She began to cry. I didn't know what to do, so I just said, 'We'll talk to you later, Sue.' We loved her like a daughter. After the divorce, when she got her house in Ardmore, we helped her paint and clean. We didn't let the divorce stand in the way, we accepted it. After her own mother died, she seemed so alone. That last Christmas she invited us for dinner. She had the house all fixed up, she had the candles lit, and she was all dressed up. She had prepared all kinds of fancy food. It was just the two children and Sue and it seemed so sad.

"The last Mother's Day of her life she gave me a silk scarf that I still treasure, and she had us to dinner. It was her first Mother's Day without her own mother. The day after Sue had called to invite us, Ken called, but we told him that we had already been invited to Sue's, and that we had accepted. We were so fond of her. We didn't want her to feel that we thought that what had happened was her fault. She was dating Bill Bradfield at that time. We knew some details about him from the kids, and we had seen him, but she would never talk to us very much about him. Anyhow, at this dinner, Sue had her crystal goblets out and I said, 'Sue, where are the good silver goblets?' I was referring to about a dozen beautiful silver wine goblets that were quite valuable, that Sue and Ken had received as a gift. 'I don't know, Mom,' she answered, 'they seem to be missing.' And then she added, 'It's the funniest thing, because nobody has been here except for Bill and the kids. I can't pinpoint it. I just realized one day that they were gone. I have no idea who could have taken them.' "

18

As Upper Merion students headed back to classes in September 1979, state police launched a massive search for Jay Smith's missing daughter, hoping the Reinert children might be with her. One state police officer said, "The search for Stephanie Smith Hunsberger represents the only remaining ray of hope for finding the children."

Wayne Jones, editor of the *Phoenix Evening* newspaper, was convinced he had another ray of hope. He had received an anonymous phone tip from a woman who said, "If you want to find the Reinert kids, look behind the white house with the six pillars, where they hold cult meetings. Look for fresh dirt piles in the area right behind the house." The woman had also mentioned something about an eight-cornered schoolhouse before hanging up, but Jones couldn't remember all of the details.

He called police saying that his reporters had not been able to find the school or the house. Jack Holtz remembered that the *Philadelphia Daily News* had run a photograph of William's apartment building. It appeared to have six pillars. Probably, Holtz reasoned, the woman had seen that photograph and had imagined the rest. But every lead had to be followed, every clue checked out. On the eleventh of September, investigators sent a helicopter to take photographs of the area surrounding Bradfield's apartment. From the photographs, Sabinson and Holtz were able to identify the Diamond Rock Schoolhouse in Chester County. The school had been built in 1818, restored in 1908, and had eight corners. It was approximately five miles from William Bradfield's six-pillar apartment house. The next day, a search was conducted. Startled residents looked out of their windows and saw nine state troopers and three FBI men digging up piles of dirt behind their homes. But law-enforcement officers, who worked in intense heat with picks and shovels for six hours, found nothing.

Jack Holtz, who ended up with a massive dose of poison ivy, was not surprised at the lack of results. "I hadn't really expected to find the children's bodies there. After all," he said, "it would be very stupid for William Bradfield to bury the bodies of the murdered children right in his own backyard."

19

William Bradfield and Vincent Valaitis were assigned to a big, dusty classroom in an abandoned elementary school. They were no longer permitted to enter Upper Merion High School or to talk with any students. Vince stared at the vacant school in disbelief.

"You have to remember the Book of Job," Bradfield said calmly, as they walked toward the empty classroom. "Like you, Vince, Job was an innocent man. You know, God didn't promise any of us a bed of roses in life. You may even have to go to jail with me."

"I don't want to hear any more," Vince moaned, alternating between anger and grief.

"Job hadn't done anything wrong either," Bradfield continued, "but he went through his trials and tribulations without complaining. If there is a trial, and you have to testify, just remember that courtrooms are battlefields, and after battles there are always bodies."

Vince banged his hand on a table. "Get out of here! Just get out," he yelled. For a long time, there was total silence. William Bradfield's steel-blue eyes swept across Vince's anguished face. Then he shrugged his shoulders, got up, and left. After that, he took a six-week sabbatical. He called it "a sick leave for an inner-ear infection."

One afternoon, Vince's old friend Bill Scutta showed up at the abandoned school. It was the first time Vince had seen him since Susan's memorial service in June. Uneasily, Scutta put his hand on Vince's shoulder. "I heard that you have been cooperating with the police, Vince," he said.

Vince nodded.

"I turned away from you when you were desperate, and I can understand that you might not want to be my friend anymore, but if you'd like to come over to my house tonight, you can."

Filled with relief and gratitude, Vince answered, "This whole mess has already caused both of us too much pain. If you're willing, I'd like to forget it and resume our friendship exactly as it was. We were both part of a situation that was out of our control and I'm glad you're back."

It was late November when William Bradfield returned to the abandoned schoolhouse. He entered the classroom casually, as if everything were normal. Angered by Bill's attitude and his silence, Vince said decisively, "I think you should go somewhere else."

"I was assigned here, and I will stay here," Bill answered stubbornly. He began moving Vince's books to another part of the room.

Vince felt the anger and humiliation swell in him. He grabbed Bill's desk calendar and threw it across the room. "God damn it," he said, as Bradfield watched without reacting. Then, feeling weak and defeated, he gathered his belongings and went downstairs to the basement. There, in an abandoned nurse's room with a mildewed cot, an old sink, and opaque windows, Vince hung his calendar. Each day he marked the date with an X, like a man in prison, and wondered how long this could continue without resolution.

20

By late December, the FBI had begun to explore its first big break in the case—a lead they would later call "the mistake that proved William Bradfield's undoing."

Among Susan Reinert's personal papers, Jack Holtz had discovered a receipt indicating that Susan had purchased 25 percent of a hundred-thousand-dollar certificate from an unnamed bank. The receipt bore the signatures "E. S. Perrit" and "M. E. McEvey." Under federal law, investment brokers must be registered with a state or federal securities regulator. However, the National Association of Securities Dealers in Washington, D.C., had no knowledge of either Perrit or McEvey; nor had the Pennsylvania Securities Commission. There was one other possible explanation: Perrit and McEvey might be lawyers, independently arranging or participating in mutual-fund sales. A check soon revealed that neither of the men was listed with the Pennsylvania Supreme Court, which registers all attorneys practicing in Pennsylvania.

Susan Reinert's brother, Pat Gallagher, and several of her friends, told Holtz and Van Nort that Susan had invested the $25,000 in a firm recommended by William Bradfield.

On February 5, 1980, Jack Holtz and Joe Van Nort paid a visit to Philadelphia district attorney John Riley, who had just become the court-appointed executor of Susan Reinert's estate. Dressed in a sport coat and slacks, Riley, a Civil War expert, looked more like a college professor than a polished Philadelphia lawyer, but he knew his job, and he did it well.

"Through searches of the house, we found certain items," Holtz told him. "One appears to be a receipt for twenty-five thousand dollars, invested in a six-month certificate, at 12½ percent interest. It's signed by two men who don't exist, but you can tell it's a fake just by looking at it. It's not even typed right.

The letters are off-line. It was also typed on an IBM Select II, Gothic Ball typewriter. Exactly the kind of typewriter that Bill Bradfield owns. Now, take a look at this,'' he said, handing Riley copies of Susan Reinert's bank withdrawals. "Seven in all, which add up to twenty-five thousand dollars. Each one matches a notation on her calendar that says 'investment—cash to B'—or 'cash to Bill.' I've also located a local office-supply shop which sells receipts identical to the one Susan's credit memo was typed on.

"Here's how I figure it," Holtz explained. "Bradfield was running out of time. On July 15, Susan Reinert's phony 'six-month certificate' would have come due. Jay Smith was going to jail, where he would be of no use to Bradfield—unable to kill Susan or to be framed for her murder. Susan was expecting marriage. The pressure on Bill Bradfield was building. He either had to kill her, marry her, or break up with her and return the twenty-five thousand dollars.''

John Riley considered the information for a few minutes. He was more than interested; he was intrigued. "As court-appointed executor of this will," he said thoughtfully, "it's my responsibility to make a thorough inquiry into this matter.''

Jack Holtz nodded. "We fully agree with you, sir.''

"Bradfield must answer every question that you have raised,'' Riley continued. "More important, he will have to appear in court to do that. No charges of theft can be made, since this will only be a hearing, not a trial. Officially, it will simply be an attempt to force him to verify that he has the money, and to return it to representatives of the estate. But unofficially, it will provide the first opportunity to demand and to guarantee that William Bradfield will answer your questions.''

21

By February 1980, both Jack Holtz and Joe Van Nort were convinced that this was a clear case of theft by deception, and a prelude to murder. They also knew that if William Bradfield said, "Yes, Susan and I were good friends; we were thinking about marriage. I took the money and made a poor investment. I was embarrassed to tell her, but here is a check for the correct amount," that would be the end of it, legally. The money would be returned, and the case could never be brought to trial. Nearly a year-long effort to hone in on Bill Bradfield and trip him up would be lost, perhaps forever.

However, when Bradfield took the stand, he did not know how much—or what—the state police had already uncovered. He was not aware of Susan's cash withdrawals, recorded by the bank, or of her own notations on her calendar, revealing that she had passed the money to him. Neither did he know that a receipt for the twenty-five-thousand-dollar investment had been found and determined to be a fake. And so, on the tenth of June, 1980, when William Bradfield appeared at the orphans' court hearing, he could not know that the account he was about to provide would damage him for years to come, formally and irrevocably; for everything he said would now be on record and would set the stage first for his arrest and trial for theft by deception, and later, for triple homicide.

"What was your relationship with Susan Reinert in May and June of 1979, sir?" John Riley asked, as he paced back and forth in front of the witness stand.

"We were very good friends," Bill answered, almost in a whisper.

"Were you anticipating marriage?"

"I was not. No, sir."

"Did you ever *discuss* marriage with her?"

"Often."

"What is that, sir?" Riley repeated, apparently unable to hear him.

"Often, sir."

"Was the marriage date planned?"

"No, sir."

"Did you ever spend evenings with her, you and her alone? I am not interested in what happened, but did you ever spend evenings with her?"

"Yes, sir. Often."

"Overnight?"

"Never."

"Never?" Riley echoed, his voice rising incredulously.

"No," Bradfield answered.

Riley beamed, then continued with new confidence.

"Now," he said, "did you ever discuss investments with her?"

"Yes."

"Her investments?"

"Yes."

"Do you know what Susan Reinert inherited from her mother?"

"No, sir, I don't."

"You have no idea?" Riley said, again with an obviously incredulous tone.

Bradfield amended his answer. "Well, I had some idea."

"Well, what was it?" Riley snapped.

"Her mother described it as her estate, consisting of a piece of land somewhere in upper Pennsylvania, and she did not discuss any money, but I know that she had a house and she said that she owned that, and I presumed the estate consisted of the land that she owned which she spoke of as being inconsequential in terms of worth, and a home."

"Do you know what Susan Reinert got from her mother's estate in terms of cash?"

"No, sir."

"No idea?" Riley spat, glaring at Bradfield. "Now tell me this. Did you discuss Susan Reinert's investments with her?"

"Yes."

"Did you advise her on investments?"

"Well"—Bradfield paused—"we discussed them. I don't know whether 'advise' would be the proper word; she was troubled about what to do about them; I'm not an estate advisor or financial advisor.''

''Did you ever discuss the fact that her investments did not give her a sufficient return?''

Suddenly, Bradfield became confused. He seemed to sense the trap being built for him.

''Her . . . her what?'' he stammered, and fell silent again.

''Her return on investments,'' Riley repeated, ''the percentage of interest.''

''What investments?''

''Her investments.''

''I didn't know she had any investments,'' Bradfield said, suddenly reversing himself completely.

''You didn't know she had any cash in the bank?''

''No.''

Riley pressed him. ''You didn't know that at all?''

''No, sir.''

''Now,'' said Riley, exchanging a rapid-fire glance with Jack Holtz, ''did Susan Reinert ever give *you* any money to invest?''

Bradfield's answer came without a pause. ''No, sir.''

Riley walked toward Bradfield and produced a copy of the certificate that had been typed on the typewriter identical to Bradfield's. ''Mr. Bradfield,'' Riley roared. ''Exhibit P-1, sir.''

John Paul Curran jumped up from his chair at the defense table and addressed the judge. ''Your Honor,'' he said, unaware of the nature of the evidence that the state had collected, ''may I ask that we be provided with a copy of it?'' Then, as he took the document and glanced at it, he added, ''This is the first chance I've had to see it.''

Riley strolled over to the witness stand.

''Mr. Bradfield,'' he continued, his voice booming, ''you're looking at P-1, are you not?''

''Yes.''

''Have you ever seen the original of that receipt?''

''No, sir,'' Bradfield answered evenly.

''You *never* saw that?'' he echoed, the earlier incredulous tone now sounding more like mock sarcasm.

''No, sir.''

''All right,'' Riley said. ''Now, referring to this, sir, this is a one-hundred-thousand-dollar investment right here, partial 25 percent payment of a hundred thousand dollars.''

Curran jumped up again. "I'm going to object to this line of questioning. The witness has stated that he has never seen this document, and is not familiar with it." And then, because Curran did not yet know that the receipt was a counterfeit, he added, "This is a bank document. I believe the official from the bank should come up and explain what these various initials mean. I object to Mr. Riley's interpreting what this document means."

"Objection sustained. You may ask the question, but not characterize the response," the judge said.

Mr. Riley nodded in agreement, and then went on. "Mr. Bradfield, did you have a discussion with Mrs. Reinert concerning an investment of a hundred-thousand-dollar certificate?"

Bradfield did not answer the question directly. Instead, he said, "I discussed with Mrs. Reinert's mother, and I think Mrs. Reinert was present, that her mother could gain interest in her investments if she were to pool her monies or whatever with someone else in a larger investment. I told her that, in my limited understanding, it was a common thing to do. The discussion arose because Susan asked me to speak with her mother, and said Susan's brother wanted her mother to sell the land that she owned and to make some investments concerning it." Apparently forgetting that he had earlier referred to the land as "inconsequential in terms of worth," he went on. "She would give the proceeds from the land and the investment to Susan and to her brother, at that point, while the mother was still living. It would give the children something with a guarantee that the mother would still be protected."

"And were there any conversations after Mrs. Reinert's death, concerning this pooling of the investment?" Riley asked.

"After her mother's death?"

"Yes."

"I don't recall any specifically, although Susan mentioned that there was an estate and wondered what to do with it, and asked me if I had an estate what I would do with it. I told her I would go and employ two securities experts, one whose job would be simply to give her advice as to what to do, and who would have nothing to gain other than to give her good advice. The second would be a person to carry out that advice, who would gain from that, thereby giving herself some kind of protection. This is what I advised Mrs. Reinert.''

Then, without revealing that the court had in its possession bank records detailing each of Susan Reinert's cash withdrawals between February 14, 1979, and March 7, 1979, withdrawals that totaled $24,500, Riley sprung the question.

''Mr. Bradfield,'' he said, pointedly, ''did Mrs. Reinert give you sums of money periodically from January 1979 until the period immediately preceding her death?''

There was a moment of silence. Jack Holtz sat still, waiting to see if Bradfield would fall into the trap. At first, Bradfield appeared slightly confused. Then he spoke calmly and with certainty. ''No, sir,'' he said.

Holtz was ecstatic. Bradfield had not only forever lost the opportunity to quietly return the money and close the case, he had, under oath, locked himself into a story that he would have to live by, and had given statements that Holtz felt certain he could prove were lies.

''We got him,'' Holtz whispered under his breath to Joe Van Nort, ''we got him now.'' Van Nort nodded.

''She never gave you any money whatsoever?''

''No, sir.''

''Did you ever give her money, sir?''

''Yes.''

''For what purpose?''

''Well, Mrs. Reinert was having trouble almost from the time I met her, making ends meet. She was divorced and was bringing up two children and would often complain to me and some other of my colleagues that she did not have enough money to buy Michael, her son, a Cub Scout uniform, or Karen, her daughter, a dress or something, and I, and I know not only myself, but other teachers, often would give Mrs. Reinert ten dollars, twenty dollars. She always seemed to be barely making ends meet.''

''Who were the other teachers?''

''Mr. Valaitis, I know for one, gave her money, I think, for her son.''

Riley cleared his throat. ''Were you aware that Susan Reinert had taken out very extensive insurance policies naming you as beneficiary, sir?''

''No, I was not.''

''Totally unaware?''

"Yes, sir."

Over the next several hours, William Bradfield continued to answer highly specific questions, still not realizing that each statement would eventually be used to convict him first of theft and, later, of conspiracy to commit triple homicide.

"Did you ever give her money to pay the premiums on these insurance policies?"

"No, sir."

Riley did not indicate that he had information to the contrary. He simply repeated Bradfield's answer in the same sarcastic tone he had used earlier.

"You never did?"

"No."

"Were you planning to go to England in the summer of 1979?"

"No, sir."

"You weren't?"

"No, sir."

"Now," continued Riley, pointing out that until the last months of Bradfield's relationship with Susan he was still married to his second wife, "did you tell Mrs. Reinert that you would be divorced in March of 1979?"

"I may have," Bradfield answered.

Riley sprung at the first concession.

"Why did you tell her you would be divorced in March of 1979, sir?" Riley said, pressing the edge he appeared to have.

"Why did I tell her that I would be divorced in March?" Bradfield repeated.

"Yes, why did you tell her that you would be divorced in March of 1979?"

"We discussed many things, personal things, and that was one of them, a change in my life, no particular reason."

"Why would you discuss a change in your marital status with Mrs. Reinert?"

"Mrs. Reinert and I discussed all matter of personal things."

"Isn't it a fact, sir, that you had promised to marry Mrs. Reinert upon obtaining the divorce?"

"No, sir," Bradfield answered calmly.

"That is not a fact?" Riley asked after more than thirty seconds of silence.

"No, sir."

"Now, directing your attention to February 1979, or shortly thereafter, did Mrs. Reinert give you fifteen hundred dollars in cash, sir?"

Bradfield paused. Riley glared at him.

"No, sir."

"Check or otherwise?"

"No, sir," Bradfield echoed.

"Directing your attention to February 20, 1979, did Mrs. Reinert give you fifteen hundred dollars either cash or check?"

By this time, it was obvious to anyone familiar with bank records that Riley knew the date and amount of each transaction. Bradfield held firm.

"No, sir, Mr. Riley, Mrs. Reinert never gave me any money."

"Never gave you any?"

"No, sir."

"Nor did she give you fifteen hundred dollars after February 21, 1979?"

"Mrs. Reinert never gave me *any* money, Mr. Riley."

"For purposes of investment?"

"No, sir."

"And your answer would also be true as with respect to March 2, 1979? She never gave you five thousand dollars to invest for her?"

"No, sir."

"And, on March 7, 1979, she didn't give you five thousand dollars to invest for her?"

"No, sir."

"Mr. Bradfield," Riley continued, moving to another area of inquiry about which he already had exact information, "what bank accounts did you have in 1979, sir?"

"Well, let's see. I had a checking account with the Elverson National Bank in Elverson, Pennsylvania. I had, I believe, a savings account at the same bank."

"And a safe-deposit box?" Riley suddenly interjected.

"Correct," Bradfield said, the pitch of his voice rising slightly. Then for a moment, Bradfield stopped. Riley stared at him, remaining absolutely silent.

"Mr. Bradfield," Riley finally said in a voice that was now completely flat and dry, "during the spring or early in the summer of 1979, did Susan Reinert give you a diamond ring?"

Almost without pause, Bradfield continued his denials. "No, sir."

"Isn't it a fact that she gave you a ring that had been her mother's? You were going to have it changed, have the styling changed for her?"

"No, sir."

"How about directing your attention to Friday, June 8. Did you meet with Mrs. Reinert on that day and discuss a wedding ring?"

"Mr. Riley, I'm afraid that my memory is not good enough to pinpoint dates of discussing rings, wedding rings."

"In the month of June, did you discuss a wedding ring?"

"Mrs. Reinert told me she had a ring, yes, and we discussed it. Would you like me to give you the discussion?"

"Yes."

"It had come from her mother, she said, and she wanted a different setting, and perhaps something done about the stone which had some defect in it, and she felt, she told me, she asked me, if I could, through business connections in the mall, and through my store, somehow reset the ring or have it reset for her or recut the stone, or have someone look at it, and so forth. My business is not really connected with diamonds. I don't deal with diamonds. I know nothing about diamonds, and I don't know anyone who does. So, I told her that I couldn't do it for her."

Once again, Riley changed the area of questioning.

"How many times did you visit Mrs. Reinert's home? Was it weekly or more often?"

"Well," Bradfield answered carefully, "the frequency of my contacts with Mrs. Reinert grew, I would say, in proportion to her demands. She was a very fine, terribly sensitive, easily hurt, intelligent young lady, but she was really troubled and she seemed more and more to feel that the situation she was in at Upper Merion was not one that she could tolerate, and she would tell me often at school, when we met, that she had to talk to me, that she had urgent problems and she had to see me, or I had to call her, and sometimes I couldn't see her, so I would say, 'Well, I will call you.' Her demands became very frequent. Several times a week, she would have terrible troubles and not know what to do with Karen or Michael. She was terribly afraid, constantly, of her husband claiming that she was an unfit mother, and getting guardianship of the children, or some such thing. So, I would stop by and see her, and I would call her as frequently as I possibly could.'' Bradfield paused. ''I couldn't stay there, spend my life there, but I went as often as I possibly could.''

Riley began questioning Bradfield's financial status.

''Did you ever tell Susan Reinert that you were wealthy in your own right?''

Again there was nothing in Riley's voice that would have told Bradfield that the FBI had studied his financial accounts. He could not know that they had already compiled a list of every bank account, of all major sources of cash, as well as a monthly summary of checking accounts, balances, and his schedule of deposits. Every transaction from savings account No. 39111 at the Elverson National Bank had been traced. Every deposit and withdrawal for his business, all mortgage papers, and residential loan applications had been collected. Neither did Bradfield know that the state troopers, the FBI, and Riley himself knew that William Bradfield was deeply in debt, and that his store was going bankrupt at the time of Susan Reinert's murder.

''Did you ever tell Susan Reinert you were wealthy in your own right?'' Riley repeated in a dry, unemotional tone.

''Susan was aware of my financial position, and it was one of several hundred thousand dollars. I don't ever recall saying to Susan, 'I am wealthy,' but, I can well understand that she may have thought that way.''

''What do you mean?'' Riley asked. ''Was she aware of your financial position, sir?''

''Well,'' Bradfield answered, ''she was aware that I owned a store in a major mall, and she knew that I owned property, expensive property, in Chester County. She knew that I owned a home.''

''Did you tell her that your business was successful?''

''I don't remember telling her it was successful. We fully expected it to be, that it would be successful.''

''Was it?'' Riley asked.

William Bradfield looked directly at John Riley. There was a pause.

''It was,'' Bradfield said, almost in a whisper.

After the hearing was completed, the judge told Riley that he would have two weeks to prepare requests for findings of fact, conclusions of law, and supporting law. After that, Curran would have an additional two weeks to respond and then the court would make a determination as to whether William Bradfield was or was not responsible for repayment of the $25,000, and return of the diamond ring.

At the close of these proceedings, no one in the courtroom knew that Chris Pappas, Bradfield's friend and former student, had been following both press and television reports of the hearings, and was now haunted by the information that he had previously withheld—information about $25,000 in cash that he had wiped fingerprints from and had helped William Bradfield hide.

22

Christopher Pappas sat frozen in front of his TV watching the reports of Bradfield's hearing. He felt his life was disintegrating around him. The notoriety of Susan's death and the questioning by the police had been more of a strain than he could bear. He had believed in Bill Bradfield, his former teacher, his wrestling coach, and close friend, without reservation—not only during the public ordeal that followed Susan's death, but in all of the strange events that had preceded it. That belief had sustained him; but suddenly, everything was in question.

For months Pappas had remained silent whenever police interviewed him. Now, the day after the hearing, Pappas was tired. His head and shoulders ached as he sat in the state-police barracks with the FBI and state troopers. He knew he could no longer avoid the truth because the foundation of his own belief had been shattered.

"Did William Bradfield ever discuss twenty-five thousand dollars with you?" Van Nort asked tersely, as he showed Pappas Susan Reinert's bank records and the receipt for the $25,000.

Pappas hedged, but only for a moment, then he said, "Bill

Bradfield never told me he took any money from Susan Reinert, but in the spring of 1979, he did tell me about having a lot of money in his possession that he withdrew from the Elverson National Bank. He told me he was hiding it from Sue Myers,'' Pappas continued, eager now that he had begun to break at last the silence that was tormenting him. "We were in the attic of Bill's apartment, when he told me that the money was in the trunk of the red Cadillac, which was his father's car. I convinced him that the money should be removed, so Bill and I went down and searched for the money, which was hidden in plain white envelopes and in a briefcase, and also in a gym bag. It took us a good while until we found all the money, which I counted—five thousand dollars in the gym bag, ten thousand dollars in the briefcase, and the rest in two white envelopes. There were six packets. It was mostly in hundred-dollar bills. Some of it still had bank wrappers on it. He told me that the bank would not let him take out the money in cash in one lump sum, so he had to make several small withdrawals of about five thousand dollars at a time.''

Van Nort exchanged glances with Holtz. For days, they had been interviewing bank tellers at the American Bank in King of Prussia, some of whom recalled that Susan Reinert had come into the bank several times and had quarreled with tellers because they would not permit her to withdraw $25,000 in cash. The bank officials had suggested a bank money order. Susan had insisted on cash, saying, "He will only take cash.'' Finally, she had settled on making several smaller transactions and had asked for large bills. One teller recalled the incident specifically, because she did not have enough hundred-dollar bills at her station and had to get more from the head teller.

"Bradfield told me he had saved the money through the years,'' Pappas explained, "and that he had also sold some property. He said he took the money out of the bank to buy a boat. He didn't trust the banks because of the present world situation. He said he didn't want to keep the money in his apartment because he was afraid the police would search his property and possessions. It seemed reasonable, especially since he was a friend of Jay C. Smith's, whose house had already been searched by the police. I suggested that he get a safety-deposit box at Southeast National Bank in West Chester.

"The following year after Susan's murder, Bill said he didn't want Mr. Curran, our attorney, who was requesting legal fees, to know he was in possession of this large amount of money. He asked me to talk to my father and my brother and to get a phony loan from them. He would pay them cash. They would write out checks. It would look like he had borrowed the money to pay his legal fees. My father and brother agreed to do this. I still have the check stubs from the money orders. I'll give them to you if you want. There are two from Girard Bank for five hundred dollars each, and a check for a thousand dollars with my name on it. I also have parts of a gun and some acid and other things I can give you. Bill says they came from Smith.''

On the night of September 22, 1980, Lou DiSantis and Jack Holtz drove to Croton Road in Wayne. "Looks like we got another convert. I think Bradfield's finally loosing his grip," DiSantis said, laughing, as they pulled up in front of Chris Pappas's house to collect the items he had promised. They found Pappas waiting outside, agitated and pacing under a streetlight.

"Bill must have come to my house and dumped out the acid and filled it with water," he said. "I had it under my boat, waiting for you to come and get it, but it was amber, and now it's clear. He told me he was going to dump it the night after the orphans' court hearing was over. He asked me to stand by him.

"Bradfield also told me that Smith would cut up bodies, pour acid on them, and wrap them in out-of-town newspapers, then tinfoil, and put them in trash bags. The thick kind. He said that Smith had two guns when he approached a victim. A large one in his right hand, and a .22-caliber with a silencer in his left. He told me Smith felt that a .22-caliber was best for assassinations because it made less noise and the bullet traveled slower. Bill explained that he had entered into a teacher/pupil agreement with Smith in order to learn his techniques and gain his confidence. He would often practice the techniques that Smith told him about. Once he put chains on my wrists and told me that you could suspend the victim with the chains to cause pain. Bradfield also said that Smith was planning to beat and torture Reinert before he killed her.''

DiSantis looked directly at Chris Pappas and spoke quietly. "Listen," he said supportively, "I know how hard it is to go back over all this.''

Pappas nodded, grateful for the reinforcement.

"And I know it's hard to remember a lot of details and I ain't pushing you to do that." While he spoke, DiSantis opened his briefcase and removed photographs of chains and locks that were taken from Jay Smith's house. "But it would help us to know if any of these look familiar to you."

"Yes," Chris answered, "the locks. If you wait a minute, I'll show you the things I still have."

Pappas went into the house and came back carrying a brown bag. From it, he took two small locks that matched those in the photographs, a ski mask, two boxes of .30-caliber ammunition, and a listening device. "You hook this up to a telephone," Pappas explained, as he handed over the device. "Bill wanted to use this to record Smith's conversations in case he had to prove at a later date that Smith was a nut. There was something else that I gave back to Bill. It was an automatic weapon cut down to appear like a pistol. The stock was just a pistol grip. Bill said he didn't remember if it was his or Smith's. I offered to take the serial number off of it, so no one could ever read it and trace it to Bill. I did that, and then I gave it back to him after Smith was arrested. Bill also said Smith would sometimes use drugs on a victim, like a truth drug, to make them talk. He would take an eye dropper with acid and drop some on the victim's arm. If the victim would talk, he would wipe it off with a damp rag. He always used cardboard or newspaper on the floor to soak up the victim's blood so no stains would ever come through."

Pappas led DiSantis and Jack Holtz into his parents' house, a brick rancher set back from the road. As they sat in the living room in front of a fireplace, which warmed them as the night air grew colder, Pappas spoke openly.

"By the spring of 1979," he explained, "Bradfield knew he was named in Susan Reinert's will and he did not want any large sums of money connected to him if Smith killed Reinert. Bill was worried about the twenty-five thousand dollars. He did not want to keep it in a bank in the area because he was afraid that the authorities would survey the banks if Reinert were killed, and they would think it was her money. Like I told you, he said the money came from the Elverson Bank and that he had saved it over the years. But we wiped the fingerprints off it anyhow. Looking back, I'm not sure why. I do know he was afraid that Susan Reinert's fingerprints might be on his red typewriter. He said he had loaned it to her and she had used it to type a receipt for the twenty-five-thousand-dollar bond investment that she made. He assured me that he knew nothing about Susan's money. He said the FBI had tapped his phone and found out that he also had twenty-five thousand dollars and they were trying to falsely connect him to Reinert.''

Jack Holtz narrowed his eyes but kept his excitement to himself. These were the kinds of facts that he needed to bring William Bradfield back to court. This time it would be more than an orphans' court hearing. With a little more information, he could finally arrest Bradfield and charge him with the theft of $25,000.

23

Susan Myers had long been a woman scorned by the man she loved. Her life with William Bradfield was, by all accounts, an emotionally and sexually barren one. She continued to live with him because she had loved him for twenty years. And, like everyone else Bill Bradfield's love had touched, Susan Myers believed their relationship was unique. She described him as a man with extraordinary qualities who, despite everything, had enormously enriched her life. At the same time, this seemingly gentle woman with cameo features, dark hair, and clear, soft skin, desperately raged against the other women in William Bradfield's life, especially Susan Reinert.

"You didn't like Susan Reinert, did you?" Jack Holtz asked almost deferentially.

"Not after she was involved with someone I loved," Susan Myers admitted.

"Did you ever call her names in school?"

"Yes, sir, I called her 'bitch' and 'whore.' ''

"Was that ever done in front of other teachers?"

"I can think of three times. The first time I called her a whore I saw no one else present. I don't know if anyone else heard. The third incident, when I called her a bitch, Mr. Bradfield was present, but there was no one else present.''

"Did you ever make her cry?"

"Yes, sir, that was the second incident."

"And how did that occur?"

"Mr. Bradfield had left school early that semester to go to New York to study Latin. For years, I had gone out to lunch with Vince Valaitis, Bill Scutta, and several other teachers. We were waiting to go to lunch. Mrs. Reinert came in and Mr. Scutta said to her, 'We're going out to lunch. Where are you going?' but it wasn't an invitation. And she said, 'With you,' and I said, 'I refuse to eat lunch with Susan Reinert,' and she burst into tears.''

"Did you ever assault her in school?"

"Yes, on the third incident, when I called her a bitch."

"You kicked her?"

"Yes."

"In school?"

"Yes."

"Was that in the presence of other teachers?"

"No, sir, no one else saw it. Mr. Bradfield was the only person present. I had seen letters, a number of letters. The first one I discovered was lying on his desk.''

"In school?"

"Yes, in school. That is the day I saw her, when I thought she was alone in the hall. The students had gone home and I called her a whore. When he came back after summer school and I saw the phone calls he made to her from New York in 1976, that Labor Day weekend I found a place to move. I went back to get my things to physically move out of the apartment, and he would not, well, he would not let me go. He convinced me that I was still in love with him and I returned.''

Susan Myers was one of the last links in the chain of cooperation that Holtz, Van Nort, and DiSantis needed. Like Vince Valaitis and Chris Pappas, she had gone through her own struggle and had kept her secrets out of pain and humiliation, and out of loyalty to the man she loved. For months before Susan Reinert's death, she had watched silently as William Bradfield became more and more a resident of the night. A man who now, according to her, cried out in his sleep, yet relished the cloak of darkness. A secret, uncommunicative creature who stayed away from home four or five nights a week, all night, saying he was helping Dr. Smith prepare for his theft case or trying to keep him from murdering Susan Reinert.

Susan Myers had her own ideas about what William Bradfield was doing. She was afraid to ask for fear of knowing, and yet she became, in those last months, a silent detective, observing every move. Now, almost a year after Susan Reinert's murder, she was still in love with William Bradfield, but estranged from him, and finally ready to cooperate fully with the police.

Conversation with
William Bradfield

I'll never forget the day I knew that it was over with Susan Myers. She had been with the police. She came home that night and she was crying. "I can't stand going to jail. I'll kill myself if I have to go to jail." Then she became very frightened. "The police say I'm next. You're going to kill me next." The next morning she said, "I think it would be better if you stayed at your parents' house for a while." I agreed to do it for her, to give her a chance to think. Two weeks later, I called and she told me that she had changed the locks and that it was over. She just didn't have the strength that it takes to resist that kind of police pressure. The problem is one of psychological toughness against authority. After that, when I tried to go there, she wouldn't open the door. She said that if I didn't leave she would call the police. You have no idea what she has of mine. My prints, a desk that I had specially built. All of my stuff on philosophy. All of my Temple, Haverford, and New York University books. I had thousands of books there. That was the spring of 1980. I stayed at my mother's and father's house. She felt that she had been wronged. We had been living together since 1974, but we had known each other since 1963. In the beginning, she was at the University of Pennsylvania. I'd stay with her for days at a time. I always tried to touch base with my second wife, Muriel. She was taking care of the kids from my first marriage and the child that we had together. But I had started spending more and more time with Sue. It got to a point where I would only spend a weekend now and then with Muriel, and the rest of the time I'd be with Susan Myers.

As I said, the three boys were still living with Muriel in the house that I had built, and we were always good friends, Muriel and I. But she couldn't keep up with the house and the kids. When you would come into the house, the newspapers and stuff would be so thick you could hardly walk through it. Then there would be a place cleared where she had brought a wounded possum in to give birth. She was great with wounded creatures. The first house Muriel and I lived in was an old eighteenth-century pre–Revolutionary War farmhouse on thirty-five acres. She just ruined that place. I was the general contractor for the new house. I designed it with a floor-to-ceiling fireplace built of fieldstone. I felt so bad for Muriel. I had nothing but love and pity for her. She was the nicest lady. Such a sweet woman. When I first met her, she had a room as neat as a pin.

As the years went by, she just couldn't cope. Part of it was that the relationship with me was not what she thought it would be. The old house was sold to get money to set up the Terra Art store for Susan Myers. And in 1982, the new house that I built was also sold. By this time, the two older kids weren't there anymore. Muriel would get bills for the house and just let them pile up, not even send them to me. I found out that the property was to be sold at a sheriff's sale just a month before the sale. At that point, Muriel couldn't pay the bills or the taxes on it and I had lost my job. I was being pursued for this murder. So I took a friend and started cleaning. Muriel hated to leave because of the deer and wild animals that lived in the woods, but she finally went out and found a place. After that, my son David wouldn't tell me where they lived. He'd always just say, "I'm sorry, Dad, but I can't tell you." She's such a dear, sweet lady. Things were good with her for a couple of years at most. A clean break might have been better for everyone. Muriel was a continual thorn in Sue Myers' side. Sue felt I was more loyal to Muriel than to her. I just hope Muriel is O.K. For someone who wanted to help everyone, I certainly ended up making a mess of things.

24

Susan Myers's voice was surprisingly steady as she sat across from Jack Holtz and Lou DiSantis. There was pain and sadness in her eyes, but also a certain calm that had come from her decision not to hold anything back, not to protect William Bradfield.

"We had a joint checking account since 1974, when we started living together. I handled our personal finances and gave him money as he needed it. I wrote all the checks so I *know* what we had."

"How much money would you estimate Bill lost in Terra Art?" Holtz asked, knowing that this woman could account for her joint assets with William Bradfield and, in the process, prove that the $25,000 was not his.

"Eighty-five thousand to a hundred thousand dollars," she answered. "The year Susan Reinert was killed, our savings account never consisted of more than a hundred dollars. It was barely enough to keep open. In fact, he mortgaged the new house that Muriel was living in, but I don't know the amount of the mortgage."

"You mean he was really broke," Holtz said as he calculated.

"Yes sir," she answered. "He sunk everything he had and borrowed everything he could, and now the store was lost.

"It was at this time that he began to tell me that Jay Smith was a nut and that Susan Reinert was going to die and he couldn't stop it. Early in the spring of 1979, it may have been a Thursday or Friday night, he came in late, three or four in the morning. I heard the filing cabinet open and close. The next morning when Bill was in the shower I tiptoed over to the closet and took the key from his pocket. I unlocked the filing cabinet, and saw the Last Will and Testament of Susan Reinert. Two days later, Bill told me that Dr. Smith was going to murder Susan before the month was up.''

"Prior to that, did you ever see any money in the filing cabinet?'' Holtz asked.

"Yes,'' Susan Myers answered, "prior to May 1979, I saw a stack of hundred-dollar bills in the filing cabinet. I never asked Bill about it and I never disturbed it. Then on my birthday, May 25, Bill gave me five hundred-dollar bills that were crisp and new. At that point, I asked him where he got the money. He smiled and kissed me and said he had saved his pennies.''

Then Susan Myers handed over several additional love letters that she had found. This time they were not from Susan Reinert, but from a former student at Upper Merion High School, Wendy Zeigler. During the same year that Susan Reinert was expecting to marry Bill and Joanne Aitken was wondering how she could bear to continue at Harvard without him, Wendy Zeigler, a shy, intellectual twenty-year-old, now a freshman at a California college, was also planning her marriage to Bradfield. She hoped to marry him in a Catholic church and had just returned from visiting her priest to discuss the possibility of an annulment from his second wife. As was the case with Joanne Aitken, Wendy's happiness and her ability to function seemed to be ruled by Bradfield's response or lack of it.

Dearest love,

I love you madly, passionately, eternally, and infinitely . . . I miss you so terribly, I sometimes think that if I can't feel your hands running through my hair, or have you pull me into your arms and kiss me, I shall scream. I tell myself I will not be ruled by my passion. That it's silly to think that I am not strong enough to get through college without you, but I'm lying. I need you to be with me. I don't see how I can survive days, let alone years. I am meant to be a mother. I am ordered to you as a wife, and so, what I feel is proper and I thank God I feel this way.

Wendy trusted William Bradfield. She adored him and, like both Susan Reinert and Joanne Aitken, this normally shy, reticent woman had become passionate and deeply romantic.

Dearest darling wonderful marvelous William,

You don't know how your phone call made my whole day. . . . Think how nice it will be when we wake up and the first thing we see is each other. The first thing we touch is each other. The first thing we taste and smell is each other. Oh, honey, I'm so impatient. You are, without doubt, the most wonderful man I know, as friend, lover, husband, and everything else.

Wendy told him she loved him immeasurably and was his, in all ways and for always. The letter was signed "Your wife, Wendolyn."

For the life of him, Jack Holtz couldn't understand the magic that Bill Bradfield seemed to wield. "What do you think, Louie?" he said.

DiSantis shrugged, then, by way of explanation, added, "He plays with their heads to get into their pants. That's how he controls 'em. I'll tell you one thing," he added, "Wendy Zeigler ain't gonna do no talking."

"Don't worry," Jack Holtz said, smiling confidently, and patting DiSantis on the back, "Sue Myers already told us what we need to know."

Conversation with William Bradfield

To have loved Susan Myers well would have been to walk away from her, but I thought that by setting down my limits I made it clear. Don't expect marriage, I'd say. Now I understand that saying that didn't mean anything. When I acted lovingly towards her, it turned into terrible hurt. I sucked those people dry. I was willing to be sucked dry, but they weren't into that. They didn't want that. I could never let anything go. Not Susan, not Wendy, not Muriel, not even my first wife, Fran.

The final, telling impoverishment Sue Myers felt I imposed on her was not giving her a child. She bound that up with marriage. Then came the realization that she was too old. When she was very young, she was a devoted mommy to her dolls. I should have seen that need and I should have released her. I had such a strong affection for her. She was a dear little girl. I guess I was as shocked and saddened by her actions during the investigation and trial as anyone. She has so many wonderful and endearing qualities. But there was a certain stuffiness as a veneer. There were so many fears that she had that she couldn't deal with. Some of the very best years of my life were with her. I had fun with her. I couldn't believe that she would think I would be involved with Susan Reinert. She'd see me visiting Susan Reinert's classroom and I'd come home at night, and she'd be crying. I'd tell her that I would never leave her. I had known her ever since 1963, when I started teaching at Upper Merion. She came into my classroom and introduced herself. In those days, she had a bouffant hairdo and wore high heels. She sort of swiveled into the classroom, pulled herself up, put her chin out, and welcomed me. God, how I feel the loss of that warmth and affection. My greatest hurt is in seeing myself through the eyes of others and in knowing how I failed in loving my friends.

It was 3:00 P.M.—visiting hours were over. William Bradfield put his face in his hands for a moment; then he looked up at me and said, "Thank you for listening, Loretta. God, how I treasure these moments with you." As he spoke, he leaned toward me and touched the folds of my skirt. Growing uncomfortable, I stood up. "You're such a wonderful friend," he said. He put his arm around me and kept it there as we walked the length of that coffin-shaped room. "When are you coming back? Make it soon. I love to see you," he added, hugging me. Again I pulled away.

I knew I was walking a thin line between my role as a reporter and the possibility that he was attempting to seduce me at some emotional, intellectual, or romantic level in order to control what I wrote. I wanted to understand as much about him as I could. At one level, I was still charmed by his warmth and the friendship he openly expressed, but I was also experienced enough, and suspicious enough, to question every statement and examine every manifestation of affection. William Bradfield had always denied the role of ladies' man that he had been assigned by the press. He told me that he never made love to Wendy Zeigler or Susan Reinert. He said his relationship with Susan Myers had been platonic for years, and he claimed his primary affection for Joanne Aitken was at an intellectual level. He never admitted that he missed women or sex. When we sat in the prison's visiting room, he would often watch as the guards pulled men away from their women. Sometimes he smiled sympathetically as the men stood up cursing and covering the wet circles on their pants. Still, Bradfield maintained that celibacy posed no problem for him. That, as much as anything, made me suspicious.

Soon after his transfer from Camp Hill to Graterford Prison, in the fall of 1985, I arrived at Graterford with an official visitor's pass which allowed us to sit in a small private room off the main visiting area. The guard looked at Bradfield and said, "No sex in there. This is supposed to be some kind of an official visit. I'll be keeping an eye on you. Any sex between you two and I gotta report it."

"Good grief," Bradfield said, laughing incredulously after

the guard had walked away. Then, turning serious, he told me that he would like me to attend a religious service conducted entirely by prisoners inside the prison walls. "I have come up with a way for us to spend time alone together," he said. "If you come in as a religious sponsor, you are allowed to attend services here even at night." Although Bradfield was a Quaker who planned to convert to Catholicism, he told me that he had joined a Jewish group.

"There are twelve of us and we have created our own little synagogue. We conduct the services ourselves."

First, Bradfield asked me if I could bring a dozen bagels and cream cheese for refreshments; then he mentioned that the head of the group and several of the members were also convicted murderers. He explained that once I had been escorted inside the walls of the prison, the guards would leave. I would be alone with twelve of these men during the religious service. Afterward I would be free to go anywhere in the prison with only Bradfield accompanying me.

"Really?" I said, thinking that it would be a terrific opportunity to get past the visiting room and to see life inside the prison firsthand. Then, hedging as I thought about the risks involved, I added, "I think I'd be a little afraid."

"But why, Loretta?" he asked, in that warm, concerned way of his. "*I'd* be with you the entire time."

PART III

The
Damned

Pray for me, pray for me. And what noise soever you hear, come not unto me, for nothing can rescue me.

—CHRISTOPHER MARLOWE
Dr. Faustus, Act 5, Scene 2

25

By June 1981, Jack Holtz and Joe Van Nort were ready for
William Bradfield's arrest. They were more than ready. With
Susan Myers's help, they had compiled a financial profile on
Bradfield that they believed would prove the $25,000 could not
have belonged to him.

From a summary of bank and mortgage records, Holtz
figured that not only had Bradfield been broke when Sue Reinert
was murdered, he had been in debt for $21,000. The only thing
he ever had, Holtz reminded Van Nort over barbecued rib
sandwiches, was his property, and he had that mortgaged,
double mortgaged. The $40,000 that Bill had gotten for his first
house had been deposited in a joint account with Sue Myers.

"Where did he get the money for the store?" Van Nort asked.

"Part of it was the forty thousand dollars," Holtz explained.
"Then in 1977 he took a twenty-five-thousand-dollar mortgage
loan from Elverson National Bank on the second house and
deposited that into the store's checking account. By the end of
the next month, that account was drawn down to $1,603.54. On
August 28, 1978, he took another mortgage. This one for fifty
thousand dollars, from the Downingtown National Bank. After
the settlement charges and payment of the first mortgage, he had
around twenty-two thousand dollars left. This was deposited
into the joint account with Myers at Elverson on August 29,
1978. But the balance of this account was down to four hundred
dollars by February of 1979. The store was failing. He still owed
the twenty-one thousand dollars. He had no more options. He
was desperate, except," Holtz added, pausing for dramatic
impact, "that Sue Reinert's mother had just died, leaving her
more than twenty-five thousand dollars in cash. Some of that
twenty-five thousand dollars was eventually funneled back to her

to pay for the premiums on her life insurance. We know that because Susan told her friends how wonderful Bradfield was to be paying for the insurance.''

Van Nort nodded, impressed by Jack's ability to put it all together.

''It's really obvious as hell,'' Holtz added. ''The man had a dream of getting a sailboat and enough money to sail around the world. Instead, he's in debt and his world's falling apart. Then he comes across this plan.''

Holtz knew he wouldn't be able to use this explanation in court, but it didn't matter, because in his own mind he was sure. Walking quickly toward the Delaware County Court House on February 11, 1981, in a new gray, three-piece suit, Jack Holtz could hardly contain his excitement. The charges for the arrest of William Bradfield were finally about to be drawn up. It wasn't the arrest for murder that he had originally hoped for. Not yet. But it was the beginning, and if he could win this conviction, Holtz was sure, absolutely positive, an indictment for murder would soon follow.

Conversation with William Bradfield

Before I began teaching, I had a tenant farm. I was writing poetry and fiction. I was married to my first wife, Fran. We had two kids. We were so poor, we were living on oatmeal and powdered milk. I could take it, but I didn't know if they could. I just couldn't rip things off for *Redbook*. I remember there was a class reunion at Haverford College in 1960. I took one shopping bag and Fran took another. We hitchhiked to get there, because we didn't have a car. It seemed like all my old colleagues were on their way to becoming vice-presidents of banks. We really just came for the food. We filled up the shopping bags and said to the kids, "You're not to eat up all the chicken. We're saving it." Those poor little kids. They were such darling kids and they loved the chicken.

I began wondering what in the hell I had to offer the world. I felt like the remiss head of a lion pack. While we were at the reunion, one of my friends suggested that I start teaching. He said I could be hired at The Deveraux School for Disturbed Children. I looked at my kids and my wife and I made the decision. I went to Deveraux. They hired me on the spot and gave me a class of troubled kids from thirteen to eighteen. I was supposed to teach them mathematics. I looked around at the kids. Some were standing on desks. One was urinating on the floor. Another was picking his face. I walked up to one kid and said, "What's your name?" He didn't answer. I asked him again. He said, "Fuck you, man, I'm busy." I clipped him on the chin. He sprawled down on the floor. The entire class stopped what they were doing. I said, "Now, sit down." And then I said, "Listen, I'm not really a teacher. I'm a student just like you, but learning can be wonderful." I didn't think I would last more than a week. I stayed four years.

Later, when I taught in Upper Merion High School, I tried very, very hard to improve education there. I had an advanced placement program in English organized around great books. I was instrumental in forming a teachers' union. I visited schools and read extensively, but at great cost to myself. I was trying to solve battles, but there were so many jealousies within the department, and so many vanities, the malaise in the public schools was so deep, that my own studies suffered. By 1979, I felt I had done all I could do with public school teaching.

26

Just when all efforts were being focused on William Bradfield's arrest and conviction, an unexpected event took place, exciting enough to pump new energy into the lagging investigation of Dr. Jay Smith. Raymond Martray, a former policeman serving time with Smith in 1981, requested a confidential meeting as soon as possible to discuss his "personal knowledge" of Smith's involvement with the Reinert murders. A background check on Martray revealed that he had headed and masterminded a group of local cops who robbed their own town blind, cracking safes and committing burglaries while off duty.

"My first reason for writing," Martray said in his letter to the state police, "is the Reinert kids, as I have a few of my own. It has taken many months before Jay Smith would let me into his confidence. Smith is treacherous and should not be let out on the streets. Contact the district attorney in Fayette County and get me there as soon as possible. I will explain everything to you then. *Do not contact me here at the Prison*. I need not tell you how important it is not to contact me, or anyone on the staff, here."

Lou DiSantis tapped his long, slender fingers on the conference table as he waited at the Holiday Inn in Fayette County until a tall, big-bellied redhead with a pudgy face and brown eyes muddied by tinted glasses was led in. Raymond Martray nodded his head and held out his hand.

"I have a strong feeling that Jay Smith was involved in the Reinert murder," the convict said.

"We need more than feelings," DiSantis answered.

Martray corrected himself. "It ain't just a feeling, it's more than that. Smith told me he's glad the body was cremated and he said he's glad the investigation was screwed up. See, he's worried about his alibi and he's been working hard on my legal papers, especially getting my perjury conviction reversed, so he has someone he trusts on the outside in case he needs help with the Reinert thing.

"He also wants me to check out an armored-car job at the Sheraton Hotel in King of Prussia. He'd been watching the Sheraton for around six months before he went to jail. The man's a criminal genius, but he goes over the edge sometimes, like this one time he was talking about the position of Reinert's body in the car, then suddenly something about sex set him off and he started carrying on how she's like the rest of them. He must have dated her. At the moment, I have so much in my head that I can't settle down and remember it all but, I'm telling you, the man is treacherous."

27

Nona Bradfield, Bill's mother, heard someone knocking on the door of her old farmhouse. At seventy-five, she was still a handsome woman with gray hair, clear, blue-gray eyes, and fine features. She put the coffeepot down on the stove, wiped her hands on the dish rag, and went to open the door. Her husband, who'd been ill, and her son, William, were still upstairs asleep.

"Mrs. Bradfield, I'm Trooper Holtz. We'd like to see your son, Bill," Holtz said gently.

"Just a minute, please," she answered politely, and the door closed. A few minutes later, she returned, opened the door a crack, and peeked out. The men were still there. Her voice faltered. "I'd like to see your identification, please," she said. The officers took out their badges. "Just a minute," she said, and the door closed again. A short time later it opened. "Perhaps I can help you," she offered.

"Mrs. Bradfield," Holtz responded, growing visibly irritated, "we have a warrant for your son's arrest."

This time, the old woman did not speak. She nodded her head and closed the door. The next time the door opened, Mrs. Bradfield held her head high and said in a firm voice, "I'd like to see the arrest warrant, please." She looked at the warrant and closed the door again.

Holtz and Van Nort got angry. They'd sat in their car for two hours, hoping to see William Bradfield out jogging so they could arrest him without having to disturb his elderly parents. "It's a good thing she's an old lady, or I'd grab her by the throat," Holtz spat. He perceived the woman's resistance as a power struggle with Bradfield and felt somehow violated. If I wanted to, I could break down the damn door and arrest him, he thought bitterly, and I'm standing here waiting while that bastard is in there giving her instructions.

Just then, Mrs. Bradfield returned. She opened the door wider this time, sighed heavily, and said, "Come in, please. My son's attorney is on the phone, and he'd like to speak to you."

They walked into the living room, which was furnished with colonial antiques and oriental rugs. Van Nort took the call. "We'll be taking Bradfield to the Emeryville State Police barracks for photographs and fingerprints," Van Nort said. "If he can't make bail, he's going over to Delaware County Prison."

Nona Bradfield, a southern Quaker, who had always formulated life's problems and solutions in religious terms, listened. For years, she had prayed nightly that one day her only son would be a man of the cloth.

Van Nort turned to her. "He's had ample time to get dressed, ma'am. We'd like to see him now."

"Look, you get Bill," Holtz added, addressing the old woman and raising his voice for the first time, "or I'm going up and get him. We have a warrant for his arrest. This is no game. We've waited long enough.''

Suddenly Bradfield appeared. Probably standing there listening, Holtz thought angrily as he watched William Bradfield walk down the stairs, meticulously dressed in a suit and carrying his coat over his arm. ''We have a warrant for your arrest,'' Holtz said, with a rush of excitement.

''Is it for murder?'' William Bradfield asked with a deathlike calm in his voice.

''No,'' Van Nort said, and read him the warrant. Theft by deception; theft by failure to make required disposition of funds received; and conspiracy. While Van Nort was reading, Holtz frisked Bradfield, then, out of respect for his mother, they walked William Bradfield out to the patrol car before handcuffing him.

Conversation with
William Bradfield

My very first memories were of my mother sitting by the side of my bed, talking about God and how she wanted me to be a preacher. As soon as I learned to read, I was reading the Bible. My favorite occupation in those days was to lie stomach-down on my wagon, put my legs on the ground, and watch the patterns of light as the branches moved. I wanted to understand why the stars went on forever. I prayed to God that I would die during the night so I could go to heaven, because my mother had told me that when I died I would be at the feet of God, so I wanted to go there and ask him all my questions.

My father never understood me. He was an enormously aggressive person, teaching me how to fight. He was like a James Cagney character, manager of Pittsburgh area Western Electric, a subsidiary of Bell. Because of his work, we moved constantly. I went to thirteen schools in twelve years. My father had determined I would be an engineer because *they* made things happen. If I insisted on wanting to study intellectual things, he said math. If I said art, he said architecture. I failed plane geometry. My father was horrified. ''Willie, how can you fail plane geometry?'' I didn't find the axioms self-evident. I was asking too many questions. After two weeks, the teacher decided I was disrupting the class. My father locked me in my room. He was a terror. Not a pleasant person. Straightforward, but such a stiff-necked bull-headed man. A great deal of what I turned out to be was a reaction against him. He didn't have the intellectual curiosity that I had, and to him education meant a union card and meeting important people. He believed in the business of America.

By the time I was in junior high school, he was wondering

what he had wrought. My father had never gone to college. His father wouldn't let him. Like all people who didn't, he had a vision of what it was. My first college major was math. When I switched to philosophy, he withdrew support. In his old age, he turned into a dear, gentle man. But through my first forty years, our relationship was really stormy.

At sixty-five, my father began to experience vertigo due to a swelling of one of the lobes of the brain that caused a lack of drainage of cranial fluid. He had a pioneer operation, inserting of a ventricular shunt. For a short time after the operation, he was much better, but by 1978 or so, he was slipping again. By 1979, when Susan Reinert was murdered, he wasn't walking and his memory was gone. When Sue Myers asked me to leave and I came home in 1980, I started teaching my father how to walk again. First I got him out of the chair and we'd walk to the door, then to the circular driveway. Finally, we got to the point where we'd walk a mile every day. Then Judge Wright decided I should be in jail. No one exercised him. He fell. The shunt was damaged. My mother was going through a terrible time. Her only son was in jail and the husband on whom she depended had become totally dependent on her. She was grieving constantly. She was denying the situation, but it seemed as if she was denying him. He died soon afterward.

I think about my father a great deal now, and I'm angry at the gods that be for not allowing me to finish my dialogue with him.

Bradfield's concern and compassion for his father were moving, but I began to wonder whether even these expressions were manipulative, part of Bradfield's attempt to win my sympathy. I became more and more consumed with the desire to understand the hidden dimensions of William Bradfield, questioning almost everything he did or said when we were together. Having lost the yardstick by which I normally judged people, the simple assumption that what they said was true, I found myself constantly ill at ease and uncertain.

Sometimes Bradfield would give me leads to follow to help prove him innocent. He wanted me to track down Alex, the black man whom he now said he thought was responsible for Susan's murder. After a day of frustrating research that led nowhere, I called John Paul Curran, Bradfield's attorney in the theft trial. "We worked on this case for four years," Curran said, "and we were never able to substantiate Alex's existence beyond the information that Bill gave us. Every lead was exhaustively evaluated, but unfortunately, the facts of the case pointed a finger at Bill Bradfield.''

At one point, Bradfield said he wanted Josh Lock to open up his files to me. Lock refused, saying, ''Bill hopes you can prove him innocent, but there is nothing in there that can help him. He'll cooperate with you only as long as he perceives it to be in his interest and only as long as you visit him.''

In an effort to gain additional perspectives, I began to question the people who still cared for him. ''I'm confused,'' one woman who had known him for thirty years admitted. ''Bill knows that. I never write to him and say 'I think you are innocent,' but I care for him, no matter what.''

''I loved him for twenty years,'' Susan Myers said. ''He enriched my life enormously, and, yes, I believe—in fact I feel certain—that he is guilty.''

''If I found out that he was guilty and that it had been a crime of passion,'' Steve Crockett, his professor from New Mexico, said, ''then I could forgive him. But if I believed that he was guilty of this, then I would say he is a monster.''

It had become more difficult for me to sleep. After I visited him, I would often awaken at three or four in the morning and lie in bed for hours trying to understand. I began talking to psychiatrists about the case. I read articles on everything from ''the fantasies of violent offenders'' to ''boyhood behavior problems as precursors of criminality.'' Then, one night, I began to read Harvey Cleckley's *The Mask of Sanity,* an acclaimed classic study of the psychopathic personality written by the coauthor of *The Three Faces of Eve*.

''Remorseless, charming, irresponsible,'' Cleckley wrote. ''They are all headed for disasters that could run the gamut from financial ruin to murder . . . they are people who on the surface appear graced with the most winning human virtues, yet who embody the darkest drives and desires.''

Describing a typical psychopath who had committed two sadistic murders, Cleckley continued, ''He wanted the victims to remain alive as long as possible to experience the agony resulting from his vicious torture. The victims were tightly bound and gagged . . . he seemed to relish the butchery particularly while the victim still remained conscious and capable of feeling it . . . his record as a charmer among the ladies was difficult to match. Many intelligent and wealthy young women considered themselves engaged to him until he disappeared after ingeniously borrowing or otherwise obtaining large sums of money.''

As I was reading, the telephone rang. It was William Bradfield calling collect from Graterford Prison.

''Hi, Loretta,'' he said. ''It's wonderful to hear your voice. I just called to say I miss you. When are you coming to see me?''

28

Jack Holtz was about to make a controversial decision. A decision to arrest Wendy Zeigler. It was understood by both the state police and the FBI that Wendy Zeigler was not an accessory to the crime. She was young, innocent, devotedly religious, madly in love, and following instructions. But, at the same time, as Holtz saw it, she had consistently refused to cooperate with police and was obviously withholding critical information. Every interview she had given had been laced with lies and denials.

Holtz thought about Wendy as DiSantis drove him home.

By the time they pulled up at Holtz's modest brick house with its neatly mowed front lawn, Jack Holtz was sure. He changed into his shorts and began to work out on his weights and exercise equipment. Even now, his mind was racing. He wanted to be thorough and he wanted to be fair. He also wanted to win this case. He knew that Wendy Zeigler had hidden that $25,000 over the summer and he knew that she had removed it from the safety-deposit box. Wendy had gone to the bank on the twenty-second of June, the same day Susan and the children disappeared. She had taken the money and signed the card. On June 27, two days after Susan's body was found, Wendy took $300 and put it back in the safety-deposit box. Holtz could verify that from the deputy access card he had managed to get from the bank. Those facts, along with Wendy's lack of cooperation, were enough, Holtz thought, to bring her to court for conspiracy. He would offer her immunity, but only if she cooperated.

The next day, when he announced his plan, FBI detective Matt Mullen was shocked.

"She's just a kid. You don't have enough on her to arrest her."

"I'll make that decision," Holtz answered, "and when I make it, it'll be final."

"But she's only twenty years old. You can't arrest her. You know she didn't steal that money," Mullen insisted. Holtz brushed him off.

"Yeah, and I also know she's lying to us. I know she hid it all summer. This is my case, I'll make the judgments."

The preliminary hearing was held on March 24, 1981, in the judge's office in the basement of his home. Although the tiny paneled room seated only sixteen people, more than forty crammed inside. Wendy Zeigler, looking even younger than her twenty years and fighting back tears, shared a chair with her father, one of them sitting while the other stood. William Bradfield, flanked by three lawyers, sat nearby, sweating heavily, but never removing his topcoat.

Attorneys for Bradfield and Zeigler argued that there was no evidence that the money had come from Susan Reinert. But young, ambitious Assistant District Attorney Edward Weiss presented eleven witnesses who testified that shortly before her death Susan Reinert had withdrawn large sums of cash from her bank account.

When the hearing was over, the judge ordered both William Bradfield and Wendy Zeigler to stand trial on charges of theft by deception and criminal conspiracy.

THE VICTIMS

Susan Reinert

Michael Reinert

Karen Reinert

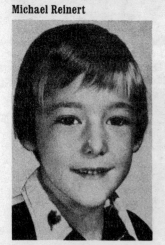

Susan on the day she married Ken Reinert (1965)

Susan and her children, Michael and Karen, in Puerto Rico, where Ken Reinert was stationed

Karen and her father, Ken Reinert

Karen and Michael on the day their father remarried

Karen and her grand-mother, Florence Reinert

The last photograph of Karen Reinert

The last photograph of Michael Reinert

WILLIAM BRADFIELD AND HIS THREE COMPANIONS ON THE "ALIBI WEEKEND"

William Bradfield, the English teacher at Upper Merion High School who was convicted of conspiracy to commit three first-degree murders

Susan Myers, the English teacher at Upper Merion High School with whom Bradfield was living at the time of Susan Reinert's murder

Vincent Valaitis, an English teacher at Upper Merion High School, the first of Bradfield's close friends to cooperate with the police

Chris Pappas, the substitute teacher and close friend of Bradfield's whose testimony was critical to the prosecution's case

The apartment house in which William Bradfield and Susan Myers lived upstairs; Vince Valaitis, downstairs

THE TRIALS

Rick Guida, the prosecuting attorney who won convictions against William Bradfield and Jay Smith

Bill Costopoulos, the defense attorney in Jay Smith's murder trial

Josh Lock, the defense attorney in William Bradfield's murder trial

Bill Bradfield's second wife, Muriel, arriving in court to serve as witness for the prosecution

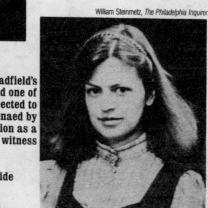

Wendy Zeigler, Bradfield's former student and one of the women who expected to marry him, subpoenaed by the prosecution as a witness

Bill Bradfield's car, outside the house in Birdsboro, Pennsylvania, where he was arrested for murder on April 6, 1983

State trooper Lou DiSantis (left) with William Bradfield, who was sentenced to three life terms for murder

State trooper Jack Holtz (right) with Dr. Jay Smith, who was sentenced to die in the electric chair

29

Three days before his theft trial on July 28, 1981, William Bradfield filed two lawsuits to collect the $750,000 in life insurance that Susan Reinert had left to him.

The publicity created by those newspaper reports, combined with the pressure of arrest and trial, convinced Wendy Zeigler that she had no choice. A few hours before the first juror was chosen, she signed an agreement to testify against William Bradfield. Charges against her were immediately dropped. Bradfield's anger was immense, though this was the kind of behavior he had expected from the police. He was, he said, deeply sorry for Wendy. He knew she loved him. He understood her position completely. He wanted her name to be cleared, and he didn't want anything to interfere with her schooling. As far as Bradfield was concerned, Jack Holtz had no interest in solving this crime. Holtz's only goal was to convict him. First of theft, and then of murder. It was on this conviction and not on seeking justice that Holtz's career goals were based. Bradfield believed that Holtz, Van Nort, and DiSantis had made up their minds ahead of time that he was guilty and their commitment was to destroying him. Under such conditions, he would give them nothing. Not even the satisfaction of seeing him take the stand in his own defense. He would fight them with all he had—tenacity and silence. This was a battlefield and William Bradfield was ready for war.

"Susan Reinert's death has nothing to do with this case," Delaware County judge Robert Wright sternly reminded the jury.

But awareness of the violent murder was unavoidable, especially during the fifty-minute opening statement made by Edward Weiss. Looking directly at the jury, Weiss said, "Wendy Zeigler will testify that three days before Mrs.

Reinert's body was found, Bradfield asked her to remove about twenty-five thousand dollars from the safety-deposit box in *case* something happened to Mrs. Reinert this weekend. He drove her to the Southeast National Bank and waited outside while she withdrew the money. Three days later, Mrs. Reinert's body was found outside a Harrisburg motel.''

"What the prosecution wants you to do is build a bridge," John Paul Curran told the jury, "because Mr. Bradfield had saved some money over a period of years that he has got to be guilty. That is what he wants you to do, and I say he cannot do it."

Curran was wrong. As soon as the court bailiff swore in James P. McMillan, branch manager for Continental Bank at the King of Prussia office, it became apparent that Edward Weiss could, in fact, build that bridge. "Before it actually got to the point where I told her, I won't let you walk out of here with twenty-five thousand dollars in cash, I asked her the nature of the investment. Directly asked her. I asked her if I could contact the person with whom she was making the investment and possibly supply him with a number of different alternatives besides cash. She responded, 'You can't call him.' She definitely used the word *him*. I remember that."

Christopher Pappas was next. The jury sat with eyes glued on William as Pappas explained in troubled tones how his former teacher told him he had more than $25,000 in cash hidden in the trunk of his car, and how they counted it. "He felt that it would be wise to remove fingerprints—my fingerprints, his own fingerprints," Pappas said nervously. "Mostly my own. For my safety, he would try to remove them. He had a pocket handkerchief and wiped the bills down after we finished counting them. Then he took the money and consolidated it into three envelopes, which he put in a filing cabinet in his bedroom. Mr. Bradfield held on to it for a period of about a week to ten days, and then he mentioned he was worried about having it in his apartment. He asked me if I would hold on to the money. I did so."

"He gave you the envelopes?" Weiss asked incredulously.

"Yes."

"And what did you do with them?"

"I took them to my house. I hid them in my bedroom behind a bookshelf, I believe."

"And how long did you keep it in your bedroom?"

"I guess I had it for about a week to ten days and during the course of that time we discussed where better it might be placed, and it was decided upon that I would open a safety-deposit box at a bank not too close to my home, and that I would put the money in it and keep it there. And about a week to ten days later, I did so."

"Whose suggestion was it that the box not be too close to your home?"

"Mr. Bradfield's."

"Did he tell you why?" Weiss pressed.

"Yes. He felt that the police might come to his home, and in the course of an investigation, he was worried that his goings-on might be observed and mine might also become suspect, since we were close friends. He asked me to take the money and open up a box someplace not too close to my home in the event that there was some sort of search."

"Okay. Now, did you, in fact, find such a bank?"

"Yes, I did."

"And do you know what bank that is, or was?"

"Yes, sir," Pappas answered. "It was the Southeast National Bank in West Chester."

"Now, at some point in time shortly after you arrived in New Mexico, did you and Mr. Bradfield have a discussion concerning money in the safety-deposit box?"

"We did. He said he was uneasy about having money in the safety-deposit box, as it might be discovered. He told me that he had Wendy Zeigler acquire the money. He also had instructed her to put three hundred dollars back into the box. In the event that the box would be discovered, there would be some reason for having it. In other words, it would not be an empty tray."

"Did he say anything else about the money?"

"He just told me that Wendy had the money. He restated that it was, you know, boat money, and that he had saved it for a long time."

"Chris," Mr. Weiss said, glancing over at the jurors to sense their reaction, "you made one final trip to the safety-deposit box, didn't you?"

"Yes, sir, that's correct," Pappas answered. "In August, after we returned from New Mexico, I went to the bank, I removed the three hundred dollars that was in the box, and then

I closed the account. I closed out my dealing with the box."

"Now, did you do anything with respect to the cards?"

"I did."

"What?"

"At Mr. Bradfield's request, I retrieved two or three of the cards and disposed of them."

"What do you mean, you disposed of them?" Weiss asked, emphasizing the word *disposed*.

"That means I destroyed them."

"Which cards were they that you destroyed?"

"I believe they were the deputy cards. You know, the cards that proved we had rented the box."

Susan Myers then took the stand. Her statement, though not as lengthy as Pappas's, confirmed the details of his account.

"Tell the jury, if you will, about the financial arrangement that you and Bradfield had."

"We had a joint checking account and savings account at Elverson National Bank. After 1973, I did all of the bill paying and financial management. On paydays, Bill would sign his check over to me and we banked primarily by mail at Elverson National Bank, which meant we had to deposit the entire contents of both checks."

"And who did that?"

"I did."

"Did he give his paycheck to you each and every pay period?"

"Yes."

"And you deposited it in the bank?"

"Yes."

"Who handled the checkbook, paying the bills and so forth?"

"I did."

"Did that go on continuously, as long as you resided together?"

"Yes."

"How did Mr. Bradfield get spending money, then?" Weiss asked, looking slightly amused.

"Usually we were together, and when we were, either I would handle the money to pay a restaurant bill, or whatever, or if he needed money if he were going to a bookstore or something. I would give him the necessary amount of money."

"And did Mr. Bradfield have any other accounts other than Elverson Bank that you were aware of?"

"I know of none."

"At some point in time, did you and Mr. Bradfield go into a business? In order to open up that business, did you need a certain amount of cash?"

"Yes."

"And how did you obtain that cash?"

"Bill had a property which he sold."

"And what did he do with the proceeds of that sale?"

"It was deposited in our savings account, and it was used to open up the store."

"Altogether, how much money did Mr. Bradfield sink into this business?"

"It would be difficult to estimate, but I would say, yes, I would say, eighty thousand dollars, from selling one home and taking a second mortgage on the second, as well as our income."

"And what profit did either of you earn from that business?"

"None."

"Zero?" asked Mr. Weiss.

"Pretty much zero, yes."

The prosecutor smiled at Susan Myers, content that he had established Bradfield's economic dependence and current state of debt.

"That's all I have," Weiss said, glancing coldly in Bradfield's direction for emphasis.

Then, a bewildered-looking young woman with shoulder-length brown hair took the stand. "Referring your attention to that Friday, which was June 22," Weiss said to Wendy Zeigler, "may I ask you some questions about the events of that day? Do you recall receiving a telephone call from Mr. Bradfield?"

In a clear, melodious voice, Wendy Zeigler said, "Yes."

"At about what time?"

"Somewhere around noon."

"And did you and he make arrangements to get together?"

"Yes."

"What time did you get together on that day?"

"I think it was about three-thirty that he came and picked me up."

Restricted by the judge from mentioning that Bradfield had

taken Wendy to a motel, where they had spent several hours "hugging and kissing," Weiss became vague. "After he picked you up, and you went wherever you went, did he at some point show you any money?"

"Yes."

"And how much money was it?"

"I don't recall exactly," Wendy said. "It was several thousand dollars, I think around four or five."

"Four or five thousand dollars?" Weiss said, feigning surprise.

"I think so, yes."

"Was it in checks, money orders, or what?"

"In cash."

"Where did he have all this money?"

"I don't know," Wendy answered, frowning slightly. "In his pocket or something. I think it was in a coat pocket, but I'm not sure."

"Was it in an envelope or anything?"

"Yes."

"A white envelope?"

"Yes."

"Normal white envelope, like this?" Weiss asked, holding up an envelope for the jury to see.

"Yes."

"Was it counted in your presence?"

"I believe it was, yes."

"Who was doing the counting?"

"We both were."

"Now what did Mr. Bradfield do with that money?"

"He gave it to me."

"All of it?"

"Yes. I mean, no. He took out a thousand dollars for his own expenses, and gave all the rest to me."

"Now, following doing all that, did you and he go somewhere?"

"Following that?" Wendy repeated.

"Yes. Where did you go?"

"To the Southeast National Bank in West Chester."

"Had you ever been there before?"

"No."

"Where did you get the key?"

"Mr. Bradfield gave it to me."

"He gave you the key?"

"Yes."

"What did you do?"

"After I signed the visitor's card, I went into the box and took out what was in the box. There were three envelopes. I put them in my handbag."

"Did you look inside them at that point in time?"

"No, not then."

"After you put them in your handbag, what did you do with them?"

"What did I do with them?" Wendy repeated, seeming dazed.

"Yes."

"I took them. I went out of the bank, back to the car."

"After you got home," Weiss continued, choosing his words carefully, "what did you do next?"

"I took the money up to my room and counted it, and separated the denominations, and put them into separate envelopes. Then I put the money in a closet in my room."

"And on June 26," Weiss said, referring to the day after Susan's body was discovered, "did you telephone Mr. Bradfield in New Mexico?"

"Yes."

"What was your reason for calling him?"

"To inform him of Mrs. Reinert's death."

"Did he advise you that he already knew about it?"

"Yes."

"And how did he already know about it?"

"A teacher at school told him."

"Following that discussion about Mrs. Reinert's death, did he tell you to do something with respect to the money from the safety-deposit box?"

"Yes."

"What was it he instructed you to do?"

"To take three hundred dollars and put it in an envelope and then put it in the safety-deposit box."

"And did he tell you why?"

"He was afraid that an empty safety-deposit box might look suspicious."

"At the end of the summer, either late August or early

September, did anything transpire with respect to Mr. Bradfield and the money?''

''I returned it to him.''

''When, where, and how?''

''Sometime in early September, at Mr. Pappas' house, I gave it to him.''

''All of it?''

''Yes.''

''Did you give it to him in the same form that you had put it in, separated as it was in various envelopes?''

''Yes.''

''Have you seen any of that money since?''

''No.''

The jury gaped back and forth between the quiet, studious girl and the large, bearded, middle-aged man who had given her over $25,000 in cash to hide for him when she was barely nineteen. But the prosecution was not counting a victory yet. They were still hampered by the judge's decision not to let them introduce the fact that Susan Reinert's certificate had been typed on exactly the kind of typewriter that William Bradfield owned. Nor were they permitted to say that he had hidden the typewriter at a friend's house in New Mexico all summer, or that his handwriting was similar to that of the nonexistent men who signed the fake certificate for $25,000.

That evening, as was his custom, Jack Holtz put his feet on his desk and chewed some tobacco. It was one of the few remaining habits that betrayed his small-town background. He spat the tobacco into a glass and swung around in his chair. ''It was a pretty good day,'' he told DiSantis. ''Nothing to feel elated about, but we shouldn't be discouraged either. Tomorrow we'll see what the defense can do.''

On the third day of testimony, William Bradfield sat absolutely still as his mother, Nona Bradfield, took the stand. The only perceptible movement were his eyes darting back and forth between the witness stand and the jurors. The old woman had summoned all her strength for this testimony, but now, as she glanced in her son's direction, her eyes seemed to moisten. She had always thought of herself as a courageous woman bolstered by religious commitment, but this nightmare, these allegations against her brilliant and treasured son, were almost more than she could bear.

"My name is Mrs. William S. Bradfield," the old woman said proudly. "My first name is Nona. William is my son."

"Where do you presently live, ma'am?" Curran asked, gently.

"I live in a two-hundred-year-old fieldstone home. We lived for several years in Haverford Township, and my husband had a yearning for a farm, so we looked for a farm property and bought a little over a hundred acres in Chester County. He wanted to have a dairy farm, so we bought a dairy herd and had a manager for the farm. We lived there for about five years."

"Did you have an apartment aside from that?"

"Yes, sir. We maintained an apartment in the city of Philadelphia, so that when we went into the theater or orchestra, we could spend the night there and did not have to drive back to the farm in the evening."

"How did you display your generosity to your son?" Curran asked, hoping to establish William Bradfield as the son of wealthy parents who had given him $25,000 over the years.

"After he was married, we often gave him gifts on anniversaries, birthdays, and other occasions."

"What types of gifts did you give him?"

"We would give him one hundred or two hundred dollars. We knew that William was very fond of the sea, and had been since a child, and he was saving towards buying a boat, so we often gave him money. My husband would say, 'Let's give Bill a couple of hundred dollars toward his boat fund.'"

"Now, Mrs. Bradfield, did you ever lend specific sums of money, or give specific sums of money in large denominations to William?"

"Yes, we did."

"At my request, did you go through your old records and try to locate canceled checks or whatever?"

"I did. I have three fairly recent canceled checks, where we gave William money at three different times."

"Do you have these with you?"

"Yes, sir."

"Could you produce those, please? Would you look at D1, please. What is the date on D1?"

"April 27, 1974."

"And who was that check made out to?"

"It was made out to W. S. Bradfield, Jr."

"And is that your son?"

"Yes, it is."

"And the check is for thirteen hundred dollars. And would you go to your next check, D2. What is the date of that check?"

"October 22, 1974."

"And to whom is that made out?"

"Made out to W. S. Bradfield, Jr."

"From whom is the check?"

"W. S. Bradfield, Sr."

"And how much is that check for?"

"For ten thousand dollars."

"And what is D3?" Curran asked, holding up another check. "To whom is that check made out?"

"Made out to W. S. Bradfield, Jr.," the old woman answered.

"And from whom?"

"W. S. Bradfield, Sr."

"And for how much?"

"Six thousand dollars."

"Thank you. Now, drawing your attention to Susan Myers, you knew your son was living with Susan Myers, did you not?"

"Yes, I did."

"Did you approve of that relationship?"

"No, I did not approve of it," Mrs. Bradfield said, shaking her head emphatically. "My son was raised in a Christian home. I did not approve of it, but I accepted it. And it in no way changed my love for my son."

"When you gave cash gifts of a thousand or so dollars a year to your son, did you give them to him in the presence of Susan Myers?"

"No, we did not."

"Why not?" Curran asked.

"Well, our son asked us for them, and we gave them to him privately at our home."

During the cross-examination, Edward Weiss held up the check for $6,000, and said sharply, "Mrs. Bradfield, wasn't Exhibit D3 actually a *loan* to your son to fix the roof on his house?"

"I did not ask him what it was for," Nona Bradfield answered, her voice quivering slightly.

"Didn't he pay you back in increments of $150?"

"A portion of it, perhaps," she acknowledged reluctantly.

"He paid you back," Weiss repeated.

"He paid me, but I don't know what he borrowed it for. I have never known."

"Was it a loan, then, not a gift?"

"Well, we considered it a gift," she answered. "If he wished to pay it, it was all right with us. If he didn't, it was all right."

"What did he need all of these gifts for?" Weiss asked coldly.

"Because we wanted to give them to him."

"Not because he asked for them?"

"Because we loved him and felt we had the money to give to him, and we were happy to be able to do that."

"You loved him very much."

"Yes."

"You still love him very much?" Weiss said, almost as if that love involved some form of treachery.

"Yes, I do," Mrs. Bradfield answered calmly.

"You would do anything for him?"

Nona Bradfield looked at her son, then shook her head sadly. "No," she said. "I wouldn't do anything. I wouldn't tell an untruth for him."

Whatever was to happen to her son, Nona Bradfield would not change her own moral code now. Nor could she have said anything to that jury to make them more sympathetic to Bradfield. Portraits of a dead woman and her two children were already so firmly etched in the jurors' minds that John Paul Curran believed they could not examine the evidence objectively. On those grounds, and others, he asked that the matter not be allowed to go to the jury.

"Your Honor," he told the judge in a private session, "the danger that exists here is the smoke-and-fire problem. Yes, there is evidence that Susan Reinert withdrew $24,500 from her account, and that is where the evidence stops. There is no proof that any money Bradfield had was her money. The only way you can do that is by mere suspicion, guesswork, and innuendo."

"That is a matter for you to argue," the judge said tersely.

Curran tried one more tactic. "The ultimate position of a

judge is to be able to stand back and say, You know, I may be criticized, many things may happen, but as a matter of law, I can't allow this to go to a jury. I know I'm asking a lot," he told the judge honestly. "I know I'm putting you in a bad spot, but I have an obligation to do it. There was no proof that her money became his money, and it's pure guesswork to allow the jury to fill that in. I think it would be an injustice not to grant my motion."

"It's a very close case," Judge Wright acknowledged, shaking his head. "I'll agree with you. Very close. But I'm going to let it go to the jury."

Tired and unsuccessful, Curran quit for the day. He had the weekend to prepare his closing argument to the jury, but when he delivered his concluding remarks, he seemed to know that the case was already lost. His speech to the jurors was brief, and half of it was devoted inexplicably to a historical discussion of how jurors are chosen, and how the judicial system works. Finally, he got to the point.

"There is suspicion, but there's no proof," he said. "When you consult on the case, I think that it will be important for some of you to stand up and say, 'Let's cut through this and let's see what evidence was presented.' If Susan Reinert loved Mr. Bradfield, as the evidence indicated, she would have given him the money. She would have given him twenty-five thousand dollars if he wanted it. It seems to me that if she were here today, she would be mortified to see the man she loved, here." It was his last shot and it was weak. He had not even chosen to dwell on the arguments he presented in court.

Edward Weiss nodded in what looked like mock gratitude and then launched into his own concluding remarks. He speculated that Bradfield began the fraud in order to realize a long-term dream of buying a sailboat and traveling around the world. He summarized the evidence, then asked, "If it was his own money, why would he wipe fingerprints off it? Why would he place it in an out-of-town safety-deposit box, in the name of Chris Pappas?" He paused and approached the jury as he began quoting a poem by Sir Walter Scott. " 'Oh, what a tangled web we weave,/When first we practice to deceive!' The defendant weaved a very tangled web," he whispered, then waited to let the impact of the concept sink in. "It is very difficult to untangle that web, but I ask you as members of the jury, to go back to the jury room, and untangle it for us, and after you consider all the facts in the law, find the defendant guilty. Thank you.''

When a jury deliberates behind locked doors for many hours, it usually means that the panel is confused or hopelessly split. On August 4, 1981, the jurors decided quickly and unanimously. Although they acknowledged that it was a very complicated case, they were back in less than ninety minutes.

"Members of the jury, have you arrived at a verdict?'' the clerk asked. "Do you find William Bradfield guilty in the matter and form in which he stands charged, or not guilty?''

"Guilty,'' the foreman answered.

As soon as the verdict was announced, several spectators burst into loud, joyous applause.

"All right, all right, let's have none of that,'' the judge said sternly. "Bring the defendant forward.''

As he stood before the judge, William Bradfield looked pale and seemed to hold on to the edge of the table for support.

Exhilarated, Ed Weiss jumped to his feet. "Your Honor,'' he said, "I suggest that bail be raised from twenty-five thousand dollars to seventy-five thousand dollars, because Bradfield might now be charged with the murders.''

The judge agreed to raise the bail, while Curran, still smarting from the verdict, objected angrily.

"This is guilt by association, the exact same situation we had when counsel began his argument.''

Then William Bradfield, who was given four days to secure the additional bail, turned to the press.

"They didn't deliberate long enough to reach a fair verdict,'' he said bitterly. "If they had taken one minute to examine each document presented as evidence, they couldn't have done it in the time they spent deliberating.'' Then he added resolutely, "I think the time to talk to the press has come.''

Pulling at the sleeve of Bradfield's suit, Curran tried to quiet him. "Let's think about releasing a statement to the press, rather than talking in the courthouse hallway,'' he said gently.

Then Curran turned to the reporters. "His emotions are running high. I think he should take a few days off to think things through calmly. We will file an appeal next week.''

30

Things were not going well for Raymond Martray. Almost six months had passed and the state police still had not contacted him again about Jay Smith. Now, claiming he had new information, Martray made an urgent request for another meeting.

Inside Room 252 of the Mt. Vernon Hotel, Joe Van Nort eyed him with the casual ease of a veteran cop who has seen every kind of con.

"Why did you request this meeting with us today?" Van Nort asked.

"Jay Smith has confessed some more things," Martray answered, lighting a cigarette with slightly trembling hands. "He told me that Bradfield said Reinert was going to blow the whistle on the Sears alibi, so they should take care of her. Smith agreed, but said he would handle it by himself. Then I asked him how he got Reinert out of the house."

"Yeah, go on," Van Nort said coldly.

"He told me that he called her and said Bradfield was in a bad accident and for her to come to the hospital emergency room right away."

Joe Van Nort listened to the statement and weighed it carefully. He was fascinated by the new details this ex-cop was providing, but he was cautious, and not without suspicion.

"Then what?" he said.

Martray hedged. Dragging deeply on his cigarette, he answered, "Smith stayed away from telling me any specific details regarding what happened except that the kids were also dead, and that there were three ways to get rid of bodies. You could take 'em in a rowboat and dump 'em in a river. You could eat 'em. He didn't give no further details on that. Or you could find a newly dug grave with a casket already in it and put the bodies on top of the casket, then put the dirt back.''

Holtz rolled his eyes. As bizarre as Jay Smith was, eating bodies, dumping them from rowboats, or sticking them in someone else's grave didn't sound like his tactics.

"What else did he tell you?" Holtz asked.

"He said he called the county radio about the body and when he talked to them he used a Spanish accent. He also said the power lines were down that night and this caused problems.''

Martray paused and rubbed his forehead. "Listen, man, it's hard as hell to remember all these details. Maybe if you hypnotized me, it would help.''

Conversation with Jay Smith

My only danger is the sexual smear. If it weren't for the smear, I would have no problems, because they know that I had no relationship whatever with Mrs. Reinert. And they know also that my relationships with Bradfield were so few that I couldn't possibly have been involved in anything. They know that from their investigation. Do you realize how much this has been investigated? Do you have any idea? Don't you think they would have come up with something years ago that would have shown that Smith had some relationship with Mrs. Reinert other than teacher and principal? Don't you think they would have found, maybe, a letter, a bank account, a phone call? In talking to all the teachers they interviewed, every teacher up there, all of her friends, all of her family? There is nothing, because there wasn't any.

I think Bradfield was mentally disturbed because of all of these women, his money problems, the insurance, this whole thing. I was a good target. Bradfield began figuring, I can get rid of all these pressures by blaming this character Smith, and that gave him, in his own mind, the go-ahead. Also, I think the information in the press gave him additional background. You might say, the specifics of the plan. I was in the military intelligence, so in Bradfield's mind that's CIA, see what I mean? So, therefore, he could project that on me, that somehow I was a CIA operative. And if he placed that comb they think is mine under Susan Reinert's body, and that sexual device, the dildo, under the front seat, the police would have connected it to me, because I was being accused of having unusual sexual practices.

So then, if this theory was correct, he would have started

eight or nine months prior to her death to have planted in the minds of his colleagues the whole concept that it was me. The thing I have trouble understanding is why he kept telling those people those things, and they didn't say something about it. One of the things I hate most is this sexual smear, but it may have been the thing that saved me too, because it proved in the minds of the police and the prosecution to be untrue. I mean, do you think they believed that I had an affair with Susan Reinert or with a student? I don't believe it. Students talk. They would gab. The very moment a girl like that left, she'd be telling her girlfriends within an hour. They never keep things quiet. It's impossible. I just keep listening to the things that the press says Bradfield was saying or his friends say he was saying. To conceive of me having a sexual affair with my students or with Susan Reinert was a big error on his part, see, because the only place that could have come from was himself, because Susan Reinert would have told everybody. Everybody would have known it in the school.

I never had anything to do with Susan Reinert. I don't even know the last time I saw her at school. Remember, we had close to a hundred faculty members, maybe seventy-five of them were women, so I probably said hello to her or something. But I would say in my whole time in Upper Merion from 'seventy-three on, I don't think I had more than five or six conferences with her as a teacher.

I didn't know what Bradfield was saying to these people. Like I'm planning to kill Susan Reinert, I'm having an affair with her, she jilted me, and all this crap. If just one of those people would have spoken up, Mrs. Reinert probably would have been alive today. I mean, if they had just said it to anybody. They didn't even have to go to the police. Remember, that English department had seventeen teachers, nine females. They could have gone to anyone. All of them knew Susan Reinert. All of them knew each other. They were teachers in the same high school. If I had known what he was saying to these people, what do you think, huh? You know what I think? I think they better keep me and Bradfield in separate prisons.

31

It was his first heart attack. Joe Van Nort collapsed without warning at the State Police Academy pistol range and was dead by the time an ambulance got him to the Hershey Medical Center. Returning from lunch, Jack Holtz, who had stopped at a red light, noticed a state police car pass him and caught a glimpse of Joe's wife, Betty, sitting in the backseat. She seemed to be crying. Holtz pulled over and called the barracks. Whoever answered told him that Joe had had a heart attack and had died almost instantly.

As he drove home, Jack Holtz felt more alone than he could ever remember. He thought about continuing William Bradfield's murder investigation without Van Nort's help and shivered involuntarily. Finally he whispered. "You trained me good. I know what I have to do. I guess I'm on my own now."

Two days later, Holtz stood at Joe's casket, wearing a class-A state police uniform—dark gray trousers, gray shirt, and black gloves, with a gun and holster on his hip. Surrounded by ceremony and pomp, salutes, and guns, swallowing his own fear, Jack thought, Joe would have liked this ceremony. He'd like the uniforms and flags. He always liked to do everything in style. Still, Jack's eyes burned and his shirt was soaked with sweat as he thought of Joe standing on his thirty acres of land on top of a mountain, building a log cabin. Joe, the dreamer, who had filled his den with the head of a lion he had killed in Africa and that of the second-largest water buffalo ever recorded. Even breaking his back when the Land Rover turned over hadn't stopped him for long.

"Thanks, old buddy," Holtz said softly as the casket was lowered into the earth. "I'll finish the job we started. I'll do it for you, I swear I will."

32

"What's your name?" Louie DiSantis asked, his dark eyes calm, almost sleepy, his voice without affect.

"Bill Penn."

"And your occupation, sir?"

"Assistant manager of the George Washington Motor Lodge for the past ten years."

It was November 10, 1981. Penn had contacted the Upper Merion police the day before, stating he had information that might aid in the Reinert murder investigation.

"I knew and was friends with Jay Smith's wife, Stephanie, for seven years prior to her death," Penn explained. Then he went right to his purpose. DiSantis listened quietly, interrupting occasionally to ask a question. The statements became so bizarre that, ordinarily, DiSantis would have dismissed Penn as a standard nut case, but by the time Penn had finished, DiSantis found the statements believable.

When he left Penn three hours later, DiSantis sat alone and drank a beer. Then he went directly to his office and typed out the following official state police report:

George Washington Motor Lodge, King of Prussia, Pennsylvania, November 10, 1981. This officer interviewed one William Penn, white male, 55. Penn stated that Stephanie Smith, Sr. once showed him a letter that Jay C. Smith was going to send. It was to a black teacher from Delaware County, and it was explicit about unusual sex acts that Smith was going to perform on her. Stephanie told Penn that there were two teachers, one black and one white, that Smith would have sex with after class. Stephanie told Penn that her husband would come home and tell her all the sordid details of his affair with these teachers. When Penn was asked what kind of unusual sex acts were mentioned in the letter, he stated that the only one he could remember for sure was "fist fucking." Stephanie told Penn that once Jay Smith used an ear of corn as a dildo after he heated it up, and she let him do it, as she was afraid of him and what he would do to her. She also stated that once, coming back from the New Jersey shore, Smith had stopped at a motel near the Tacony-Palmyra bridge and met another couple for a swinging party, but that Stephanie didn't get involved. Penn stated that there was a teacher in New Jersey that he had sex with and he would tell his wife about it. . . .

Once, Mrs. Smith had gone into her husband's private room and found a black cape, a cheap devil's mask which appeared to have been bought at a five-and-ten-cent store, a pair of gloves, a cheap set of handcuffs, an enema bag, a flesh-colored dildo, and a large black dildo, which could squirt water and had a manual crank on the inside. There was a whip in the garage.

Mrs. Smith also told Penn that Jay Smith would watch his daughter, Stephanie, and son-in-law, Eddie, while they were in bed downstairs having intercourse. Mrs. Smith did not like it, but was unable to prevent Jay from watching. It was her opinion that Stephanie and Eddie were not aware of being observed.

Penn stated that Mrs. Smith was convinced that Smith had killed [Stephanie Smith, Jr., and Eddie] and that she did what Jay told her to do, for she feared that he would kill their other daughter, Sherwin, if she talked to the authorities. Then, in February of '78, Mrs. Smith told Penn she thought that Jay had cut her daughter and son-in-law up with a chain saw and dumped them in acid, as she saw these things in the garage and the private room he had in the basement. She thought this because after they disappeared, she was not allowed in the garage or downstairs at all.

Conversation with Jay Smith

My daughter Stephanie was a cheerleader, a very active, lively, attractive cheerleader. I don't know when she got into the heavy stuff. I think when she went to California she really became a heroin addict out there. I guess that was 1974, 'cause I had gotten her a good job at Western Electric, in King of Prussia. She was a secretary. She'd been accepted by Penn State but turned it down. She was very bright and well read, but I think the drugs and attractiveness of that culture were pulling her in. It was a lot more fun, a lot more exciting than going on to school. When she came back from California, she was a heroin addict. She was living at my house, down on the lower level, in the den. Bradfield and the newspapers called it a basement. We never used that word, we always called it the lower level, or the den. That's how I know Bradfield picked up this stuff from the papers.

Anyhow, in July 1976, my daughter said, "I'm not going to live here anymore." She moved down into Philadelphia and got into the methadone clinic. My daughter was now living in a hotel near there and was streetwalking. Then she met this Eddie Hunsberger. Eddie had nothing to do with Stephanie's problems. They just met each other at the methadone clinic and started living together. It was a very bad situation because they were living in Kensington and had to travel every day across Philadelphia from Kensington to West Philly to get their methadone. They were living in a very bad, sordid, squalid apartment. Roaches all over the place. Burnt mattresses, arguments, fights, noise, people, urine all over the hall, people lying around in the hall, zonked, drugged, this kind of stuff. I went down there, and I would end up a lot of times paying their apartment rent. The FBI checked this and I did pay their apartment rent. The FBI knows all this. And my wife and I were getting back together and Stephanie would call my wife and talk to her because she didn't want to talk to me except when she had a problem. I'd go down there and try, you know, to help. She and Eddie would fight because Eddie was having problems with his potency because of the drugs and he was blaming the drugs, and she was blaming him.

I would try to get men to stay away from my daughter because she was both attractive and an addict. Meanwhile, Stephanie was prostituting and using the money for heroin, and Eddie was back to using the heroin. They were taking their medical cards and food stamps and buying heroin with the food stamps. I went to the methadone clinic and argued with them about this, and this counselor says, "Well, you're acting very unprofessional, and you can't see what our professional team is trying to do." And I said, "Your professional team is a lot of bullshit." I was really upset because, well, you gotta know heroin. Heroin is not like other drugs. I mean, heroin is master, it's king, it dominates your whole life. I mean, if you are on heroin, it's like the wildest kind of love affair you could ever think of. You could do anything for heroin. Die for it, kill for it. It's the same as some beautiful woman. It gets into your blood and skin and body, and you can't get it out of your mind and everything. And you can't do anything without it. Heroin is master.

My daughter was the start of all my problems—the beginning of the end. If it wasn't for trying to help her, I never would have gotten into trouble with the police in the first place. And I never would have ended up where I am now.

33

Raymond Martray ran his fingers nervously through his thinning red hair, and adjusted his tinted glasses. The cops had turned down his request to go home for Christmas and had consistently told him that they could promise him nothing in exchange for his testimony against Smith. He was almost certain that his information was not being taken seriously, and he was becoming desperate. Martray still had one thing left in his pocket and he was about to use it.

"Why are we here again today, Mr. Martray?" Jack Holtz asked, on December 29, 1981.

"Jay Smith confessed," Martray answered, narrowing his eyes and removing his glasses. "He told me that he killed Susan Reinert. He never told me he killed the kids. The only thing he said was more like a hypothetical question. He said, 'If you were to do something and there were witnesses, what would you do?' Then, another day, a couple of months later, he repeated himself, only this time he told me a little different. This time he said, 'I killed that fucking bitch, Reinert.'"

Jack Holtz suppressed a whistle. Finally, there was something substantial—a confession. "Would you say that in court? Would you testify against him?" Holtz asked, trying to cover his growing enthusiasm.

Martray shrugged. Sensing that the cards were finally on his table, and hoping again to cut a deal, he answered the question indirectly. "Listen, man," he said, without committing himself, "if Jay Smith ever gets out of prison, I'm dead."

Holtz was eying him more cautiously now. Either the state police were being handed a plum on a silver platter or it was a piece of rotten fruit on a tin plate. He needed more.

"Did Smith ever tell you how the body or the car got to Harrisburg?"

Martray paused. "Well, he never said he drove the car to Harrisburg, but he led me to believe it. He said the police never checked the buses in the area to see if anyone came back from Harrisburg. He also said he was very familiar with the Host Inn. But he wouldn't tell me how he did it. I mean how he killed her, uh, except to say that she died from an overdose of morphine. He did say that."

"You said that the first time he told you this was months ago. Why didn't you tell someone sooner?"

"Listen, man," Martray answered, his voice heavy with emotion, "I was afraid of Jay Smith. I didn't know what your reaction would be, and I didn't want to take a chance or use his exact words till I was sure I could trust you."

"That's a shame," Holtz said, uncharacteristically cold and

sarcastic. Martray's answer didn't ring true. He was in jail for burglary and for perjuring himself under oath at his own trial. Jack Holtz didn't want to be played with, especially not about this. There was too much resting on it.

Polygraph test results are inadmissible in court, but Holtz wanted to see Martray's reaction to taking one. "Would you submit to a lie-detector test?" he asked.

"Yeah, sure," Martray said. Then he chuckled nervously. "Only I'm upset right now. I need a few days to get my mind together." He shifted his weight in the chair. "Next week would be good. Yeah, definitely."

34

"It's my opinion," wrote FBI polygraph examiner Lawrence Bria, seven days later, "that the recorded physiological responses of Raymond Martray are indicative of deception. Whenever he was asked questions regarding specific statements Smith made to him concerning the Susan Reinert killing, Martray immediately backed off. On each occasion, he said he could not recall specifically what he was told by Smith, but that he definitely knew Smith was the one who killed Susan Reinert. He did continue to insist that one time Smith said to him, 'I killed the fucking bitch,' but admitted that Smith did not specifically make reference to Susan Reinert when he made this statement."

Constant attempts were made by this examiner and, later by Jack Holtz, to pin Martray down concerning specific statements Smith made to him, but Martray's answers became more and more general rather than specific.

"Jesus Christ," Martray finally said, sweating heavily and wiping his forehead with his shirt, "I'd like to review the notes."

"What notes?" Holtz asked.

"You know, the notes you guys made of my previous statements. Just to help me remember what Smith told me."

Bria brought out a March 19, 1981, copy of *Philadelphia Magazine* and turned to an article entitled "Murder on the Main Line." "Maybe this will help you remember what you told us," he said. Martray laughed. "Oh, yeah, right." Then Bria challenged him.

"Most of the information you furnished to the police was taken directly from this article, rather than from conversations you had with Mr. Smith, wasn't it, Mr. Martray?"

"Well, I read it," Martray stammered. "I mean, I'm familiar with it. But that ain't the reason I can't remember. It's because I couldn't take any goddamn notes."

"And you just can't recall what he told you?" Bria asked, his tone heavy with sarcasm.

"Yeah, that's right," Martray answered defensively. "Listen, man, Smith led me to believe he killed her. That's definite. He may not have used those exact words, but he led me to believe it."

Raymond Martray had let them down. But this was an important case. The state police, the attorney general's office, and the public wanted it settled without delay. Besides, since polygraph results are not admissible in court, the results were basically irrelevant. One month after Raymond Martray failed the polygraph test, the Pennsylvania State Police decided to "use him" anyhow, in an attempt to elicit a taped confession from Jay Smith.

At this point, the account becomes confusing. Despite adamant assertions by the state police that Ray Martray would receive nothing in exchange for his cooperation, according to a state police report of February 8, 1982, Martray was to be "released from jail as soon as all the necessary preparation for the wire tap and mail cover could be made." It was also decided at that time that on his release Martray would report to the state police in Uniontown every day by telephone, or in person, and he would be required to obtain a post-office box for all mail coming from Jay Smith. State police would keep the keys to this box and collect the mail. A double tap would be placed on Martray's home phone, one that Martray himself would control to tape all conversations with Smith and another that Martray would know nothing about. If Martray visited Smith in prison,

Martray would wear a wire body tap to be monitored by the state police. The reason for the detailed monitoring technique was clear: Raymond Martray would not be permitted to testify in court unless he succeeded in reversing his conviction for perjuring himself at his own burglary trial. But, if a confession could be recorded, the prosecution could present tapes to a jury.

By April 1982, the arrangements to release Martray had been completed. Early on the afternoon of April 21, Raymond Martray, looking heavier and far more relaxed than he had at his last meeting with the state police, appeared at the office of his attorney in Uniontown to sign an affidavit: "I, Raymond Martray, hereby consent voluntarily, and of my own free will, to allow interception of my oral and telephonic communications with Jay C. Smith and others. I have personally spoken with Trooper Holtz of the Pennsylvania State Police and other law-enforcement officials about my desire to cooperate. I have not been coerced, threatened, or promised any consideration to induce me to engage in the interception of my communications."

Ray Martray hesitated for a moment before signing the affidavit. There was a wild look in his eyes. He seemed to want to say something. But then he smiled, his thin lips curling around his nicotine-stained teeth. He picked up a pen from the table and signed the affidavit of consent. It looked as if Raymond Martray had finally cut himself a deal.

That night, April 21, from his cell in Camp Hill, Jay Smith wrote a letter to Raymond Martray, thus sending it directly to his archenemies, the Pennsylvania State Police. "Hi, buddy, just a quick note to let you know I do have your address. I'll be sending you little notes from time to time, but nothing much. Keep your freedom. Within a year, even if all things are lost, I will be on my way out of this place. So, have fun with Deb, but don't let her get you committed to marriage. Believe me, it will come on subtley at first, then openly, but it will be good humping while it lasts, and necessary. Stick with her as long as you can, but keep all contacts, even a bad fuck is better than none. That's why you keep friends with all females. No need to make enemies. Future looks real good."

Jay Smith had reason to be optimistic. For nearly three years, the best efforts of the state police and FBI had failed to come up with enough evidence to make a single arrest in the Reinert murder case. Smith, who still had three years left to serve from his theft and weapons convictions, was unaware that the office of the Pennsylvania attorney general had recently decided to assist state police with the murder investigation. Richard Guida, an intense, ambitious young deputy attorney general, had been assigned to the case. Guida had spent three years in the district attorney's office, and five in private practice before accepting the job with Attorney General Leroy Zimmerman, his former boss in the DA's office. It was the challenge of a seemingly unsolvable murder that drew him in.

"Anytime that a child is killed, it's always a special case," Guida said when he accepted the job. "All homicide cases are important, but the death of a child is particularly tragic." Guida placed two small photographs of the Reinert children on the wall beside his new desk and dedicated himself to succeeding where eighteen FBI men and a team of state troopers had failed.

At thirty-four, Guida was thin, dark-eyed, and youthful. He could joke and drink all night with his men and still astonish juries in the morning with his commanding presence and tough cross-examinations. He also had a unique talent. He could take the complex and bizarre and make it direct, simple, and understandable to the least-educated and -informed juror. On May 20, 1982, under Guida's supervision, Jay Smith was subpoenaed to appear before a multicounty grand jury.

"I plan to take the Fifth," Smith wrote to Raymond Martray. "The only purpose of the grand jury is to try to catch you up in a misstatement, hence a perjury charge, where they can impeach your credibility if there is a trial, and you try to testify. Also, they get leads to pin something on you. They find out if you have any defense and they knock it apart before the trial. The grand jury nowadays is just another tool of the prosecutor."

With that statement, Smith had minimized the approaching danger. His letter then reverted to instructing Martray in subjects he found more enjoyable. Once again, Jay Smith revealed the strange split between the public persona of high-school principal and U.S. Army colonel, and the man who stood accused of bizarre and perverted sexual behavior.

About fucking Gloria [he wrote], if I read you correctly, you want some kind of hints regarding how to throw a special fuck to her, or something like that. This is a complicated task. We'll have to talk more about this. I need to know a little more. Every woman is different even though they are all alike. First you have to give me some more facts. For example, does she have a regular menstrual cycle. This is important, for it is a way to track down the times she is hot by nature. It can guarantee you a top-notch, hot fuck with her. There are a number of other things. I will get to them as we talk about it, BUT STAY AWAY FROM KINKY SHIT. Most of that is made up by men who get hardons thinking about nutty stuff—leather, bondage, chains, whips, shit. They jack off thinking about that stuff. DO NOT TRY ANY OF THAT STUFF. All the efforts to show nude men with big dicks to women in magazines have failed. Porn is man's shit. If you want to get a good hardon, okay, but if you want to hot fuck Gloria, stay away from the nut stuff. There is a lot of kinky stuff in magazines, *Penthouse*, etc., but believe me, buddy, except for the very unusual woman, in very unusual circumstances, it is a turnoff. We'll go into more of this if you want, and if this is what you had been referring to, you can get what you're after, in fact, it is the way you'll have to go, as you get older. For you'll find that most fucking gets to be less fun unless you approach it properly with Gloria, or anyone else. If you are still fucking Val, study her also. Try the same things with her. Gentleness in all things. Get a good look at her cunt when you are sucking it, especially the clit. Eventually, in the future, with other women you will be able to tell the differences in the clit and really get them on. No kinky shit is needed. Just your tongue, dick, and fingers, are the best sex organs, plus kindness, consideration, and love talk as they are getting hot. In the middle of fucking them, say "Oh, fuck me hard, hon, fuck me real hard." Say this gently and they will get hotter. Concentrate on their signs, such as heavy breathing, changes of color of tits (aureole-nipple and underside), little murmurs, etc. This is so you know when they are hot. I'll call you on Sunday.

35

"It's a cold case, but not a totally dead one," Attorney General Leroy Zimmerman announced at a news conference. "We want to take a fresh look at it."

On May 11, 1982, thirty Montgomery County residents were chosen to serve on the new grand jury. Operating on a budget of $25,000, the grand jury was to hear evidence in several cases that law-enforcement agencies had been unable to solve. Its function was to decide if there was reason for indictment. Members of the district attorney's office and the grand jurors themselves were sworn to secrecy. Then Judge Louis Stephan told the jurors what their responsibilities would be. "The investigating grand jury will be called upon to undertake some of the most important investigative work ever undertaken by a grand jury in this county. I suggest to you that it will be an honor to serve on it."

After hearing the evidence in the Reinert case, the grand jury could vote to indict or to dismiss William Bradfield and Jay Smith for murder; or they could take no action at all. They could also recommend that a succeeding grand jury continue to study the matter. Theoretically, a grand jury has extraordinary power. It can even elect to investigate something itself, going over the heads of the police and the attorney general. Usually, however, it is an obedient servant of the attorney general, doing what it is told to do, and condemning the men or women it is told to condemn.

36

The news had come in one terrible flood. Just two days before Christmas, 1981, William Bradfield, who had been out on bail since his conviction for theft, stood before Judge Robert A. Wright. After listening to witnesses, the judge would decide how much time Bradfield had to spend in prison and if he could continue to be free on bail while his case was appealed.

Susan Reinert's brother, Pat Gallagher, was among those who testified. Looking directly at Bradfield, Gallagher said, "He took all of the money my sister had. This was the betrayal of deep personal trust built up over a period of time."

Judge Wright listened without expression, then sentenced Bradfield to serve from four months to two years in prison for stealing $25,000.

Jack Holtz stood up. "Your Honor, Susan Myers is convinced that harm will come to her at the hands of William Bradfield. For that reason, I request that the defendant's bail be increased."

John Paul Curran jumped to his feet, and for a quarter of an hour he pleaded for leniency, describing William Bradfield as a man whose career and reputation had already been ruined. "My client has been fired from Upper Merion High School. He has applied for eighty-three other teaching jobs, but probably will never be able to teach again. He does not have the additional money that he needs to remain free while I appeal his sentence to the State Superior Court."

Despite Curran's repeated objections, and the judge's acknowledgment that Susan Myers's statements might be those of a rejected lover, Judge Wright raised the bail from $75,000 to $150,000. Then, William Sidney Bradfield, overwhelmed with rage and helplessness, allowed himself to be led by sheriff's deputies to the Delaware County Prison.

Conversation with
William Bradfield

A prison guard came and got me from the hole and escorted me
in handcuffs. It was an exercise in childlike role playing.
Everything worked toward the assumption that I was a bad
person. The average prison kid views this kind of treatment not
as instructional, but as punitive. It hurts him to sit there and
listen to the way that he's described. He looks around and says
to himself, "Hey, man, who the fuck they talkin' about?" It is
the sociology of the pack in wolf's clothing. A short, fat guard
will come toward a beautiful, mahogany, six-foot-three black
man, and as the guard approaches, the black man will slump
and become smaller.

When they came to get me, it was almost as if they were
saying, "Come on, Bradfield, play the game right." The guard
said, "Sit down." I said, "Oh, do you want me to sit here?" He
said, "Come on, Bradfield, come on. I've got some forms for
you here." "Who are you?" I asked. "Who am I?" he
repeated, shocked. I said, "Yes, I'm William Bradfield, who are
you?" "I know who the fuck you are," he said. It was obvious
that he did not want to tell me who he was, but he could not
think of the reason why. I said, "Do you think you could take
these handcuffs off?" There were about five of these guards
standing around, and just me in handcuffs. "You're asking me
to sign away my power of attorney," I said. "I can't really read
this form, let alone sign it, with these handcuffs on." They had
a big debate. Finally, they took the handcuffs off. Small
victory. In prison, we live by small victories. I said, "I can't
understand this form." "You don't have to understand it, man,
you just have to sign it," he answered. "It's so you can get mail
and money." I said, "But it's coercion to sign when it is totally

incomprehensible.'' I crossed half of it out and then I asked some questions. The guards were amazed. This is not a situation in which there is the expectation of questions. It's a unilateral situation. The dominant and the submissive. Finally, when we were finished with the forms, they took me over and weighed me, then took me back to the block. As they did that, the lieutenant told me I was a pain in the ass and he'd be glad when they moved me.

That afternoon, they took me down to another environment. The C Ward. It was entirely different there. Now the game changed. The whole world-view was different. Now, it was a psychologist. The psychologists are there to help. Mr. Shank, a nice, scholarly man, graying at the temples, was there with about twenty-five prisoners. Twenty-two of them were black. First there was a spelling test. I could see all of the defense mechanisms in action. The hisses of exasperation. ''Jesus Christ, man, is that English?'' they said. They made little comments to relieve their sense of failure. When they started out, they were trying, but as the words got harder and harder, so many of the little structures for failure that helped those who were in charge came into play.

The guards reasserted their dominance. One guard stumblingly asked me if I knew any psychology. Had he been more verbal, he would have said, ''How familiar are you with modern psychological testing categories?'' Then we sat at a table where the psychologist actually introduced himself. We began to talk about Graterford Prison. I told him it was my first choice for permanent placement. He said he had spent two years there and that it was a bloody den of Philadelphia criminals, both large and small. ''I'll put it to you straight,'' he said. ''It's a goddamn black jungle. The inmates run it.'' I smiled and told him that I'd rather put up with an angry black with a knife than an ignorant, red-necked, prejudiced guard kicking young blacks around. Then I told him that if I had to stay in prison, I'd give Graterford a shot. ''I'm going to make the best of it,'' I said. ''I'm going to try to think of it as a long sabbatical and while I am there, I want to study languages, because language is the most significant aspect of man. Through it, I will find a key to the interior of man's soul. What better place is there than prison for capturing the human analogue of pain, what T. S. Eliot called the ''objective correlative,'' and how does the pain of separation, loss, and longing for days gone by manifest itself in these men who are captured behind bars?

William Bradfield's intellect and use of language constantly amazed me. He sounded more like a Classics scholar who had just stepped out of the last century than a convicted killer. Extraordinary as his intellect was, it was also the least challenging aspect of him because it was verifiable. During our prison visits, Bradfield would often digress from our conversations about his life or his case and begin a long, didactic lecture about art, religion, language, philosophy, or poetry.

His interests were obscure, strangely out of touch with most of the rest of the world. His hero was the poet Ezra Pound. While most people consider Pound anti-Semitic, mentally disturbed, and difficult to understand, Bradfield idolized him. "I never saw Pound exhibit any anti-Semitism or racism of any kind, ever," Bradfield assured me. Then he explained that when he was a student at Haverford College a classmate had handed him Pound's *ABC of Reading*. "I read it and reread it. For thirteen days straight, I didn't go to class. I was also supposed to be wrestling, but I didn't wrestle. Pound made statements of urgency. I felt bound, at least, to investigate."

Bradfield explained that during his years as a student at Haverford College, he would frequently visit Pound at St. Elizabeths Hospital for the Criminally Insane near Washington, D.C. "I offered to help him escape," Bradfield said. "But he dismissed me, saying, 'No, I'm very comfortable here.' I showed Pound the things I had written. He told me they had promise. They showed good craft, but not that I was a great poet." Clearly dissatisfied with his own artistic and intellectual achievement, Bradfield added, "I'm the eternal student, not the scholar. The scholar not only has the enthusiasm but the ability. I don't have the ability. All the things I have done, I've done with incredible effort. I'm really a slow learner. I have some talent in poetry but it's a small talent."

A sense of failure seemed to pervade all aspects of Bradfield's life. He described himself as a willful, isolated kid with a harsh father and an intensely religious mother. As an adult, he said, he had failed his women, his children, and his own dreams of creative success. Instead of writing great literature, he was teaching high school English and struggling for economic survival.

I believe that when life was hardest for William Bradfield, it was his sense of connection with, and his escape into a scholarly classic tradition that sustained him. In a draft of a letter addressed only to "Love," dated April 28, 1980, and seized by authorities from a box in his mother's house, William Bradfield expressed his anguish. First admitting that he was terribly lonely and "white with fear for the future," he said, "I shall not come out of this as I went in. I am too long in the land of the dead waiting Tiresias . . . I rage against this dying but how rage against Proteus." Later in the letter, as if the identification with classical figures had in itself lifted his spirits, Bradfield wrote, "But the trace of hope remains, however faint, for which a seed waits birth to become a silver tree." The letter was signed "Forgive me, I love you, Pax Christi, your William."

In February 1985, when I asked him some probing questions about his possible role in the murder and why he had refused to talk to Jack Holtz, he became angry and distressed, and his voice rose. "This is intolerable, Loretta," he said. "I don't want to see you anymore if you don't believe me." I dropped the questions, but when I got home I wrote to him explaining that as a journalist it was my job to ask hard questions and to understand all aspects of the case. He immediately wrote back, thanking me for my letter but ignoring what I had said. Instead, he went on for page after page, writing about the suffering and persecution of Ezra Pound. In great detail, he described Pound's arrest in Italy on May 2, 1945, and how he was turned over to Americans who chained him to an accused rapist-murderer and took him to a detention training center near Pisa where thirty-six thousand men were confined. Of all those men, Bradfield said, Ezra Pound was treated the worst. Pound was among ten men who were put in wire-mesh cages. "The other nine incorrigibles were allowed out for an hour a day for exercise, but," Bradfield continued, "Pound was never allowed out of the cage . . . within a month, he couldn't see, could barely stand, couldn't pass urine."

It seemed to me that William Bradfield found solace in his identification with Pound and other famous prisoners and martyrs throughout history. He felt inferior to them, but at the same time the identification lifted him from what he considered the mundane world of people like Jack Holtz and Lou DiSantis.

He steeped himself in intellectual traditions that isolated him from reality, became his refuge in despair, and justified his rage. While he could get along well with the toughest, most illiterate prisoner, William Bradfield considered himself an intellectual. Nevertheless, he seemed to feel that he had failed the final test of greatness, the ability to create despite adversity.

What he admired most about Ezra Pound was that Pound *never* stopped writing. While in his cage in Pisa, Bradfield told me, Pound had talked a guard into breaking regulations and giving him paper and pencil. "He folded the paper down the center," Bradfield said, "and began what would become the *Pisan Cantos*. . . . Later, at St. Elizabeths Hospital, Pound continued to write cantos, some of which are utterly magnificent."

While incarcerated at St. Elizabeths, Ezra Pound also translated the work of Confucius. It was Pound's translation of Confucius that police ultimately seized from William Bradfield's apartment. Bradfield had used the book to devise a secret code, which was later cracked by an FBI cryptologist. The code, which referred to Susan Reinert's murder, said, "Immunity improbable. My danger conspiracy."

37

The ethics of the technique are questionable from an outsider's perspective, but it is routine to those in law enforcement: just another way to explore every possibility and press every advantage. Every cop or prosecutor who knows his way to the courthouse knows that prisoners can often be "encouraged" to cooperate with the authorities. Now that William Bradfield had been locked up with other inmates, some variant of the method that Raymond Martray was using to entrap Jay Smith might also be employed to gather evidence against Bradfield to present to the grand jury. On February 10, 1983, Jack Holtz and Lou DiSantis contacted prison officials to see if William Bradfield had spent time with any particular prisoner to whom he might have confessed.

They were informed that during his brief stay in prison in January 1982, Bradfield had been seen frequently with Proctor Nowell, a twenty-three-year-old, uneducated black man. On the surface, they were unlikely companions: the upper-middle-class philosophy, Greek, and Latin scholar, and the black street kid from Chester County who'd been in and out of prison from the age of sixteen on weapons, stolen property, and aggravated-assault convictions. But Proctor Nowell was also a heavyweight Golden Gloves boxer, and a good friend to have in a world of tough, angry convicts.

"I was on Block D in Delaware County Prison," Proctor Nowell explained. "I was sitting there playing chess one day and William Bradfield walked over to me an' he said, 'I'd like to find out how to play chess, so if you have time, would you teach me?' An' I said, 'Yeah, man, I'll show you how to move the pieces, but you have to do the rest.' So the next night I was in my cell, me and this other dude, an' we was playing chess. We was just finishing up from playing a game an' Bradfield walks past my cell, an' I call him, 'Yo, Bradfield,' I say. 'Do you want to learn how to play chess? You can come in and I'll show you.' He entered my cell an' I began to show him how to move the pieces. After that, we used to sit in my cell and talk. One time, there was an inmate who said he was gonna hurt Bradfield an' I told him, 'Man, you ain't gonna do nothin' to him; that's my friend,' because we was pretty close friends."

When Lou DiSantis and Jack Holtz got the word that Nowell had been Bradfield's prison buddy, they interviewed Nowell in a private room in the visiting area of the prison. The troopers introduced themselves and explained why they were there. Nowell's eyes hardened. Holtz thought he saw a look of pride and loyalty cross the prisoner's face.

"I got nothin' to say to you," Nowell spat, then turned on his heels and spun toward the door. Holtz was on his feet in an instant.

"You don't have to say anything, man," he said smoothly. "We just want you to listen to a few things." Knowing that Nowell had two children, Holtz added, "You know, a pretty little girl, eleven years old, named Karen, and a little boy named Michael, who was only ten, were murdered. It's our job to find out who their killers were. We're wondering if you have any children of your own, Proctor.''

"Yeah," Nowell said, "I got children."

"We were wondering if Bradfield told you anything that could help us to locate these children."

"He was only here for about three weeks before he raised his bail, but we was friends," Nowell acknowledged. "We'd rap, only we agreed we'd never tell on each other. I want some time to think about it."

"That's fine," Holtz said casually, not wanting to scare him off. "We'll contact you again. Like I said, we'd just like to know if he said anything to you about those kids."

Suddenly, this tough man looked scared. "Listen, man, Bradfield laid some heavy shit on me about his case, but I don't know if I wanna talk to you or not."

"O.K.," Holtz said, secretly pleased that Nowell was somewhat reluctant to talk. He was more leery of guys like Martray who seemed overly eager. "Take your time, think about it. Here's a telephone number where you can reach us if you decide you want to talk. Let me ask you this," Holtz added, seemingly as an afterthought, but actually as an inducement, with the unspoken promise of more to look forward to. "Would you be more comfortable if we talked about this at a location outside the prison?"

"Yeah, man," Nowell said, smiling for a moment, "I sure would."

On February 25, 1983, Proctor Nowell called the state police and said he wanted to talk. Holtz had Nowell's name placed on the court sheet so the other prisoners would think he was leaving prison for a routine court appearance. "The kid interests me," Holtz said to Deputy Attorney General Rick Guida, on the morning of the meeting. "I don't know what we have here, but he interests me."

"How are you doing?" Holtz asked casually, after removing Nowell's handcuffs. "Everyone thinks you're in court, so you don't have to worry, and you won't have any trouble when you get back to the block." Nowell laughed, obviously impressed by the power and ease with which these state troopers had taken him out of a maximum-security prison.

"How 'bout some lunch?" asked Holtz. Sandwiches were brought in and DiSantis winked at Holtz as he watched Nowell say grace before he began to eat. Jack Holtz never asked Proctor Nowell why or even if he had decided to talk. He just waited until Nowell was relaxed, then began with casual questions.

By the end of the day, Nowell had not only decided to cooperate with Holtz and DiSantis, he had also agreed to repeat his statements before the third multicounty investigating grand jury.

38

More than $625,000 of taxpayers' money had already been spent in the effort to convict William Bradfield and Jay C. Smith of the Reinert murders. Two previous grand juries had ended without indictments. Adding to Jack Holtz's frustration, by the middle of January 1982, Joanne Aitken had raised the additional bail money Bradfield needed and he had been out on the street ever since. It was time, past time, as the troopers saw it, to bring this man to trial for the murders they were certain he had committed.

The third grand jury's term was running out, but Holtz and DiSantis hoped that they finally had what they needed to indict William Bradfield. As the hour of Proctor Nowell's testimony approached, Jack Holtz grew less confident. His face showed the excitement and strain of a man who was taking a risk that was almost breathtaking in its magnitude. If the jurors found this tough, almost illiterate convict believable, it would clinch the case. On the other hand, if the grand jury discarded Nowell's testimony, the probability was that they would be less certain than ever who was guilty. They might even begin to feel that Bradfield was being persecuted, not prosecuted. If they ended their term without an indictment this time, Holtz was pretty sure he would never get another chance.

On March 23, 1983, Proctor Nowell was led in. He looked directly at the men and women in the jury and, for a moment, a wild, haunted look passed through his dark eyes. He was like a cornered, frightened animal.

Rick Guida spoke softly. "Mr. Nowell," he began, "during the time you were at the Delaware County Prison, did you have an opportunity to talk with William Bradfield on a number of occasions?"

Nowell nodded, and Guida continued without waiting for a verbal response.

"Now, I'm going to skip ahead to the last conversation you had with him while you were in the Delaware County Prison. Do you remember that conversation?"

"Yes, I do," Nowell answered, becoming more controlled, even cocky, as he adjusted to his surroundings.

"All right," Guida said evenly. "Was there any event that occurred just before you talked to him?"

"Yeah," Nowell answered, "he came back from court an' I was looking for him earlier because I got some coffee from the commissary for him, an' when I walked out I seen him standing there lookin' up in the cell, real depressed, with the veins popping out the side of his head. An' then he was looking down to the floor an' I said, 'Yo, Bradfield,' an' he turned, like I had caught him at a surprise, an' I said, 'Hey, come here for a minute, man.' He came into my cell an' I went on to tell him that I had got the coffee an' I asked him, I said, 'How did it go for you in court today?'"

Guida interrupted, sensing in advance Nowell's reluctance to use four-letter words in front of a middle-class white jury. "All right, I know that there were some words used that are not pleasant for a courtroom setting, but we want you to be able to quote him as best you can, so if you have to use the words that he used, I repeat, that he *himself* used, it's all right to use them in front of these people."

Nowell shifted uneasily. "I said, 'How did you make out in court today?' An' he said, 'Well, man, they're fucking me over. They denied my bail reduction.' So I said, 'Well, Bradfield, all that money you was making as a teacher, couldn't you use that to make bail?' An' he said that 'I owe. I lost thirty-eight acres an' two cars. I was forced to close down a store in Montgomery County. If I wasn't in a financial bind, I wouldn't be here now, nor would any of this shit have had to happen to Susan.' Then Bradfield said, 'I was there when they were killed, but I didn't kill anyone.' An' I said, 'Damn, Bradfield, the children too?' An' he said, 'None of this was meant for the children, only for Susan. It was a shame they had to suffer like this, but there couldn't be a stone left unturned.' After he told me that, I just stayed away from him 'cause I didn't like the idea of him saying that about the kids.''

Rick Guida paused for a moment to let the statement have its impact. It was important that the jury accept the portrait of William Bradfield as a man who could see children murdered. Then he said, ''I believe there were two other conversations that you had with him in prison. One was after a letter you received from your wife. Now, tell us what happened after you received that letter.''

''I got this letter from my wife and it was real disgusting. Like, she said, 'I'm sorry, baby, but I don't want to hang in there this time,' and at that moment I was sitting there thinking about how hard I had worked to provide for her an' my two children. An' I tol' Bradfield, I said, 'Bradfield, read this letter.' He read the letter an' then I said, 'Know what, man? I'm gonna kill her.' An' he said, 'No, you don't ever want to kill anyone, man. If you do that, they ain't never gonna get off your ass.' He said, 'You know what I'm here for?' I said, 'No, not really.' An' he said, 'I'm here for theft of twenty-five thousand dollars.' An' I said, 'Well, why don't you just pay back the money?' An' he said, 'It's not that simple. It's not the twenty-five thousand dollars. They're trying to indict me for murder, but they'll never convict me.' I said, 'Why?' He said, 'They don't have no evidence,' an' he smiled.''

''Did you have any conversation with him after that?'' Guida asked, glancing over at the jury members to see their reactions.

''Yeah. Bradfield said, 'I can't believe after all I've done for those people.' He mentioned some names like Chris and Wendy and he said, 'After all I've done for them, I can't believe they are testifying against me.' He told me that he'd threw parties and that he'd entertained them, and now they're all getting up on the stand and testifying against him, an' he said, 'I'd like to get a fucking groat around their neck.' ''

''What do you mean by that?'' Guida said, feigning ignorance. ''Is that a wire?''

''Yeah, exactly,'' Nowell answered. ''I said, 'Bradfield, you don't want to do that, man. You're in enough trouble now.' An' he said, 'Yeah, I guess you're right.' "

"Mr. Nowell," Guida said, responding to a look of skepticism on one juror's face, "when you were originally questioned by the police, did you give them this information?"

"No, I did not."

"Why was that?"

"Well, because me and Bradfield was good friends, and I didn't want to get involved in it because I felt as though maybe I would be hurt or something. I just didn't want to be no witness and I made this aware to the troopers that had asked me. I said, 'No, I don't know nothing about it,' although I was lying. And the troopers said, 'Well, why don't you think about it. This is concerning two men and some kids.' I went back to my block and I laid in my cell and I thought about how I had two kids, and I thought about how I would want somebody to come to my kids' rescue if it happened to my kids. I just got the feeling like, you know, no matter what it takes, I'm going to tell the truth about it. And so I called the troopers on the phone and I said, 'Look,' I said, 'I want you to come out here and see me, 'cause I want to tell you exactly what he tol' me.' "

Rick Guida approached the witness stand. "Mr. Nowell, are you telling this grand jury today the absolute truth without embellishing it, or adding anything to it at all? Is that exactly what happened?"

"Yes, yes," he said, "I am telling you exactly what happened."

"So help you God?"

"So help me God."

"One more thing. It's difficult for you to read, isn't it? You have a tough time reading?"

"Not really," Nowell answered. He sat upright and his face hardened.

"What I mean," Guida added quickly, "is when you mentioned the names Wendy and Chris, those are names you never read about in the newspapers. Never heard of before, right?"

"Yeah," Proctor answered, still defensive. "I never heard of them before until Bradfield told me."

"Now," said Guida, addressing the jury, "I'm going to ask Mr. Nowell to step outside and see if we have any questions."

"Questions?" Guida asked, turning on his heels like a

leading man who has just taken a bow in a Broadway show.

"Yes," a grand jury member said. "Did he remember those names, or was he fed those names by you?"

"As a matter of fact," Rick Guida responded, "he just answered that question. The names were not told to him by us. He came up with the names Wendy and Chris himself. I believe he also knew Vince's name, but he didn't say that today."

"I must say," another grand jury member added, "that's surprising testimony. But when he said that Bradfield admitted he was there when Susan and the kids were killed, but that he didn't do it, are you saying that's all his testimony is? Just that he was there at that time."

"Well, yes, that is the statement," Guida answered.

Several of the male jurors still seemed uneasy. This huge, black, illiterate convict was not their kind, and his testimony startled them and left them uncomfortable. "How long was Bradfield in prison?" one of them asked.

"Almost a month," Guida answered. "He went in on December 23, I believe, and he was out toward the end of January. Anything else?"

"Yes. When did Nowell come forth with his 'voluntary information'? Did he tell you this when you interviewed him the first time, or didn't he?"

"Obviously, we're not going to have somebody make up testimony, you know," Guida answered, becoming noticeably impatient. "He wouldn't talk to us the first time. Would not talk to us."

"So when did he voluntarily come forth with this information?" the juror asked, still uncertain.

"As he told you," Guida answered, "he went and thought about it and was so upset because two kids were killed that he finally contacted Jack Holtz and asked him to come down. But don't think that this guy was ever anything other than a reluctant witness, because he wasn't. He did not want to cooperate with us and initially he didn't."

"He has nothing to gain by volunteering this?" the grand juror pressed.

"He got no deals," Guida said, "nothing."

"He's still in prison?"

"As a matter of fact, we had to move him out of Delaware County Prison because of the fact that he's testifying. He's gained nothing. Anything further?'' Guida asked, moving along, appearing confident and unshaken.

''No further questions,'' the jury foreman said.

When Rick Guida sat down, beads of perspiration were dampening his crisp white collar. Nowell's testimony had not elicited the overwhelming response Guida had hoped for, but he still believed that it had had an impact, that it would be the final push that convinced this grand jury to indict.

He was right. Later that day, an indictment was returned, charging William Bradfield with three counts of murder, three counts of solicitation to commit murder, three counts of conspiracy to commit murder, three counts of kidnapping, three counts of conspiracy to commit kidnapping, and three counts of obstruction of justice.

PART IV

The Price

Is that how men do murders? Do men go to commit a murder as I went then? I will tell you someday how I went. Did I murder the woman? I murdered myself. Not her. I crushed myself once, for all, forever.

—FYODOR DOSTOYEVSKY
Crime and Punishment

39

Lou DiSantis spotted William Bradfield's battered blue Volkswagen on East Sixth Street in Birdsboro, a suburb of Philadelphia. Holtz, DiSantis, Guida, and a female trooper assigned to the case had spent most of the night staking out the guest quarters of Bradfield's mother's house in Downingtown. They knew Bradfield was living there with Joanne Aitken and trying to find work. At almost midnight, Holtz had seen a light go on in the upper floor of the guest house. The female trooper had called the house and asked for Bill. Joanne Aitken had answered. "He's in Birdsboro," she'd said. Now, triumphant at the sight of the car, DiSantis mumbled, "He's the only asshole I know who parks in the middle of the goddamn street." Then he added, "Now it's definite, we're gonna take him tonight."

When the rest of the team arrived, armed with shotguns and tear gas, and backed up by helicopters on standby, they found the Birdsboro police chief nervously observing DiSantis's unmarked car. DiSantis promptly presented his trooper's identification. Then he showed the Birdsboro chief a photograph of William Bradfield, advised him of the charges against Bradfield, and offered him the opportunity to help with the arrest.

It was 2:52 A.M. on April 6, 1983, when the arrest team arrived at the bi-level frame house that they had been watching ever since learning that Bradfield had become friendly with the owners and frequently stayed overnight. Four men took the rear and the sides of the house. Three went to the front. Rick Guida, who was officially present only to give legal advice to the troopers, remained in the car. Holtz knocked on the front door, prepared to take it down if he had to. A sleepy-looking, middle-aged white male, peaked out. He identified himself as Robert Wells.

"We have an arrest warrant for William Bradfield," Holtz said, his voice quivering slightly with excitement.

"He's in the garage," the man stammered. He opened the door and stepped back. "His dog's been hurt, he's sleeping down there to keep it company." Holtz had heard about the dog from another trooper. A goddamn doberman. He was prepared to kill it if it attacked.

The men walked down the steps, opened the garage door, and flicked on the light. The dog jumped up, startled. Holtz spun around, gun in hand. "Shoot it if it moves," he shouted. Bradfield was lying on a cot beside the dog; his hands were under the covers. "Put your hands up," Holtz spat. But Bradfield, afraid he'd be shot if he moved, lay still. "Stay where you are," Holtz yelled, ripping off the blankets and pointing the gun at Bradfield's head.

"Watch out for the dog," Bradfield said quietly. "His leg has been hurt."

For the first time, Holtz noticed that the "fierce doberman" was a young English setter, wagging its tail.

Outside, unable to bear the suspense, Rick Guida started up the driveway. One of the neighborhood cops, called in by the Birdsboro police chief for the detail, heard the footsteps. "Freeze," he shouted, his voice echoing through the darkness. Rick Guida's hands went clammy.

"Oh, shit," he mumbled. "Now someone's gonna get killed. Wait a minute, let me identify myself," he said, louder. "I'm the deputy attorney general."

Apologizing profusely, the local cop let him pass.

"As soon as I walked in, I saw Bradfield's eyes," Guida later recalled. "There was something about those eyes. I never felt anything like it. Almost like some part of him had reached out and touched me. I felt his power. It's hard to describe. I literally had a sense of a struggle between good and evil. I was uncomfortable, shaken. I had lines rehearsed, things I was planning to say to Bradfield. I simply forgot what they were. Then I found myself sitting on the floor of the garage in my three-piece suit, playing with the dog. To this day, I don't know why I was playing with the dog and why I didn't do what I had planned to do. I looked at him again. My hands were shaking. My hands never shake. Oh, I know there are other explanations, and I'm not superstitious. I can only say it was very strange."

"Get dressed, Bill," Jack Holtz said quietly. Bradfield

looked at Holtz, then at the other men in the room. "Did you hear me, Bill?" Holtz asked, casually dangling the handcuffs. He put his polished shoe on the cot and rested his elbow on his knee. For a moment, the gazes of the two men locked. "Did you hear me, Bill?" Holtz repeated, his voice hardening with the power of his victory. "I said, get dressed."

40

Awaiting trial on charges of murder, William Bradfield had been held without bail in Camp Hill Prison for less than three weeks when inmate Arnold Weidner contacted state police, claiming he had important information on the Reinert murder. "Hot damn, another stool pigeon who wants to run off at the mouth," DiSantis mumbled when he got the word. The Pennsylvania State Police were no longer desperate for leads. They already had Proctor Nowell and they could afford to be choosy. Still, it was always worth hearing what a convict had to say.

"We understand that you have requested to talk to someone in law enforcement," Holtz said when the twenty-three-year-old black prisoner was led into a private interview room.

"Yeah," Weidner said, nodding vigorously. "Me and Bradfield, we was friends and we talked many times. I was a runner. It was my job to take food and stuff to the other prisoners, an' he was looking for a flunky to talk to. He was desperate and not very wise about jail, so I started taking notes every time he'd talk to me. He was panicked about this dude, Nowell, testifying against him and he asked me if I could have him killed."

DiSantis frowned and lit a cigarette. "How did he happen to get on the subject of his case and the murder of witnesses?" he asked, already feeling bad vibrations.

"He started sayin' that if he went down, he wanted somethin' to kill himself with, as he could not do the time."

Holtz interrupted. "What did he want?"

"Poison or something that would be quick and not just blind him or make him a cripple. He asked me if I knew somebody who could kill three people for him—Nowell, Valaitis, and Pappas. I told me yes. He said Nowell was the main one, because Nowell was going to testify that he killed Reinert. We was going to put poison in Nowell's food through an outside plant, and if that didn't work, we'd have shot him on his way to the courthouse. Bradfield was gonna pay fifty thousand dollars for his elimination. Pappas and Valaitis was also to be killed because they betrayed him an' didn't deserve to live. He offered me one hundred fifty thousand dollars for the three lives. He said it would come through offshore investments. I wouldn't get the whole amount, but Bradfield said it would make me a million before the year was out. I never exactly understood the deal. I contacted the prison deputy an' I said I need to talk because, you know, I had gotten in deeper than I wanted. I was stalling. I requested to be transferred out. When Bradfield heard they was transferring me, he snapped. He jumped out of the bed an' grabbed the bars like a wild man. 'What's goin' on with you?' he said. So I said it was nothin'. They was just transferring me, but I didn't know why. I swore I would not testify against him."

"Did he say anything about Susan Reinert?" Holtz asked casually.

"Yeah," he said. "She was a bad fuck. Always dressed down, not freaky with her sex habits, but she was an opportunity. Then he said, 'It's Karen I dream about. I'll never forget the look in her eyes when she was killed. She screamed and screamed.' He told me bailing twine was used to strangle someone and that wasn't his idea of class. He said he never murdered anyone because there was a big difference between murder and justified execution."

Weidner swore the statement he made that day was true. He said that he sent letters to his sister explaining and documenting it. But when Holtz contacted Weidner's sister, Eleanor, she said she had never received any letters from her brother.

That night, long after everyone else had left the office, Jack Holtz sat alone at his desk, chewing tobacco and thinking about how a jury would respond to Arnold Weidner's story. If the jurors didn't buy it, they would also probably discredit Proctor

Nowell, who had convinced the grand jury and could be expected to convince another jury as well. Besides, Arnold Weidner was pressing too hard and openly for a deal. He had made deals before with cops that had led to convictions. He had been out of prison for a short time, then had gone back in on a new burglary charge. Now he wanted that charge lifted. There was another problem, a tactical one: would a jury believe that the suave, educated, upper-middle-class William Bradfield had confessed not to one, but to *two* illiterate black men?

The next morning, Jack Holtz walked over to Rick Guida's office and knocked on the door. "In my opinion," he said, "Arnold Weidner isn't worth the risk."

41

On the eleventh day of October 1983, jury selection for William Bradfield's murder trial began. For five days, ninety-four prospective jurors filed through the Dauphin County Courthouse. Judge Isaac J. Garb, president judge of Bucks County, a wiry man in his mid-fifties, presided. Garb was a former college football halfback, army counterintelligence officer, assistant U.S. attorney, and public defender. He still saw himself as a man with a public mission. He drove a beat-up Plymouth, smoked a corncob pipe, and thrived on difficult legal situations. Described by his colleagues as brilliant, the five-foot, five-inch judge seemed more than six feet tall in his courtroom.

Garb, who had been especially assigned by the Pennsylvania Supreme Court because of the complexity of the case, greeted each of the prospective jurors personally. They were, by no stretch of the imagination, a jury of William Bradfield's intellectual peers. They were a microcosm of American life, ordinary people who, for the most part, had no knowledge of the judicial system, of violence, or of the bizarre workings of the criminal conscience. Many of them had gleaned fragments of information about the case from television or newspaper articles, and had already decided that William Bradfield was guilty. Those men and women were dismissed.

Because Rick Guida was seeking the death penalty for Bradfield, prospective jurors were asked their views on capital punishment.

"If this is such a case as I suspect it is," said one middle-aged woman, "I *would* believe in capital punishment, but not until I searched my heart."

"Your heart? What about the evidence?" Garb quipped.

"Based on what you have read, do you have an opinion about the guilt or innocence of the defendant?" he asked another.

"Yes, I do. I'm afraid I believe he's guilty."

"What is that based on?" Garb asked.

"Intuition. I am a believer in ESP."

"Can I talk you out of it?" the judge inquired.

"No," the man answered, "it comes through the walls and everything."

"All right," Garb said, shaking his head and leaning back in the huge leather chair embossed in gold. "I thank you, sir. You are excused."

The parade of prospective jurors continued. Each time one was accepted, William Bradfield, pale and unsteady, looked as if another nail had been hammered into his coffin.

"I have no compassion for someone who kills someone," a thirty-four-year-old supply systems analyst for the navy said, glaring angrily at Bradfield.

"Yes, I have formed my opinion," announced an elderly, tight-lipped woman.

"And what is your opinion?" Garb asked.

"I'd rather not say," the woman responded.

"I'm sorry," the judge said, "we must know."

"The authorities accumulated the evidence; therefore, I assume he is guilty."

"You are excused, but let me say something for you to take with you. If all people believed that everyone brought to trial was guilty, there would be no reason to have a trial. Certainly, you know that some people are brought to trial and it is determined that they are innocent. If it is a foregone conclusion, then we are wasting our time here."

Rick Guida spent most of his twelve strikes trying to eliminate jurors who might be sympathetic to Bradfield. He was searching for people with great respect for police authority and a willingness to impose the death penalty. Guida operated smoothly and easily in this environment. He wanted women on the panel, but only those who would be likely to identify with Susan Reinert and the children and be repelled by Bradfield's multiple relationships. If even one woman was drawn in by Bradfield's charm and power, she could present a threat to the entire panel.

Joshua Lock, a young, hardworking private attorney, accepted a court appointment to defend William Bradfield after Bradfield declared bankruptcy. Lock was already worried about the way things were progressing. Public sentiment was clearly against his client. Lock had hoped that the hundreds of hours for which he would barely be paid would establish Bradfield's innocence and advance his own career and public image.

Lock's courtroom demeanor was a decided contrast to Guida's easygoing, soft-voiced approach. Lock seemed to snap at the prospective jurors. He badly wanted a bright, educated jury that could understand the unconventional lifestyle of an eccentric suburban intellectual. But almost without exception, the men and women he would have liked to choose were opposed to capital punishment and were, therefore, ruled out by the prosecution.

Nine men and three women were finally chosen. They were not the jurors Lock wanted, but he had used up all of his preemptory challenges. Most had graduated from high school, but only four had attended college. They ranged in age from twenty-four to sixty-nine. They had a total of twenty-four children. Among them were a twenty-nine-year-old computer operator who lived with his grandmother and read only comics; a fifty-three-year-old female machine operator who seldom read newspapers, but enjoyed *True Story* magazine; and an unemployed electrician. They were law-abiding, blue-collar citizens, men and women whose lives seemed to be devoid of culture, scholarship, and sexual shenanigans. They were ordinary people who, Rick Guida hoped, would be able to recognize a cold-blooded plot to destroy a woman and her two children.

For the next nine days, from October 15 to October 24, 1983, the prosecution presented its evidence. Much of it was devoted to demonstrating the complex links in the chain of circumstantial evidence that connected Bradfield to the murders. The jurors listened to the strange tale of love, fear, manipulation, and death. They were told that Susan Reinert wanted to marry William Bradfield, and that he was having an affair with her while living with Susan Myers and engaged to Wendy Zeigler. They were also told that Bradfield appeared to be afraid that Jay Smith was going to murder Susan Reinert but did not tell her or the police. Bradfield, the jury was told, had been named as beneficiary of almost a million dollars in life insurance. Then the jurors, who listened to the evidence during the long, tiring days, were told that a tiny fiber found in Susan Reinert's hair matched fibers found in a carpet in Jay C. Smith's house. An FBI laboratory specialist said that a strand of hair that microscopically matched Susan Reinert's hair was found on the same rug. Jurors were also told that a blue comb inscribed *79th USAR COM*—the Seventy-Ninth Reserve Command, in which Smith served as colonel—was found under Susan Reinert's body. Rick Guida made no attempt to link Bradfield directly to the hair, comb, or fiber findings. Instead, the testimony was used to suggest that William Bradfield had participated in a conspiracy with Smith.

The jury was then introduced to Susan Reinert's neighbors, who testified that two or three nights a week, they observed Bradfield's car parked in front of Susan Reinert's house all night.

"She was a great mother and they were real good kids. Very bright and lovable," Florence Reinert, the children's grandmother, testified. "Michael told us they were going to get a van when they went to Europe with Bill. I asked them who Bill was," Mrs. Reinert added, her eyes filling with tears as she glanced directly at William Bradfield, "and Michael said, 'Bill Bradfield, my mother's friend.'"

"Is he here today?" Guida asked gently.

"Right over there," she said, wiping her eyes and pointing. "He's the man with the beard."

"In April 1980, we distributed a wanted poster searching for the children," Jack Holtz explained, trying to establish that, although their bodies had never been found, the children were dead. "It went to every police department in the nation. We requested the assistance of the FBI. We had our state police divers diving in ponds. We dug up landfills. We even had special probes made in an attempt to find the graves of the children. I myself traveled from Delaware to New Mexico, looking for them.''

"The effort was massive," Donald Redden, a roughhewn FBI man, told the jury. "Eighteen agents were assigned to the case, along with two stenographers and two state police officers. The FBI assigned a code name to this murder. We called it SUMUR, for Susan's murder. Almost all of our eight thousand agents were aware of the search for the children."

"And was there ever any indication as to the whereabouts of those children?" Guida asked.

"None whatsoever," Donald Redden said softly.

"Is there any indication that those children are alive today?"

"None whatsoever," he repeated.

It was difficult for the defense to assess the impact of the prosecution's witnesses upon the jurors, but many of them appeared to be moved by the tragedy of the loss. Josh Lock remained quiet; at no time did he cross-examine any of the witnesses who suggested that the children were dead. It was not until Proctor Nowell took the stand and repeated what he had said before the grand jury that Josh Lock's style of cross-examining became active, contemptuous, and aggressive.

"As I understand your testimony, while you were in prison you got a letter from your wife, is that right?" Lock asked, studying Nowell's face carefully.

"Yes," Nowell answered.

"And in that letter she told you she had had about enough and was not going to be waiting for you when you got out this time."

Nowell hedged. "Not exactly," he added.

"Well, what exactly did she say?"

"It was, uh, you know, something like, I'm tired baby and, you know, I don't know if you and me is gonna make it again, but I'll bring up the children to visit you, things of this nature."

"You became very upset upon receipt of that letter," Lock said.

"Yes, I did."

"So upset that you threatened, at least in anger, to kill her, isn't that right?"

Nowell nodded. "Yes." Then he added, "I just said that out of anger, you know. I never really entertained that thought to carry it out."

"Because of the letter you received, did you think it was important that you get home and patch things up with your wife?"

Nowell remained silent.

"Mr. Nowell, the truth of the matter is, you were thinking about that when the police came along and told you to think about the children, weren't you?"

"No," Nowell said defensively.

"You had totally put this threat to kill your wife out of your mind?"

"Well, I had got other letters from her after that letter, and you know, they wasn't as harsh as the first one."

Turning his attention to Nowell's criminal record, Lock said, "It is true, is it not, that you were originally arrested on an excess of a dozen charges?" Lock added, "And it is also true that the burglaries, the aggravated assault, the simple assault, the recklessly endangering, as well as the crime committed with the firearm, and the prohibited offensive weapons, and the terroristic threats and the like were all dropped, weren't they?"

"I don't really know."

"You don't know?" Lock repeated incredulously. "You were given a furlough to an alcohol and drug rehabilitation center, weren't you?"

"Yes."

"Did you forget that?"

"No, I didn't."

"Mr. Nowell, you are not serving your sentence in jail, are you?" Lock said, pointing out that despite the prosecution's adamant denials about deal-making, Proctor Nowell had been removed from Delaware County Prison and placed in a minimum-security rehabilitation center in upstate Pennsylvania. "Now," Lock continued sarcastically, "do you remember being taken out of Delaware County Prison *after* you gave your statement to the police?"

"Yes, I do," Nowell conceded.

"Well," Lock said, "let me go back a little bit. Mr. Bradfield comes to your cell on the day of his bail-reduction hearing or whatever it was, and tells you what?"

"Do you want me to explain it from the beginning?" Nowell asked.

"I understand he was standing on the tier, and his veins were popping out,'' Lock answered. "Let's take it from there."

"Well,'' Nowell responded, "he is staring at the ceiling like I said, looking out the window. His veins is like popping out of his head. He starts to say if he wasn't in a financial bind, he wouldn't be here, nor would this have had to have happened to Susan. And I just said, 'Damn, Bradfield, the kids, too.'''

"You knew nothing about this before his disclosure, did you?'' Lock spat.

"Yes,'' Nowell answered.

"Because you read it in the paper, didn't you?''

Nowell hesitated. "Well, I previously read over it, and I also overheard a few other inmates, you know, talking about it.''

"And you knew about the missing children, didn't you?'' Lock asked angrily.

"No, not really,'' Nowell answered.

"Then how did you come off saying to him, 'Damn, Bradfield, and the children too'?''

"Well, yes, I knew about it,'' Nowell conceded. "But, you know, it was through, like, hearing it on the grapevine.''

"But you knew about some of the details of the case, didn't you?'' Lock pressed.

"Yes, I did,'' Nowell admitted.

"Your cooperation was brought up before the judge when he sentenced you on July 25 to the alcohol and drug rehabilitation program, isn't that right?''

"I don't know, I don't think so. But if it was brought to his attention, it was brought, maybe, by the papers and TV as far as I know.''

"Were you there, at your sentencing?'' Lock asked.

"Yes, I was there,'' Nowell said. "I'm pretty sure that they made the judge known of my cooperation. But as far as him asking to take me into consideration, I don't really remember hearing that.''

"The point I'm getting at,'' Lock said, "is that the original charges were much more serious, weren't they?''

"Yes, they was.''

"They were robberies, weren't they?''

"Yes, they was robberies.''

"Did you know on February 25, 1983, how much time accumulatively you were facing for all of your offenses?''

"No, I really didn't know.''

Rick Guida jumped to his feet. "Objection," he shouted, apparently concerned that the jury would think Proctor Nowell had been given a lighter sentence in exchange for his cooperation.

"Overruled," Judge Garb said sharply.

"You knew you had eighteen additional criminal offenses filed against you, isn't that right?" Lock continued. "You discussed your case with your attorney, didn't you? You told him you wanted out of jail, isn't that right?"

"Yes," Nowell repeated reluctantly.

Then, in a final effort to discredit Nowell's testimony, Josh Lock said, "And then you decided to take matters into your own hands, isn't *that* right?"

Nowell sat there confused and frozen.

Josh Lock smiled triumphantly and said, "That is all, Mr. Nowell, thank you."

Conversation with William Bradfield

Proctor Nowell is an ignorant, weak, young black who grew up in a terrible situation. What he did was understandable. Jack Holtz knows Proctor Nowell's testimony is false. I reject Holtz. I reject the system for which he and the others are the cutting edge. I reject the court. I already testified and told the truth. I was mocked. I'm livid about this. They don't want the truth. They didn't get the truth out of Proctor Nowell. These people are playing power games and cloaking it in respectability. They arrested Wendy, knowing she hadn't done anything. She told them that she knew I was innocent. She knew what they made Chris do. She knew what they made Proctor Nowell do. That's the prosecution. We *know* they lie. Do you think Jack Holtz thinks I would go to Proctor Nowell and tell him those things after five years of staunchly defending myself? During those years, I didn't believe that I could end up in prison for something so heinous, that I didn't do. In my view, Jack Holtz is every bit as bad as Jay Smith, because he's in a public position. He has betrayed a sacred public trust.

They made a deal with Nowell. In the midst of the trial, our team learned that someone from the Dauphin County prosecutor's staff was talking to Nowell's judge. In addition to all the other charges, Nowell had two gun charges. That's five years each, ten years for those charges alone. He got a year and a half total at a rehabilitation center. Proctor Nowell knew he was looking at ten years or more in prison. The police deny it, but they offer rewards for favorable testimony. From start to finish, this has been a farce. They even told Josh Lock that without Proctor Nowell there would not have been an arrest. Proctor Nowell got this case into court and Jack Holtz's tactics got me convicted. Now I have to work on who I am, not where I am. I have to view prison life as secondary.

I was working closely with the state police. Often, I would leave William Bradfield and spend the next day or two going over the official evidence that had been used to indict William Bradfield as well as some that had never been used in court or become public record.

Jack Holtz handed me a photograph of Susan Reinert. It was taken on the morning of June 25, 1979, before Holtz arrived at the scene and before Susan's body was lifted from the hatchback of her car. Photographed from behind, she was still in the fetal position and the rope marks, the bruises, and the chain marks across her back were clearly visible.

"Poor Susan," I said.

"No," Holtz replied, handing me another photograph, this one revealing her face and body. "This is poor Susan."

Then, for the first time, I saw the swollen eyes, the mouth open and filled with blood, the slender, bruised arms. It was obvious that Susan had been fighting to fend off her killers.

"She was hit with the chain," Holtz explained, "and she was probably tied in the fetal position for a number of hours before she was killed. That way she could have been sexually assaulted from behind."

Suddenly, Susan's death had become graphic. I thought of William Bradfield and the way he had seemed the evening before. He begged me to try to find Alex, the real killer, to prove that he, Bradfield, was innocent. Then we said goodbye. As the last slanting rays of winter sunlight hit the barbed-wire fence, I watched him turn and walk back toward his cell until he was lost among dozens of other men dressed in brown prison suits. Now, sitting in Jack Holtz's office, I felt I had to know the truth. I wanted to believe everything that William Bradfield had told me: he was not Susan's lover; she had fantasized the whole thing; she had taken out life insurance and named him the beneficiary without his knowledge or consent. She had imagined the engagement and the wedding plans. But had she typed her own receipt for twenty-five thousand dollars and invested her money in a nonexistent firm? Had she lost her diamond ring and arranged for the disappearance of her children? How could Bradfield have known with such certainty that Susan was about to be killed, if the murder was not, as he now claimed, even committed by Jay Smith?

Interrupting my thoughts, Jack Holtz handed me a letter. It was dated December 9, 1978, and written by Susan Reinert. She was posing a question to a life insurance salesman who had just sent her information on a term policy that paid the beneficiary an additional two hundred thousand dollars in the event of an accidental death. Susan thanked him for the information and said: "For clarification, please tell me what is covered under accidental death. If I fall off the back of a sail boat or if I am shot, are these considered accidents?" Was it a coincidence that Susan had told a friend that she and Bradfield were planning a boat trip?

Before I left Jack Holtz's office that afternoon, he also read to me from the sworn statement by inmate Arnold Weidner reporting that Bradfield had said to him, "It's Karen I dream about. I'll never forget the look in her eyes when she was killed. She screamed and screamed."

"It's convincing, isn't it?" Jack Holtz said.

"Yes," I answered honestly, "and it's terrifying."

That night, after falling into a troubled sleep, I had my first dream about William Bradfield. He had escaped from prison and had come directly to my house. I was alone. When I opened the door and saw him, I was surprised, but greeted him as a friend. He put his arms around me. "I've waited a long time for this," he said, and then he lifted his hands to my throat.

PART V

Duplicity

. . . there will be time
To prepare a face to meet the faces
   that you meet;
There will be time to murder and
   create . . .

—T. S. ELIOT
   "The Love Song of J. Alfred Prufrock"

42

Spectators jammed the courtroom, arriving early and frequently standing in line to await an open spot in the rows of wooden benches. "It's better than a soap opera," said a woman from a nearby country club, as the long list of Bradfield's former lovers and friends filed through.

"Christopher Pappas, Your Honor," said Deputy Attorney General Guida, as the bailiff led in another of the prosecutor's star witnesses. Despite eight days of testimony from nearly sixty witnesses, it was Pappas who Guida hoped would establish Bradfield's guilt beyond a reasonable doubt.

Bent at the shoulders and quivering, Pappas told the jury that William Bradfield had become a "disciple" of Jay Smith's. "It was," he said, "advantageous for Mr. Bradfield to maintain a friendly relationship with Smith, and to help that relationship, Bradfield was learning Smith's assassination techniques."

"Did he have any particular garment that he used to practice this type of thing with?" Guida asked, feigning ignorance.

"He did," Pappas answered. "It was a blue jacket that Mr. Bradfield often wore. It was dark blue and had four rather large pockets on it, and in each of the pockets there was something different. There was a ski mask in one pocket and tape in another pocket, and chains and locks in another pocket, and in another pocket, there were plastic bags. After making assassinations, the plastic bag was placed over the person's head and then tied, to restrain the flow of blood."

"Why did Mr. Bradfield have these articles—the tapes, chains, locks, and plastic bags? What was the purpose of having these in his jacket as he told you?" Guida asked.

Chris Pappas searched for his answer. After glancing at William Bradfield as if to refresh his memory, he whispered,

"Mr. Bradfield said that he wanted to enter into a teacher/ disciple relationship with Smith to gain Smith's confidence, so he imitated the things that Smith suggested and practiced with Smith at times, things that Smith had done."

"So," said Guida, the now-familiar sarcasm in his inflection, "that's what the jacket and the filled pockets were all about. Bradfield was practicing things Smith was doing?"

"Yes, and Smith had recommended a particular type of plastic bag," Pappas said.

"Is that what Bradfield told you?"

"That's correct."

"Go ahead."

"Mr. Bradfield went out and bought some of those particular types. I don't remember the name. I remember they were dark green. He was testing the strength. Just playing with them, so to speak."

Next, Guida produced a small scrap of paper which had been turned over to police by Chris Pappas. On it, Bradfield had written dozens of words and phrases. Under the heading "Enemies," Bradfield listed "state," "FBI," "Reinerts people," and "Vince." Also on that small, torn scrap of white paper, which seemed to reflect his assessment of his own vulnerability, Bradfield had written, "fingerprints on money," "I was there, during insurance man's visit," "perjury at St. David's." Finally, most damaging, Bradfield had written six words that the press and the jury would now believe reflected his actions, the actions of a murderer: "lured and killed kids, taped her."

43

The afternoon session was cut short when William Bradfield became ill. Red-eyed, complaining of nausea and dizziness, he was led unsteadily from the courtroom. It was clear that Bradfield, who had demonstrated no emotion at the trial until this point, was badly shaken. He seemed to understand, finally, that unless he took the witness stand and convinced this jury that he was innocent of Susan Reinert's murder and not responsible for the disappearance of her children, he would be found guilty of three first-degree murders and he would, in all probability, be sentenced to death in the electric chair.

The next morning, still ashen and shaky, William Bradfield walked to the witness stand. After being sworn in he began to speak in a voice that was barely audible. The jurors were silent, almost transfixed, as they strained to hear his explanation of events. Josh Lock gently led him with patience and courtesy.

"Mr. Bradfield, was your relationship intimate with Ms. Myers?" Lock asked, almost apologetically.

"It was, up until the time we came back from Europe in 1973," Bradfield whispered. "Until then, we were living together as lovers."

"When did you first meet Wendy Zeigler?"

"Wendy was a student in the advanced-placement English class [at Upper Merion High School], in 1977, I think. We had tenth-, eleventh-, and twelfth-grade advanced placement. She was also in my Latin class and my Greek class. She was one of my favorite students."

"And did you develop another aspect of your relationship after graduation?"

He nodded. "Yes. Romantic, after that."

"What was the basis of the relationship with Joanne Aitken?"

"We shared interests in artistic and intellectual matters," Bradfield answered.

"When did you first see Susan Reinert?"

Instantly on guard, Bradfield answered, "There was never any romantic interest on my part. I had made it quite clear to Sue the first time she mentioned me in that context, which was nineteen seventy-four or -five, and through the period in which she grew more demanding and insisting I see her more, that kind of thing. I made it real clear to her. There was never any doubt about that."

Lock turned his attention to Jay Smith. "Did he ever say he was going to kill anybody?"

Bradfield ran his fingers nervously through his hair. "He never directly said that to me," he answered, contradicting what he had told Vince Valaitis and Chris Pappas. He paused, and then he amended his answer. "The kinds of things he had been involved in, he categorized as 'screening for elimination.' Dr. Smith spoke in a very cautious, circumspect way. He had spoken about the fact that if harm came to people by people who were professionals, it happened during holiday weekends.''

William Bradfield seemed to want to give the jurors a picture of the bizarre world of Jay Smith, but he was softening it, becoming more general in his descriptions and presenting that world as a realm he himself had only intermittently entered.

''Dr. Smith was an unguided missile,'' Bradfield added pensively, ''and with my being there, at least I could see what he was being guided toward. I was spending more and more time with Smith by Christmas of 1978. I was also spending more and more time trying to be near Sue Reinert . . . to see if she was O.K. I was at the point of taking Dr. Smith seriously enough that I checked on Susan Reinert, almost constantly.''

''Why didn't you go to the police at this point?'' Lock asked, wishing he could avoid the subject, but knowing it was on the minds of the jurors and knowing it would look better if he, not Guida, asked the question.

Bradfield hesitated. When he finally spoke, the answer was halting and uncertain. ''Vince and I especially, and Chris to a lesser extent, talked about what we should do every other day. We, number one, didn't know whether we really believed it; number two, we didn't, at that point, think we knew enough to be able to trust the police in light of what Dr. Smith had said. We tried to test what he was saying to me against the reality and often it seemed to make sense. . . . Chris said, 'Well, find out if he knows about this, and ask him if he knows how to do this, ask him how this is done,' and I would come back and report what Smith had said and we would think about it. And the more those things began to make sense, the more terrified we became. And the more seriously we took him, the more afraid we became to do anything. We were prisoners of our own fear.''

Lock walked back to the defense table and whispered to an assistant. He rifled through a stack of folders, then, deciding not to take that line of questioning any further, he approached the witness stand again with a new set of questions.

''Can you tell us what this is, please, Mr. Bradfield?'' he asked, holding up the scrap of paper that had visibly affected the jurors and had made newspaper headlines with the phrase ''lured and killed kids, taped her.''

"Yes," Bradfield said, clearing his throat, "it's a two-by-two note that I made at Mr. Curran's, my attorney's, concerning various things that I had heard from Vince, heard from Chris, or that John Curran told me he had heard."

"Where did the information contained on this particular note come from?"

"This particular note?" Bradfield repeated, as if he were trying for the first time to remember something so insignificant that it had slipped his mind.

"Yes," Lock said.

"I think it came from John Paul Curran. These are things that Curran told me were of central interest to the authorities at that time."

"Why did you write those down?"

"Because, as we would go over them, he would say, 'This is a concern.'"

"Is there any information contained on that note that was not given to you in this instance, at least, by Mr. Curran?"

"I don't remember what some of the things referred to. It's been four years. They all look as though they came from Mr. Curran's meeting."

Guida jumped from his seat, fearful that the jury might believe this explanation, and anxious to cut it short. "Your Honor," he said, "he's answered the question."

"I'm going to ask him about a specific notation on the note," Lock replied, unwilling to drop the subject. *"Lured, and killed,* with a line through the *killed,* and then the word *killed* repeated, *kids, taped her,* do you see that?"

Bradfield nodded. "Yes."

"What can you tell us about the presence of that notation on the note?" Lock asked, with great deference and courtesy.

"This is what John Paul Curran told me was the theory that the authorities were then working on," Bradfield said. "That I had lured Susan Reinert from her house and killed the children and taped Susan Reinert."

"When you wrote this out, did you in any sense at all mean to imply this is what you had, in fact, done in this instance?"

"Oh, no, no," Bradfield answered, looking amazed.

Hoping again that the jurors would take Bradfield at his word, Josh Lock now said, "Did you kill Mrs. Reinert?"

"No, I did not," Bradfield answered.

"Did you plan to kill Susan Reinert?"

"No."

"Did you kill either of her children?"

"No."

"Did you kill both of them?"

"No."

"Did you plan to do either of those things?"

"No, I did not."

"Are you responsible for the deaths?"

"Absolutely not. I never hurt Mrs. Reinert or her children in any way."

"Are you guilty of these crimes?"

"I am not."

"That's all I have," said Lock.

Some of the jurors glared at William Bradfield. Others seemed to be hanging back, confused, or still weighing what they had heard. Suddenly, Rick Guida jumped to his feet.

"Who did kill Mrs. Reinert, Mr. Bradfield?" he shouted.

"I don't know," Bradfield answered, noticeably intimidated by Guida's manner.

"In 1979, you told a number of people that Jay C. Smith was going to kill her, and you were so afraid," Guida continued sarcastically, "that you went to the shore, just to have an alibi. Now, don't you think Jay C. Smith killed Susan Reinert?"

"I don't know who killed Susan Reinert."

Guida threw his hands in the air like a man who was so disgusted that he could barely go on. "Do you *believe* that he did, Mr. Bradfield?"

"Do you want me to speculate?"

"Sure, just tell me what you think."

Josh Lock bounced to his feet. "Objection," he called out.

"Overruled," Garb responded, just as quickly.

"He may have," Bradfield said, answering Guida's question.

"He may have," Guida said mockingly. "Now what about this other person that you identified in the summer of 1979, while you were in New Mexico? Do you think he may have killed Mrs. Reinert?"

"I think he may have," Bradfield whispered.

"Who was that?" Guida asked. "What was his name? If you think he killed her, I'd like to know how you know that."

Bradfield tensed. "Mrs. Reinert mentioned the name in the

winter of 1979, the name Alex, among four names that she mentioned over the years as men whom she'd gone out with and met through her association with Parents Without Partners. She mentioned four names only. No last names. Jay; Alex, Ted, and Graham. She said they were into group sex, that they were advocates of bondage and discipline. And they were advocates of deviate sexual practices, such as urination during the sex act and oral sex, and such as that. That's where I learned about them. In the spring of 1979, I baby-sat for her and she came in at four-thirty in the morning, and said she had seen him. He was the next-to-the-last person that I heard her mention.''

"So, even though you told everybody Jay C. Smith planned to kill Susan Reinert, you still think now that somebody else did it, is that right?''

"He . . .'' Bradfield stammered.

Guida interrupted. "Just answer the question. Yes or no. You still think somebody else did it?''

"I don't know who did it,'' Bradfield said resolutely.

"Do you *think* somebody else did it, Mr. Bradfield?''

"Do you want me to speculate on who might have?'' Bradfield said.

"I want you to answer the question. Do you think somebody else did it? Yes or now, please.''

Bradfield sighed deeply. "I don't know who did it.''

"The question was, do you *think* somebody else did it other than Jay C. Smith? Yes or no, please.''

"I think someone else may have. Yes.''

"Even in spite of all of those threats that Jay C. Smith made, is that right?''

"Yes.''

"And why do you think that Jay C. Smith didn't do it?'' Guida demanded.

"Because, I found out more from the newspapers, first, that it was in Harrisburg, that's where she said Alex was from. Secondly, it seemed to involve some kind of sexual misuse. There was a dildo found in her automobile.''

"Where was that found?'' Guida asked, hoping to catch Bradfield off guard and get him to admit something the newspapers had never reported. "Where was that dildo found?''

"Found?'' Bradfield repeated.

"Yes,'' Guida said. "Where was that found?''

"I don't remember," Bradfield answered, pausing. "It was part of the things that were recorded early on. Thirdly, the thing that made me really wonder about Dr. Smith doing it was that nothing he had ever told me indicated that he would kill in this way. It didn't seem to be his style. There were chain marks on her. And, in addition to this, under her body was found a comb from the same outfit as Dr. Smith, and that certainly didn't make any sense to me, that he would do it."

"Does it make any sense," Guida asked, looking directly at the jury, "that Alex, an unnamed person, would come all the way to Harrisburg to get Jay C. Smith's comb and plant it in Susan Reinert's car? Does that make any sense?"

"I never thought he planted it there," Bradfield replied defensively.

"Then how do you think it got there?"

"Well," Bradfield said, appearing confused, "Susan told me that she was meeting somebody named Jay. This was one of the reasons early on, that I didn't know whether there was a relationship between her and Dr. Smith. His first name was Jay. Later, after I'd been arrested, I found out that there was another man named Jay that she knew of."

"You didn't answer the question," Guida snapped. "The question was, How do you think that the comb got there? How did Jay C. Smith's comb get into the car, unless it was planted there by Alex from Harrisburg?"

"I wonder about it. Perhaps he lost his comb," Bradfield responded, shaking his head and appearing puzzled. "Why the comb was where it was, I'm not sure."

Having taken that subject as far as he could, and satisfied that Bradfield's explanations were confused and unconvincing, Guida returned to a topic he had raised earlier. "At the beginning of your testimony," he said, "you indicated that you ceased to be romantic with Susan Myers in 1973, is that right?"

"Yes, we were never really lovers after we returned from Europe," Bradfield answered.

"Why did you move in with her then for six or seven years? Why did you do that if you were no longer lovers and not intimate?"

"Susan Myers offered me the first real comfort of a home base that I have had since leaving home for college. She and I had what I thought was a real close, warm, and comfortable relationship. That was the place where I felt the most at home.''

"The question was, Mr. Bradfield, you got an apartment together, is that right?''

"Correct,'' Bradfield answered.

"The question is, if you no longer cared for her, why did you bother to live with her for six or seven years after your return from Europe?''

"I did care for her, I cared for her very much.''

"You were not in love with her?''

"I loved her,'' Bradfield insisted.

"You were not intimate with her?''

"Correct,'' Bradfield said.

"How did she perceive the relationship, if you know. I believe you heard her say on the witness stand that she loved you.''

"I think we loved each other,'' Bradfield answered quietly. "I cared very much for Susan Myers. Sue was one of my dearest and closest friends. We had for years talked about her problems with teaching. Not that she wasn't a good teacher. She is a good teacher. But she didn't feel comfortable about teaching. It was really a privilege to be able to try to give her something that she could fall back on and get out of teaching.''

Guida looked surprised. "A privilege to give her something like Terra Art, is that what you're saying?''

"Yes,'' he answered.

"And a privilege to put forty-five thousand dollars of your own money in it, is that right?''

"That's right.''

"At the time, you were dating Joanne Aitken, weren't you?''

"I was seeing Joanne, yes.''

"Why would you put forty-five thousand dollars into a business for a woman that was basically just a friend, when you had another active and involved relationship with someone else, can you tell me that?''

"I cared very much for both of them,'' Bradfield responded.

"And Wendy Zeigler, too?'' Guida snapped.

"Yes,'' Bradfield answered. "I offered with Joanne, for example, to go and buy property down in Annapolis. I was going to take the boat fund and sink it into property with Joanne Aitken, because I cared very much for her. I offered to lend Mrs. Reinert ten thousand dollars in order to have her buy a house and lend her that money with no interest, because I cared about her. I was going to spend what I had."

"From the boat fund," Guida said mockingly.

"Yes," Bradfield answered.

"So, you were going to buy a business with Ms. Myers, a house with Ms. Aitken, and you were going to lend Susan Reinert ten thousand dollars with no interest?"

Once again, Guida glanced at the jury with an expression of total disbelief on his face.

"Those were at different times."

"Now, I believe you described your relationship with Aitken as artistic and intellectual, is that right?

"Then how did you spend a four-day weekend in Cambridge with her at Thanksgiving? A romantic holiday, or whatever you want to call it. What happened?"

"Well," Bradfield said, "we went to see a number of art exhibits in Cambridge. We went to see the glass flowers at Harvard, in the exhibit there. We attended a lecture. We went to the Museum of Art."

"Where did you stay?"

"With Joanne."

"In her bedroom?"

"Yes."

"But this wasn't . . . you're not characterizing this weekend as intimate or romantic. Is that what you're telling me?"

"I don't mean to suggest that the relationship with her, or with any of the other people in my life, was either orthodox or proper. What I'm trying to tell you is that if you try to characterize them all as flaming affairs, that is simply not true."

"Speaking of that weekend, what did you do that weekend to protect Susan Reinert?"

"Nothing," Bradfield answered.

"Now Mr. Bradfield, this jury has been told that you drove around her house and did so many things over that time period when you found out about this threat, even to the point of sending Susan Myers away because Smith would kill on weekends; why," he asked, pausing for effect, "did you just bother to take that *critical* weekend off and go to Massachusetts, if Susan Reinert was in such danger?"

"I tried to spend as much time as I could," Bradfield shot back angrily, "to do what I could about the situation with Dr.

Smith. I couldn't do so much that I gave up my life, and I was, by Thanksgiving, alarmed and concerned and afraid. At Christmas, I went away again. I was even more alarmed and desperately tired. Memorial Day, I tried to go away and rented a camper, and I had an accident, and—''

Guida interrupted. ''What I'm saying is, if you were so interested in protecting her, so interested in making sure nothing happened to Susan Reinert, why did you go away in the time periods which you described as the critical ones, when this man would kill? Why did you go away on those weekends—Christmas, Thanksgiving, and you tried Memorial Day?''

''I couldn't park in front of Susan Reinert's house during the whole holiday weekend, without simply moving in. I couldn't do it,'' Bradfield said, his face becoming flushed with anger.

Guida glanced at the jury, then back at Bradfield. ''So you just *gave up* on the critical weekends and went someplace else, so you wouldn't even be anywhere near her house, or near Jay C. Smith, is that right?''

''It was more than I could do,'' Bradfield answered, between clenched teeth.

''You just couldn't handle it,'' Guida said mockingly. ''On critical weekends, you couldn't handle protecting her, is that right?''

''I wasn't always sure which weekends were going to be critical,'' Bradfield said, trying to regain his composure.

''Didn't you tell Sue Myers that Smith always killed on holiday weekends? Didn't you say that?''

''No,'' Bradfield snapped. ''Like so many things in this case, for four and a half years, a little twist here and a little difference there, and a definition of this here.''

Guida interrupted again. ''Mr. Bradfield, please answer the question. What did you say, if I characterized it incorrectly?''

''When Dr. Smith characterized, in his very circumspect way, the methods that were used by the professionals with whom he had come in contact, one of the things he indicated was that the time for that kind of assassination could very well be, was very often, on weekends, or on an extended weekend or a vacation. That's different from saying that Dr. Smith told me he always killed on weekends. I didn't say that.''

''Maybe I'm wrong,'' Guida countered, ''but didn't you say, 'You better get out of town on Thanksgiving weekend'? Didn't you say that to Susan Myers?''

''I told Susan that she'd be safer away, yes,'' Bradfield acknowledged.

Guida smirked. ''Was she in danger too?''

''I was afraid so,'' Bradfield answered.

''She was in danger because you believed that Smith would do this on holiday weekends, right?''

''Yes.''

''But you would leave on every holiday weekend in spite of all your efforts the rest of the time, riding around Mrs. Reinert's house, and watching her house, and calling her on the phone, is that right? I'm going to ask you to justify both positions if you would.''

''Looking back,'' Bradfield said quietly, ''there are a number of things that I would do differently, not the least of which is I would try to be more protective of Mrs. Reinert.''

''In other words,'' Guida snapped, ''you mean watch her house a little bit more?''

''I don't know if I could have,'' Bradfield answered earnestly. ''I really don't know how I could have done much more and not ended up in the hospital.''

Guida turned to the jury again. ''How about calling the police?'' he said.

Bradfield frowned. ''Looking back, I wish that I had. I think we all wish that.''

''How about telling Mrs. Reinert that someone is going to kill her? You could have done that too, couldn't you?''

''I did tell Mrs. Reinert she was going to get killed, or beat up.''

Guida nodded. ''You indicated to Mrs. Reinert that she may be in danger from these people she was dating. Isn't that right?''

''Yes.''

''My question is, why didn't you go to her and say, 'Sue, Jay C. Smith has chains, he has locks, he has guns, he has silencers, he has all these things and, by the way, he's threatening to kill you. You better do something about it.' Did you ever say that to her?''

''No.''

''That could have been another way you could have protected her, could it not have been?''

''I don't know that that would have worked, but it could have.

I'm not sure whether there was a relationship between Sue Reinert and Dr. Smith. I could never find out for sure.''

"Wouldn't that be all the more reason to tell her, if this person you think she's having a relationship with was going to kill her, was threatening to kill her? Wouldn't that be all the more reason to tell her, so she could protect herself?''

"Looking back, I think it was.''

"But that didn't occur to you at the time?''

"No.''

"It occurred to you to tell the police, but you dismissed that, is that right?''

"It occurred to us to speak to Reinert also, but we decided not to do that.''

"*We*,'' Guida repeated angrily, jumping up from his seat. "Weren't *you* the one? You keep saying *we*. Wasn't it *you* who was bringing all this information to Mr. Pappas, Ms. Myers, Mr. Valaitis, and Ms. Zeigler? *You* were the one that brought all the information back, isn't that right?''

"Yes,'' Bradfield admitted.

"And you were the one that was making the decision, you were the leader, weren't you?''

"I was not making the decision solely,'' Bradfield answered. "I sought their advice in everything that I did.''

"Then the group of you were making the decisions on the basis of your facts, isn't that right?''

"Yes,'' Bradfield conceded, so softly that the response was barely audible.

"Now, you indicated on your direct testimony that you didn't want to tell the police because they were corrupt, is that right?''

"Correct, and involved with Dr. Smith,'' said Bradfield, sounding more confident.

"That would have been the Upper Merion Township police?''

"No, not just them.''

"Oh, how many police departments did he control?'' Guida asked, his sarcasm rising again.

"Well, he mentioned that he knew someone who was involved with the West Chester police. He mentioned several people in the Philadelphia police.

"Isn't it a fact, Mr. Bradfield, that the Upper Merion Township police arrested Jay C. Smith for some stolen-property violations, and some other things, isn't that right?''

"Correct," Bradfield said.

"If they went so far as to arrest this man with all his power, why wouldn't he be in danger if you went to the police department and told them about these threats?"

"They were potentially connected to him," Bradfield insisted.

"Did you ever hear of the Pennsylvania State Police, Mr. Bradfield?"

"Yes."

"You've heard of that organization?"

"Yes."

"Are they listed in your telephone book at home, or were they in 1979?"

Bradfield frowned. "Looking back, I wish we had gone to them."

"You could have picked up the phone, could you not, and called the Pennsylvania State Police, and said, 'I don't trust the Upper Merion Township police and I'm going to tell you people about these strange goings on.' You could have done that, isn't that right?"

"Any one of us could have done that."

"*You* could have done that, couldn't you?"

"We all could have," Bradfield insisted.

"But you could have?"

"Yes, indeed."

"*You* didn't, did you?"

"None of us did," Bradfield said.

"Have you heard of the Federal Bureau of Investigation?"

"Yes."

"Did you call them?"

"No."

"Did Jay C. Smith have contacts in the state police and the Federal Bureau of Investigation?"

"He never indicated that."

Rick Guida smiled, looking satisfied, and nodded as Judge Garb said, "Let's take a ten-minute recess."

Convinced that he had cast serious doubt on Bradfield's innocence, and his judgment, Guida was now confident that this would be the kind of victory he had dreamt of ever since he finished law school.

After the recess, Guida began again. "Vince Valaitis described for us an incident where you had a gun with a silencer and you shot it five times near your apartment complex. Did that happen?"

"Yes."

"But why did you need a silencer for protection? Tell me that. Why did you need a silencer to protect yourself?"

Bradfield hedged. "Because both Chris and I felt that if Smith were to threaten me while I was in the car, I would have to try to wound him or disable him, or kill him. And the very first thing that I would do, we agreed, was that I would call Chris, and he would come immediately, and at that point, we would figure out exactly what to do. If I were to try to defend myself with a .357 magnum, with the cannon reproach that it has, I would have alerted half of Chester County and that would not have worked."

"It probably wouldn't have worked," Guida said, "but when you're talking about protecting yourself from an armed man who threatens you with a weapon, why did you need a silencer?"

"Because I wanted to do more than simply disable him," Bradfield replied, a new level of intensity creeping into his voice. "I wanted after that to be able to call Chris and for Chris and me to decide where we were going to take Smith. We talked about what public official we could be absolutely sure we could trust, or whether we should do away with Smith."

"Were you planning on murdering him?" Guida gasped, feigning a look of shock and horror.

"We talked about it, Chris and I talked about it."

"If you had a plan to murder him," Guida replied, "and he threatened you with a weapon in self-defense, why didn't you just finish him off right there, Mr. Bradfield, and be done with the situation?"

"We didn't know what the best plan would be."

"And you say that this contraption, this gun and the silencer, you carried around, concealed on your person?"

"Not on my person, no," Bradfield said, correcting Guida.

"Where did you have it?"

"I had it in a plastic shopping bag in which I had several items kind of stacked around it, and I carried the shopping bag with me so that I could reach into the shopping bag to get the automatic quickly."

"So," Guida said, shaking his head incredulously, "you carried this silenced automatic around in a shopping bag whenever you were with Smith?"

"Correct," Bradfield answered.

Changing focus again, Guida asked, "Did you tell any other people that were on this list of Smith's that they might be harmed?"

"Not except by attempting to confront Sue Reinert twice with the fact that she was in danger. I never mentioned that it was from Dr. Smith, but I told her once again when I baby-sat for her in the spring of 1979. She was out till four or four-thirty and came back and talked about having been with this fellow, Alex, and some of the things that apparently he was interested in, and I said to her, it was not the first time I said it, 'You're going to get beat up or killed.' I was concerned about her having been out so late. Not only in view of those kinds of activities, but I didn't know where she was and I couldn't stay with Karen and Michael and check where Dr. Smith was at the same time."

"How many times did she leave you at home and go out until approximately four in the morning, and do whatever she was doing? How many times?" Guida asked.

"Very seldom," Bradfield answered.

"Now Mr. Bradfield, can you explain to me why she would do that, leave you at home with her children while she was out until four in the morning, when she had, as you expressed it, such a great romantic interest in you?"

"Do you want me to try to explain it?"

"I'd like you to, yes."

"My feeling about it at the time was, when Susan would tell me about the fact that the people whom she was associated with believed in group sex or bondage or whatever, she used a kind of emotional blackmail on me, and I think the reason she did it was in order to nudge me into the position of saying, 'Don't go out with these people. I don't want you to go out. I'll go out with you.' And I think that's why she did it."

"In other words," Guida said, frowning, "she was dating all of these people and doing all of these weird things to make you jealous. Is that what you're telling us, basically?"

"I don't know. I don't think it was jealousy," Bradfield answered.

"Well, you had told her on many occasions that you didn't want anything to do with her as far as your romantic relationship was concerned. Isn't that right?"

"That's correct."

"You were concerned about Jay C. Smith's threats, is that right?"

"Yes."

"But you never told her about Smith?"

"Not directly, no."

"Did you tell her about the chains?"

"No."

"Locks?"

"No."

"Ski masks?"

"No."

"Trash bags, did you ever tell her about that?"

"I never saw any trash bags."

"Never?" Guida repeated. "Now, you heard Mr. Pappas tell us that you actually went out and bought some of these trash bags."

"You have to remember," Bradfield said, barely controlling his anger, "that someone like Chris has been interviewed year after year by the FBI, and by the state police, and by the federal grand jury, and the state grand jury. And Chris Pappas must have, judging from the material that we have, must have had seventy-five interviews. It's understandable that after four and a half years Chris would, last month, suddenly remember trash bags. I'm not suggesting necessarily that it was something that he made up, but it's simply something that did not happen."

"So," Guida said, his voice rising, "you're telling us that the FBI and state police planted that information and told him to say it, encouraged him to lie, is that what you're telling us?"

William Bradfield didn't take his eyes off Rick Guida. "Yes," he said, "I think it's merely as simple as that. Chris has misremembered the trash bags. I never had trash bags in any of my pockets. I never spoke to Chris about trash bags, and I never tested any trash bags, and Dr. Smith never showed me any trash bags."

"Let's go back to the pockets. You're talking about your blue jacket now, aren't you?"

"Yes," Bradfield answered, scowling.

Guida spun around. "Did you have tape in that jacket pocket?"

"Sometimes I did."

"Did you have chains in that jacket pocket?"

"Yes I did."

"Did you have gloves in that jacket pocket?"

"Occasionally, I may have."

"Why did you have a jacket with all of these things in the pockets? What were you doing with tape, chains, gloves, and locks?"

"We were trying to test them against some kind of reality to see whether this man was telling me an absolutely bizarre fabrication. We were trying to see whether they really worked. I'll explain to you about the gloves."

"Let's take the tape. Did you tape up Pappas to see if it worked?" Guida asked.

"Yes," Bradfield answered.

"Did you use the chains?"

"Yes."

"Did you lock him up in chains?"

"Yes."

"Is it the same jacket you had on the night of June 22, 1979, the night that Sue Reinert was murdered?"

"Yes," Bradfield said, adding, "and almost every other evening. I wore it constantly."

"Mr. Bradfield, after Dr. Smith had indicated to you that he was going to do dangerous things, a lot of dangerous things, you thought he was a threat, did you not?"

"I wasn't certain that he was. None of us was ever certain. He was not simply deranged. It's easy to look back now after a murder and see danger. But it was not easy to see for any of us at that point. To conclude that such bizarre tales were really real."

"They weren't just tales, Mr. Bradfield," Guida reminded him. "You saw him with a sawed-off carbine, didn't you?"

"Yes."

"He had a silencer for the length of the gun, didn't he?"

"Yes."

"He was shooting it off in the parking lot, right?"

"Yes."

"And you don't think that that indicates that he might be dangerous, is that what you're telling us?"

"It indicates that he *might* be dangerous."

"Given that belief, Mr. Bradfield, why did you appear as an alibi witness for him and attempt to have him absolved of his criminal activity?"

"Because I knew where he was at a time when he was

accused of being somewhere else, and he could not physically have been able to make it from Ocean City, New Jersey, at around three o'clock to a Sears store in St. David's by, I think it was a quarter to five or five.''

"Mr. Bradfield," Guida said, "didn't you and Chris Pappas have a contingent plan to murder Jay C. Smith?"

"We did."

"So you testify for him as an alibi witness and contemplate actual *murder* in order to stop him from committing the crime, is that right?"

"That's correct."

Rick Guida smiled. He seemed confident that he finally had William Bradfield where he wanted him, floundering in the midst of his own bizarre story. Guida paced himself carefully, convinced that the longer he questioned Bradfield and the longer Bradfield talked, the stronger the prosecution's case would be. Now, seventeen days into the trial, he was more than guardedly optimistic. He was certain that Bradfield's own words would convict him.

At that point, something seemed to click in Guida's mind. He whispered to an assistant, who began to look for a particular section in a document.

"Mr. Bradfield," he said, as he produced a cohabitation agreement that Bradfield had presented to Susan Myers in the fall of 1978. "You told us that the reason for this document was to protect Sue Myers from people finding out that you were living together, is that right?"

"I thought it might help, yes."

"Now, I believe that you said that there was only one paragraph in here that you were concerned with, is that right?"

"Primarily concerned with, yes."

"Read it, please," he said, handing Bradfield the document.

Bradfield put on his glasses and began to read. "The parties hereto have done nothing to demonstrate any present intent to cohabit or live as husband and wife, nor do they desire at this time to cohabit and live as husband and wife."

"And you say the rest of it, the rest of the five pages of this, is just surplusage, is that right?"

"That's correct," Bradfield answered.

"The rest of this document was forced on you by a lawyer, is that what you're telling me?"

"Suggested by him, to make the document a legal, binding, and meaningful instrument, as he put it. He said it needed a legal boiler plate. They were his words."

"Let's go to the assets page," Guida said, first pointing to what William Bradfield had listed as a two-hundred-and-fifty-thousand-dollar inheritance. "It also says, insurance policy beneficiary, $500,000. Now," Guida asked, hoping the jury would recall that this was the precise amount of term-life insurance that Susan Reinert had taken out during the four months that preceded her murder. "Where did these figures come from?"

Bradfield hesitated briefly. "They came from my thinking about what possible assets might be mine in terms of my family's wealth."

"Whose insurance policy was that?"

"I don't know," Bradfield stammered, looking uncomfortable. "I don't remember specifically because it doesn't say here."

Guida was satisfied that he had made his point, and that the judge and jury would see that the matching figures went well beyond the possibility of coincidence and condemned William Bradfield.

He hoped that the jury would also remember the "coincidence" of Bradfield's hastily executed divorce agreement with Muriel Bradfield that same spring. Like the cohabitation agreement with Sue Myers, it precluded any claim on a possible inheritance.

Guida paused. When he resumed his questioning, his voice was unusually soft. "Did you telephone Susan Reinert at home on the last night of her life, Mr. Bradfield?"

"No," Bradfield sighed.

"Were you concerned that she might be injured that weekend?"

"I had been concerned for some time," he said.

"Did you telephone her at all during the day of June 22, 1979?"

"No," Bradfield acknowledged.

"Did you telephone her after you saw Jay C. Smith on the night of Susan's death and tried to follow him?"

"No."

"Why not?"

"I had done all I really thought I could do."

"But you told us how you used to call her and sit by her house and do all of these things to the point where you were exhausted. Why didn't you just pick up the phone and call her and see if she was all right sometime on this day when you were doing all these things in the event that she might be murdered that weekend?"

"I had really come to the end of what I could do. Looking back, I wish I had."

"You just didn't have one more telephone call in you," Guida roared. "Is that what you're saying?"

"I just didn't do it," Bradfield answered, grimacing.

"Vince Valaitis says that in the car on the way down to the shore, you told him that you had followed Smith around Reinert's block fourteen times and lost him in a hailstorm, and that this was the weekend that it was going to happen. Did you say that, Mr. Bradfield? Did you tell Valaitis that you followed Smith around Reinert's block fourteen times and lost him in a hailstorm?"

"I said that I should have followed him, and that I should have, if necessary, circled Sue Reinert's house fourteen times."

"Why the number fourteen?"

Bradfield shrugged. "Oh, that was just a . . ."

"*Why*, sir?" he demanded, his voice commanding the attention of the entire courtroom.

"My comment was meant to imply that I hadn't done every last thing that I might have."

"Did you call to say goodbye?"

"I said goodbye to Susan when I last saw her."

"When was that?"

"It was the week preceding her death. It was at school."

"The week preceding her death in school?" Guida repeated incredulously. "I am talking about at her house. Did you see her there the weekend before her death? Did you see her there?"

William Bradfield edged forward in his seat, frowned, closed his eyes, and shook his head in despair. "I can't recall specifically whether I did or not," he finally said.

44

On the morning of October 28, 1983, Josh Lock began his closing argument. For nearly four hours he spoke to the jurors.

"I have tried my best throughout these proceedings to provide you with those facts that I thought were important for you to know so that you could see this entire matter for what it is," he said. "I will try my best now to suggest to you why those facts compel a verdict of not guilty. . . . At the beginning of the trial, I suggested to you what I believed was a very real possibility in this case, and that is that you should be presented with a façade, with an appearance, with an illusion of wrongdoing. The evidence doesn't tell us much, if anything, about Bradfield's guilt, but it may tell us a great deal about his innocence. There is no proof presented that Bradfield carried on an affair with Reinert. There is no objective evidence of marriage plans. There is nothing in his background that would lead anyone to conclude that Bradfield would callously lure Reinert's children away from her."

Then Lock turned to the jury and asked them why such an intelligent man would confess to Proctor Nowell or have himself named the beneficiary of the insurance policies of a woman he knew was going to be murdered. He pointed out that Reinert's final policy did not go into effect until June 25, 1979, the very day her body was found. As he spoke, he walked toward Bill Bradfield and said sarcastically, "And he thinks he's going to collect on that policy. You'd have to be very, very foolish to make that assumption. Very, very foolish.

"If that is what someone wished to do, if they were willing to turn their backs on their entire life, reject education, reject literature, reject teaching for money, if they were willing to do that, then marry the woman, go to England, get a boat, go out into the English Channel, and let something happen. You don't have to be a genius to figure that out.

"There is a book written by Theodore Dreiser called *An American Tragedy* where that exact scenario was played out on a woman named Roberta in a place called Pass Lake in upstate New York.

"You have to believe all the other stuff to believe that there is anything going on. You have to buy the illusion and the appearance of wrongdoing in the absence of any evidence that supports it. It is not there.

"The man aligned himself in characteristic fashion with two people whose lives did not appear to be on converging paths: Jay Smith . . . and Susan Reinert. . . .

"At one point, those two lives converged, and it was exactly as if someone took two live wires and crossed them. Who was caught in the middle? Maybe it was done for profit. Maybe it was schemic and calculated, but where is the evidence? There is no evidence. It is only illusion.

"Now, there's the money, there's the will, there's the life insurance, and there's the motive," he said finally. "But *where,*" he repeated, "is the evidence that supports the motive? Isn't there just as much evidence, isn't there *more* evidence, that supports a contrary motive? It looks terrible, it feels terrible, it creates a sense that something is wrong, but what else is there besides that façade?"

It was Lock's last chance to dismantle the prosecution's case and present his client as an innocent man, with an unconventional, eccentric, lifestyle, who had tried to prevent a murder and who had then been exposed to years of harassment and suffering. But, as the morning wore on, Lock seemed to be losing ground.

"Efforts were made to protect Susan Reinert," he said, almost pleadingly. "Efforts were made to control Jay Smith."

With new lines of fatigue showing on his face, Lock added, "There is no need for me to keep going over fact after fact after fact. The analysis of the case, our analysis of the case, is apparent. The inevitability of that interpretation is apparent as well. I merely wish to highlight a couple more things, then I will sit down. . . .

"I suggested at the beginning that the facts of this case were truly bizarre and indeed they are. Much stranger than you could ever believe if you saw it on a television program. Does that mean he's not telling the truth? Does that mean that it is an impossibility?

"Look at the facts," he added passionately, "because the facts make it apparent that the explanation most consistent with all of those facts is an explanation most consistent with innocence. A four-and-a-half-year investigation, extensive and commendable efforts by the authorities, who have done everything they can, and what do you have, what is left for you? As a consequence, your job, your responsibility is clear. It is apparent under all the facts in this case, there can be but one verdict. It is a verdict of not guilty, and I ask you to return that verdict."

With that, Josh Lock rested his case. He turned, walked slowly away from the jury, and then sat down.

45

There was, in Rick Guida's manner, a quiet intensity that immediately told everyone in the courtroom that he did not intend to waste an instant of his final hours with the jury.

"Ladies and gentlemen," he began, "when you analyze what Mr. Bradfield said in his own defense, it can do two things. It can eliminate some of the commonwealth's proof or it can strengthen it. . . . You saw him on the witness stand. I want to talk to you about some of the things he said in a minute. But you saw him sit here and say things that I submit to you are ridiculous and you can judge whether the defendant was too smart to commit the mistakes that you saw in this case. He told you he didn't want the insurance money, yet, the defendant sued for $750,000. If he didn't think he was going to get it, if he didn't want it, why did he sue for it? Does that make sense to you?

"Mr. Bradfield told you a long and involved story on the witness stand about how concerned he was about Susan Reinert, how he tried to help her. She was following him, she was chasing him, she was writing him notes. He was so worried about her for seven months. So worried, that his health deteriorated. And he was very nervous, and he couldn't sleep, and had violent nightmares, and all of these terrible things happened to him because he was so concerned about Susan Reinert. But where was he when his concern was greatest? What does he do? He leaves. The pressure just gets too great. Right when he thinks it's going to happen—he leaves. He's gone on Thanksgiving. He's gone on Christmas. He plans to go away on Memorial Day and the weekend before Jay C. Smith is to be sentenced. He is so concerned that the pressure just happens to get too great whenever the danger is greatest. What does that tell you?

"He comes home from the shore and he's concerned about Susan Reinert, so he rushes into his apartment. And who does he call? He calls Jay C. Smith's lawyer, to find out if Susan Reinert is still alive. Why didn't he call Susan Reinert? Why didn't he call her on Friday, on Saturday, on Sunday, or on Monday, *if* he was so concerned? He told you on a number of occasions how he called her house all the time, rode by her house and parked the car outside. Yet, on the fatal weekend, the weekend when the plan is complete, where is he? He's at the shore and he never talked to her. Does that make sense? If it doesn't make sense, it goes on the pile.

"His physical exhaustion can certainly be explained by the degree of activity during that spring. Joanne Aitken is in town. He's meeting with Smith three nights a week. He's meeting with Pappas and . . . Valaitis until late at night and, as Susan Reinert's neighbors told you, he was sleeping there. Anyone would be tired with a schedule like that. But I submit to you it was not because he was worried about Susan Reinert. If he were worried about Susan Reinert, if he were *truly* worried about Susan Reinert, *we wouldn't be here today.*

"He's telling all his friends that Smith was going to kill Reinert. Smith's a madman. Smith has killed two hundred people. Smith is crazy. Even to the point where he is contemplating murdering Smith. . . . And yet, Mr. Bradfield testifies as his alibi witness. Morally compelled? Does it make sense that somebody who is contemplating *murdering* another individual because he is so dangerous, he doesn't deserve to live, would go and testify as an alibi witness in that case? Does it make sense? And if it doesn't, it goes on the pile.

"On June 22, Susan Reinert leaves her house at nine-thirty. She is a happy woman. She is finally not going to be lonely anymore. She finally has got the man she wants. Three days later, she's at the Host Inn, dead. If this man Smith is so dangerous, if William Bradfield is telling all these people that Susan Reinert is going to be killed, and he doesn't know what to do about it, why doesn't Susan Reinert find out about it? Why don't the police find out about it? . . . A dangerous killer, as Mr. Bradfield described for you. What does he do? He spends three nights a week with this man. Doing what? Building silencers. Planning his defense and planning his alibi. Again, does it make any sense? Isn't that a pebble you have to put on the pile? Think about it.

"Let's look at the sailboat fund for a second. Chris Pappas is in Bill Bradfield's attic and Bradfield says to Pappas, 'Guess what? I've got twenty-five thousand dollars in the trunk of my car.' So they go down there and they find it in separate envelopes, and Bradfield's explanation to Pappas is that the bank wouldn't let me take it out all at once. 'I had to take it out in periodic payments.' Isn't that interesting that that's the exact same way that Susan Reinert had to take her money out of the bank? Periodic payments. Again, we are talking about a substantial sum of cash in the trunk of somebody's car. Does it make sense or is it a circumstance that goes in the pile? Now, what does the sailboat fund have to do with Susan Reinert's murder, unless, as you can infer, it was her money?" Rick Guida paused, shuffled through some papers, and took a long, serious moment to glare at William Bradfield. "Are all these coincidences? Is the fact that he knows that she's going to die a coincidence? Is the fact that he has the exact amount of money in a sailing fund that is taken out of her bank, is that a coincidence? Is the fact that this money has to be hidden in the closet of a nineteen-year-old girl all summer, is that a coincidence? You think about it. That's what a circumstantial case is all about. Eventually you say, 'Wait a minute.' In the words of Mr. Lock, something's wrong here, this looks terrible. And, it begins to look more than terrible when you put all of these pebbles together. Who wipes fingerprints off money? Why do you wipe fingerprints off money? Unless it's because Susan

Reinert's fingerprints are on that money. Actions of an innocent man?''

For a moment, Rick Guida stood silently in front of the jury. When he resumed, his voice was softer, his cadence slower, and his demeanor even more confident.

"Ladies and gentlemen, you remember the defendant admitted, there's a special jacket that Smith told him to use, where you put all these things in separate pockets. You put chains in one pocket, you put tape in another pocket, you put gloves in another pocket, you put a plastic bag in another pocket. All these items were so that you could mobilize, kill, and dispose of the body. What did Sue Reinert's body show? Chain marks, tape marks, a plastic bag under her body. Is it just a coincidence, that on this one night in June of 1979, he just happens to put on the exact jacket that was used to practice abducting, killing, and disposing of people? And do you remember Vince Valaitis saying he spoke to Bill Bradfield? And what did Bradfield say to him? 'Don't talk to the police. If you do, you'll put me in the electric chair.' Ladies and gentlemen,'' Guida said leaning forward, his voice almost a whisper and filled with sadness, ''you don't get the electric chair for stealing twenty-five thousand dollars. . . . You don't get the electric chair for stealing a ring, or even attempting to defraud an insurance company. You only get the electric chair for one thing in this state, and that is a cruel, premeditated, barbarous act of murder in the first degree.

"Whoever helped in the commission of this crime, whoever did it, was careful enough and had enough savvy to make sure that those children's bodies would never be found. But he took the awful chance, the awful chance of driving a dead body all the way to Harrisburg and parking it in a public parking lot. Walking around behind that car and opening the hatch for the world to see the exposed body of Susan Reinert. Now, why would a killer take a chance to do that? Who benefits from that? Does Jay C. Smith benefit from that according to the way Bradfield has explained his situation? What if Alex had done it? Why would Alex do it this way? Why would he transport her to the Host Inn and expose the body to the world?

"Do you know why her body was exposed?'' Guida asked, walking toward the jury, then pausing to look at each member individually. ''Because this body is worth, to only one person in the world, seven thousand dollars a pound, and it has to be found during the alibi weekend so that he can say to the world, and to a jury, 'I couldn't possibly have done it. I was away.' No other person out of six billion people benefits from this scenario, no one else would have taken this chance unless they did it for Bill Bradfield. Because her body had to be found. Because nobody collects on insurance unless they have a body. The children weren't worth anything, they were disposed of in some other manner. And the real irony, perhaps the real measure of justice is that the children's lives were not sacrificed in vain, because their absence at this scene speaks so loudly of the defendant's guilt that it is impossible to ignore. No one else benefits in this terrible chance of exposing this body *except* the defendant. . . . What is significant about this case is that today is October 28, 1983. Five years ago today, Susan Reinert's mother died, and the plan to kill her began." Rick Guida paused and glared at William Bradfield, every eye in the courtroom followed, every ear was waiting for his next word.

"Today the conspiracy ends. We're going to leave this to you."

Guida continued with the same sad trusting intensity. "The defendant has exhibited to you on the witness stand and in his actions through the witnesses, callousness that is beyond belief, and I ask you to listen to the law and come back with the appropriate verdict, which is murder in the first degree. Thank you."

46

It was the fastest decision reached in a capital case in recent years. After only an hour and fifteen minutes of deliberation, the jury had reached a decision. William Bradfield sat with his eyes riveted on the door through which the jurors would return. The first juror entered with his eyes downcast; the second, a young woman, dragged behind sniffling. But William Bradfield did not have to look at them to know that they could not have returned so quickly with a verdict to acquit him of three murders.

The judge opened the folded slip of paper delivered to him by the dry-eyed, controlled jury foreman, Jack Philips. He read the words, then hurriedly refolded the paper and leveled his dark, intense eyes on the jurors.

William Bradfield was found guilty of conspiring to commit three first-degree murders. Rick Guida rose triumphantly and asked for the death penalty on the grounds of three aggravating circumstances: killing during commission of a felony; killing of a witness and killing that endangered the lives of other people. Lock jumped up from the defense table and passionately disagreed, claiming that there were no aggravating circumstances in the murders that would legally justify the death penalty.

Judge Garb thanked the jurors. Then, in an unusual move, he dismissed them and took the final judgment of life or death out of their hands. He said that because Susan Reinert had been killed by a massive dose of morphine and because the children's bodies had never been found, there was no evidence that other lives were in danger. He also said there was no evidence of the perpetration of a felony and there was nothing that proved the children had witnessed the murder of their mother.

"I'm satisfied that the state has failed to prove aggravating circumstances," he said calmly, "and *I'm* directing a verdict of life imprisonment."

Bradfield smiled at Josh Lock as a man and a woman in the spectators' section called out, "Bill Bradfield, we love you." Several others broke into sobs of relief.

"Have you anything to say?" Garb asked.

William Bradfield rose and stood before the judge, his hands folded in front of him. "I am compelled to say again some simple truths," he told Garb quietly. "I did not kill Mrs. Reinert and I did not kill her children. I cannot show remorse for something I did not do."

The eyes of the two men met and then the judge spoke.

"What I find," he said firmly, "is that you are highly intelligent and creative, with more than just a modicum of charm. . . . It is also safe to say that you are extremely destructive. It has been decided, the only way we know how to decide these things, that you took three lives for financial gain and nothing else. A word that hasn't been used here today is *diabolical*. *Diabolical* is a word that does apply and that is certainly the kind of crime we're dealing with . . . I guess it must be said that you are some kind of an anomaly to us, a charismatic Rasputin . . . a cold and calculating mind bereft of human sympathy and compassion. An extremely dangerous person.''

With that, Garb imposed three terms of life in prison to be served consecutively, not concurrently—the harshest penalty, except death, that he could inflict.

William Bradfield said nothing, betrayed no feeling. He held out his arms for the handcuffs. After they were snapped in place, he turned, and his eyes met Joanne Aitken's as she sat alone in a far corner of the courtroom crying quietly. For an instant, a look of intense pain and longing seemed to flood his face. Then, as a guard pulled at his arm, he shook his head sadly, turned away, and was led quietly out the rear door.

47

Spurred by the victory of Bradfield's conviction, the attorney general's men were more determined than ever to keep the Reinert case alive. The week after William Bradfield was convicted, the prosecutor's office made an announcement: ''We have closed one chapter, but the book is not yet over. This is a continuing investigation. We will now focus on finding the person or persons unknown who helped Bradfield carry out the killings.'' Unofficially, the word was out that it was Jay Smith they were after.

On November 10, 1983, less than two weeks after William Bradfield's conviction, Jack Holtz and Lou DiSantis traveled to Wilkes Barre, Pennsylvania, to meet with Charles Montione after learning from Raymond Martray that Montione and Smith had become close friends.

Montione, who was in prison for armed robbery and burglary, was brought to room 239 of the Wilkes Barre Holiday Inn. There, away from possible observation by other inmates, Montione informed the troopers of his willingness to cooperate. After returning from the meeting that afternoon, Jack Holtz wrote:

> Smith told Montione that he would be arrested for five murders, Susan Reinert, Michael and Karen Reinert, and Stephanie and Eddie Hunsberger. Smith felt that he would be arrested after he appeared before the Grand Jury. Montione recalled that once Smith wanted a picture from Hustler magazine. Smith stated that the picture must be one with a girl on her knees with the head down and her ass exposed, but her legs must be together with the cunt closed, because this is the way Reinert's body was found in the car. Montione also stated that at one time Reinert had her hands tied behind her back. Montione recalled that he showed Smith several pictures from magazines before Smith found the right one. . . . Montione also recalled Smith stating that the best way to kill someone is by injection because the police will think it was an overdose. (It should also be noted that during this interview, Montione stated he did not know the cause of Reinert's death). . . . At the end of this interview, Montione furnished these officers with handwritten notes that he made detailing numerous conversations that he had with Smith.

Montione's cooperation heralded a major break in the state's case against Smith. Not only was the soft-spoken, twenty-four-year-old former medical student a believable witness, but Holtz was convinced that a jury would find him likable. He seemed to be an essentially honest young man who had somehow been drawn in and used by the wrong people.

On January 17, 1984, while troopers were still assessing the depth of the impact that Charles Montione would have in a courtroom, Joseph Weiss, a forty-eight-year-old white male with sentences totaling thirty years, contacted them.

"One morning," Weiss said, "I was out running in the

prison yard and Jay Smith was waiting for me. He took me by the arm. He kept talking very fast. Just babbling on uncontrollably, like he couldn't stop. He gave me information concerning the murder of Susan Reinert and the two children. He told me that Bradfield had lured Mrs. Reinert out of the house on a Friday night and that he, Smith, met them and then took over. I think they were his exact words, he took over. . . . Smith was to keep the woman and her two children for twenty-four hours and then he was to kill them. Sometime in that twenty-four hour period, he would get a phone call from Bradfield. I got the impression the phone call was the go-ahead. He took them to a building, an industrial building. I think he said the 8000 block of Rowland Avenue. He had a set of keys for the building. He had a contact. A friend or associate of some kind owned the building or worked there. He wasn't clear on that. He kept them there Friday to Saturday night. In order to keep them from running away, to keep them quiet, he gave them all a shot of heroin. The industrial building was called the Penncraft Building. Saturday night he rigged up what they call a hot shot, an overdose of heroin, for each of them. He injected them and killed them. He told me that he buried the two children in the building. He said he undressed Mrs. Reinert to make it look like a sex crime. He drove the body to Harrisburg, where it was found. I asked him why Harrisburg. He said something about that's where his hearing was to take place and that would be the last place they would expect him to take a body. That would throw suspicion off of him. . . .''

DiSantis checked Norristown and the surrounding area for any company with the name of Penncraft and could find none. He then checked the county tax assessors. Again, with negative results. Finally, he contacted the chamber of commerce in Norristown. They had never heard of such a building.

On February 3, 1984, Raymond Martray called Jack Holtz. The break they were looking for had finally come. It was ''practically'' a confession, the troopers agreed, or at least as close to one as they were ever likely to get on tape. In a phone conversation recorded by police, Martray told Smith that the authorities had contacted him about the case and asked him if he would take a lie-detector test.

''I'm worried,'' Martray told Smith. ''I mean, what happens if they ask me the big question. What if they say, 'Did Smith ever tell you that he killed Reinert?' ''

"Well, uh," Smith replied, "I'll have my people tell them you're not taking any lie-detector test."

That was a statement Holtz knew he could use in court. If Smith was not guilty, if he had not actually told Martray he had committed the murders, as Martray claimed, then why would he say, "I'll have my people stop the test?" Equally important, Martray's buddy Charles Montione had agreed that he would testify against Smith at the next statewide investigating grand jury.

48

On Tuesday, June 25, 1985, exactly six years after Susan Reinert's nude, beaten body was found in the trunk of her car, Jay Smith was charged with her murder and the murders of her children.

Arrested in his cell at the state prison in Dallas, Pennsylvania, he was led in handcuffs and leg-irons to state police headquarters under tight security by Jack Holtz, Lou DiSantis, and half a dozen uniformed policemen.

The arrest was recommended by the statewide investigating grand jury shortly after they listened to Raymond Martray's tape-recorded conversations with Jay Smith and heard the testimony of Charles Montione.

"While you were at the state correctional institution in Dallas, Pennsylvania, did you meet a man by the name of Jay C. Smith?" Rick Guida had asked soon after Montione was sworn in before the grand jurors.

"Yes, I did," Montione answered softly. "I met him sometime in 1981, when I was transferred to F Block. Ray Martray was another inmate who did time with me in Dallas. And because I was friends with Martray, I became friends with Jay also. I was introduced to Jay so he could help me with my legal work. Jay was mostly a loner. He didn't trust anyone. He didn't like to talk with people because he was always paranoid that they might go later and try to set him up," Montione said, apparently unaware of the irony of the statement. "He knew I was going to be getting out soon, and he wanted to know if once I got out, I would help him escape from whatever prison they had him in at the time, either Dallas or Camp Hill."

"Were there different plans or just one plan for these places?"

"No, there were different plans. If he was at Dallas, he spoke about getting a gun inside the prison. Then he changed his mind, because we'd have to trust somebody else. But he finally settled on escaping from the visiting room. I was to come up in a car with Martray. Smith would give us the signal. What we were supposed to do was go inside the guard's house where the guard interviews and visitors come in, tie up the guards and anybody else who was in there, disarm them, and put a cover over their heads. And then, Smith would calmly walk down while we pried the door open with a crowbar. He'd walk out to the car and we'd drive down the road where he'd switch cars and then go into hiding.

"If he was at Camp Hill Prison, he said I was supposed to be dressed up as a guard. I would go up and take Jay out of there at gunpoint and also take Jack Holtz and Lou DiSantis as hostages, and we were to take them down the road and then kill them, and when we were done with them, throw them out of the car."

"Why did he want to kill Holtz and DiSantis? Did he tell you that?"

"He said he hated them. That they were part of the Reinert investigation."

Guida paused. He was delighted that Montione had mentioned murdering Holtz and DiSantis and he wanted that statement to have the greatest possible impact. "Throughout the spring and summer of 1983," he said finally, "when you were talking with Smith, did he ever discuss homicide or how homicide could be committed, or anything of that nature?"

"Yes. He usually brought it up in every conversation we had. He went over the actual way to kill a person. He said, 'Never kill anyone unless you can make the body disappear.'" Apparently unaware that this directly contradicted what he had just said about disposing of Holtz and DiSantis, Montione continued. "He said one of the best things to do with the body once you kill it was to just leave it sit for three days. After that, the blood coagulates. He said when you make the body disappear, you want to dismember it and put it in different cans, oil cans or something, weight them down, and throw them in bodies of water. This way, if the police find one of them, they might identify only a torso with no hands or head, and that would make identification almost impossible.''

"Now," Guida said, "I'm going to direct your attention to the dates of October 29 and 30, 1983. Did you have a conversation with Jay Smith at that time concerning the Reinert murder case?''

"I did,'' Montione answered, looking, for a moment, directly at Jay Smith. "Jay was pretty shaken up that day. When we walked in the yard he told me that Bradfield had been convicted of the Reinert killings. He was pretty sure that the indictments were going to come down on him for murder, and he was pretty sure that he would have to go through with an escape plan. He made a lot of comments on how stupid Bradfield was. He said if Bradfield did what he was supposed to do, we would have been okay. According to Jay, the stupidity and the mistake was that Susan's body appeared. He said, 'Look, five years have passed, two more and she would have been declared legally dead, and the insurance money would have been paid.' I said, 'Why the kids? If she had to be killed for the insurance money, why the kids too?' And he said the kids were a mistake. He said they were killed because they were there. He said they were witnesses. He said they'll never be found. I said, 'Don't you think Bradfield might make a deal with the government in exchange for his freedom and say where the kids are?' And then he stressed that Bradfield didn't know where the kids are because you never let your *partner* know everything.''

Now, on June 25, 1985, as he was led into state police headquarters for fingerprints, Jay Smith turned to reporters and said, "I had nothing to do with the murders of Susan Reinert and her two children." Then, unaware of Montione's testimony and the fact that Raymond Martray had been recording their telephone conversations and allowing their prison visits to be videotaped since 1982, Smith added, "I talked to nobody at any time about this case.''

"Do you know Raymond Martray or Charles Montione?'' one reporter asked.

"No, I don't know those names," Smith said. Then he amended his answer. "Well, I know they were inmates at Dallas, but I never discussed the Reinert case with anyone, any inmate at all."

49

After four days of preliminary hearings before District Court Justice Mary Cross, Jack Holtz was convinced that Charles Montione and Raymond Martray could convict Jay Smith in any jury trial.

Wearing a black suit, brown work boots, and leg-irons, Smith sat silently during the preliminary hearings until one taped telephone call that was being played stopped in midconversation.

"Play the damned thing," Smith shouted, struggling to stand in his leg-irons. "Play everything. I had nothing to do with it."

"It's pretty hard to stomach," Smith added, as they handcuffed him for the noon recess. "After all I did for Ray Martray and Charles Montione, to sit here and listen to them lie. I should be angry, but I feel sorry for them."

Later that day, after Justice Mary Cross ordered that Jay Smith stand trial for the murders of Susan, Michael, and Karen Reinert, Florence Reinert, who was sitting in the spectator section of the courtroom, said sadly, "I'm glad it's coming to trial." Then she wiped her eyes and added, "But I'm also very sad. If I had any hope at all that my grandchildren were still alive, after listening to Martray and Montione, it's gone."

"Come on," her husband said, taking her arm and leading her out, "it's time to go home."

50

On March 31, 1986, the prosecution began presenting its evidence. Judge William Lipsitt, a seventy-year-old World War II Bronze Star recipient, presided. Lipsitt, who graduated from Harvard College and Harvard Law School, was a quiet, shy man who had waited fifty-six years to marry, and who, after twenty years as a judge, still sat like an awkward boy in the judge's huge black padded leather chair. Just the same, he was a force to be reckoned with in the Harrisburg legal community and when he personally asked William Costopoulos to defend Jay Smith, Costopoulos felt he could not refuse.

With his dark hair swept back and his beard flecked with gray, Costopoulos had a theatrical, commanding courtroom presence. The broad-shouldered Harvard graduate, who neither drank nor smoked, rode horses on his three-hundred-acre ranch and woke up every morning at 5:00 A.M. to train so that his body would be as tough and quick as his mind. A trial lawyer for fifteen years, Costopoulos instantly recognized that the county would pay him only a fraction of his usual fee. Yet he eagerly took the case: "We have a man who is charged with the murder of a woman and her two children," said Costopoulos. "He has maintained his innocence from day one and he stands alone."

Costopoulos had had seven months to prepare his case. Now that it was actually under way, his first concern was the jury. He wanted "just, fair, and impartial people who didn't seem to have a prejudice." To help find them, he had hired psychologist Arthur Patterson, president of Jury Analysts Inc.

Patterson set up an elaborate juror questionnaire in an effort to find "intelligent, logical jurors who would decide the case solely on the evidence that came out in court." He examined everything about each candidate: the clothes they wore, the way they walked and talked, and the time it took them to respond to each question, especially those related to their feelings about imposing the death penalty. At the end of the first day, every prospective juror had been rejected.

"They all sucked," Costopoulos told Skip Gochenour, a tough, smart former cop who was now serving as private detective for the defense. "I'm afraid that every one of them would come back in forty minutes with the death penalty," Costopoulos said sadly.

Over the next six days, ninety candidates were rejected. The twelve men and women finally chosen represented the usual cross-section of ordinary Americans. There was a sewing-machine operator, an electrician, a retired steel worker, an aviator, a mechanic, and a bank teller. Costopoulos's main concern was that this lower-middle-class assemblage of law-abiding blue-collar citizens would not be sophisticated enough to see through what he regarded as the state's thin case.

Despite his private pessimism, Costopoulos cut a fine figure before the jury. His voice rumbled like thunder as he opened for the defense.

"Ladies and gentlemen of the jury," he began, "Jay C. Smith has been charged with three counts of murder and he is not guilty of *any* of them. This isn't just a murder trial, this is a high-profile media event in which a man's life is at stake for something he didn't do. . . ."

As he spoke, Costopoulos looked at the jury intently, studying each face. In his fifteen years as a trial lawyer, he had come to believe that juries send out vibrations in the earliest moments of the trial. This jury barely looked at Smith, who sat frozen at the defense table, his lips purple, his face impossible to read. Smith had grown so much thinner, his hair so much grayer since his last court appearance, that some of the spectators thought he had deliberately aged himself for the trial. He looked now like one of those anonymous old men with rounded shoulders who creep through life afraid of being noticed.

Addressing the jurors' indifference, Costopoulos said, "There is frequently one individual who is overlooked always by the prosecution and too often by the defense. That person, ladies and gentlemen, is labeled the defendant. That person has a name like you and I do. His name is Jay Smith."

Then Costopoulos walked over to the defendant's table and put his hand warmly on Smith's shoulder, as if he were a close

friend or relative. "Jay Smith is fifty-seven years old. He is
a widower after twenty-eight years of marriage. Of that marriage were born two children. Prior to August, 1978, he had
two distinguished careers. He was a full colonel in the United
States Army, having served his country for almost three decades,
and he was a principal for thirteen years in an upper-
middle-class high school in the suburbs outside of Philadelphia. He was recognized in his community as a pillar, as
an educator, as an administrator, as a college professor. In
his capacity as colonel for the United States Army, he served
with, and was friends with Brigadier General John Eisenhower."

Costopoulos could feel the jurors respond more favorably
toward Smith. "That was prior to 1978," he said, his voice
filled with regret as he referred to the arrest and convictions for
theft, which "had thrust Smith into the media spotlight, cost
him his life work, stripped him of his dignity, and made him an
object of ridicule and scorn."

Costopoulos paused in his opening remarks, preparing to give
the jury the main thrust of his argument. "What happened in
August of 1978 also resulted in his being targeted by a man who
was *very, very* good at deception, not as good as he thought he
was, but good. Ladies and gentlemen, I am talking about none
other than William Bradfield. The Bradfield accomplices are an
interesting group. I call them accomplices, I call them a group.
A book author might call them a cult. You," he said, glancing at
the jury, "might call them co-conspirators. They slept with
him. They gave him sexual favors. They lied for him. They
practiced killing Susan Reinert with him. This group had
possession and control of the instrumentalities of crime consistent with Susan Reinert's death. Their names were Susan
Myers, Wendy Zeigler, Vincent Valaitis, Chris Pappas, and
Joanne Aitken.

"You see," he went on, waving his hand toward the
prosecution, "when an investigation focuses on a suspect too
early, obvious evidence is sometimes overlooked or put aside.
Sometimes, ladies and gentlemen, in a brutal, highly publicized
murder, particularly when there are two children involved that
haven't been found, the prosecution can get too desperate. They
are willing to accept almost anything as proof to make someone
accountable, especially when that investigation is billed as the
most massive investigation in the history of Pennsylvania, when

millions of tax dollars have been spent to justify it, when thousands of man-hours over a seven-year period have gone by and the prosecution has the same evidence they did within the first fourteen months. In this case, that desperation caused them to reach into the bowels of our prison system and emerge with a guy by the name Raymond Martray, a convicted felon, a former police officer who victimized the very people he swore to protect by setting up a burglary ring in his own community and looting the homes. We have, in this courtroom, taped recordings and two videos where Raymond Martray was instructed and coordinated by the authorities to tape telephone conversations between Smith and himself. But I am telling you, ladies and gentlemen, within those tapes and within that film lies the *acquittal* of Jay Smith."

51

For Rick Guida, it was different this time around. The case against Smith was harder to prove and riddled with unanswered questions. Guida couldn't tell the jurors why Jay Smith would leave Susan Reinert's body in Harrisburg when he was to appear there for sentencing that very day; nor why, if the crime was so carefully planned, Smith would leave, under the body, a blue comb inscribed with the same army reserve unit in which he served. He couldn't even give them a crystal-clear explanation of Smith's motive in killing Reinert. Nor could he tell the jury where Susan was killed or where the bodies of the children were. Even more ominous was a nagging question: Would the jury believe Raymond Martray and Charles Montione?

Guida was also concerned about the prospect of burdening this jury with the entire Bradfield story. As he approached them to deliver his opening remarks, his presentation seemed tentative, almost apologetic.

"What we will be doing in this case, although there is only

one defendant present," he explained, "is trying two. We will be presenting evidence concerning Mr. Bradfield's involvement, his connection with Mr. Smith and, unfortunately, the result . . . the first two, maybe, three weeks of the case you will barely hear Mr. Smith's name mentioned. You are going to be looking at me, saying, 'What are we doing here?' But it is necessary that I show you the first half before I show you the second. These things are intricately linked together and without showing you the connection, I can't show you the case."

For the next fourteen days, the prosecution presented its evidence against William Bradfield. It brought back every witness who had testified at Bradfield's trial and re-created every scene. It reconvicted Bradfield. This time without the defendant or his attorney. A great deal of the state's evidence was designed to link Jay Smith to the already convicted Bradfield and every bit of this evidence was challenged by William Costopoulos. With probing questions and intense sarcasm, Costopoulos went after each of the state's witnesses.

"Just look at him, this dangerous hit man, the ultimate assassin," Costopoulos said, as he put his arm around the sagging shoulder of Jay Smith. "And you—you, Mr. Pappas—what instrumentalities of crime did *you* turn over to the authorities?"

"I believe I turned over some ski masks, some chains and locks that went with them, and a bugging device that worked on an FM frequency," Pappas said. "Also, I turned over a .357 magnum. Those are the items I immediately recall."

"You testified on direct that you removed the serial numbers from a .30-caliber with acid. Is that correct?"

"Actually, I took the numbers off by grinding them on a grinding wheel. I attempted to grind all the way through to the other side hoping that it might cause the gun to malfunction."

"You did all this to protect Susan Reinert from Dr. Smith?" Costopoulos asked. He pointed toward Smith, hoping the jurors would see him the way Costopoulos wanted them to, as a pathetic, defeated creature, mercilessly framed by Bradfield.

"Yes, sir," Pappas answered.

"And did you have a silencer in your possession after the murder of Susan Reinert that you asked Wendy Zeigler to destroy?"

"Yes, I had a silencer in my home," Pappas admitted, "on

the weekend of the twenty-second through the twenty-fifth, and then when I went to New Mexico I asked Wendy Zeigler to destroy it.''

"Did you tell her to do that so you could protect Reinert from Mr. Smith?"

"No," Pappas answered.

"You ordered the destruction of that silencer to protect yourself, didn't you? And everything you've testified to in this courtroom about Jay C. Smith came from William Bradfield, didn't it?"

"Yes," Pappas reluctantly admitted.

During the first two weeks of the trial, the defense team was exuberant. Each day, after cross-examining the witnesses, Costopoulos would leave the courtroom feeling that Smith's chances of acquittal were stronger than the day before. "The jury doesn't even know what Smith is doing here," Costopoulos told his assistants, happily. "I can see it in their faces. They think this is a soap opera and William Bradfield is the star."

When Joanne Aitken appeared and took the witness stand, the women jurors scrutinized her carefully as if she were a new arrival at a local cocktail party. Her chestnut hair fell softly on her shoulders and she wore no makeup. The men looked her up and down, obviously fascinated, somehow expecting she would lead them into the sordid canyons of illicit sex, murder, and the quest for money.

"Miss Aitken," Costopoulos began, "because of your romantic interest in Mr. Bradfield that has continued until this day, is it fair to say that you communicate with him now that he is in prison?"

"Yes," she answered evenly.

"After Susan Reinert was murdered, did you and Bill Bradfield develop a code system for communications?"

"No," Joanne Aitken answered without hesitating.

Then, referring to a book of William Bradfield's that Susan Myers had turned over to police because it had been heavily marked with numbers representing a code, Costopoulos asked, "Then what was the purpose of the Ezra Pound book?"

"I don't know what the purpose of the Ezra Pound book was."

"Miss Aitken," Costopoulos asked sharply, suggesting that she was lying under oath about her knowledge of the coded book and of the actual murder, "when did you receive immunity from the government?"

"When I first talked with whoever the authorities were."

"Were you given immunity to the point where anything you said could not be used against you, even if you had a role in the murder? Or was your immunity limited to anything you said presuming you didn't have anything to do with the murder?"

"I really don't remember at this time," she answered.

"You had how many years of schooling?" he asked.

"Nineteen and a half."

"You have had a lot of conversations with your lawyer, haven't you, regarding this case?"

"Yes, that is correct."

"It was only after you got immunity that you agreed to give any statement whatsoever, isn't that right?"

"I believe that is correct, yes."

"And my question is," he said, pausing to steal a glance at the jurors, "did the immunity you were given assume you had no role in the murder of Susan Reinert or her children?"

"You will have to look at the statement," Joanne answered dryly. "I really couldn't tell you."

"What is cryptology?" Costopoulos asked, referring again to the coded message in the Ezra Pound book.

"Cryptology is the study of codes."

"And was there a letter from William Bradfield to you congratulating you for becoming an expert in cryptology?"

"No."

"Was there a letter," he repeated, "while you were in Boston, Massachusetts, a letter in code from William Bradfield instructing you to destroy, burn, and scatter the ashes of the typewriter ball that was in your custody and control?"

"No," Joanne answered.

"Do you understand enough about immunity to know that if you testify untruthfully under oath in a prosecution of this nature, you can be charged with perjury?"

"Yes, I understand that," she said, showing no more fear than a housewife facing a census taker's clipboard.

William Costopoulos was exultant. Not only was he certain that the coded message had been sent to Joanne, he believed that as soon as the cryptologist testified, he could link her directly to the crime.

"Can you tell us what a crypt analyst does?" Costopoulos asked confidently as soon as the FBI cryptologist had been led into the courtroom.

"A crypt analyst takes codes and tries to make sense out of the messages," Jacquelyn Tachner explained as she pointed to the state's exhibit. "At the top of that document there are some numbers that don't appear to make any sense. I was asked to try and decipher these numbers. The cipher is based on the Confucius book by Ezra Pound. The way it works is you number along each line. Whatever letter appears next to the margin is the number that corresponds to the letter . . . In this book, there are numbers written along the margin, the first one says 2–12. That means I turn to page 12 in this book and that's where I start decrypting. . . . When the numbers and letters are decoded, this message says, 'immunity improbable, my danger conspiracy.' Then it goes on to say, 'Does FBI have typewriter? Does FBI know V has it? Have B remove ball and destroy, or better, claim whole thing stolen, then get rid of it. FBI must not get it, especially ball.' "

"Do you know who V is?"

"No, there is no indication as to who V is."

"On the other side of the message there is a letter. You don't have to be a cryptologist to be able to read that. All you have to do is to be able to read English."

"That is correct."

"I would ask you to read the letter that appears on the back side."

"The entire thing?" she asked, surprised.

"Yes," Costopoulos said.

"The letter says, 'Miss you hon, and love you terribly. Wish I were there with you seeing things, thinking things, talking and, of course, making love. Love you, love you so much. Hurt for you. Hope I can see you soon, but lawyers say going up there now could be grounds for unlawful flight to avoid prosecution. Lawyers warn there will be FBI plant near you soon. Chris has been subpoenaed for grand jury. He will say nothing much. He must maintain this all the way up through possible, probable trial, hand on Bible, etc. or be in for perjury five to ten years. If you are in same position, you know practically nothing about case and nothing at all about Smith. You must maintain this all the way up through trial, hand on Bible forever. Did we mention

Smith to Crockett [at St. John's College in Santa Fe]? Try to remember. We can't be inconsistent about what we told them. Love you. Remember that we made it. Love you. I wish I were lying next to you and holding you.'"

The cryptologist paused. Costopoulos smiled, certain that the jurors would realize that this was a letter to Joanne. After all, he reasoned, no one else knew Steve Crockett. "Go on, please, read the rest of the letter," he said.

The cryptologist nodded and said, "The next paragraph reads, 'First, congratulations, you're on the way to becoming an expert cryptologist. Can you take more rules? Hope so. Lawyers assure us we are dealing with the best the FBI has. So we better be fairly sophisticated, O.K.? Use no punctuation except between characters. P of D means Smith, D equals dash, KW, question mark. Leave out vowels wherever intelligible. . . . Destroy messages after receiving them. Don't let anyone know you are receiving or destroying code. Repeat, destroy completely. If ashes are left, grind them underfoot.'"

52

When court recessed that afternoon, Bill Costopoulos was riding high. "We are way ahead," he said privately. "It's obvious that Joanne knew about the code and knew more about the crime than she's admitting. The jury thinks William Bradfield is the biggest liar that ever walked the earth. I think they believe he framed Smith." When Costopoulos strode into the Dauphin County Courthouse on the morning of April 23, his ruddy face alive with the energy of an anticipated victory, he did not yet know how soon his optimism would be shattered.

An hour later, amid heavy security, the court bailiff led in Raymond Martray. Looking heavier than he had during his previous courtroom appearances, the former cop swaggered to the witness stand.

"While you were incarcerated at the state correctional institution in Dallas, Pennsylvania, did you meet the defendant in this matter?" Rick Guida asked. Jay Smith watched as Martray nodded quickly. For a moment, Smith's face flushed with emotion—the anger of a parent who has been betrayed? Then he looked away and regained his composed mask.

Martray, whose perjury conviction had recently been reversed by the state superior court, repeated his allegations to the packed courtroom.

"Smith said, 'I took care of her.' Another time he slipped off the edge again and confessed, 'I killed the fucking bitch, Reinert.'"

Then Martray stood by as the state prepared to play the tapes of Smith's conversations with the inmate. He had proven to the state police that his word was good and that he could be trusted. Raymond Martray was glad to be on the "right" side of the law again. He smiled with pride as the lights were lowered and the courtroom was transformed into a public theater. Jurors and mobs of spectators strained to see and hear the final drama of Jay Smith's undoing played out on a tape recorder and screen before them. It did not matter that Raymond Martray had led Smith on; that on virtually every one of the tapes and films, Smith denied that he had anything to do with the Reinert killings. The jurors were shocked and horrified.

"I'm in the cell alone," Smith said in one recorded conversation with Martray. "I think the best time to get me out would be about eleven-fifteen because everyone is up in court . . . If you could say that the sandwiches were ready, they might open the door for you."

"O.K.," Martray answered.

"But also have a crowbar . . . I mean, when I'm down in that place I'm free. There is no handcuffs on me and there is only one old guy."

"I got you."

"Get the key, take your time. Open it, get me out and lock him in and we're gone. If they indict me with Bradfield testifying against me you should go ahead and plan. . . . Of course, you definitely have to be armed. Now, the old guard in there is not armed, but he may have a young guy with him and he will be armed. He's a deputy sheriff."

"Well, that's no problem," Martray answered. "If we've

come this far, we might as well take it the whole way."

"Yeah, get him away from the phone and onto the floor and then into the cell. Exchange him with me and then we leave. It wouldn't be more than three to four minutes."

After a brief recess, Rick Guida introduced the next piece of evidence, a videotape filmed by state police from a van in the prison parking lot.

"It was approximately 140 degrees in the van when this film of Jay Smith and Ray Martray was made," Rick Guida explained, as he lowered the lights and prepared to show the videotape to the jury.

The figure of Raymond Martray on the screen was blurred but recognizable. "Listen, man," he said gruffly. "I don't want this Reinert thing coming up and kicking us in the ass. If you get screwed up, throwed back in jail, where am I?"

"Well, I don't know," Smith answered pensively as he paced back and forth in the prison's visiting yard, "but, see, the Reinert thing shouldn't come up with me."

"O.K.," Martray answered. "But what if it does? What if it comes up and kicks you in the ass, then what do we do?"

"We have to work it out somehow," Smith answered.

"All right," Martray said abruptly. "If *he* does anything I'll take care of him."

"Who? Bradfield?" Smith asked. He sounded uncertain where Martray was headed.

"Yeah, you know, Bradfield could disappear and never show up again forever. You just get the word to me," Martray said, breathing heavily now, "and he's done. That sucker, I don't trust him."

"That's right," Smith said, nodding in approval.

"I am not in no police eye right now," Martray managed to say, inadvertently glancing toward the van where Holtz and DiSantis had the video equipment, "but, you know, soon I'm gonna be. I have been thinking about this very seriously. I could turn around and Bradfield could disappear. The motherfucker would never show up. What's everybody gonna think? He took off. The heat is on and he knows it. I'm just afraid he's gonna crack."

Jay Smith interrupted, "Well, but you see, there's nothing they can do about me 'cause I had nothing to do with it."

"Well, O.K., Jay, O.K.," Martray said, his frustrated sigh

loud enough for the microphone in Holtz's van to pick it up. "Just remember what I said before. I'm putting all my eggs in one basket. What happens if they nail you for Reinert? Then what do we do? Where am I gonna be at?"

"You mean if they try me?"

"Yeah."

"And convict me?" Smith added, anxiety raising the pitch of his voice. "Well, then they will probably send me to the electric chair."

"No shit," Martray said. "And look what that does to *me*."

"Yeah," Smith acknowledged, squinting thoughtfully in the summer sunlight. "It's a problem."

"Like I said before, it's a loose end. We got to get rid of loose ends."

"I guess if they were to arrest me with Reinert, the best thing for you to do is to go kill Bradfield and make him disappear."

"That's it," Martray bellowed, glancing again toward the van from which he was being filmed, and barely able to contain his excitement. "You made the comment. That's it."

"But, see . . ." Smith continued.

Martray interrupted. "You don't have to say any more." He raised his hand to quiet Smith at least long enough for the statement to have its dramatic impact.

"But, see," Smith insisted, "that would be very hard."

"They would never suspect," Martray answered. "I'll go find out my information for myself. I don't want you to tell me any more about him than you already told me except one thing. Just in case . . . I get rid of Bradfield, do you, uh"—Martray paused, searching for the right words—"do you have any suggestions on how I could make *sure* he never shows up again? You know, just to help me. I'll do it even without the suggestions. But if you have something good so I can make sure he never shows up again. . . ."

"Well," Smith said, falling into Martray's trap. "I think your best bet is to get him back in your car, kill him, and take his body into the woods in Fayetteville or someplace, but nobody should know where his body is but you. You should never let anybody else know. Now, do you see the advantage of that?"

"Yeah," Martray answered, looking over toward the van. "If nobody knows, then who could ever tell on you?"

53

That evening, as was his custom, William Costopoulos held his own court at the Club 21. There, Gus Giannaris, a forty-two-year-old immigrant from a tiny village in Greece who now ran the most successful political hangout in town, immediately welcomed Costopoulos and his defense team with a huge tray of hors d'oeuvres. Costopoulos sampled a potato skin and sipped his iced tea. "It was a tough day," he said. "We really took a beating today. They hurt us, man, there's no doubt about it, they hurt us. We gotta be ready to roll on Thursday with the defense."

"Maybe we should put Smith up on the stand the minute the state rests," suggested Nick Ressetar, Costopoulos's bright young assistant.

"I'd trust him on the stand talking about the tapes," said detective for the defense Skip Gochenour. "He's memorized the goddamn things, but in the other areas he's an unguided missile."

Costopoulos looked weary. Three weeks into the trial, the prosecution was winding up its case against Jay Smith, and Costopoulos knew he had very little of substance to defend him with. "You're right," he said. "I don't want to put him up to cross-examination and have him start denying the Sears thefts. Nobody will believe that."

"Until today, we were way ahead," Ressetar added, sipping a double Scotch, "but it still doesn't look like a death-penalty jury. A death-penalty jury doesn't smile and laugh. They look too happy."

Then, over a second and third round of drinks, the defense team grew rowdy. "How about Bradfield?" someone suggested. "Let's put Bradfield up there and ask him who did it."

"Shit," Gochenour said, "I've got a better idea. Bradfield

says Alex did it. Here's what we do. We find a black guy, put him up there and say, 'Is your name Alex?' He says, 'Yes.' We say, 'No further questions.'"

Costopoulos laughed, as did everyone in the room. But their laughter had the cutting edge of defeat. They knew that the tapes had been extremely damaging to their case and that the prospects of winning were slim now.

Later that evening, Costopoulos got a call. It was not a man named Alex; it was Proctor Nowell, the black street kid from Chester County who had become Rick Guida's star witness against William Bradfield.

"Listen, man, I gotta see you," Nowell said.

"Come on over, Proctor," Costopoulos answered. "I'd be very interested in whatever you have to say."

When Nowell arrived, he was obviously nervous as he looked at the immaculately groomed lawyer across a huge marble-top desk.

"What can you tell me, Proctor?" Costopoulos asked.

"When I was in the cell with Bradfield, he told me things an' I testified to them."

Costopoulos rephrased his question. "And why are you here?"

"Because that's not all Bradfield told me." Proctor Nowell paused. "See, I said, 'you're in a lot of trouble, man' an' he said, 'Yeah, but I ain't worried about it because I put it on somebody else.' I axed him who he put it on, an' he said, 'I framed Jay Smith.'"

Costopoulos jumped up from his chair. He could hardly contain his excitement. Suddenly, when the case was all but lost it appeared that he was going to get Rick Guida's star witness in Bradfield's trial as his own star witness for Smith's defense. "Jesus Christ," he thought. "If the jury believes him with a statement like this, we can blow the whole case out of court and get Smith an acquittal."

"That's great, Proctor," he said. "That's just great. Now, let's go over it again."

"Wait a minute," Nowell said, raising his hand to slow Costopoulos down. "My girlfriend's got sickle-cell anemia. She needs help bad and I'm really jammed up for cash. I need $1,500. If you help me out, I'll help you out."

Costopoulos hedged. He wanted to believe that Nowell was

sincere, but suddenly he became concerned that he was being set up. This was a high-stakes game. Giving money to a witness was strictly forbidden. If he agreed even to lend Proctor Nowell money, and if word ever got out, or if Nowell had been sent by Guida and Holtz, Costopoulos could be accused of bribery and obstruction of justice; his career could be destroyed. "Listen, man," he said gently, leveling his gaze at Proctor Nowell, "there are things I can do to help you and there are things I can't do. I'll pay your expenses. If you miss work, I'll pay for that. Your time has got to be worth $10 an hour." He looked down at Nowell's torn shoes and dirty clothes. "I'll set you up in a nice hotel with good food. You can bring your girlfriend, or if you want, I'll get you a woman."

"I need the $1,500," Proctor repeated.

"Proctor, I can't do it," Costopoulos said. Proctor Nowell stood up and turned to leave. "Let's think it over and talk in the morning," Costopoulos added, desperate not to lose him.

It was shortly after midnight when Costopoulos's home phone rang.

"It's me," Proctor Nowell said. "I'm here at this phone booth an' no one can hear me." Instantly, Costopoulos wondered if Nowell was wired and the call was being taped. "Are you going to keep our deal and pay me the $1,500?"

An image of Raymond Martray's tapes and videos flashed before Costopoulos. He imagined this conversation being played to a jury in an obstruction-of-justice trial. "Proctor," he said, "there's no deal, there never was, you *know* that. But this is a death-penalty case, and if you have information that can save a man's life, you owe it to him to speak up."

"Don't give me that guilt shit," Nowell said angrily. "I'm in trouble, man, an' I need your help."

"Proctor," Costopoulos repeated, "let's sleep on it. I'll talk to you in the morning."

"Don't bother," Nowell answered, and his voice had turned hard. There was a brief silence and then he hung up.

PART VI

The Children

The children dance.
They sing to the timbrel, and the
    harp
And rejoice at the sound of the pipe
And peacefully they go down to the
    grave.

—Job 21:11–13

54

Then came the day on which the children testified. It was the twenty-fifth day of the trial, April 24, 1986. Girls and boys who had attended Chestnutwold Elementary School with Karen Reinert created images of a pretty eleven-year-old sixth-grader, and remembered the day she went with her class to the Philadelphia Museum of Art.

"They gave each of us a green pin with a white *P*. We put them on our shirts and wore them," one boy said.

"Do you remember if Karen Reinert went on that trip and was given a pin?" Rick Guida asked.

"Yes," the boy answered.

"Why do you remember Karen?"

"She was very cute. A lot of people in the school had a crush on her. I was one of them."

"Now, I'm going to show you what has been marked as commonwealth's Exhibit No. 109. I'm going to ask you to look at it and I want to ask you if that pin is similar to the pin you received when you visited the Art Museum in March of 1979."

"Yes," he said. "It's the same pin."

Karen Reinert's young classmates, adolescents now, vividly recalled for the jury what the enormous volume of circumstantial evidence was really all about. The promise and hope of three lives had been lost forever. Unlike their classmates, Karen and Michael Reinert had not lived to be teenagers. "Most of us have children of our own," one juror later explained. "And when we heard Karen's classmates, we knew we could never forgive a man who could kill children. If he could kill children, he deserved to die."

Elizabeth Brook, the granddaughter of Susan's neighbor Mary Gove, was the ninety-sixth and final witness for the prosecution. She swore that on the evening Karen Reinert was last seen alive, the evening she and her grandmother had watched hailstones together, Karen was wearing a green pin with a white *P* identical to the pin she had received at the museum and identical to a pin later discovered by police under the front seat of Jay C. Smith's car.

55

Exhausted and discouraged, William Costopoulos sought to convince the jury that the evidence against his client was insignificant. He pointed out that over 600,000 green-and-white pins were given out by the Philadelphia museum each year. But the pin was not the only evidence Costopoulos had to persuade the jurors to dismiss. Rick Guida had also called in Michael Malone, an expert from the FBI's Washington crime laboratory. Malone testified that red fibers found clinging to Susan Reinert's hair when her body was discovered perfectly matched a rug with red fibers found in Jay Smith's house, and that a single strand of brown hair found in Smith's basement matched Susan Reinert's hair.

Costopoulos had one last, diminishing hope for Smith's acquittal in this bitter evidentiary struggle. To refute the FBI, he had flown in Samuel Golub, a hair and fiber expert with a doctorate from Harvard University. After an hour and a half of highly detailed scientific explanations of the pigments, medullar fibers, and ovoid bodies that compose hair, Golub turned away from his charts, pointed at Jay Smith, and said, dramatically: "There's a better chance of it being his hair than her hair. If Smith lived in that house he was going to shed an awful lot of hair in that house. There are no two hairs in a brown-haired person's head that are identical. So what you have to do is simply look at the hair and see if it is the kind that could possibly have come from a certain population. But the trouble with brown-haired people," he continued, "is that their hair has such a wide range in color from brown to practically black, that you can do that with practically any brown-haired person in the world. So how can you say a hair like that comes from a specific person?"

Guida interrupted. "One second, Doctor. Is it your testimony," he asked incredulously, "that the hair found in Jay Smith's basement could have come from any brown-haired person in the world?"

"That's correct," Golub answered, "and given the fact that the hair on the slide was about four and a half inches long, which is about the length of Mr. Smith's hair, and in view of the fact that all the hair found on Susan Reinert's brush and comb and in her car was six or seven inches long, I find it a little difficult to say that this hair came from her head. But nobody is ever going to know because you can find this kind of hair in any brown-haired person in the world."

"Thank you, Doctor."

"Now," Golub said. "Do you want to go on to the red fibers found in Susan's hair? I could not determine if they were from a red rug in Smith's house or not. You see, the prosecution would not let me perform tests on the fiber samples that would have given me that information." Rick Guida, who later claimed that he thought permission had been granted, looked surprised and upset. "I called Mr. Costopoulos," Golub continued, "and I said I wanted to test these fibers to find out if they were the same kind of polyester, or if they had the same type of fluorescence, or any dye variation in them. To do that, I had to be permitted to test half an inch of one of those fibers. I never got permission to do it. I waited all day for the telephone call from the prosecution to come in and I never got it."

Later that afternoon, April 26, 1986, William Costopoulos quietly and undramatically rested his case. Golub's testimony highlighted the efforts of the defense. Costopoulos had given the jury experts. He had tried to refute the evidence of the hair, the fiber, and the pin. He had torn Bradfield's alibi apart and he believed he had done a good job of discrediting Bradfield's friends. No doubt, it would have helped if he had been able to risk putting William Bradfield or Smith himself on the stand. But neither of these men could be counted on. Guida had made the same decision not to call Bradfield as a witness for the prosecution. No one knew what he might say.

Costopoulos was not happy with the picture of Smith he'd been able to present to the jury. Although he had established that Smith was married, a high-school principal, a colonel in the United States Army, and a pillar of the community, Costopoulos could find nothing to prove that the now frail and aging man had lived a private life in keeping with his public image. Costopoulos knew that if the jury came to a verdict based on Smith's character, his case looked bleak. As the deputy sheriff took Smith's arm and prepared to lead him away, Smith began to hum quietly. Then he turned to Costopoulos and said, "Thank you, I am glad my life is in your hands."

With eyes red from lack of sleep, and new lines of worry etching his face, William Costopoulos stood on the courthouse steps in Harrisburg, Pennsylvania, and spoke openly to the mobs of reporters.

"I have a real sense of anxiety, a real sense of fear on his behalf," he said. "I am just wondering now if there are some things I might have overlooked. I don't think so, but you never know. I would like to say that Jay Smith, who is fifty-seven years old, is holding up very well considering the defense has maintained that he is innocent. If I were him, I would be very concerned because in the hands of this jury lies the power of life and death."

When asked why he didn't put Smith on the stand, Costopoulos answered, "Jay Smith spoke to that jury on those tapes for eight hours. They heard the most private, the most privileged of conversations. They heard the worst of him and they heard him say over and over again that he did not kill Susan Reinert. We could not supplement the record any further."

Costopoulos thanked the reporters and headed to the office to work on his closing argument and to prepare for the worst eventuality. He also began to write his plea to the jurors to spare Smith's life.

A few blocks away, Rick Guida, Jack Holtz, and Lou DiSantis ordered drinks at Catalina's Waterside restaurant and bar, one of the nicest spots in town. They mocked the testimony of the hair and fiber expert, Samuel Golub. Toward evening, DiSantis became restless. He chain-smoked for a while, listening to the others talk. Then he walked out of Catalina's, without even bothering to say goodbye. Later, sitting in Gus's restaurant, he rubbed his forehead and closed his eyes. "Man, I don't feel good," he said to Gus. "My head's been racing all day." Seven years of work were coming to a close. No more living out of suitcases. He'd just be a Philadelphia cop again. An ordinary guy, with a wife and two kids. Probably assigned to small-time burglaries. He shrugged. "I don't know if it's the case ending or what. I just ain't in no mood to talk." Then, Lou DiSantis walked next door to the Holiday Inn, swinging his long arms toward the sky. He drank some good whiskey and was asleep by ten.

56

If William Costopoulos slept for an hour the night before he delivered his closing remarks, his face did not show it.

"May it please the court," he began, "Mr. Guida, Mr. Smith. Ladies and gentlemen of the jury, very soon you will retire to deliberate the fate of Jay Smith. And in your hands lies the power of rendering the only appropriate verdict in this case, based on the evidence, which is 'not guilty.' In your hands lies the power of life and death. It's going to be tough sitting over there after I am finished, because when I sit down, ladies and gentlemen, procedurally, I can't refute anymore and it's going to drive me crazy when the prosecution starts taking things out of context."

Then his voice filled with sorrow as he began to speak of Jay Smith.

"In August of 1978 when Jay Smith was arrested, he was charged and he was convicted for two thefts of Sears stores. His world fell apart and the truth of the matter is he brought it down on himself. There's no sympathy for you, Jay," he said, shaking his fist at the defendant. Then, turning back to the jury, he added, "Whatever Smith did to ruin two careers and end up where he's at, he brought on himself. Nobody made him do that but, doggone it, ladies and gentlemen, he didn't murder anybody. In 1978 and 1979, Bradfield had a plan, he had a scheme, and Bradfield's motive and plan and scheme was to get Susan Reinert to take out $750,000 in life-insurance policies, which she did. All four of those policies were taken out within 120 days of her death. Two of them were taken out in the month of June. One the same week.

"This William Bradfield is a character study. Codes, telephone systems, living with Sue Myers, having an affair with Susan Reinert since 1974, getting her entire estate turned over to him, getting four life-insurance policies to the tune of $750,000, having an affair with a high school student, Wendy Zeigler, who flies in from California on June 22, 1979, and enters a safety-deposit box two hours before Susan Reinert is last seen alive. You think a guy like William Sidney Bradfield isn't capable of working out this plan in such a way as to take a man like this down? He was a fallen man. Use your common sense. Why in God's name would Jay Smith, if he was in any way involved in this thing, want the body to be left outside the Host Inn in Harrisburg, the very city where he was to appear for sentencing? That woman wasn't just murdered for the purpose of collecting insurance proceeds. She was disgraced. She was left lying nude in the fetal position in the back of a hatchback car with the hatchback up, three rows from the front door [of the motel]. Who, psychologically, based on the evidence in this courtroom, had this character of disgracing and demeaning women? William Sidney Bradfield.

"Does Smith have an airtight alibi for that weekend? Not even close. But neither do I. Neither do you. I can guarantee each and every one of you that you have a brown hair in your house on the floor that matches Susan Reinert's, and the chances are real good that each and every one of you has red fibers in your house that microscopically match the red fibers in Susan Reinert's hair."

Costopoulos paused, glanced at the jury, checked his notes, and began again.

"Raymond Martray shows up in 1981. He did not have any concrete evidence to help the authorities in their investigation at that time. He was a former cop that had burglarized the very community he swore to protect. But on December 29, 1981, when the cops had about had it with this guy, they said, 'Look, do you know anything or don't you?' Martray said he was told by Smith, 'I killed that fucking bitch, Reinert.' Now you got something there, Ray. Good boy, now you've got a confession.

"Jay Smith talked to you, ladies and gentlemen, for eight hours the other day on those tapes, and you learned what he knew and didn't know about the death of Susan Reinert and the disappearance of her two children. Self-serving statements, hogwash. The guy was on the phone talking about an escape. He doesn't want to be tried for something he didn't do. Anything but that. Martray's scaring the hell out of this guy. He keeps telling him that Bradfield's going to lie. Bradfield's going to roll over. Bradfield's going to get you, man. Martray is the one that's saying he wants to kill Bradfield. 'I could turn around and Bradfield would disappear,' Martray says. 'There's nothing they can do to me because I had nothing to do with it,' Jay answers.

"So what do you have left, ladies and gentlemen? You've got a comb laid under the body. What does that prove? Nothing. If anything, it's a telegraph of where Bradfield is coming from. You've got the pin in the car of Jay, wiped clean of fingerprints. You've got everything that Bradfield said before and after, but use your common sense. Make no mistake about it. William Sidney Bradfield is the biggest liar that ever walked the face of this earth and anything he says deserves no belief.

"And that takes us down to the fibers and the hair. Dr. Golub has been working with fibers and hair for the past thirty years. He told you that the single hair found in Jay Smith's basement could have come from any brown-haired person in the world. He demonstrated it for you. And the fibers, they don't even know if they're polyester and that's their case. The comb was clean, the pin was clean, the fibers and hair mean nothing. Ladies and gentlemen, you have the power to render the only appropriate verdict in this case based on the evidence we've all heard. And that is Jay Smith is *not* guilty. It's in your hands. Thank you.''

57

That afternoon would be among Rick Guida's best hours in a courtroom. From the first moment, his grave, intense manner made it clear that he intended to win.

"What we have here, ladies and gentlemen, isn't a normal murder case," he began. "What we have are two relatively well-educated individuals, people with doctorate degrees and master's degrees and military background and every bit of intellectual ingenuity they could muster. And they plotted a crime. I submit to you, and Mr. Costopoulos has told you this, Bill Bradfield is a liar. That is right. He's right. We didn't introduce Mr. Bradfield's statements to his friends to show you the absolute truth of those statements. This case was a conspiracy within a conspiracy. Bradfield had a plan. He knew he was going to be a suspect, so before Susan Reinert was murdered, he started covering himself. He started saying J. C. Smith might do it because that's *his* insurance." And here, Guida began to use his "pebble in a pile" metaphor as brilliantly against Smith as he had against Bradfield. "The pebbles start and the first one is this. A comb, a simple comb. It doesn't have Harry's Bar and Grill on it. It doesn't have Joe's Garage. It just happens to have on it the unit which the defendant belonged to. The court will also tell you that escape plans are substantive evidence of guilt. It shows consciousness of guilt, and what did you hear on those tapes? 'Find a place to hide me. Open the visiting room with a crowbar.' A pebble on the pile.

"Most telling of all, perhaps," Guida said, pacing back and forth in front of the jurors, "is what Mr. Smith said about William Bradfield. 'I think if they were to arrest me for Reinert, the best thing for you to do is go kill Bradfield and make him disappear. I mean, get him back in your car. Kill him and take his body up to the woods, up in Fayetteville someplace. See, nobody should know where his body is but you.' 'Yes,' says Martray, 'if nobody else knows, then who can ever tell on me?' And in the same paragraph Smith says, 'When you deal with a body, only you should know. You should never let anyone else know.' Then he says, 'Now, do you see the advantage of that?' Unfortunately, for the father and grandparents of Karen and Michael Reinert, we do see the advantage of that. Does an innocent man plot to kill a person he did not commit a crime with? Does an innocent man plot to make his body disappear . . . do you see the advantage in not telling your partner where you put the bodies? Who's the only person who knows for sure that William Bradfield couldn't walk in here and tell us where the bodies were? *He* is the same person, the only one person *does* know. That's more like a rock than a pebble, but how else would Smith know that Bradfield doesn't know? And what about the rest of the evidence? Martray says, 'What if they ask me to take a lie-detector test? I'm worried about the big question, you know. "Did Smith tell you he did it?"' And Smith says, 'What I'll do is this. I'll have my people tell them that you are not taking any lie-detector test.' Now what does that tell you about Raymond Martray's credibility? If Smith didn't tell Martray that he killed Susan Reinert, why would he tell Martray that he would stop a lie-detector test?"

Toward the end of his argument, Rick Guida paused. He looked at the jurors' faces slowly, one at a time, and then he said, "On June 22, 1979, Karen Reinert went out on her porch steps. She and her brother Michael collected hailstones. Elizabeth Brook lived next door. Elizabeth was their baby-sitter, she knew the children well, and told us that Karen, dressed in a little scoop-neck shirt and a pair of yellow shorts, had a green pin on, nothing special to any one of us. Nothing special to an adult." Now the sadness in Rick Guida's tone echoed through the silent courtroom. "But Karen was a little girl. An eleven-year-old girl. This wasn't a pin. It was like an emerald to her because that's what she had. For a little girl this wasn't something insignificant. It was something prized. One of her prized possessions, even though it was worth virtually nothing. So on that night, Karen Reinert, with her little green pin and her little white scooped-neck shirt and the little pair of shorts, gets into the car of her mother and drives away. Not just in the vehicle, but into oblivion, never to be seen or heard from again.

A little girl. And on August 21, 1980, Victor Dove, trooper from the Pennsylvania State Police reaches under the front seat of Smith's car and what does he pull out? Karen's emerald.''

Once more Rick Guida paused, and when he spoke again his voice was softer, his cadence even slower. ''There's an old children's story. It talks about children walking through the woods and leaving things behind them on the ground so that they can find their way back home. On the night of June 22, 1979, Karen Reinert knew she wasn't coming back and either her, or that force that looks in on little children, left something behind for us. Not so Karen could find her way back home, but to tell us where she went and who sent her there. The last pebble is in. When I stop talking, the criminal investigation into the murders of Susan Reinert and her two children will have ended.''

Rick Guida stood in front of the jury. Every eye was on him; many, filled with tears. ''I am asking you now to do the right thing,'' he said, his voice a mere whisper, ''and you *know* what that is. Thank you.''

58

The night after Rick Guida's closing remarks, the defense team gathered at Skip Gochenour's plush office suite. There was a spirit of camaraderie, as people made sandwiches from a delicatessen platter, drank beer, and waited for the jury to return. But there was also a sense of dread. William Costopoulos lay stretched out on a couch exhausted, afraid, and wondering when the phone would ring. Despite the fact that all of these people had worked hard, it was Costopoulos who would finally take the responsibility for saving or losing Jay Smith's life. A young attorney and a reporter began singing in harmony. ''I was on your side, Bill, when you were losing. I never schemed and lied, Bill. There's been no fooling. But am I ever going to see my wedding day? Come on and marry me, Bill. I've got the wedding-day blues.''

"I am sweating blood and they're singing," Costopoulos said, waving good-naturedly. But there was a note of despondency in his voice, and the words of the song were not lost on him. At ten o'clock, a court clerk called. The sequestered jury had not yet made its final decision and were returning to their hotel rooms for the night.

Shortly after 11:00 A.M. the next morning, after six and a half hours of deliberation, the call Costopoulos was waiting for finally came. Weary and anguished, he turned to Gochenour and said, "You drive; I'm too shaky." The jury had deliberated just long enough to stir some hope in him, but not very much.

Within half an hour, the entire cast had reassembled. Jay Smith was led in, leaning heavily on the arm of a deputy sheriff. As they took their seats at the defense table, Costopoulos patted Smith on the back, then buried his face in his hands.

"Good morning, ladies and gentlemen," Judge Lipsitt said. "The court has been informed that the jury has reached a verdict. Would you hand the verdict form to the court clerk, please."

"In the case of the *Commonwealth* versus *Jay C. Smith,* criminal docket number 1677, on the charge of murder," the court clerk droned, "how do you find the defendant?"

With her voice barely audible, the forewoman whispered, "Guilty of murder in the first degree."

Jay Smith sat without moving as the jurors were polled.

"Is there any further evidence you wish to present before the jury decides on life in prison or death?" Judge Lipsitt asked the attorneys.

"None, your honor," Guida answered, his voice resonating with the excitement of victory.

Lipsitt turned to Costopoulos. "Any further evidence?"

"Yes, your honor," Costopoulos said as his voice cracked, and then he held out his hand and walked toward the defense table. "Mr. Smith."

It was a long shot, the last chance he had, but it was, he felt, a man's right to plead for his own life. Jay Smith, who had sat before the jury for four long weeks without making a sound, rose, and walked to the witness stand. Bill Costopoulos approached him with deference and sympathy. He began with the simplest questions, hoping finally to establish Smith as a living, breathing man who, though the jury had found him guilty, should not be condemned to die.

"Mr. Smith," he said, "please state your full name for the record."

"My name is Jay Charles Smith."

"Your age, sir."

"I will be fifty-eight on June 5 of this year."

"For how many years were you married before your wife passed away?"

"Twenty-eight years."

"From the date of your imprisonment, what have you done in the institutional environment in which you live?"

"I have been involved in a large number of activities," Smith began, his voice remarkably steady. "I was known as a jailhouse guidance counselor, because a great amount of my activity was helping individuals with their personal letters and personal problems. I worked with a large number of Hispanics who couldn't speak English. I taught a class for inmates called How to Get a Job. I taught that for three years to over 150 inmates, showing them how to make out applications and how to construct résumés. I worked on a lot of church activities, not that I'm an expert on it. I was more of an organizer. I was president of the 'God squad' for three years. I handled the Bible study and, of course, I did my regular prison job in the dayroom. My main activities would be in helping the prisoners themselves."

"With respect to Mr. Martray, did you help him?"

"Yes, I began working with Martray early because he came to me about his child, who was having trouble in school. He was also having problems with his wife. I gave him what I call a 'Vatican roulette lecture.' You know, on getting back with his wife. Then he asked me about his case. He was convicted of perjury. I'm the one who got him his conviction for perjury removed. I won the case for him. Of course, that made him eligible to testify against me. That's what we talked about in addition to the Reinert case. But I never said to him that I killed Mrs. Reinert, never."

"And did you ever tell Charles Montione anything that would

have incriminated you in the death of Susan Reinert or the disappearance of her children?''

"He can say what he wants to, but I never made any admissions."

"Mr. Smith, since your arrest for the death of Susan Reinert and the disappearance of her children, what have your living conditions been?"

"I have been kept in the hole ever since. I am not allowed any communication or telephone calls. I'm not allowed to visit with my relatives except one time every two weeks. They are behind a screen. I get no religious activity whatever. It's the only place in the United States where you are not permitted to have any church services. I never heard of that until I got into the hole. My only communication is by mail."

"Mr. Smith," William Costopoulos said, facing the jury directly, "if this jury would spare your life, are you aware that you would spend the rest of your natural life in the prison system of this commonwealth?"

"I don't think there is any doubt about that."

"If this jury would spare your life, what would you do within the prison system until your natural death?"

"I would go on as I am. Trying to help people when I could. Trying to work as closely as possible with my family so they could get over the disgrace."

"Mr. Smith, are you asking this jury to spare your life?"

"Absolutely, of course."

"You may cross-examine," Costopoulos said, turning to Rick Guida.

Guida jumped to his feet. "Where are the bodies of Karen and Michael Reinert?" he spat.

"I do not know."

"You don't know?" Guida said sarcastically.

"I do not know," Smith repeated calmly.

"Where did you kill Susan Reinert?"

"I did not kill Susan Reinert or her children. I had nothing to do with Susan Reinert."

"In other words," Guida said acting startled, "you're telling this jury they made a terrible mistake? Isn't that right? That's what you are trying to do?"

"All my life, I've lived in the American system," Smith answered. "I think they made their decision honestly on the basis of what they were given. I accept their judgment. They say I'm guilty, I'm guilty. You ask me do I think I really did it. I didn't do it. I respect their judgment. They've made their judgment. I respect that.''

"I didn't ask you if you *thought* you did it," Guida said mockingly. "Did you do it or didn't you?"

"I said I did not."

"It's not a thinking process," Guida added. "You know you didn't do it and these people made a *horrible* mistake, but it's just the American system, is that right? Let me ask you this. Are you telling us that you're not upset, even though you have been unjustly convicted of three counts of murder in the first degree?"

"Yeah, I'm upset," Smith answered, his voice trembling for the first time. "But I'm not the kind who falls apart. I have enough military training. I can take whatever happens to me."

59

"Dr. Smith has always maintained to me, as he has to this jury," Costopoulos said, "that he did not murder Susan Reinert. He did not murder those children. I think you can appreciate the frightening position I am in. I am asking you on his behalf to pause when you go back this time to determine what the penalty shall be. The Supreme Court of Pennsylvania has found capital punishment to be legal in this state; thus, in your deliberation on the question of punishment, you are to presume if you sentence Jay Smith to death that he will be executed. You are to presume if you sentence Jay Smith to life imprisonment, he will spend the rest of his life in prison. You will make no other presumption. The life he will lead in prison is no life at all. For all practical purposes, he began his life term on June 25, 1979, and for the past ten months the man has lived in a hole. He lives by himself. He's got minimal contact. They transport him in handcuffs and shackles. He has elected between the options—of death, and of life—to die in our prison system.'' Costopoulos's voice cracked. A sob seem to rise in his throat. He walked over to the jurors, then paused to wipe his eyes. ''I'm asking you to let him do that. Thank you.''

''When we picked this jury a month ago,'' Rick Guida said sternly, ''I told you this day might come and it is here. The defendant is no longer a defendant. He is now the convicted murderer of a woman and two small children. When he took the stand a few moments ago, what he did was ask you to question your verdict. That should not be part of your deliberations in this matter. You have found him guilty. He *is* guilty. He is a murderer. Your vote is life or death. That's it. That's what we are talking about. It is a very serious, very grave, very important decision.

''I am not standing here to tell you that I like the death penalty, or that I want people to die. I don't think that any one of you feel that way either. The question is not how we feel, but what the law requires. If we liked the death penalty, if we felt we really wanted people to die, we wouldn't be in these chairs, we'd be in Mr. Smith's chair. I know that I have feelings myself. I sat in my office alone, because this is something to think about. I have never done it before and you've never done it before. What we're talking about here is the law, not each one of your individual feelings about the death penalty. You all have said that under appropriate circumstances, you could come back with that verdict. What we are talking about is the collective conscience of the jury.

''Make no mistake about it, ladies and gentlemen, those children were killed, brutally murdered because they were there when their mother was to be abducted and killed for $750,000. The horror of the situation is when they showed up with their mother, *he* had a choice. The choice was to let two young lives continue, let these children be what they could be and give up the money because it wasn't worth it. The decision that he made was contrary to that. The decision was to trade those children's lives for $750,000 worth of insurance. They were witnesses to what had to be done and they were killed so they could never come in here and take the witness stand and point the finger at this defendant and say that he did it.''

Rick Guida stopped, and when he began to speak again, his

rhetoric was as eloquent and elegant as it had ever been. "Can there be any murder greater than the murder of children? Can there be any crime more despicable than the theft of innocence? Can there be any greater crime against society than a crime which steals our collective future, which is our children? You made a commitment to us from the very beginning of this case to obey the law. And it is now your *obligation* to do that. Sympathy, bias, prejudice should not be part of your decision. . . . For the children, I thank you."

When the jurors reentered the courtroom five hours and twenty-five minutes later, every head was bowed. Even Judge Lipsitt's voice shook. "The court has been informed that you have reached a determination." He continued, addressing the forewoman of the jury, "Would you please give the special verdict forms to the clerk. Have you reached a verdict of life or death?" There was a pause that seemed almost endless. Finally she answered, "We have reached a verdict of death."

Jay Smith locked his glacier eyes on the jury. Suddenly, his head fell back and his mouth opened in a silent scream. Involuntarily, he raised both his hands and, for an instant, they trembled, helplessly clawing the air. Then, as each of the twelve jurors were polled, the sound of the whispered word *death* echoed, floated, and lingered in the hushed courtroom—like ashes on a windswept night.

EPILOGUE

THE CASES AGAINST
BRADFIELD AND SMITH

For Rick Guida, Jack Holtz, and Lou DiSantis, Jay Smith's conviction marked the end of an era. Guida, a bachelor, who often referred to Karen and Michael as "my kids," emerged from the courtroom after Jay Smith was sentenced and said, "I feel like my kids have left home for the last time." The next day, he removed the photographs of Karen and Michael from his office wall. "It's over now," he said quietly.

But it's not really over. Just two days after Jay Smith was sentenced to die in the electric chair, on May 3, 1986, a Pennsylvania superior court raised questions about William Bradfield's three life sentences. According to the three-judge panel, a review is necessary to determine the prejudicial effects of the judge's failure, on the final day of Bradfield's trial, to instruct the jury that, as an accomplice, Bradfield was responsible for the children's murders only if he shared an intent that they be carried out. If, on the other hand, Smith had killed the children spontaneously because they were witnesses, Bradfield could be held responsible only for Susan's murder.

That same day, William Costopoulos filed an appeal stating that Jay Smith deserved a new trial because of legal errors made by Judge William Lipsitt. Publicly, Costopoulos maintained that the judge should have permitted the defense to make known to the jury Raymond Martray's perjury conviction even though it was overturned. Privately, Costopoulos wasn't certain that even that would have helped. "When those jurors went out to debate Smith's fate," he later recalled, "half of them said they didn't know if he was guilty or innocent. Yet, within a matter of hours, those people had decided he should die in the electric chair.''

Another ripple in the case occurred following Proctor Nowell's release from prison. Nowell, the state's key witness against Bradfield, was arrested and held without bail for stabbing his girlfriend to death.

The appeals and counterappeals will probably span a decade, and even when they are finally over, countless questions will still remain unanswered. No one is sure how or when the murders took place. Police think that Bradfield may have called Susan Reinert at about 9:00 P.M. Friday night and somehow lured her out of the house, then delivered her to Smith. Bradfield himself maintains that he had driven to his ex-wife Muriel's house to say goodbye before leaving for summer school in New Mexico. Finding no one at home, he says, he waited there for about an hour, then left a note. When questioned by the authorities Muriel said she never found the note.

Another theory popular among reporters is that Jay Smith telephoned Susan Reinert and told her that Bradfield had been in an accident and that she should come immediately. Police believe that, one way or another, Susan Reinert was taken to Jay Smith's basement sometime before she was killed. That notion is supported by the hair and fiber evidence presented at Smith's trial. But no one, except those to whom Bradfield or Smith allegedly confessed, will say with any certainty how or even when Susan and the children were killed.

Nor has a convincing motive ever been established for Jay Smith. In the months before her murder Bradfield claimed that Smith wanted to kill Susan because she had jilted him after a brief affair. Raymond Martray and Charles Montione have maintained that Smith killed Susan because she knew that Bradfield lied at Smith's theft trial and was threatening to go to the authorities.

Rick Guida suggested to the jury that the murder was performed for a share of the insurance money, but others close to the case believe that Jay Smith simply enjoyed killing and would murder without a motive. They cite as evidence the mysterious disappearance and presumed death of Smith's daughter and son-in-law, Stephanie and Eddie Hunsberger. Meanwhile, that investigation and the search for the bodies of Stephanie and Eddie continues.

For the handful of friends who still believe in William Bradfield's innocence, his conviction will continue to be incomprehensible. "The only thing I knew Bill Bradfield to spend money on was books," said Alice Campbell, an elderly woman who has known him for twenty-seven years. "I would bet my life on his innocence. To think of him murdering anyone for profit is simply impossible. He was interested in everything except money. He was a Thoreau-like character who liked to go out in the woods and live on nothing."

THE AFTERMATH

For most of the former friends and lovers of William Bradfield, life has returned to a semblance of normalcy. *Vincent Valaitis* was reinstated at Upper Merion High School in 1980. At first, he was permitted to come back into the school only for a limited time each week and was not allowed to have any direct contact with the students. For months, when he walked through the hallways, kids would call out, "Murderer. There's that murderer."

Valaitis has been scarred but not broken by the experience. "I know more about people now," he explained. "I've learned that the only thing that can destroy me is me. I also know that I'll never trust anyone completely again. Imagine Bill Bradfield telling me he would never be interested in Susan Reinert and then going over there and making love to her while planning to kill her. At the same time, taking Wendy to the apartment he shared with Sue Myers and saying, 'Someday all of this will be yours.' While also carrying on an affair with Joanne, living with Sue Myers, and still being married to Muriel Bradfield. He manipulated people. He abused people's trust. He wanted it all. He committed the most monstrous, horrendous sin. All of us aren't lying, *he's* lying. I didn't know what I was doing. I listened to him. I felt concerned about him. I trusted him. There was no reason not to believe him. I still don't know why he had to move me into his sphere of mystery. The police think it was because he was schizy and, in his view, I represented a very moral person to answer to that struggling side of him that wanted to be normal. I'll never fully understand him and I'll never understand Jay Smith. I always thought Jay Smith was demented. Years ago, when a janitor found Smith sitting behind his desk naked, in the middle of the night, I nicknamed him the Prince of Darkness, but who would ever have dreamt that the pathology of those two men would mesh and then explode.''

Susan Myers, too, has struggled to regain her hold on life. Like Vince, she was reinstated at Upper Merion High School once it was established that she had cooperated with the police. She, too, is scarred by years of loving William Bradfield. She has recently moved out of the apartment they shared. She has begun dating and is trying to create a new life.

Wendy Zeigler has finished college and is teaching in California; *Chris Pappas* is doing construction work in New York City; and *Joanne Aitken* still waits for William Bradfield.

WILLIAM BRADFIELD

William Bradfield has adapted well to Graterford Prison. He says he is a better Christian now and closer to God than he has been at any time in his life. To this day he maintains that he is innocent, despite the ''facts'' of the case.

''There is no doubt,'' Rick Guida recently said, ''that Bradfield wrote a note that said, 'Lured and killed kids, taped her.' There is no doubt that he told Christopher Pappas to lie to the authorities. There is no doubt that he wasn't at the shore on Friday night but wanted a receipt. There is no doubt that Susan Reinert did not die until she had life insurance worth $750,000; there is no doubt that Bradfield had $25,000 and that Reinert lost $25,000, or that he told people that Susan was going to be killed but never went to the police. Nor is there any doubt that the children's bodies were not found but Susan's was, and that William Bradfield, the sole beneficiary of Susan Reinert's will, was the *only* person who stood to gain from that arrangement.''

''Loretta,'' Jack Holtz said, ''Bill Bradfield was trying to use the same technique with you that he used with all the other women. You are the real link to understanding how all of them were seduced and how Susan Reinert was killed.''

As Jack Holtz spoke, I recalled the first time William Bradfield had looked at me and said casually, ''You have such beautiful long hair. I love long hair.'' On other occasions, he said, ''What a trim little figure you have'' or ''It was so good of you to come way up here to see me. I treasure these moments with you." I remembered the letter, the telephone calls, how the handshake became a hug and then an embrace, and how, as the years passed, I became his "trusted friend" and finally his "life-line."

Perhaps Jack Holtz was right. Perhaps I was a link to understanding how William Bradfield worked his destructive magic. Certainly, I had gone as far as I could go. I had followed Bradfield's tangled paths much farther than I had ever intended. He had permeated my life and my view of life for more than three years; and I knew I would never again be certain that anyone was what he or she appeared to be. I recalled a letter that he had written as he prepared to leave solitary confinement and begin serving three life sentences at Graterford, the toughest prison in Pennsylvania:

> I keep wondering who I will meet in the general prison population. What occasions for charity will be laid before me? Whose sorrow I might be able to soothe at Graterford? I hope my faith and will and courage are adequate to whatever awaits me. There is, of course, a great deal in me that shudders at the prospect of what lies ahead, but there is also an almost joyous expectancy. I would not have thought that possible, it has caught me somewhat by surprise.

No, it is not over. The enigma of William Bradfield, the death of Susan Reinert and her children, and the future electrocution of Jay Smith; the promise, the loss, the vulnerability; and the brutal, needless murders will haunt me always, as they will haunt dozens of other men and women who knew and loved the victims or the convicted killers.

—L.S.N.

Sue was extremely sensitive and terribly, easily hurt.
I tried to put limits on the relationship.
"I'll babysit for you," I said.
"But we're not dating."
We never went to a show, a movie, an orchestra.
She thought she loved me,
But she was too sick to love in a good way.
She begged me to make love to her,
But I never did.
She thought if she married me, it would solve her problems,
But we were never engaged.

—WILLIAM BRADFIELD